HEY JUDE

LENNOX VALLEY CHRONICLES
BOOK 1

HANNAH BRIXTON

Cover art by Hannah Brixton using custom graphics in combination with other images and illustrations available via the Free Media License Agreement on https://www.canva.com/.

First edition 2023

Editor: Myranda Bolstad: https://www.mjbolstad.ca/

ISBN: 978-1-7380101-1-0 (paperback)

Hannah Brixton

https://www.hannahbrixton.com/
Hannah Brixton's books are available on Amazon

CONTENT WARNING

This work of fiction is intended for adults and describes mature situations which may be triggering or upsetting for certain readers.

Topics dealt with in **explicit** detail include:

PTSD-like flashbacks, panic attacks, nightmares, armed robbery, attempted physical assault, self-defense (including physical restraint), and sexual activity.

Topics dealt with in **moderate** detail include:

Anxiety, addiction to drugs and alcohol, physical threats to safety, stalking, and interaction with law enforcement.

Topics dealt with in **minor** detail (including brief mentions and off-page events) include: driving under the influence, motor vehicle accidents, and unexpected and traumatic parental death.

Please read at your own discretion.

For the humans who are too hard on themselves.
You are enough.

1

OLENA

Standing alone in the middle of the room, I peer at the menu card on the tiny table next to me. *"Lincolnshire poacher and pancetta stuffed gougères."*

As if those words offer any explanation.

I opt not to take one, uncomfortable with the idea of biting into the unknown, and instead scan the room for Bradley.

Wine-drinking intellectuals huddle in reverent groups around the paintings in the Gareth Mason Art Gallery. Hushed conversations hum throughout the room and, although I can't hear exactly what they're saying, it's the suffocating type of chit-chat that makes me wonder if boredom can actually kill a person. The amount of self-important beard-stroking going on in this room is enough to make me question why I agreed to come here in the first place.

I spot Bradley waiting near the small bar at the back of the gallery. A staff member weaves around him carrying a platter of more pretentious appetizers, depositing it on one of the small tables scattered through the center of the clean, minimalistic space. The subtle aroma of roasted garlic in the air makes my stomach rumble with a hunger I try to ignore.

I rub my hands over my upper arms. I'm not cold; I just don't know what to do with myself. *Where do I stand? What do I do with my hands? I wish this damned dress had pockets.*

I tug at the dress, smoothing the drape of the tunic-style, royal blue fabric over my leggings and hug my long ivory cardigan around me. Then, feeling self-conscious that I look too closed-off, I release the grip on my sweater and run my fingers through the ends of my long brown hair as I look around. Sweeping the soft waves forward over one shoulder in a way I hope looks pleasing, I decide my standing here alone and fidgeting is starting to look strange.

Adjusting my purse on my shoulder, I drift to a nearby painting that doesn't have many people in front of it, not wanting to chance having to make small talk with the type of person who hangs out in an art gallery. *Wait.* I'm *in an art gallery*, I think to myself, and realize with a private smirk that maybe *I'm* insufferable as well. The painting before me is abstract, but I carefully plaster a thoughtful look on my face, furrowing my brow as though I see something more profound than blocks of color and bold, dark lines.

I do not.

If I had a beard, I would stroke it. *I could paint that.*

Bradley appears at my side and holds out my glass of wine with a polite smile. He's slightly taller than I am, with short-cropped brown hair that's parted at the side and combed stylishly. He wears squared, wire-frame glasses and a tailored dress shirt over dark jeans and brown leather shoes. He looks like he fits in here. I take the wine and we smile awkwardly at each other, breaking eye contact as we each take a sip. I'm sure we couldn't look more conspicuously uneasy together unless we were wearing huge sandwich board signs bearing the text *"here on a first date."* He turns to observe the painting I've been pretending to admire.

"Oh, this is a bold one," he says.

I nod.

"You know the artist, Pietr Alamain-Cortez, apparently painted this after spending three years in a Kenyan prison," he explains in a conspiratorial tone, leaning in slightly like this is a juicy secret.

"Really?" I say, then sip my merlot. I opted for the merlot because it sounded like the kind of wine a serious, fancy person would drink. I turn again to the painting as Bradley continues.

"Yes. I can't remember why he originally went to prison. Some political misstep or another. But the painting is meant to represent the contrast between the richness of the outside world and the bleak and repetitive nature of prison life."

This date is starting to feel like a prison, I sigh inwardly.

"Oh," I say. My brain is starting to make a foghorn sound—just a long, droning honk. Or maybe that's what's coming out of Bradley's mouth.

"Should we make the rounds?" he offers.

"Sure," I agree, smiling, and we walk at a painfully slow pace to the next painting. This one has a small group of admirers gathered in front of it, deep in discussion about the painter's choice of brush strokes and how they do or do not evoke the emotion of the piece. I suppress a smile when I realize they are dead serious.

One of them, an unusually tall man with sharp features and a shock of black hair, clocks Bradley's presence and greets him warmly with a handshake. The man, who I overhear is called Dale, asks Bradley how his research is going, ignoring my presence at his side. Dale stands beside a bored-looking woman with braided gray hair wearing a turtleneck and a long, floral-print skirt. She doesn't look at me.

I absentmindedly fidget with the hem of my cardigan while

they catch up and, when it's clear no one is going to bother to introduce me, I tap Bradley on the shoulder and tell him quietly I'm going to keep looking around.

I pass another table and check the menu card: *"Blistered shishito peppers with sriracha aioli glaze."*

Unbelievable. I'm hungry enough to eat, but the food here feels too foreign. I walk past, taking a long drink of my wine, and momentarily regret ordering a red; it always stains my teeth and I end up looking like a ghoul. *Damn it. Too late.* I run my tongue over my teeth self-consciously.

A sudden eruption of laughter from a large group across the room makes me jump. I turn sharply to see what the commotion is about, holding a hand to my chest as I struggle to steady my nerves. The abrupt, jarring sound is still ringing in my ears and my shoulders are up at my neck, bracing for more. I force myself to exhale and consciously lower them, but I still feel on edge. I continue walking, fixing my gaze in the direction of the loud group, monitoring the source of the threat.

No longer watching where I'm going, my face and right arm connect suddenly and forcefully with a wall of a man wearing a scratchy wool blazer. He twists around in alarm at the unexpected impact, knocking my wine glass into my chest. Merlot upends onto my dress and the glass tumbles from my hand, shattering on the floor.

"Oh! I'm so sorry! Are you alright?" I hear him say through the thick buzzing in my senses, the sound of the breaking glass echoing in my head.

When I finally look up, beady eyes stare back at me, distorted to appear even smaller through glasses with thick, smudged lenses. The man's round face, framed with thinning hair and a bushy gray beard, is etched with concern.

"Miss? Are you okay?" he tries again.

I'm frozen. My eyes dart around like an animal trapped by a

predator. All eyes in the gallery are turned on me. My pulse races. *No, no, no... not here.*

My breath is coming rapidly now and sweat prickles on my scalp. Onlookers start to exchange hushed comments. I can't bear the weight of so much scrutiny, though I can't move my feet to get away. Bradley walks rapidly over to me, nervously shifting his eyes between me and the other patrons. He looks embarrassed. He pulls me by the arm and I find myself shuffling along with him to the coat check area, gasping for breath. Out of the corner of my eye, a nonplussed art gallery employee pulls a broom out of a nearby closet.

"What the hell was that, Olena?" Bradley speaks in a hushed voice, probably to avoid any further attention. The ringing in my ears intensifies, and I can't quite hear what he's saying.

"What? I just... What?" I mumble between gasps. My heart-beat feels like it's in my neck. The lights are too loud. I blink repeatedly, then squint at him. His mouth is moving but I am not taking anything in. I try to focus and slow down my breathing. After several breaths, my brain starts to come back online and I can hear him again.

"You have to understand: Dale and Remy are important colleagues of mine. I'm just trying to make a good impression," he is saying with a disappointed look.

I frown, meeting his eyes somewhat blankly. "I need to go to the washroom."

"Good idea. You're covered in wine. You should clean yourself up." He points behind me to a nearby door.

Grateful to break away from Bradley's monologue, I duck into the washroom and lock the door, pressing my back against it as I take deep breaths. A flash of memory hits me—my window breaking, voices shouting just outside—and I wince, pushing the thought out of my mind. More deep breaths. I can't let the panic take over. Not here.

Breathing slowly, I note my heart rate gradually slowing down. *Close call.*

Oh, my God, Olena, can't you just operate like a normal person for one night? my inner critic screams. I shouldn't have come here. Who was I kidding, thinking I could fit in with the art gallery crowd, anyway? I obviously have nothing in common with Bradley. He seemed nice enough when we chatted online but this... this isn't for me. What on Earth had he seen in me that made him think this was my kind of crowd?

I splash cold water on my face and dry off with one of the rolled cotton towels on the counter, tossing it into the wicker basket below the sink. Looking at my reflection, I notice with detachment that I hadn't even bothered to clean my dress; the deep purple stain will probably set before I get home. I don't care.

Stalling, I pull out my phone and scroll through my notifications, immediately regretting showing my parents how to set up a group chat.

DAVID MACMILLAN

Any leads on work yet?

LYNN MACMILLAN

If not, we are always here to help you out. You know that, honey.

DAVID MACMILLAN

I can always fix up your old room if you need to move home for a little while.

LYNN MACMILLAN

Right. And of course we'd be happy to have you here. Are you sure you can afford rent this month, sweetheart?

Oh, Lord. I wince. *I need to get my shit together—and fast.*
I can't face moving back in with my parents at twenty-seven.

And I don't want to lean on them too much either after they've already helped me so much with getting out of Seattle. This is *my* life. *My* fresh start.

My fingers fly over the on-screen keyboard, my jaw tightening with determination as I hit send.

OLENA MACMILLAN

Thanks, Mom and Dad... but I'm making it work.

I take another deep breath and pocket my phone, silently resolving to face one crisis at a time, and open the washroom door. Bradley is still waiting nearby, looking put out.

"I need to leave," I say to him quietly.

"What? We just got here."

"I'm sorry, I can't do this. It's not my scene," I say, searching for the front door over his shoulder.

"Not your *scene*?"

My eyes return to his. He looks insulted.

"Yeah, I mean, maybe these are your people... but I don't belong here. Thank you for inviting me, but... I just... I gotta go. I'm sorry." I pull the sides of my cardigan around me, hopefully hiding the worst of the wine stain, and make for the front door, avoiding the eyes of the murmuring gallery crowd. I push outside and reach into my purse, intent on calling a cab.

Bradley follows me outside. "Olena..."

I turn to face him, wishing I could be literally anywhere else.

"I'm sorry about your dress. And... are you... are you okay?" He shifts his eyes to the smattering of other people standing out front. He looks back to me, keeping his voice low. "I mean, that was kind of an overreaction back there; it was just wine." He chuckles awkwardly.

Fire heats my cheeks. "No. I mean, yeah, I'm fine. I just need to get out of here."

"Do you need me to call you a cab?" he offers, frowning.

I'm still rummaging in my purse. *Where the fuck is my phone?* "No, I'm good," I say. "And actually, I'm gonna walk home. I don't live far and I could use the fresh air."

Before he can respond, I excuse myself as I push between a couple of serious-looking hipsters on the sidewalk who appear briefly alarmed by my abrupt intrusion into their cigarette break.

I walk the seven blocks home to my apartment, fighting back tears and wishing I wasn't such a colossal mess.

2

OLENA

I wake up curled into a ball with my blanket stuffed under my chin, the light seeping into my room around the rectangle of my drawn window shade. It looks like it's glowing; the contrast hurts to look at. Rubbing my eyes and sitting up, I recall the events of last night with a wave of shame. *Why did I make such a fool of myself? I thought it'd be different after I moved home.*

Clanging sounds coming from the kitchen tell me my roommate, Wyatt, is already up, preparing breakfast for himself. My stomach grumbles. I didn't eat much last night when I got home; I had a crust of leftover banana bread my Mom had sent home with me the other night and a glass of milk—one of my more pitiful excuses for a meal.

A quick check of my phone reveals it's after 10am. I'd go back to sleep, but my stomach protests that I need real food for once. Reluctantly disentangling my limbs from my blanket, I pull on a pair of questionably clean sweats and a wrinkled t-shirt I find on the floor next to my bed. *I need to do laundry.* Throwing a hoodie overtop of my Hot Mess Express outfit, I drag my knotted hair into a loose bun and secure it with an elastic I find on top of my dresser. Shoving my phone in the front pocket of my sweatshirt, I leave my room, blinking dramatically when the bright light of the kitchen hits my eyes. The smell of something savory elicits another hunger pang.

"Morning, sunshine," Wyatt says as he glances up at me from his pan of scrambled eggs. He's wearing a dark green polo shirt with the words *Riverside Deli* embroidered in white on the left side of the chest. His dark blond hair is getting long on the top and flops over to one side, making him look like a moody fashion model. He reaches a long arm across the counter, grabbing a handful of chopped ham from the cutting board and tossing it into the pan.

"How'd the date go last night with what's-his-name?"

I slump down heavily into a chair at the kitchen table, rubbing my face. "Bradley." My voice is scratchy. I frown and clear my throat.

"Right, right, Braaadley," Wyatt draws out his name dramatically while tracing a swirl through the air with the spatula, teasing.

I rest my chin in my hands and look up. "Great question. Let me answer through the medium of interpretive dance," I say with a sarcastic deadpan.

"Oh, please do." He pauses stirring his eggs, looking amused.

I hunch my back over the table and rest my forehead on its cool wooden surface, my bun flopping forward. I let out a dramatic groan.

"Dude, it can't have been that bad," Wyatt says, looking at me with concern.

"It can and it was," I reply in a muffled tone, my lips smushed against the table. I roll my head slightly to the side, meeting his eyes with a pitiful expression.

"Well, then, dish. But make it quick; I need to get to work. My babies are waiting." He tips the frying pan to coax the scrambled eggs onto a plate.

With effort, I sit up. "Your teenage employees at the deli are hardly babies," I say as he walks over and sits down next to me.

"That's what you think, but they look up to me like the wise mother hen that I am." He places a hand to his chest and flutters his eyelashes.

I roll my eyes. "Wisdom. Sure."

"Okay, out with it. What happened? Nutshell version." He stuffs a forkful of eggs into his mouth and looks at his watch.

"Nutshell version? Art gallery snobs, pretentious food, red wine ghoul mouth, smashed into a stranger and broke a glass." Wyatt's eyebrows lift as he chews. "Then I almost had a panic attack and fled the scene in tears. Also, Bradley turned out to be a dick."

"Oh, shit," Wyatt mumbles around another mouthful. He squeezes my shoulder. "You gonna be okay?"

"Fucking peachy." I slouch back in my chair and fold my arms across my chest.

He shoots me a skeptical look.

"No, really, I'll be fine," I say, more reassuringly this time.

"Okay, good, because I gotta run. You want the rest of this?" He slides the plate toward me as he stands, moving to the door to put on his coat.

"Thank you, thank you, thank you." The words rush out of me as I greedily dig into the rest of Wyatt's breakfast. "I'm so hungry, I'm dying," I groan with my mouth full. I'm terrible about feeding myself properly.

Wyatt smirks. "That's like... your whole thing."

"Oh, my God, this is so good." My eyes roll back in my head. Wyatt is an incredible cook.

"I call it *real food*," he says with raised eyebrows. "It's the latest craze!"

"Yeah, well, cooking has too many steps." I push the eggs around on the plate.

"Hey, you know, Sam's cousin is the exact same as you with food—gets overwhelmed by all the steps and then forgets to eat. And she just got diagnosed with ADHD." He pauses, crouching down to tie his shoelaces. "Did you ever end up taking that self-test you mentioned?"

"It's on my never-ending to-do list," I say, feeling guilty for putting it off. I sigh heavily and scrunch up my face. "Might as well add it to my growing collection of mental health issues." I gesture at myself from head to toe.

"Hey, I didn't mean it like that." He zips up his jacket and walks over to me, giving my shoulder a squeeze. "I just want things to be easier for you."

"I know." I put my hand over his.

His voice is quiet as he adds, "Also, procrastination is kind of an ADHD thing... just saying."

"Wyatt!" *Now's not the time.*

"Okay, okay!" He throws up his hands, backing off, then suddenly pauses like he just remembered something. "Before I forget, my Uncle Charles is gonna call you today."

"What? Why?"

"He has this big old house up on the cliff-side, and apparently the gardens are kind of a mess. He got excited when I mentioned what you do, so I gave him your number."

"He's going to call me *today*?" I look down at myself, almost worried my rumpled attire will show through over the phone. I frown. "I don't know, Wyatt—" I start, but he waves a dismissive hand at me.

"Too late; wheels in motion. He's calling you and you're taking the job," Wyatt declares with finality, his eyebrows raised.

I press my lips together. I know I need to. I've been trying to get my landscape design business going again; after shutting down suddenly when I fled Seattle, I've got no contacts and, most importantly, no money coming in. The last client I worked with before I moved home still hasn't paid me and my car's in the shop, held hostage by the hefty balance I owe for its repairs.

"Okay," I say with a brave face.

"That's my girl." Wyatt kisses my forehead quickly and opens the door to leave, then stops, turning back to me. "Oh, and hey, if you like real food, there's more where that came from on Friday. Don't forget. I'm gonna make a feast for us." He shrugs his jacket over his shoulders, grabbing his keys off the hook near the door.

Sam's birthday dinner, I recall with a smile. "Can't wait. Sam's lucky to have you, *daahling*." I flutter my eyelashes.

"I'm gonna get so many great boyfriend points," he says and sticks out his tongue coyly with a wink.

I grin at him as he leaves and shuts the door.

I finish the eggs and get up, dumping my plate in the sink with a clatter that makes me wince. My phone buzzes in my pocket. I pull it out and read the text from Natalie.

NAT

Want me to pick you up? Dying to hear about your hot date last night. xo

I remember with a whimper that I'd agreed to go rock climbing with Nat this morning. Exercise is the last thing I want to do right now, but I can't let my best friend down. I text back.

ME

Yes please very much thank you. See you in 15? Date tragic. Will fill you in on the mountain.

I open the fridge with a sigh and ponder eating a bit more than just a half-serving of abandoned eggs. My eyes pass vacantly over the options before I give up and head to the cupboard. Opening a box of cookies, I cram one, whole, into my mouth.

Maybe the sugar will help fuel some clear thinking for once. I return to the fridge for a glass of milk, then head to my room to change and locate my climbing bag.

Midway through rummaging through my closet, my phone rings from my pocket. Worry prickles when I don't recognize the number but I force myself to ignore the alarm bells going off in my head; Wyatt said his uncle would be calling.

"Hello?" I answer tentatively.

"Hi there, I'm looking to speak with Olena MacMillan, please," an older voice replies.

I exhale quietly. "That's me, hi."

"Hi, this is Charles Faulkner, Wyatt's uncle. He gave me your number when we saw each other at a family dinner recently."

"Oh, yes, he mentioned; that was nice of him," I say.

"Yes, well, I'm calling because I may have a project for you."

Panic threatens. *Why am I so nervous about a new project? What's with me?*

"Oh, wow, great!" I force a casual and pleasant tone. "Tell me more." I remind myself I *do* want to know more.

"Well, my wife, Carol, and I inherited this rather large property fairly recently and it needs some work—both the house itself and the outdoor area. It's gotten a bit... *overgrown*, shall we say."

"Right, Wyatt mentioned that." I find my purse and sift through its contents, searching for a pen to jot down some basic details. Not having any initial luck, I peer inside, catching a glimpse of the keychain Nat bought for me that says *"Boss Bitch"*. I smile to myself, knowing she'd remind me to own my awesomeness. I locate a small notebook and, finally, the elusive pen.

"Yes," he continues. "Anyway, when Wyatt mentioned that his roommate is a brilliant landscape designer, I thought to myself, well, this is just perfect timing!" He chuckles softly.

I fight the urge to refute the compliment. "Yeah, it sounds like the stars aligned," I say, trying my best to echo his warmth.

"They did, indeed!" A pause. "I should say, the situation is somewhat unusual."

As I fidget with my pen, he tells me the property was originally his oldest brother's, left to him by their grandparents. The brother and his wife had kept the old Tudor-style house and grounds in decent shape for a few decades, treating it like a family home despite its size. They'd never had children of their own.

"Realistically, that's probably how they afforded to heat that drafty old house," Charles adds. He goes on to explain his brother had passed away quite suddenly from cancer a few years ago, and his wife's health had taken a serious turn after that. She died last year and left the house to Charles and Carol.

I listen with a furrowed brow. "I'm so sorry for your loss, Mr. Faulkner."

"Thank you. It was a very hard time, obviously," he says sadly. "But, in any case," he clears his throat, audibly shaking off the weight of emotion in his voice, "I didn't call you to tell you a tragic tale!" He forces a small laugh, as if trying to lighten the mood for my sake.

"No, no, it's okay. Thank you for telling me; I'm very sorry, again."

He pauses for a moment. "You have a kind heart, I can tell," he says softly. "And your work really caught my attention, you know. Wyatt showed me some photos from your website. I think you have a great creative eye. Really beautiful work."

I smile. "Oh, thank you," I say with a self-conscious chuckle. I'm never sure how to accept praise graciously.

Charles lets out a sigh. "Anyway, I was hoping you could come by to have a look. I could show you around and you could get a sense of the scope of it all. And I can point to things and wave my arms about while I explain what we're looking for," he adds with a good-natured laugh.

"Oh," I say, smiling, "yes, that would be great."

I'm a bit caught off guard to have a new client wanting to move forward so quickly, but I need this job, and I can't think of a reason to say no.

But... It sounds like this will be more than just a garden makeover. Most of my projects in Seattle were smaller scale updates to personal residences; retirees who wanted to grow their own flowers or produce in their backyards were frequently among my clients. Mr. Faulkner described *this* property as *rather large*. I've done larger contracts before, but taking on something big right now feels... well... big. Especially after I'd just moved and when my life is a mess.

"Wonderful. Are you free Thursday morning?"

"Yes! That's perfect," I say.

"Great. I'll try to get the landscaper there too. And you can meet Carol, as well. I can already tell she'll like you. Here, I'll give you directions. It's a little tricky to find."

We settle the details and I scribble them down on a page in my notebook.

"Thank you, Mr. Faulkner."

"Please, call me Charles."

"Okay. Thank you, Charles." I grimace slightly. Calling him Charles feels too familiar, but calling him Mr. Faulkner makes me feel like a child. *Ugh. Stop overthinking this.*

After I hang up, I smile to myself despite the nervous tightening sensation under my ribs. *This is good. This is going to be good.*

I'm grateful for a lead on some work. I make a mental note to buy Wyatt a bottle of wine as a thank you for helping me get a foot in the door with his uncle... when I can afford a bottle of wine, that is.

3

OLENA

Nat's yellow Jetta pulls up to the curb right as I step out the front door of the apartment building. I duck into the passenger seat, chucking my climbing bag behind us with an overly dramatic flourish.

"What's with you this morning?" Nat asks with raised eyebrows, rummaging in her purse. "You look pretty chipper for someone fresh off a tragic date."

"Well, perhaps my fortunes have changed!" I narrow my eyes mysteriously, wiggling my fingers at Nat like I'm casting a spell.

"Yeah? Okay, then, spill," she says, putting a hair elastic between her teeth and gathering her small black braids up into a ponytail, a few of the shorter ones escaping her grasp and falling back down in front of her eyes. She looks at me expectantly, her dark eyes gleaming with curiosity.

"Wyatt's gotten me a job lead with his uncle. He just called and I'm meeting him on Thursday to see the property." I smile nervously.

"Seriously? That's excellent!" Nat breaks into a grin, doing a little happy dance in the driver's seat; the girl loves a celebration. "See? I knew you could get your mojo back."

"Well, so far nothing's confirmed, but it sounds promising. So my mojo level is still TBD."

"Tell me everything. How'd the phone call go?"

"Good. Actually, really good. Wyatt clearly did quite the job talking me up. His uncle was so kind. He said my work was beautiful." I pull an awkward, embarrassed face.

Nat lets out a whoop and slaps my arm gently.

"Proud of me?" I ask, knowing the answer. I smirk to myself, cautiously letting the good feelings simmer in my gut. I won't let myself worry about the specifics yet.

"Abso-fucking-lutely, Len!" She's giddy and her enthusiasm is contagious.

I can't help but grin. "Thanks." I take a deep breath and blow it out, dropping my head back on the headrest and turning toward her. "Just tell me I'm brilliant and it'll all be smooth sailing, please."

Apparently, I need some reassurance that I can do this—a little push to help me kick the self-doubt monster's ass.

I don't know why I'm so hesitant to embrace this job. I was plenty busy with my business in the big city, so getting back on the horse shouldn't feel this intimidating. I guess, on some level, I have always attributed any success I had to the talented people I worked with. Now that I'm starting over from scratch here in small town Lennox Valley, all while knowing no one in my field, I'm feeling so... *vulnerable.*

"Girl, you're gonna be fantastic at this job. You'll have all the beautiful, creative wisdom, the unique ideas, and the professional plans... and you're gonna blow this guy away with your charm and skill. And, most importantly, you'll be getting *paid* again! Congrats. Seriously, I love this for you." She waggles her eyebrows at me, sporting another huge grin. Nat's the best at hype.

I inhale another huge breath and let it out. "Okay, yes, thank you. I *can* do this. I *will* do this." I try to fill my mind with the kinds of thoughts I assume successful people think, telling myself it'll be rewarding, interesting work. That I have a handful of creative ideas I've been holding onto for just the right project and how maybe I'll get to implement some of those hidden gems at the Faulkners' property. The place sounds pretty huge, so the possibilities could be vast.

"I do usually love the beginning of a brand new project," I say to Nat.

"Yes! Exactly. The creative juices get flowing..."

"Yeah."

I sigh. There's something beautiful about starting from scratch with a landscape. I know going to see the property on Thursday will ignite my designer brain in the best way. Plus, being outdoors and getting that first look now—just as early signs of spring show up—will be beautiful. An old Tudor revival home on a misty cliff-side overlooking the river has a certain dreamy appeal, any way you slice it. I smile to myself, but it fades when I realize I will need a way to get there.

I turn to Nat, scrunching my nose. "Hey, uh... my car's still in the shop and I can't cover the repairs yet because I still haven't gotten paid by that last deadbeat client—"

"Ugh, rude," Nat interrupts in solidarity, shaking her head.

"I know." I roll my eyes. "So, my lovely best friend," I continue, placing my palms together in front of my chest, "would you be a beautiful soul and maybe consider lending me your car for the Thursday thing? It's pretty far outside of town."

Nat's eyes widen—the visual equivalent of the word *duh*. "Oh, one hundred percent. Perks of working from home, right? Zero commute. So yeah, I don't need my car. No such thing as a local government policy emergency. None that I need to drive for, anyway," she chuckles.

I smile broadly, truly grateful Nat is my best friend. Ever since we met in Geology 101 in our first year of college, we've had each other's backs.

"Thank you. I should have money coming in soon, so I won't need you to rescue me for much longer," I offer apologetically.

She waves a dismissive hand my way. "Girl, it's not an issue. I'm just happy to help you get back on the work train!"

"Thanks, again. Seriously. I owe you one." A beat passes and I realize we've been talking about me a lot. "So, what's new with *you,* anyway?"

"Well," says Nat, "Graham finally booked the week away in Portland for our anniversary!"

"Yes! The boyfriend delivers!" I exclaim, though I'm not surprised he came through. Graham, an old friend of mine and Wyatt's, is as dependable as they come. He and Nat have been inseparable ever since I introduced them on Thanksgiving weekend a couple of years back, when she tagged along with me on a trip home from Seattle to see my folks. It wasn't long before she decided to move here. I have Graham to thank for my best friend living in my hometown—another reason moving back here was a good decision.

"I know, I'm so excited. Especially with how much he's been working lately. So much overtime! They've got some new, big-deal client, so they're all working ridiculous hours. His boss just keeps piling more work on him, and he's having trouble saying no."

I shake my head, smirking at Graham's over-the-top work ethic. "You know, he's always been like that. Even in high school! He'd bring his homework over to my house and get it done before doing anything fun." I smile at the memory of Graham as a lanky teenager hunched over his assignments at our dining room table.

"Well, he's not allowed to bring any *homework* on this trip." She sighs. "Anyway, it'll be great to get away." Nat grins, tugging down the sleeves of her bright yellow athletic top. The color is gorgeous against the deep brown of her skin.

"Love that for you both. Sounds very romantic, may I add." I pump my eyebrows to accentuate the point, and she scoffs, though I know she loves it.

A buzzing comes from inside my hoodie pocket. I pull out my phone. There's a new text from a number that isn't saved in my contacts. My heart falters for a beat. Glancing at Nat, I open the message.

UNKNOWN NUMBER

Olena, it's Sean.

Heart suddenly kicking in my chest, I quickly delete the message and slide the phone back into my pocket, my hand shaking slightly.

"Nat?" I swallow and try to steady my breathing.

"What is it?"

I'm silent for a moment, my brows knit together with worry.

"Len? Everything okay?"

"Um…" I look out the car window but no one's there. My eyes search up and down the street, only seeing the usual rush of traffic and people on the sidewalk going in and out of shops and apartment complexes. "Maybe? Or… No? I don't know." I turn to Nat again. "Sean just texted me."

She pauses before responding, her eyebrows raised in shock. "What the *fuck?* Not okay. You told him specifically not to contact you." She frowns deeply. "What a dick. Are you alright?"

I take a breath. "I don't know," is all I can say in reply, my eyes still scanning the sidewalk outside the car, all the work-joy suddenly soured.

"Is there anything I can do?" she asks carefully. "Break his knees? Knock out his teeth? Send him anthrax in the mail?"

I can't help but smile half-heartedly. "Thanks," I say in a quiet voice. "Tempting. But no physical assault or acts of domestic terrorism, please," I say dryly. "Too messy."

Nat sucks her teeth. "Details, details." She pauses. "So, what'd he say?"

"Just *Olena, it's Sean*. I don't know what he wants. I deleted it."

My kingdom for a way to delete him—and what happened to us—from my memory.

"Good," Nat says. "Man, *fuck* that guy."

"Yeah."

We sit in silence for a moment.

"Hey, have you eaten breakfast?" she asks in a motherly tone. I'm sure she suspects I haven't fed myself properly, as usual.

"Sort of," I hedge. "I had half of Wyatt's eggs and a thinking cookie. Does that count?"

She looks at me blankly. "Did the cookie actually help you think about what else to eat?"

I laugh sardonically. "No. Never does."

Nat lets out a breath, clearly not at all surprised, and starts the car. "Figures. Well, that settles it. I'm buying you brunch after climbing." She pulls out into the street.

I look at her adoringly. "See, this is why I love you."

Nat gives me a look, her eyebrows raised. "Now, about that date last night..."

I grimace. "Buckle up."

GASPING, I bolt up out of bed with my face and neck dripping with sweat, my t-shirt soaked through and goosebumps prickling over my bare arms. I'm shivering, heartbeat pounding in my chest. A sudden lurch in my stomach sends me bursting out of my dark bedroom, racing to the bathroom down the hall just in time to vomit into the toilet. I grip the sides of the seat with white knuckles as my head spins.

Moments later, Wyatt comes in, flicking on the glaringly bright light. I wince. Once my eyes adjust, I see concern etched on his half-asleep face.

He rubs my back. "Another nightmare?"

I swallow hard and nod, wiping my mouth on a piece of toilet paper and shutting the toilet lid. I flush, still kneeling on the floor.

Sam appears at the door. "Everything okay?" he asks with matching concern in his eyes.

"I'm fine," I manage to say in a hoarse voice. "I'll *be* fine."

"You sure?"

"Yeah." I clear my throat as I push myself up on shaky legs to get my toothbrush.

"Do you need anything, babe?" Wyatt asks, rubbing my back again. "Glass of water? Heating pad?"

Shaking my head, I reach for the toothpaste with a trembling hand. I send them back to bed with promises that the awful part is over now. I'm still shivering, but I know once I change my clothes, I'll warm up again. I always do.

I really need to go see that therapist Nat recommended, I think numbly. Trauma, anxiety, nightmares, panic attacks... and, hell, probably ADHD in the mix. I really need to look into that. *Shit.* My mental health isn't stellar right now. But neither is my bank account, so it'll have to wait.

I watch from the bathroom as Wyatt rubs Sam's shoulders reassuringly, mumbling something I can't quite hear as they shuffle back to Wyatt's room. Sam looks back at me over his shoulder and gives me a small smile, a mix of sympathy and worry on his face. I turn to finish brushing my teeth as they shut the door.

4

JUDE

"John Harwood! Didn't expect to see you here," I call out as I approach the two men, cutting a path through the tall grass. John is standing on the cobblestone pathway next to an older man I presume is Charles Faulkner. John and his wife, Susan, live next door. I've been taking care of their property for years now; they were some of my first clients when I started my landscaping business, and I have them to thank for referring Charles to me for this job.

"It's the man himself," John replies with a grin. "We were just talking about you."

"Good things, I hope!" I shake his hand and clap him on the shoulder, then turn my attention to the other man, who holds out his hand.

"Charles Faulkner," he says, gripping my hand in a firm shake. "Nice to meet you, Jude."

"Likewise," I say. "Quite the view you've got here." I tilt my chin at the nearby cliff that looks out over Black Bear River, then take a moment to look around at the large property. It looks fairly neglected. Overgrown garden beds edge the perimeter of the old

Tudor house. A central yard is flanked by various leggy, half-dead plants, as well as several well-established but overgrown trees, including an enormous horse chestnut and several arbutuses.

"Thank you," Charles replies, following my gaze. "It's all new to us but it's quite something, isn't it?"

Before I can respond, John interrupts. "Listen." He claps his hands together decisively. "I'll get out of your hair. Let you two talk about the project."

I nod in his direction, smiling.

"Alright, John, take care," Charles says. "Don't be a stranger."

John nods and gives us a small wave before turning toward the driveway, ambling home.

"Jude, I'm glad you could pop over. I don't have a ton of time to chat," he says, looking at his watch, "but I figured it would be good for you to lay eyes on what we've got here."

"Oh, no problem. I was actually just finishing up next door."

"Well, that *is* convenient!" He raises his eyebrows. "I trust you didn't encounter any trouble on the commute," he adds with a chuckle.

I smile. There's an easy kindness to him that reminds me of Dad. A familiar heaviness settles over me at the thought, but I manage to shake it off. While the pain has never fully gone away, those once-sharp claws of grief have dulled over the years.

"So, you're looking for a big overhaul?" I ask, crossing my arms over my chest.

He nods enthusiastically. "Yes, and it's quite overdue, as you can see." Charles gestures around us, then motions for me to follow him across the grass. We cross the yard to a spot where the land dips down near the cliff-side.

"Can I ask... What's the story with this place? You said earlier it was all new to you."

"Yes, my wife and I inherited the property from my late brother. He—"

"Charles," a woman's voice sings out from an upstairs window of the big house, stopping us. "The roofers just called; they'll be here any minute!"

I shield my eyes from the light of the white, overcast sky and squint back at her.

She offers me a quick wave and I raise my hand in return.

"Be right there!" Charles calls back, then turns to me again. "Well, that was the shortest tour imaginable. Sorry about that," he says with an apologetic smile. "Are you free to come back Thursday morning, by any chance?"

"Yeah, Thursday works for me."

Over Charles' shoulder, I notice a roofing van pull into the driveway and park beside my truck.

He follows my gaze and sighs, looking back at me with a resigned smile. "That woman is running me ragged."

I smile uncertainly.

Seeing my reaction, he explains. "Carol's got all manner of contractors and suppliers coming by right now," he says, looking tired. "This place needs so much work and she's in full-on project mode. Meanwhile, I'm running around like a chicken with my head cut off trying to juggle it all." He smooths down his thin gray hair.

I nod. "I can imagine." *Well, sort of.* Fixing up my rural cabin has been a lot of work, but the scale of the project here is something else.

He watches me for a moment. "You married?"

"Married? No," I reply quickly, chuckling. *God, far from it,* I think to myself. *It's been years since Alexis left me.* So, no. Not married. Life is just simpler on my own. Besides, I'm only thirty.

"Ah, well." Charles leans in, eyebrows raised. "Happy wife, happy life, or so they say!"

I can't help but smile. "So, Thursday morning?" I try to steer us back to the topic at hand.

"Yes, that should be good." He rubs his hands together. "I've got a landscape designer coming by then too," he adds, his eyebrows raised. "It'll be great to get you both here at the same time."

"Sure," I say, nodding. We walk back toward the house. "Hey, and I should ask... would you be comfortable with my dog hanging around on-site while my crew is here? He's old and quiet and doesn't do much other than sleep." I pause, realizing I may be jumping the gun. "Assuming this is all goes ahead, of course."

"Oh, absolutely!" Charles brightens. "My grandfather used to breed Irish Setters! Carol and I both love dogs."

"Thanks," I say, reassured. Bringing Murphy to work with me is a comfort for us both. He's been with me since... *Well, he's the only one who hasn't left, anyway.*

"I'd better talk to these folks." Charles gestures at the roofing van. "Great to meet you." He reaches out his hand.

"You too," I say, shaking it again.

"See you Thursday!" He smiles and starts to walk away, then turns back to face me. "And honestly, Jude..." he adds, "as for things going ahead? Based on what I hear from John and Susan, the job is yours."

5

OLENA

I find myself staring into the fridge Thursday morning, chewing on the inside of my cheek and wishing breakfast could choose, prepare, and clean up after itself. Wyatt shuffles out of his room to join me in the kitchen. He's still in his pajamas and slippers, his rumpled blond hair sticking out at strange angles, pillow creases lining his face.

"Someone's looking fancy today," he says, taking in my outfit.

I shut the fridge and look down at my clothes. Shrugging, I smooth down the fabric of my fitted silk blouse. I stuff my hands into the pockets of my cropped dress pants and bite my lip, hoping my appearance hides the stomach-churning anxiety I feel about this new job with Mr. Faulkner.

I scoured the internet last night for images of the property but it remains elusive. With no idea what I'm walking into, I feel uneasy. I shrug again nervously.

"Yeah, I wasn't sure what to wear; it's always tricky to dress business-casual when meeting clients outdoors. Don't want to lose a heel in the muck, you know?" I fidget with my lucky sitka tree pendant. "I hope I look like a proper, dignified business-woman," I add, putting on an air of formality as I do a small twirl.

Wyatt nods appreciatively and approaches me with a contemplative expression.

"What? What is it?" I'm suddenly on the defensive.

"I just..." Wyatt reaches for my hair and pulls it back, holding it up behind my head and letting a few strands fall back down at the front. He leans back a bit to take in the effect.

I frown.

"Hmm. What if you wore your hair pulled up, babe?"

After much contemplation in the mirror this morning, I settled on wearing my hair down, the long brown waves tumbling around my shoulders.

"What? No." I roll my eyes and swat his hands away before smoothing my hair back down. "It's fine like this. And don't call me *babe*, babe." I throw him a snarky look.

"Okay," he says defensively, "I was just thinking, you know, outdoors, big property up on that cliff way out there... I'm seeing wind and I'm seeing that gorgeous hair of yours *whipping* all around..." He trails off, squinting at me. "I'm just saying, it might not create the professional *je ne sais quoi* you're going for. *Babe.*"

He winks and I roll my eyes again.

"Well, too late to change it now because I need to get going." I check the time on my phone and realize I'm cutting it too close. "Shit."

My stomach twisting, I dash to the door to grab my purse and portfolio.

Wyatt slowly pours himself a coffee and turns to watch me rushing around, scrutinizing my every move.

I stuff my feet into my ankle boots and pat my pockets, muttering to myself as I mentally go over my checklist of things to bring. I grab my coat and scarf off a chair by the door.

He sips his coffee, eyeing me over a mug that reads *"Gay and tired"* below a sleepy-looking cartoon rainbow.

"Wait, isn't your car still in the shop?" he asks with a confused furrow of his brow.

"Nat's letting me borrow her car. Damn it, where are her keys?" I rummage through my purse frantically, panic rising. There's no time to go on a *what the fuck have I done with the car keys* this *time* hunt. I swear, the interior of this purse is a portal to another dimension, and all my belongings have been taken captive in the blackness, evading my desperate clutches. I walk to the table with my bag and remove the items one by one to help me see what's left. Lip balm, tissue packet, wet wipes, two pens, sunglasses...

Wyatt sits down at the kitchen table and puts his feet up on the chair next to him. He stretches out his long limbs and runs a hand through his hair, the picture of relaxation. He watches me with amusement.

"Wow, you still carrying this around?" He picks up my small canister of bear spray, turning it to read the label. He raises his eyebrows at me.

I snatch it back from him. "Yes."

He gives me a look but says nothing.

I narrow my eyes at him. "Look, ever since the robbery... It just helps me feel safer, okay?" I let out a frustrated groan. "Ugh, where are those keys?" I sweep all my belongings back into my purse with my forearm and scan the apartment.

"You mean *those* keys?"

I freeze. My eyes snap up to his, then quickly follow his gaze to the nearby counter—where Nat's keys are sitting in plain sight. Because of course they are. I huff out an exasperated breath, then dive over to snatch them up. I whirl around to leave, jamming them into my pocket.

"Wish me luck!" I call over my shoulder.

"Kisses, vibes, colors and light, babe!" Wyatt croons, raising his voice as I make my hasty escape down the hall.

PULLING ONTO THE HIGHWAY, I take several breaths in an effort to steady myself after my frenetic exit from our apartment. Eyes on the road, I reach into the Purse of No Return and feel a crinkle of paper; finally, an object is where it's supposed to be. I hold the small note against the top of the steering wheel and squint, my eyes shifting back and forth between the scribbled directions and the highway. I can't decide if I enjoy or resent the handwritten directions, but I have no choice but to use them as the rural property wasn't searchable when I tried using my phone.

"Right on Blackriver Road," I read out loud, "left on Elmwood Avenue, then right again on Dogwood Road. Follow it all the way up until you see a sign that reads *'Faulkner'* on your right."

Okay, I can do this, I think to myself. I am a professional adult, I am good at what I do, and I can take on a big project. Mr. Faulkner —Charles—was so kind so this'll be fine. I'm fine. *This is fine.*

The sun is bright but, I notice with mild concern, dark gray clouds are gathering up ahead. They look ominous. I realize I completely forgot to check the weather forecast before I left this morning. *That would have required foresight, you bonehead,* I grouse to myself. That's what proper adults do: check the weather forecast and choose sensible attire accordingly.

Not me, apparently. I glance over at the light jacket I brought and frown.

Two quick flashes of bright light in my rear-view mirror pull my attention away from the weather. I flick my eyes up and see a large, forest green pickup truck following behind me, closer than I'm comfortable with. From my comparatively low vantage point, I can't see much other than the front grill. I frown again, returning my eyes to the road and sliding the wrinkled note paper into the cup holder beside me. I check my side-view mirror to see if I can get a look at the driver. The sun is behind us, and I can't decipher much beyond a vague man shape. I bite my lip and keep driving.

Tiny raindrops pepper my windshield and a shadow quickly envelops the car, as if all the warmth and light suddenly got sucked down an invisible drain. *Ah, shit.* I turn on the wipers as the rain picks up quickly.

I try to ignore the guy riding my ass, relieved when I see my exit up ahead: Blackriver Road. *Good. At least this shithead will get off my tail.* I flick on the turn signal.

Seeing his matching turn signal flashing in my mirror, I roll my eyes. *What is this guy's problem?* I do not have time for this. As we slow down along the exit ramp, he flashes his lights once more, derailing me again.

"Oh my God, *what?*" I grit out through clenched teeth. "Why won't you just pass me already?" I ask out loud, like the empty car will give me an answer.

Some women might get nervous about being followed by a strange man in a dark truck, but I'm so keyed up with nerves already that this guy is straight-up pissing me off. I've gone from anxiety mode into anger mode like a video game character getting a power-up.

Huge raindrops splat against my windshield as though a rain cloud from a cartoon is suddenly dumping its contents here and only here. It's getting harder to see where I'm going and I click the wipers up to full speed. Distraction and anger nagging at me, I find myself repeatedly glancing at my mirrors, trying to figure this guy out.

Squinting quick glances at my crumpled-paper copilot, I prepare to make the left on Elmwood. A fresh wave of exasperation hits me when the asshole honks his horn behind me.

Are you kidding me? I am so done with this jackass and I *do not* need this stress right before arriving at work. I complete the turn and pull over to the side of the road, fuming. Readying myself to watch him pass me, I imagine his self-important, big dickhead truck roaring around my inconvenient little car and tearing down the street. Instead, I'm met with the crunch of gravel as he pulls over behind me.

Shit.

I twist in my seat and scowl over my shoulder. The rain is too intense to see anything through the bleary back window. Turning back around, I take a deep breath and let out a string of profanities as my fingers dig into the steering wheel. *Am I really going to have to get out and face this prick?*

Muttering to myself, I snatch up my coat, fighting to coordinate arms, sleeves, and my wayward hair within the tiny space between the seat and the steering wheel. I yank up the hood with a grumble, not bothering to put on my scarf. I didn't even bring an umbrella. I can feel the weather forecasters laughing at me.

I swing open the door and heavy rain pelts my thighs. Stepping out and slamming the door in one surprisingly coordinated movement, I whirl around and stalk back toward the truck, my arms out at my sides in the universal sign of *"what?"* with a hefty side of *"the fuck?"*

The truck door opens and a large black umbrella emerges, followed by its owner.

"Hey, what the hell is your problem?" I yell. "You're flashing your high beams and honking at me?" I fling an arm behind me in an exaggerated gesture in the general direction of my car—Nat's car. "I'm going to be late for work and I—"

My words falter as he lifts his umbrella and I stop, a few feet separating us. The rain splats loudly against my jacket's hood and soaks rapidly through my sleeves. I blink at him, my mouth frozen open as I try and fail to finish my forgotten sentence. My rage ebbs for a beat as I take him in.

He's... impossibly gorgeous. Intense green eyes look out at me from under tousled, dark brown hair. A trim beard covers a square jawline that's clenching slightly. And the *size* of him. Standing at least six foot three, he has the build of a lumberjack; his broad, muscular chest and arms are just missing the suspenders and chainsaw. Otherwise, the look would be complete. He's wearing well-worn jeans and a dark gray t-shirt with a warm-looking blue flannel jacket overtop. His rolled-up sleeves reveal large hands and strong, tattooed forearms.

Fuck.

I stare as his arm muscles flex, his grip tightening on the umbrella. My eyes meet his again. He looks more than slightly taken aback at my reaction.

"Whoa, hold up, *my* problem?" He frowns at me, holding his free palm up toward me with a look of cautious defensiveness on his face. "I was just trying to—"

I cut him off. "Trying to what? Piss me off?" I ask, forcing myself to find my voice and my indignation once again, shoving aside the distraction that momentarily wiped out my ability to speak. "Or make me late? Well, mission accomplished. On both counts."

"Okay, look, you've got this all wrong," he says in a tone calmer than I can match.

"Oh, do I? You were following me way too closely in this rain! Do you know how dangerous that is?" I try to justify my reaction with logic.

"I was just trying to make sure—"

"That we both died in a rollover?" The sarcasm oozes forth; even *I* know I'm being a bit much. Still, I can't stem the flow of salty words coming out of my face.

"No, I—" he tries again.

"Because I need to get to work, and I don't have time for some asshole with road rage trying to get us both killed!"

Now he looks pissed. Good.

"Would you stop interrupting me and let me explain?"

"Explain what? I think I have a pretty good idea. You and that huge truck... You think you own the road!" I fling an arm in the general direction of the asphalt, my eyes wide with accusation.

I know his type. Handsome jerks are the worst kind of jerks.

He rolls his eyes. "You don't understand."

My jacket is soaked through and rain drips from the ends of my hair despite my hood. He looks perfectly dry under his umbrella. *Smugly* dry.

I narrow my eyes. "Oh, I don't? Well, then go ahead. Explain yourself." I fold my wet arms over my chest and raise my eyebrows, waiting.

He takes a measured breath. "I was following closely to make sure I didn't get cut off by another car. I didn't want to get cut off because I needed to tell you—"

"That *what*?" I groan, bending my knees and dropping my arms in a full-body show of impatience.

"That you have a brake light out!" he shouts in frustration, pointing at the back of the Jetta, his eyebrows raised.

My mask of righteous indignation falls at his words, my eyes widening suddenly. *Oh, shit.*

I turn quickly to look at the car, then back to him. Heat rushes to my cheeks and I flush, instant regret flooding through me. *Why do I always fly off the handle like this?* He was just trying to help.

"Oh," I manage sheepishly. "I didn't realize... that's why you were... I thought... shit."

He's watching me with eyebrows raised as the puzzle pieces come together, one by one.

A grimace of regret is painted on my dripping face.

"Yeah. Well, message delivered," he says with his eyes narrowed. "Don't let me keep you."

I look at him with momentary confusion.

He exhales. "You said you were going to be late for work, right?"

"Oh, yes! Oh my God." In my frustration, I'd gotten carried away and almost forgotten. I turn to leave, then whirl back to him after a step. "Sorry. Thank you. Sorry..."

My embarrassed words tumble out in a pleading tone; I have no way of taking back what I said. And, more importantly, no time.

Without looking back again, I rush to the Jetta and get inside. My heart is racing and I feel nauseated as I start the car. Before I can pull back onto the road, I hear the roar of the truck's engine as he pulls out around me and takes off, disappearing over the hill ahead.

Appalled at my impulsive diatribe, I numbly pull back onto Elmwood Road and continue on. My stomach rumbles, bringing me back into my body. *Right, I forgot to eat breakfast. Classic Olena fail*, I think to myself, shaking my head.

The roads are mercifully uneventful the rest of the way up to Charles Faulkner's cliff-side property. The rain is letting up, so I chance a few glances in the rear-view mirror to paw at my hair and try to tame the mess. I find a roll of paper towel jammed in the pocket of the door, and do a decent job of squeezing the water out of my hair with one hand, the other on the steering wheel as I slowly wind my way up the mountain road.

Out the window, the river snakes along far below, revealed in the gaps between a stand of birch trees to my right. I finally see the worn wooden sign marked *"Faulkner"* and pull into the long gravel driveway. It cuts a path between densely packed evergreen trees; their uniform darkness seeps into my awareness, taking the edge off my nerves. I vaguely remember I had been looking forward to seeing this place for the first time.

As the driveway dips down and around a bend, the trees clear to reveal a stunning view: an enormous yet slightly run-down

Tudor-style home sits perched before an expansive panorama of misty... *nothingness.* The landscape drops away on the far side of the house and I can see the river clearly now, hugged by rolling mountains on the opposite bank.

My stomach drops. Parked in Charles Faulkner's driveway is a familiar large, dark green truck.

6

OLENA

This is not happening. He can't be here. What's he doing here? My mind spins with questions. Our chaotic roadside encounter suddenly lurches back to the forefront of my awareness, regret once again gripping me by the throat. But I'm late showing up; I can't linger in my car any longer than necessary. I park beside his truck, which bears the business name *Sharpe Blades Landscaping* in bold, white lettering with the shape of a saw blade emerging from the bottom. *Clever*, I think vaguely as I try to pull myself together.

A jolt of panic hits me. *Is he the landscaper Charles mentioned? Shit. Shit shit shit.* It would be just my luck to get stuck working with him after humiliating myself.

Shame threatens to wash over me as I recall my accusations from earlier. *You called him an asshole*, my inner voice screams. I scrunch my nose, stuffing the memory down; I can't think about that right now. *Just focus on getting out of the damn car.*

The rain has now stopped completely, giving me a sliver of hope. Small white clouds drift across the blue sky and it's clear the gray monstrosity that drenched me on the way here has passed. Sunlight cuts through the nearby trees.

I awkwardly peel off my jacket and realize, with relief, that I'm not as drenched as I felt when wearing it, the damp having made me feel colder and wetter than I was. Careful to extract my portfolio first, I throw the jacket in a crumpled heap onto the passenger seat and pull my purse onto my lap. With closed eyes, I inhale what I hope is some semblance of bravery and calm. Holding my breath, I step out of the car to face reality.

Those green eyes instantly meet mine before we both look away. He turns his attention back to the gray-haired man opposite him, who is gesturing enthusiastically at the landscape.

I know he must have spotted me pulling in; Nat's ridiculous yellow car doesn't exactly blend into the background. Plus, I'm sure he couldn't forget it after following me on the road for so long—especially after what I said to him. I can't imagine what this guy must be thinking about me showing up here. I risk a glance at him but his expression is unreadable. I'm not sure I can do this.

I push the doubt aside and give myself a quick mental shake, determined to forge ahead. I hope plastering on a cheerful demeanor will effectively mask my inner reality, which is clearly a total raging mess.

"Hi, Mr. Faulkner?" I meet the older man's eyes with a genuine smile as I remember his kindness from our phone call the other day. I grip my portfolio in one hand and readjust the strap of my purse with the other, then reach out to shake his hand.

"Olena," he replies, his kind eyes crinkling. "Lovely to meet you in person. And remember, please call me Charles." A smile spreads over his round face.

I nod quickly. "So sorry I'm a bit later than expected," I venture with a weak smile, pointing a thumb behind me toward the road. "I got... held up."

Operating against my will, my eyes jump to the man I called an asshole only ten minutes ago. He returns my gaze with one dark eyebrow raised. He looks like he's enjoying watching me explain myself. I can't bear to face the reminder of my earlier behavior and decide to focus my full attention on Charles. Mercifully, he doesn't press me for details.

"Oh, nonsense." He waves dismissively. "You're here now," he adds, patting a weathered hand on my forearm. The gesture is reassuring in a fatherly way, and I smile gratefully, remembering again why I liked him so much when we spoke on the phone. "Olena, this is Jude Sharpe, my landscaper." He turns, gesturing at the man before returning his gaze to me. "Jude, this is Olena MacMillan, the designer I was telling you about."

No one speaks as we consider each other a moment, my jaw hanging slightly open in a silent expression of understanding.

"Nice to meet you," Jude says politely.

Jude. Well, it's a better fit than 'Asshole', I think wryly to myself. I inhale as if to say something professionally relevant, but find I have no idea where to begin. Charles and Jude are looking at me.

"Hi, nice to meet you too," I blurt out, because that's how normal people respond to being introduced to someone new in a work setting. I'm kicking myself for letting that dead air hang.

Jude smiles and holds my gaze with a quiet intensity that brings a hint of heat back to my cheeks.

I bite my lip.

Charles glances between us, a question in his eyes. "Tell me," he ventures, "why do I get the feeling you two know each other? Have you worked together before?"

Jude looks at me with a slight smirk, both of us clearly calculating how much to divulge in this professional scenario.

I contemplate my words for a moment before he rescues us.

"No, actually, we hadn't met before today," he says, pinning me with a knowing look that Charles doesn't catch. *Carefully chosen words.*

A slight smile touches my lips as I direct a sharp nod to Charles, showing my agreement. This seems to satisfy Charles' curiosity and he moves on. I throw Jude a grateful look.

"Would you like to see the property?" Charles smiles.

꧁

CHARLES LOOKS to be in his element as our tour guide, gesturing broadly and often to punctuate his ideas for the place. I scribble notes furiously and snap photos with my phone to document the layout and problem areas he points out along the way. A pang of dread hits me as I realize how extensive the work will be for this project. But I continue smiling.

Charles had said the previous owners, his brother and sister-in-law, had lived here for over forty years before they got sick and couldn't keep up with caring for the property. I can see now he understated that point. The place is in really rough shape. The house itself needs a ton of major work done: moss creeps over the roof shingles, the mortar between the stonework is crumbling, and the painted wood trim is peeling. Nature is also slowly reclaiming the cobblestone path, which is overgrown at the sides and riddled with dandelions.

The rest of the grounds are even worse. There are forgotten vegetable beds with dead and crushed plants, weeds pushing between their skeletal stems and bent stalks. The trees are all sprawling and weighed down, their branches brushing near the ground in several areas, a few of the evergreens sporting dying sections of brown or gray where they should be green. The perimeter of the main yard is surrounded by various ornamental plants and shrubs that have grown wild and unruly over the years, and the grass brushes against my knees.

None of this dampens Charles' enthusiasm when articulating his vision for the property. He and Carol have always dreamed of running a bed-and-breakfast. They want to turn this mess into a beautiful garden oasis: a romantic retreat on the cliff-side. I admit this place has potential, but the work is going to take a while. And it's not going to be easy. Or cheap.

I fill pages in my notebook with wild and often disconnected details—some, Charles' ideas or instructions, others, my own inspiration—to remember for later. Tiered planters for succulents, sapling trees to order, raised flower beds, ornamental grasses, bistro seating area, an arbor covered in white wisteria... My head spins trying to keep track of all the information.

The three of us agree the first step is a lot of clearing out: cutting down the sick trees, pruning any overgrown plants worth saving, cutting the grass, digging out particularly nasty sections entirely to start fresh...

Jude and his crew can start this part the following week while I work on the design planning. Charles is delighted.

Jude is quietly attentive as Charles articulates his plans, sketching and jotting his own notes diligently on a pad of graph paper. His brow furrows slightly in concentration as he writes, a lock of dark hair tumbling in front of his face. My eyes drift to his arm muscles, working as he moves the pencil, then to his strong chest. I imagine what it would feel like to run my hands over his—

My cheeks flush as I catch myself staring. Thankfully, I look away before he catches me in the act. *What is wrong with me?*

I grip the edges of my portfolio tighter. Scanning my surroundings, I force myself again to focus on the project at hand, banishing any unprofessional thoughts from my mind. *Get it together, Olena.*

I make note of a large oak tree touching the roofline that will need trimming, then snap a quick photo of two maples that are showing signs of disease and will need to get cut down.

Yes. Good. Just focus on the work.

Having made a rough circle of the property, we return to the driveway, the tour complete. Charles grins with satisfaction and clasps his hands together, looking at each of us expectantly. He explains he wants my vision for the design and for Jude and his team to do the execution. He's seen our work and trusts us to do the job right. Throwing around some quick numbers, it sounds like we can make it work within Charles' admittedly generous budget.

"You two will be working very closely together over the next few weeks," Charles says. "There will obviously be a lot of logistics to work out between you... the division of labor, so to speak." He smiles at us.

Jude and I share an uncomfortable glance.

I assume he must have a usual designer he prefers to deal with but is now stuck working with me instead. Back in Seattle, I had worked closely with several landscaping companies, but the truth is, I'm out of my comfort zone here in Lennox. Rebuilding my professional contacts from scratch isn't going to be easy, so having this piece of the puzzle already decided is kind of a relief.

"I'm up for it," Jude offers with a professional smile to Charles, then directs his attention to me, waiting for my response cautiously.

I silently remind myself I need this job and will just have to deal with the awkward mess I've made between me and Jude. "Absolutely." I nod with a brave face, looking quickly away from Jude. I turn to Charles. "Let's do it."

"Wonderful!" Charles shakes hands with each of us then mentions he needs to go tell Carol the good news. "Well, I'll leave you to it; you probably have a lot to discuss. Thanks again for coming. I have a good feeling about you both," he says with a smile. "I look forward to seeing your design plans, Olena."

I smile gratefully and promise he'll have them before the end of next week.

He excuses himself and ambles back to the house where a tall brick chimney works a lazy stream of smoke up to mingle with the clouds. I take a moment to look at the old home once more. Taking it in properly, I can see it must have been beautiful in its prime.

Jude and I drift over to our vehicles in awkward silence. He quickly busies himself writing a few more notes, and I follow his lead, both of us conspicuously avoiding eye contact. Charles' magnanimous presence now gone, we are left to face each other alone for the first time since my explosive roadside performance. I grimace at the memory again and try to think of words that might smooth the situation over.

I close my notebook. "Listen, I'm so sorry about earlier—" I start.

Jude raises his head from whatever he was writing, a smirk tugging at the corner of his mouth. He places his pencil behind his ear and folds his arms across his broad chest, fixing his green eyes on me patiently. He was waiting for this.

"You were right. I totally misread the situation and I overreacted," I continue, hating my past self for being such a dramatic, interrupting jackass. *What a great first impression that was*, I snark inwardly. I forge ahead, trying to repair it. "I was running late already and feeling the stress of this new project," I explain, gesturing vaguely around us, "and then I saw you following me, and the lights flashing threw me off. I think I was just surprised. And they were extremely bright. Did you know they are, like, exceptionally bright headlights? Practically blinding... Anyway, I couldn't figure out what you wanted, and I thought you wanted to pass me, and I was thinking *why doesn't this guy just pass me already...*"

Good Lord, Olena, are you still talking? Why isn't he saying anything? Oh, God, please say something to shut me up.

He says nothing.

The words keep tumbling out. "Oh, and I think my blood sugar must be low; I didn't eat any breakfast this morning. So that's part of why I think I was a little extra *on edge*, you know?"

Jude is still just staring at me, not speaking. His calmness and silence are enviable. He's giving me nothing.

Against my better judgment, the words keep coming. "So, anyway, again, I really apologize, and I hope we can start over from the beginning, because I'm not usually that irrational, and I don't make a habit of swearing at men I've just met—"

"Are you done?" he asks, cutting me off.

Oh, thank God.

"I... Yes. Sorry. Yes." I shake my head and press my lips together, trying to physically stop the flow of my pathetic monologue.

He turns away from me and opens the door to his truck. I instantly deflate; he doesn't even want to speak to me any more than necessary. I can't blame him, not after how I treated him when he was only trying to help me out. My gaze drops to my feet and I send a wish to the universe for the magical ability to transport myself away from here, into my bedroom and under my covers, where I could safely shame-spiral in private.

"Heads up." I hear him say.

I snap my head up just in time to see the small object whizzing through the air toward me, which I manage to snag awkwardly with a free hand before it hits me in the face. I drop my gaze and turn it over in my confusion, the plastic wrapper crinkling in my hand. It's a protein bar.

"What? Why?" I manage quietly as I look up at Jude in utter bewilderment.

"You said you hadn't eaten breakfast, right?" He shuts the door and leans with his back against the side of his truck, crossing his arms again as he looks at me with an eyebrow raised.

I furrow my brows, then relax them, letting out a breath. "Yes, but—"

"But what? You're hungry and you need to eat. So eat." He gives me a small smile.

"Why are you being nice to me?" I ask, narrowing my eyes. I don't understand what his game is. I've been awful to him, blathered on endlessly... and now he's feeding me?

He smiles ruefully and looks up at the trees, then back at me. "That's a weird way of saying *thank you*." He tilts his head quizzically as he smiles at me. He's definitely enjoying this.

I close my eyes. "Of course, thank you. I'm so sorry." *Could this be more humiliating?* I meet his gaze again. "I should go." I need to get the hell out of here before I embarrass myself any further. Unlocking the Jetta, I throw my belongings, protein bar included, onto the passenger seat.

"Wait," he says.

I slowly turn around to face him, bracing for what he'll say next.

"I'm sorry too."

I furrow my brow, feeling thrown off.

"For following so close earlier. You were right. It was a bit dangerous." He stuffs his hands in his pockets. "That was my bad."

"Oh," I say. "Yeah." I shrug, trying to brush it off. I'd rather just forget about everything that happened on the road earlier.

He lifts his chin. "What was that book you were holding onto earlier?"

"What book?" I look at him in confusion.

"The one you held a death grip on but never opened. You had that thing with you the whole time we walked around the place. What is it?"

"Oh, my portfolio?" I turn to see the book on the seat of the car behind me and briefly note that it's avoided landing directly on top of my sopping wet jacket. *Small mercies.* Relieved, I turn back to Jude.

"Lemme have a look." He reaches out a hand expectantly, like a teacher who's caught his students passing notes in class.

"Oh, no, you don't need to," I start, smiling nervously. "I just thought Charles might want to look through the photos but he didn't ask to. It's fine." I'm hoping he'll drop the subject.

He doesn't. "Come on, Olena," he says, holding my gaze.

The sound of my name on his lips makes my breath hitch. I quickly shake it off and hope he hasn't noticed.

"We're going to be working together here. I wanna see what you've got up your sleeve." He raises his eyebrows, hand still outstretched.

I reluctantly turn around and open the passenger door to retrieve the book, feeling Jude's eyes locked on my movements. Turning back to him, I cautiously hand it over.

His silence as he flips through the before-and-after photos of my past projects unnerves me, and I find myself needing to fill the air yet again with my infernal talking.

"I was surprised Charles didn't ask to see it, to be honest; I didn't realize he'd already made up his mind about hiring me," I offer.

He gives a soft grunt in response, focusing fully on the photos.

The truth is, I have no idea what makes Charles so sure I can do this project; his blind trust makes me uncomfortable. Why did he choose me instead of someone else? Why didn't he ask Jude to recommend whatever designer he normally works with? Maybe he's just doing Wyatt a favor by hiring me. But, then again, this property is massive and the work will be long. And expensive. Charles seems wiser than that. Hiring just anybody for a job this big would be a huge risk.

Jude's expression is unreadable as he looks through my work.

I feel vulnerable with my creative choices under his scrutinizing gaze. I find myself hoping he's pleased with what he sees.

As he peruses my portfolio, I look around me at the trees and out at the cliff-side vista, absentmindedly twisting the ends of my hair between my fingers. I'm not sure what else to say or do with myself as he takes his time judging my work. Judging *me*.

Please hurry up, I plead silently.

"Nice work." He tosses the casual comment my way with a blank expression and closes the book, holding it out to me. I take my portfolio, hugging it protectively against my chest.

"Oh, thanks," I say with uncertainty.

Nice work? That's it? I'm not sure what I was expecting. Not for the first time today, I can't figure this man out.

"Listen, I've gotta run," he adds, turning again to his truck, pulling open the door and climbing in. He rummages around for something beside him, then looks at me through the open window. "Here," he reaches a hand toward me, proffering his business card. "I guess we'll need a way to be in touch with each other."

I hesitate a beat before tentatively reaching up to take the card. "Right. Thanks," I reply, suddenly self-conscious. He's rushing out of here like he can't wait to put some distance between us.

"Great. See you soon." He throws me a smile that doesn't reach his eyes. Then, before I can respond, he quickly starts the truck and pulls off down the treed driveway, disappearing around the bend.

I stand there another moment, staring after him with my mouth hanging slightly open, until I hear his truck's engine roar onto the roadway.

Stunned and confused by Jude's abrupt departure, I climb into the driver's seat and let out a long breath. I drop the business card into the cup holder next to my scribbled paper directions.

Frowning, I open the damned protein bar.

7

JUDE

G lancing in the rear-view mirror as I pull out of the driveway, my eyes linger on Olena's quickly receding form, frozen in place beside the yellow Jetta, my business card in her hand. My hasty exit was probably not my smoothest or most professional move, I realize with a grimace. If there hadn't just been a downpour, I would have literally left her in my dust. You know, like an asshole.

I run a hand through my hair and blow out a long breath, stretching my neck from side to side as I grip the steering wheel. *Shake it off, Sharpe,* I think to myself with a frown. *You have a job to do.*

I turn on the radio. The weather forecast is wrapping up.

"More rain to come," the voice says.

A flash of memory from the roadside hits me: Olena's soaking wet jacket, her hair and face dripping as she gives me hell in the rain. *Explain yourself,* her voice echoes in my mind, her eyes so full of fire. I find myself smiling.

Later, watching her as we toured the property with Charles, she was much more reserved. Even slightly awkward. She was obviously thrown off by finding me there after having chewed me out so thoroughly on the side of the road. I have to admit, it had been satisfying to watch her scramble to apologize and explain. I enjoyed watching her squirm.

I wonder what else might make her squirm...

Get your mind out of the gutter, my rational brain reminds me. *She's probably got a boyfriend anyway.* I try to shut down the lewd images served up by my animal brain. *God, I must be hard up.* It's not usually this difficult to shake off attraction. Must be because it's been months since I've been with anyone. *I guess I haven't scratched that itch in a while.*

The inane banter of the radio personalities starts to grate on my nerves and I turn off the chatter. I open the window for some fresh air and take a deep breath. The cool wind whipping into the cab is refreshing, helping to clear my head. And I need a clear head. I need to focus on the job. What I *don't* need is anything complicating my work. Or my life, for that matter.

Driving the familiar route home, my brain goes into autopilot. I try to focus my thoughts on the new project, but thinking about work does nothing to get Olena off my mind. Having looked at her portfolio, there's no denying those before-and-after photos were truly impressive—unlike anything I've seen before. And I've worked with plenty of designers. Those images were not what I was expecting. Or, if I'm honest, what I was hoping for.

What I was hoping for was to be able to justify ignoring the undeniable pull drawing me to Olena, from the first moment she stalked angrily over to my truck in the rain to her rambling apology after Charles left. I was hoping to discover she was, well, uninteresting. Just a pretty face. I'm a grown man with self-control, after all, and I've been around plenty of beautiful women without losing my senses. On top of that, I know professional relationships need to be kept at an arm's length so the job runs smoothly.

But a stunning woman with a stunning mind? That's going to be much harder to ignore.

If anything, knowing she's brilliant just makes me want to stand a bit closer, stare a bit longer... It makes me want to get to know her, to figure her out. I think about watching her absent-mindedly fidgeting with her pen while Charles talked, as well as the adorable way she couldn't shut up when trying to explain all the reasons she'd lost her mind this morning in the rain. I'm smiling again now, picturing that fiery intensity under very different circumstances.

Realizing with a jolt that I've nearly missed my turn, I pull the truck sharply onto the sleepy rural road that leads to my house in the woods. *Fuck. Get it together, man.*

I run a hand over my beard. I don't know what's wrong with me. I've driven this route home from the Harwoods' on Dogwood Road a thousand times. I give my head a shake and blow out a breath. *Right, the Harwoods...* Thinking of John and Susan, I make another mental note to thank them for the referral. This is going to be a pretty lucrative project for me and my crew. And with Olena's unique talent on board...

Olena. She flashes in my mind again. Her flushed cheeks as she bit her lip... My rational brain is failing miserably at keeping my thoughts professional.

Oh God. I'd only met her this morning and I already want to do unspeakable things to her.

I pull the truck into the driveway of my secluded log cabin home and kill the engine. I take a moment to look at the place, wondering, before I can stop the thought, what Olena would think of my house. It's beautiful here, overlooking the river's edge. Would she like the rustic, cabin-in-the-woods vibe?

I shake my head. *Why does it matter? She's just your colleague.*

Gathering my notes and sketches, I climb out of the truck and exhale a long breath, rubbing my forehead. I'm going to have to find a way to work with her—*very closely*, as Charles had said—without letting myself get distracted. For weeks.

Locking up the truck, I head for the front porch. My ten-year-old Golden Retriever, Murphy, lumbers toward me slowly from his semi-permanent perch there. I crouch down, giving him a good scratch behind the ears.

"Thanks for waiting, buddy. Let's go get some lunch."

He yawns.

I unlock the front door and Murphy trails inside behind me. I hang my keys on the hook and kick off my work boots, heading to the kitchen to grab some leftovers. Leaning against the counter, I cross my arms over my chest as I wait for my food to reheat. The microwave buzzes, the dish inside rotating hypnotically. I stare past it, frowning, trying yet again to get my head on straight about this new job.

Lunch in hand, I settle onto the couch and let out a sigh as I look around the room. I like my routine here, just me and Murphy. Our life is predictable and comfortable. Uncomplicated.

But, after this morning, something tells me I'll need to figure out how to keep Olena from becoming a major complication.

8

OLENA

"Glad you could make it; was the commute hellish?" Sam winks at me, reaching out for a hug. I embrace him tightly, rocking us side to side in the small apartment hallway. Balloons and streamers hang from the corners of the ceiling in the kitchen and living room nearby.

"Oh, just brutal, all ten feet from my bedroom." I pull back, sporting a sarcastic deadpan expression, then break into a grin as I squeeze his hand. "Happy birthday, darling. You don't look a day over twenty-five. What's your secret?"

Sam's youthful glow is enviable. "Asian genes and overpriced skin care products." He adjusts his Happy Birthday tiara with a coquettish pout and smooths down his silky black hair.

We crack up and head over to the kitchen where Wyatt is busy using every pot and pan in our possession, stirring and flipping a variety of dishes. The aromas wafting through the apartment are already making my mouth water.

"Wyatt, you're killing me; it smells *so* good in here." I put my arm around his shoulders and give him a squeeze.

He glances at me quickly before returning his attention to the multiple pans and bowls sprawled out in front of him. "Beats crackers and cheese, right?" he teases me pointedly with a raised eyebrow. I'm famous for treating every meal like a picnic.

"Oof, shots fired," says Sam from behind us as he loads a small plate with appetizers from the kitchen table. "Let's save the drama for hearing about Olena's new hunky lumberjack." He pumps his eyebrows suggestively at me, grinning.

"Sam!" I exclaim in alarm. "He's not my hunky lumberjack!" I try to keep my cool. "He's not *my* anything, either. Except maybe my coworker," I say primly.

Sam rolls his eyes, still smiling. "Uh-huh."

"He's a landscaper, too, by the way, not a lumberjack," I add, a bit defensively.

"That's not what I heard from Wyatt," Sam says.

I shoot Wyatt a look; he gives me a guilty smile.

"But seriously, Olena, we need the whole story. Consider it a birthday gift to me. All the juicy details, please and thank you." Sam sits at the table, patting the seat beside him.

I pour myself a glass of wine and narrow my eyes at him good-naturedly, shaking my head. I don't sit down.

"Okay, fine, but no more lumberjack talk." I raise my eyebrows and point a threatening finger at each of them.

The door buzzer sounds. Wyatt wipes his hands on a tea towel and answers it, letting Nat in, then turns back to his post at the stove.

"Alright, don't worry," says Wyatt, "we'll be on our best behavior. I want to hear more about how things went with Uncle Charles, anyway."

Because Wyatt had been so busy preparing for tonight, I'd only had time to give him a quick summary of what happened yesterday at the property. Somehow, what seems to have stuck is

Jude's appearance. I may have likened him to a lumberjack, but I definitely did *not* use the term *hunky*.

I cautiously sit down beside Sam as Nat lets herself in. "Best behavior," I remind Sam with a stern look.

He raises his hands in an obedient pose.

"Remember, I'm a consummate professional," I add, holding a hand to my chest, the picture of restraint.

Nat shrugs off her coat, dumping it and her purse on the chair near the door, then kicks off her shoes.

"Who's a consummate professional?" she asks. "Ooh, are we hearing about Olena's new job?" Nat catches up quickly, joining us at the table. She rubs her hands, then wraps her arms around Sam's shoulders from behind. "Happy birthday, Sammy," she adds quietly as she gives him a squeeze, a few of her dark braids falling forward over his shoulder.

He smiles up at her.

"Yes, I've been roped into recounting the whole messy tale," I say, glancing pointedly at Wyatt. He's drizzling sauce into the skillet, steam hissing up from the pan.

"I want to hear everything," Nat squeals, sitting down with us.

Wyatt begins clearing away the appetizers to make room for the feast he's prepared. He's been teaching himself how to cook traditional Vietnamese dishes lately, even secretly calling Sam's mom from time to time for guidance on technique so he could get everything right for the party.

I take a long, steadying breath. "Well, I guess everything started on the drive out there..."

"Wait, so, he just left in a huff for no reason?" Wyatt asks, looking confused and surprised.

"Well, I wouldn't say he was in *a huff*, but I guess it was kind of abrupt?" I'm still not sure what to make of Jude's behavior; he'd taken off so suddenly yesterday.

"Huh, that's kind of... dramatic and weird," Sam notes.

"Probably just realized he was stuck working with me for the next few weeks," I joke.

"Shut your face; he should be so lucky," says Nat. She takes a sip from her glass of wine.

I smile sheepishly. "I don't know," I say, pausing to think for a moment. "I'm probably overthinking everything. Classic me, right?"

"I mean, you would qualify for Olympic gold in that sport," Wyatt teases, now sitting with us at the table. The remnants of his incredible main dishes sit in front of us: bánh mì sandwiches, phở noodle soup, and bún chả—pork meatballs. Needless to say, there isn't much food left. "I remember back in high school we'd stay up until two in the morning talking on the phone about exactly what Brandon Gregson meant when he signed that note *'love, Brandon'* or analyzing Taylor Copeland's body language in math class to figure out who he was going to ask to the dance."

"To be fair, they were both total dreamboats," I say wistfully.

"You're not wrong," agrees Wyatt with a sigh.

Sam clears his throat, looking pointedly at Wyatt.

"Not as much of a dreamboat as you, honey, *obviously*." Wyatt leans over to plant a kiss on Sam's cheek.

Sam flutters his dark eyelashes dramatically. "I was worried that, maybe, now that I'm twenty-eight, you'll have eyes for the younger guys." He pouts jokingly.

"Oh, God, not a chance. Have you spoken to the youths lately?" Wyatt asks, rolling his eyes. "Because I spend all day with them at the deli. There's no way. Too much drama. I'm constantly helping them figure out their little baby love lives. There's not much upstairs just yet, you know what I mean?"

"So, you prefer my brilliant mind, do you?" Sam flirts, leaning toward Wyatt suggestively.

Wyatt smiles and kisses him.

"Ugh, get a room, you two, shoot!" Nat interjects, ripping off a piece of her bread roll and tossing it at them. It hits Wyatt on the shoulder, and he looks up at her in alarm and amusement.

"Oh, leave them be," I say, coming to their defense. "They're cute. Plus, it's Sam's birthday. No bread pelting allowed."

Sam looks at Nat smugly, agreeing with me.

The reality is, Sam and Wyatt are the most solid couple I know; they've been together three years now, and often talk about getting married. Their plan is to move in together once Sam finishes business school and Wyatt can get a better job than managing the deli. For now, Sam's living with his parents, and Wyatt's saving money by splitting the rent with me.

I watch their easy closeness with envy. The contrasting image of Jude high-tailing it away from me flashes in my mind, and I frown to myself.

My phone buzzes in my back pocket and I pull it out. Another text from a number I don't recognize.

UNKNOWN NUMBER
Why won't you respond? Talk to me.

The crease in my brow deepens as I delete the message and quickly block the number. I feel queasy.

"So, when do you start work for Uncle Charles?" Wyatt asks from the kitchen, breaking into my thoughts. He's gotten up to take dishes to the sink, so he doesn't catch the look on my face as I stare at my phone. I glance up. Nat and Sam are busy talking to each other and haven't noticed either.

I blink and force myself back into the present with my friends, pushing Sean's text out of my head. I put my phone back in my pocket. "Oh, um, right away, basically. I'm going to be taking measurements and working on the designs this week."

"So, you'll be back at the job site on Monday?" Nat cuts in with a knowing look on her face. She pops a bite of bread into her mouth, grinning. "Will *Jude* be there?" She draws out his name, pumping her eyebrows.

I swat her in the arm, then take a deep breath. Yes. Yes, he will.

9

OLENA

I'm already regretting getting out of bed as we pull up to the curb next to Lyons Park, last night's merriment having carried on late enough that I could have used a few more hours of sleep. Natalie parks under a large oak tree. Black Bear River flows calmly along the opposite side of the park, a paved footpath following the river's edge, the burbling sound of the water a familiar backdrop for our Sunday morning runs. I unclip my seatbelt and cram my phone and keys into the overflowing glove compartment. The lid takes a couple of shoves to latch shut.

I reach around the back of the seat and twist, trying to wake my body up with the stretch. "It's not too late, you know," I say to Nat dryly, releasing the stretch and slumping back against the seat. "We can still bail and go get greasy drive-thru breakfast instead of"—I gesture in the general direction of the river in mock disgust—*"this."*

Nat smirks. "As tempting as bacon sounds at this fine hour, I'm gonna need to remind you that you agreed to train for that 5k in the fall."

"Ugh, rude of you to bring that up!" I direct a scowl at Nat.

She rolls her eyes. "Olena, my darling," she says patiently, "we are going to be fabulous, fit babes." She flips down the sun visor to look in the mirror, rubbing her eyes. She's as tired as I am, but she was born with the gene that lets her overcome such things in favor of being practical. "You know," she continues archly, "the kind who *enjoy* exercise and talk endlessly about endorphins and protein shakes and collagen supplements."

"Oh, please promise to shoot me if I ever become that person." I close my eyes and let out a deep, soul-level sigh. I reconsider. "Well," I say, "maybe I can accept the fit part and the babes part, but that's it. No insufferable carrying on about it. I wouldn't be able to live with myself." I open my eyes, bringing my knees up to hug them against my chest. I seem to be having an enthusiasm malfunction this morning. "And you'd better not become that person either or I will disown you!" I narrow my eyes and level a serious glare at Nat.

She raises her hands in defense. "Okay, okay, shoot. I won't. But we signed up for that 5k together, so let's muster up the..." Nat trails off and looks past me out the passenger side window, seeming to search for the word in the park beside us. "Strength? Energy? The... chutzpah?" She turns to me with a hopeful expression.

The prospect of mustering up chutzpah hits me in a fresh wave of dread, and I whimper dramatically, pulling my hood up over my head as if I can shield myself from reality. I zip up my hoodie with a scowl and yank on the laces, cinching the hood almost shut so only my nose sticks out.

"Oh, come on," says Nat, "it's not gonna be that bad."

"It's going to be *the worst* and I don't wanna." My whiny toddler voice is muffled against the inside of my sweatshirt, but there's no turning back; I'm committed to my petulant performance and Nat knows it. I expect her to play the part of responsible adult now. That's how this always goes. But I don't hear her cajoling me along like usual.

"Nat?" I ask uncertainly, wondering what the dead air is all about.

"What? Oh, yeah, right." She sounds distracted.

"Aren't you going to convince me to get out of the car? This is normally when you're like 'Olena, running always makes you feel better, come on,' or 'Olena, get your ass out of the car and put on your big girl pants' or—"

Nat interrupts my childish impression of her with a gentle swat. "Len, shut up; what did you say that landscaper guy's business was called again?"

"What? Oh. Something Knives? No, Blades? Grass Blades? No... I can't remember. Why?" I ask from inside my hoodie cocoon.

"Sharpe Blades?" she asks tentatively.

"Oh, yeah, that was it. Why?" I try to get us back on track. "Nat, focus up. I need some more mustering help here." This is how it works between us: I'm the hot mess and she's my voice of reason.

"Oh, wow. You didn't mention..." Nat sounds like she's smiling. Then, more alarmed, I hear, "Oh, shit."

The sound of her keys jingling reaches me through my morning fog, penetrating the combined layers of sweatshirt and soul-crushing ennui. The automatic window whines softly as it rolls down beside me. I absentmindedly lower my legs to the floor of the car, now thoroughly confused.

I shift the fabric aperture of my cinched hood to line up with one eyeball as I turn to Nat, trying to figure out what has caught her attention. When I finally align my little window correctly, it reveals Nat sporting a massive grin, her eyes shifting rapidly between me and the open window to my right.

"What's going on? Nat—"

Nat discreetly shoves my arm.

"Olena?" A deep voice from outside the window startles me and I jump, realization hitting me in slow motion. Jude. Jude is here. *Why is Jude here?*

In a panic, I claw at the edges of my hood, tugging it open, snagging a tangled section of my hair along with it.

"Shit, ow," I mutter under my breath as I sweep away my hoodie and hair as fast as I can. In my rush to free myself from my sweatshirt prison, one of the laces whips up and drags across my open mouth. Frantically inhaling at exactly the wrong moment, I get a mouthful of hair and hoodie lace. I recoil, coughing and spluttering as I rip the hood down and attempt to spit out several errant hairs my fingers are failing to drag out of my face. Finally, smoothing my hands over my hair and face a half dozen times proves successful; I return to some approximation of my normal appearance, though I know I must look disheveled. I take a steadying breath and look up.

"Jude. Hi," I manage to say, although my voice comes out at a higher pitch than normal, as if contrived cheerfulness can help me recover my dignity. I clear my throat and look away, the eye contact intolerable as my cheeks flush in humiliation. I can feel him grinning down at me, his forearm braced over the passenger side door.

I send a fervent wish to the universe for a sinkhole to swallow me up. But, knowing my luck, it'd swallow us all up together and we'd have to continue this cringefest at the bottom.

I turn wide eyes on Nat. She's pressing her lips together, her shoulders twitching forward as she tries to suppress a laugh. My eyes shoot silent daggers, pleading with her to save me from this moment. But there's clearly no escape.

"You okay?" Jude asks, and I turn back to him reluctantly. I lift my eyes to meet his with an expression that hopefully reads *I'm not deranged.* His smile tells me he's as delighted as Nat is at my suffering, his green eyes shining with amusement. "Did I... interrupt something?"

Oh, just me humiliating myself. Nothing to see here. Move along, citizen. Please, *please* move along.

Jude remains in place, looking down at me under his arm. A breeze drifts through the open window and carries with it the scent of him; he smells of freshly cut grass and sawdust mixed with something deeper, smokier. My eyes linger a moment too long on his broad chest, then I snap to attention when I realize I haven't answered his question.

"Oh, us? No, no. I mean, we were just... we're going for a run. We were just talking and I was—" I gesture weakly at Nat, trying to convey meaning with my hands because my mouth can't put words into a coherent sentence.

"I recognized your car from the other day," he says to me, then nods to Nat.

"I'm Natalie, hi." She waves.

I scrunch up my face as I realize I have, yet again, forgotten how to be a human with even the most basic grasp of social graces.

"Yes, sorry, Jude, this is my best friend, Natalie; Nat, this is Jude, from the work... thing." I shift my eyes to Jude's briefly, cringing at my weak reference to how we know each other. *The work thing?* I should stop talking. My inner critic is logging all of this in furious detail to be replayed later. Probably when I'm trying to fall asleep tonight.

"Nice to meet you." Nat leans over me from her perch in the driver's seat and flashes a friendly and somewhat amused smile. "And this is actually my car; Olena was borrowing it for a bit."

"Right," he says, nodding. "Well, it's hard to miss. Not many yellow cars around." He flicks his gaze to me for a thoughtful moment, then inhales and breaks eye contact.

"What are you working on over there?" Nat asks as she looks

past Jude, saving me from having to open my own mouth and risk whatever humiliating nonsense might come out.

With a half-glance behind him, he gestures over his shoulder. "Just finishing this job at Lyons Park before we get going on the Faulkner property."

I feel him look at me. Avoiding his gaze, I scan the park and see a small crew of workers building a retaining wall alongside a freshly paved footpath. A half-dozen saplings stand sentinel, waiting to be planted, their root balls covered in burlap. A familiar dark green truck is parked beside them.

I swallow and smile weakly at Jude, then look away. My embarrassment is still too potent to shift into small-talk mode. I envision myself fleeing the scene without looking back. Diving into the river. Building a new life in the mountains, surrounded by animals who don't care that I'm an awkward bonehead.

"Well, I should let you get on with your plans, ladies," Jude says as he gently taps the car frame with his fist and pushes off to take a couple of steps back. "Have a great run." Then, to me: "See you at the work... thing." He raises an eyebrow and gives me a crooked half-smile.

As he turns and walks back to his crew, Nat's eyes follow him for a few paces, then widen as she turns to me with her mouth agape. A delighted and knowing grin spreads across her face.

"O-le-na!" She punctuates each whispered syllable with a slap to my upper arm, devolving into suppressed cackles. She's clearly relishing the delicious horror of having witnessed me making a fool of myself in front of Jude—Jude, who, I now realize, I had neglected to describe to Nat last night. The look on her face tells me she wasn't expecting... *him.*

With a muffled groan, I slowly slouch down into my seat, lower and lower, until I'm sure I've disappeared from view altogether. I let the last few minutes wash over me and feel a fresh twinge of self-loathing.

Sinkhole, take me now.

10

OLENA

Alone in my bedroom that evening, I open my laptop to check my bank account for the tenth time this weekend. I've been watching my balance steadily circle the drain, feeling more and more anxious about my dwindling funds with each passing day. When the page loads this time, however, I almost yelp with joy at what I see: my last Seattle client has finally paid me. Relief washes over me. I immediately call the repair shop that's holding my car hostage and tell the man who answers that I'll be there tomorrow morning to pay what's owed and pick it up. I hang up and exhale loudly.

Thank you, universe. Finally, I'll have my own way out to the Faulkner property on Monday. This is perfect timing so I can get to work. At the property. With Jude.

Jude. Images of him float into my mind. That first moment when he lifted his umbrella and I saw those green eyes. The way his hair fell in front of his face when he was concentrating on his notes. The devilish grin on his face after he gave me the protein bar.

I open my portfolio and pull out his business card. *Sharpe Blades Landscaping.*

I type it into the search engine before I can think better of it. His website loads to show smiling faces in beautiful gardens, happy customers standing on pathways, and laughing families picnicking on grass. I click through the gallery of images but don't find any of Jude. I catch myself feeling slightly deflated and search for *Jude Sharpe Lennox Valley* instead. No social media profiles. *Weird.* I find one tiny, low-quality group photo from four years ago, evidently from a fundraiser for the Lennox Valley Conservation Society that was profiled in the local paper. Zooming in on the photo just makes it blurrier. I squint at the screen, trying to make out which guy in a ball cap is him...

I jump at the knock on my door, slamming my laptop shut in a panic.

"Yeah?" I squeak, my strange voice giving me away. I clear my throat.

What the hell am I doing?

Wyatt opens the door and peers in with a puzzled expression. "Everything cool?"

"Yup, just working. You know, getting things ready for Monday." I smile awkwardly with over-exaggerated pleasantness.

"Okay..." Wyatt eyes me suspiciously. "Anyway," he says, gesturing to the door with his thumb, "I was just gonna let you know Sam and I are heading out to grab dinner in about ten minutes."

"Oh, awesome, have a great time."

He turns to leave.

"Oh, and hey, I finally got paid!" I do jazz hands to accentuate the significance of this news.

"Oh my God, it's about time!" he says, sagging with relief against the doorframe. "So happy to hear that."

"I know. Now I can get my car back tomorrow," I add.

"That's perfect timing with the new job."

"I know, right?"

Wyatt steps into my room to give me a quick hug, reminds me not to get sucked into working late, then leaves, shutting the door.

I open the laptop again and immediately close the browser tabs with Jude's website and the news article. Digging out my notebook, I take a breath to reset myself, reviewing my scribbled notes from the tour. I try to jot down some additional ideas, but nothing comes to me. Pulling up my design software instead, I hope that will work to get me in the zone. I stare at the screen blankly and try to force my brain to think through the design steps that are usually second-nature to me. *Uh, trees. There were trees.*

I'm having trouble focusing. Thoughts of Jude's abrupt exit on Thursday are hogging all my mental bandwidth, my humiliating hoodie mishap this morning coming in at a close second. *Why do I always embarrass myself in front of him?* I get as far as saving a blank file in a folder named *"Faulkner"* before giving up on work.

I grab my favorite stress ball, the one with green glitter gel inside, and pace the room. Squeezing it and watching the green sparkles bulge out between my fingers, I try to channel some of my nervous energy, but all my thoughts return to one person.

What was going through Jude's mind, anyway? First he gave me a snack, then turned cold and bolted. Then, this morning at the park, I could have sworn he was almost flirting with me...

He probably thinks you're ridiculous. Because you keep acting ridiculous.

I'm still pacing when there's another knock at my door.

"I'm back! I'm coming in!" Wyatt's muffled voice calls out, as if concerned about what he'll walk in on.

"Come in!" I call back impatiently, and Wyatt opens the door, peeking in at me again.

"Hey, did you want me to—" He stops mid-sentence, stepping into the room fully. "Are you sure you're okay, babe?"

"Why wouldn't I be?" I ask.

"Uh, well, first of all, you're about to pop that stress ball."

I look down and release my death grip with a self-conscious smile.

"And when I came in here before, you looked like I caught you watching porn. What gives?" He smirks at me.

"I don't know what you mean; I'm fine," I lie with a weak smile.

"You just look like you're... working out some tension," he says carefully.

"Just some job stress, is all. Butterflies, I guess." I know I don't look the least bit convincing.

"Uh-huh," Wyatt says slowly, narrowing his eyes at me. "This wouldn't have anything to do with that tall drink of water who was giving you bedroom eyes while you choked on your hair this morning, would it?" He smiles knowingly.

I roll my eyes and let out a groan. "Nat told you?"

"Oh, every glorious detail." He's grinning at me. "It sounds like *hunky lumberjack* was a bit of an understatement." He raises his eyebrows.

I collapse on the bed in defeat. "Ugh, Wyatt, what am I going to do? I have to work alongside this man. And I can't go five minutes without acting like a total mess in front of him."

"Oh, honey." Wyatt sits down on the bed beside me, rubbing my back. "Don't give yourself a hard time about being... *yourself.*"

My eyes widen and I turn to see Wyatt grinning and bracing for impact. I tackle him, slapping playfully at his arms and chest as I knock him over onto my bed. "Rotten human!"

"I take it back!" Wyatt gasps between fits of laughter. "I couldn't help myself! Mercy! Mercy!"

"How dare you!" I shriek, laughing despite myself as he cackles below me. Defending himself, he finally catches both my forearms in his hands, stopping us both.

His eyes are watering from laughter. "Seriously," he gasps. "Seriously. I didn't mean it. How can I make it up to you? Tell me your demands. Anything."

Still perched over Wyatt on the bed, I narrow my eyes in mock resentment and think for a moment. "Bring me dinner when you come home and we're even."

"Deal!" He lets go of my arms and wriggles out from under me. Standing, he straightens his shirt and wipes his eyes. "I really didn't mean it, you know. You're not a mess; you're perfect." He leans over to kiss me on the cheek.

"That's more like it," I reply, giving him a rueful smirk. "Now, go get me dinner, errand boy." I lift my chin at the open door.

He retreats in supplication, averting his eyes, and I throw a pillow at the door as he closes it.

I fall back on the bed and stare at the ceiling, sighing deeply. *What am I going to do?*

My phone rings and I get up to grab it from the desk.

Fuck. I don't recognize the number. Again.

Nausea suddenly replaces all the giddy energy from wrestling with Wyatt. I reject the call and put the phone down. I wait a minute, frozen in place, my heart beating rapidly, to see if I'll get a voicemail notification. Instead, the text notification chimes.

UNKNOWN NUMBER
I know this is your number. Stop ignoring me.

I feel ill. I delete the message as fast as I can, block this new number, and toss the phone back onto the desk with a clatter. Inhaling a steadying breath, I walk back to the bed and sit down slowly. I look warily across the room at my phone, as if sheer force of will can make Sean stop trying to contact me.

What the fuck am I going to do?

11

JUDE

"Alright, folks, Steph'll flag any trees and plants needing inspection or showing signs of disease." I grab a roll of flagging tape from the truck and throw it to Steph, who catches it deftly. I raise my eyebrows and point a finger at her. "Impressive reaction time for a Monday morning. Nice." Steph gives me a smug look from under her ball cap, crossing her muscular arms over her chest.

Clipboard in hand, I scan down the list of tasks to assign to my team, absentmindedly drumming my pencil along the edge as I delegate.

"Dimitri, you're pulling up the dead stuff and invasives," I say, lifting my chin at the dead plants across the clearing. "I'll set up a tarp for you."

"Okay, boss," Dimitri says, a look of determination crossing his sharp features. He reaches up and runs a hand through his dark hair. Dimitri is easily the hardest worker on my team and looks it: his wiry frame is packed with lean muscle, and he has a perpetual air of exhaustion about him.

I still smile when I hear Dimitri, or any of my team, call me *boss.* It was initially a tongue-in-cheek thing a few years back when I'd hired him, fresh out of college, but the nickname ended up sticking. Then the rest of the team picked up the habit.

"Mitch," I continue, directing my attention to the oldest member of my crew. He's in his late forties, with bristly, graying hair and deep creases in his forehead, the years of working out in the sun having made him look older than he is. "You can start marking out the utility lines." I pull a map of the property out of my back pocket and hand it over. "Then you can help me flag out the section we're going to be calling the *too far gone area.*" I gesture with the clipboard across the clearing, pointing to a lumpy section of rock, weeds, and tall grass.

Mitch glances over his shoulder and gives me a quick nod.

"And Teddy, you're on branches. Grab a ladder."

Teddy, a barrel-chested guy in his mid-thirties with thinning blond hair, holds up his lopping shears. "Can do," he says with a smirk. He has the appearance and personality of an overgrown kid.

The team moves off to get started as I climb into the truck bed to grab a tarp and some stake flags.

A vehicle rumbles toward the driveway and I look up, expecting Charles or Carol with their groceries, or possibly another work vehicle for something related to the house renovation. A small silver hatchback I don't recognize emerges from the trees, and I stand slowly, my vantage point atop the truck giving me a better view. I don't know why I'm so curious; plenty of tradespeople are coming and going from the site as the renovations get underway.

Except that's a lie. I know exactly who I'm waiting to see.

I look away and take a breath, determined to focus on the job in front of me. Jumping down from the truck bed, I circle around to the passenger door, letting Murphy out to join us. It's an unusually warm, spring-like day, and he can amble around out here comfortably while we work. Our unofficial mascot, he joins me on the job site most days. He never gets underfoot, just alternates between sleeping and receiving head scratches and belly rubs from anyone who will indulge him.

Behind me, I hear a car door closing.

"Is he yours?"

I know her voice before I even turn around and catch myself smiling. I don't want to seem too eager, so I take my time closing the door before turning to face her. When I do, Olena is standing outside her car, Murphy lumbering over to her to say hello. She stoops down to meet him, extending her open hand, which he nuzzles and licks.

"Hi, there," she says softly, crouching down now and ruffling the fur around Murphy's neck with both hands.

I can't help but smile.

He is loving the attention. He noses Olena's face, licking her cheek.

"Oh, wow, that tickles, buddy," Olena laughs and rubs at her face with her sleeve.

"Sorry, he's not normally like that with people," I say.

"Oh, I don't mind." She throws me a quick smile.

It's true. Murphy's gotten old enough that this puppy-like display of affection is rare for him. He's normally not fussed enough by anyone to even get up—unless they have food for him.

"Do you have a dog? Treats in your pocket or something?" I'm a bit baffled that he's acting so excited.

"No, no dog, no dog treats." Olena smiles again and shrugs as she scratches around his ears and under his chin. Her eyes lift to mine at the same moment that Murphy pushes his face into hers again, knocking her off balance. She stumbles a step in her crouched position, catching herself with an outstretched hand. She looks back to me, laughing. "What's his name?"

"Murphy," I reply, entranced by watching them together. "And yeah, he's mine."

"He's beautiful." Olena beams, still stroking his fur affectionately.

You're beautiful, I stop myself from saying.

I run a hand through my hair and tear my eyes away from Olena and Murphy, making a point of rummaging through a bag in the truck instead.

"Hey, boss, you got that tarp?" Dimitri calls out from across the clearing, holding a few dead plants he's already hauled up.

"Yeah, be right there!" I call back, then turn back to Olena. "I assume you're here to do a bit of recon?"

"Yeah," Olena says, standing, then adjusting her footing with a smile as Murphy slumps heavily onto his side at her feet. "I thought I'd get some measurements and take more photos, take a plant inventory, that kind of thing." She tucks her hair behind her ear and readjusts the heavy-looking bag on her shoulder.

"Okay, well, let me know if you need anything from me," I say.

Something in her expression changes for the briefest moment before she looks away. "Sure, sounds good." She starts looking through her bag and pulls out a notebook and measuring tape.

I blow out a breath and plod across the tall grass to Dimitri, leaving Olena in the driveway. Passing by the base of Teddy's ladder, I hear his voice from above my head.

"Who's that?" Tilting his head in Olena's direction, he raises his eyebrows.

I stop and turn back to look at her. "Olena MacMillan. The designer," I reply, then look up at Teddy.

"Murph's sure in love already," he adds, smirking.

"Yeah, he's a sucker for a good head scratch, I guess." Murphy's now rolling at her feet as she rubs his belly indulgently, her hair falling softly forward. I shake my head at my old dog's unexpected antics.

"Ah, I dunno," Teddy says, cutting a branch and letting it fall to the ground. "Dogs can tell, man."

"What do you mean?" I squint up at him, the sunshine filtering through the branches of the tree he's working on.

He shrugs. "You know, they can tell if people are good or bad... like, on the inside," he says, looking at them appraisingly. "And from the looks of it, old Murph isn't finding any red flags." He grins at me. "Just saying. Dogs can tell."

By MIDMORNING, we've got two tarps full of debris to haul out between the dead plants and the cut branches. I'm taking stock of our progress, surveying which trees need attention next, when my eyes settle on Olena across the main yard. She's near the house, crouching down and squinting through a DSLR camera to photograph the overgrown pathway and nearby garden beds.

As if sensing my eyes on her, she turns briefly from the viewfinder and meets my gaze with a small smile. She looks back through the camera and snaps a few shots, then lowers it, standing to look at the preview on the screen. I realize I was so focused on keeping my shit together when she arrived that I haven't introduced her to my team.

Her back is turned to me as I walk over. I drink in the sight of her as she gathers her hair in both hands and pulls it back, twisting it up into a messy bun. I slow my pace and take a deep breath, trying not to stare at her neck as she secures her hair with an elastic and readjusts her camera strap. Small, wispy waves bounce loose from her haphazard topknot, falling around her ears, glowing auburn in the sun. Her movements seem to be happening in slow motion and I shake my head, returning to reality.

Just act normal. Pretend you're talking to Teddy.

As I approach, she turns toward me and smiles. She looks... almost shy.

I clear my throat. "Hey," I say, "if you've got a minute, I thought I could introduce you to my crew." I gesture over my shoulder with my thumb in the general direction of my team.

"Oh, sure." She grins bravely and picks up her bag to follow me.

I have to remind myself to stop staring at her mouth. *That smile is going to be the death of me.*

Steph is tying flagging tape around the trunk of a tree not far away, so we head toward her first. As we walk, the silence between us feels thick. I have no idea what to say or do around this woman. I try to look anywhere but at Olena, though I can feel all my senses heightened just being next to her.

Olena finally breaks the tension. "For what it's worth, I promise not to call anyone an asshole today."

Her quiet joke takes a second to land due to the swirling thoughts in my head.

I let out a breath, both surprised and amused. "Well, it would be poor form on day one, for sure," I tease, relieved I managed something remotely smooth in response.

"Ooh, ouch!" She feigns offense, wrinkling her nose at me.

"Too close to home?" I raise an eyebrow.

"No, I absolutely deserved that," she says as she lowers her eyes, letting out a soft chuckle and tucking a fallen wisp of hair behind her ear.

I'm immediately desperate to hear her laugh like that again. I look away. *Keep it together.*

Steph turns as we approach. I'm relieved to have another human to help me keep my mind on the work. As they shake hands, I try to focus and silently vow to steer clear of any flirtatious territory with Olena. I've got to keep this professional, though her sweet scent at my side is pulling my thoughts in a very different direction.

Because damn, I can't stop imagining pulling her against me, tangling my hands in her hair.

"So, Jude," I hear Steph say, and quickly snap back to attention. She takes off her ball cap and smooths down her short hair before putting it back on. "I wanted your opinion on this oak branch over here." Steph leads us to a nearby tree she's already flagged. She uses a laser pointer to show me the partially broken branch hanging at a precarious angle above the side of the house, a few other branches taking its weight.

I cross my arms and study the tree, frowning. "Oof, definitely need to get that out of there," I comment quietly, almost to myself. *Yes, think about the branch. Only the branch.*

"That looks like it could cause serious damage to the roof if it fell," Olena agrees.

Steph nods. "Exactly. But I also noticed there's some die-back at the crown. See up there?" She points to a small section of bare branches at the top of the tree. "Do you think the tree will need an assessment? I'm thinking there might be rot."

"Could be," I say.

"It might have to be cut down?" Olena asks.

"Hope not." Steph shrugs.

"That'd be a shame." Olena furrows her brow. "Especially for such a big tree, providing shade to the house," she adds, squinting up at the tangled branches and shielding her eyes from the sun with one hand. Then she looks down, taking in the surrounding area. "But you know, if the oak did go, we could plant a line of cedars along this face of the house... or even bamboo would grow quickly and provide some shade."

"We'd have to figure out what's infected this one before choosing anything new... and consider the soil." I run a hand over my beard. "And we wouldn't want to plant right on top of the ground-out stump."

"Totally," says Steph.

I'm feeling good now; this is appropriate, professional territory. No more mooning about my dog's adoring instincts or staring longingly at Olena's neck.

"Well, let me know if you get word from the arborist; I'll be making a design call for that area this week." Olena looks in her element too; I can see the wheels turning as she takes in the area and jots some quick notes before stuffing her notebook back into her bag. She lifts her camera and snaps a few photos of the area.

I make sure to focus on the tree as I wait. Steph moves to get back to work, and I take that as our cue to carry on.

I lift my chin, indicating the other side of the clearing. "Come on, I'll introduce you to the guys," I say, then add under my breath, "Apologies in advance about Teddy."

Olena's eyes shine with curiosity, then she places a hand over her heart with a solemn look. "Hey, a promise is a promise."

"WHAT DID YOU SAY?" shouts Teddy over the sound of the small excavator. We're standing a half-dozen feet away but the rumble of the machine is intense.

"Dude, turn it off so you can hear us!" I cup my hands around my mouth. Teddy squints at me, trying to read my lips. I roll my eyes and make a key-turning gesture. He finally gets the message and kills the motor on the digger. I sigh and shake my head. "Thank you."

I lean toward Olena and gesture at Teddy, smiling. "See, Teddy here never quite grew out of wanting to play with toys all day." Teddy's worked for me for years and never tires of using the heavy equipment.

Olena lets out a soft chuckle, pulling her eyes from mine to watch Teddy, amusement playing on her face.

He clambers out of the digger and grins. "It's true. This is my favorite part." A pause. "You must be Alanna! Nice to meet you!" Teddy enthusiastically offers his hand with a boyish grin.

"Olena, actually, but that was very close," she replies good-naturedly, shaking his hand. Seeing the regretful expression on Teddy's face, her eyes widen as she quickly adds: "Happens all the time."

He looks reassured.

She gestures to the area he's been excavating. "What's happening here?"

"Teddy's digging this area out to get rid of the boulders. I've been calling this spot the *too far gone area,* but I think in a few days we'll need a new name," I explain.

Olena smiles and looks at the mini-excavator, then at Teddy. "Well, Teddy, I'm with you. That thing does look like fun to drive."

Teddy's eyes light up. "You wanna try? I can show you how it works!"

"Oh, I don't need to—" Olena starts, shaking her head.

He turns to me. "That okay with you, boss?"

"If you're up for it," I say to Olena, raising an eyebrow.

Would she be? This is an interesting development.

She looks hesitantly at me, then at the machine, then back at Teddy, whose enthusiasm rivals Murphy's from earlier this morning.

"Come on, it's great!" he says.

"Oh, okay." She chuckles nervously.

Brave girl, I think to myself, pleasantly surprised. *What else is she up for?*

"I'll leave you to it," I say, grinning at Olena.

Her eyes widen at the realization that I'm leaving her with Teddy.

Walking away, I call out over my shoulder. "Don't worry! You're in excellent hands!" I head for the truck to get a drink of water. Leaning against the tailgate and taking a swig from my water bottle, I smile at Teddy's enthusiastic arm-waving and Olena's nervous posture.

She climbs into the cab of the digger and listens intently to Teddy's instructions. Her eyes meet mine briefly and I give her an encouraging smile.

I'm so focused on watching the scene unfold that I don't notice Steph appear at my side.

"Hey," she says, resting beside me against the tailgate.

"Hey. Didn't see you there," I reply, turning again to watch as Olena gingerly controls the digging arm. It jerks forward suddenly and she startles, then laughs.

Steph is quiet for a moment. "She's got you good, huh, boss?" She elbows me.

I frown. "What do you mean?" I ask, although I know exactly what she means.

"Oh, come on. I mean, even *I'm* in love with her already."

I raise my eyebrows and look at Steph, who gives me a knowing look. With a roll of my eyes, I look away. "I'm just supervising my crew member using heavy equipment, Steph; I have no idea what you're talking about." I take another drink, keeping my expression carefully neutral.

Steph follows my gaze, locked on Olena in the excavator.

"Sure you are." She pats my arm and walks off, chuckling and shaking her head.

12

OLENA

After surviving my first day on site with Jude and, miraculously, not making a raving fool of myself, I'm feeling more optimistic about the project. Maybe there's hope for me and Jude to have a proper working relationship. Maybe I didn't ruin everything with my temper and my unstoppable rambling. Maybe I *can* keep my cool standing next to this gorgeous man and pretend I'm not constantly aware of every move he makes.

I've spent the last two days working from home on some initial design sketches, creating a proof-of-concept mockup for Charles and Carol. And for Jude. I haven't seen him since Monday; my eyes are already searching for him as I pull into the Faulkners' driveway. I spot him talking with Dimitri at the far end of the yard and gesturing to various points along the garden border at the cliff's edge. He's wearing a black t-shirt and jeans and looks delicious, even from far away. I sigh.

He turns as I drive in and immediately makes his way over to me.

Oh, God, he's even better up close, my treacherous brain pipes up.

I step out of the car and hurry to put my jacket on, shivering in the morning chill. I reach behind my neck to flick my hair out from under my jacket collar.

"Hi," Jude says, sticking his hands in his pockets.

I grab my bag from the car and circle around to where he's standing. "Hey," I say.

"I was hoping you'd show up today." He smiles. "I wanted to ask you about your plans for the space."

"Yeah, I actually brought the initial design sketches with me to show the Faulkners." I glance at the big house. "And you, obviously," I quickly add. I catch myself playing with the ends of my hair and quickly stuff my hand in my pocket, not wanting to look as nervous as I feel under Jude's gaze.

"Oh, yeah? Let's have a look." He raises his eyebrows expectantly.

Opening my bag and pulling out my folder of sketches, I glance around the work site. "Have you got a smaller crew today?" I ask, tilting my chin at the two workers I can see.

Steph is demolishing the rotten wood frames of old raised vegetable beds, a sledgehammer leaning up against the bed beside her as she pries the wood apart with a crowbar. Dimitri is using an edging tool, creating clean-cut lines along the sides of the cobblestone walkway. No sign of Teddy or Mitch.

Following my gaze, Jude nods. "Mitch booked a few days off months ago, and Teddy is at a dentist appointment. He'll be here later."

Pulling the sketches out of the folder, I hold them in front of me. Jude walks over to stand at my side, peering at them over my shoulder. He's so close; the heat of his body radiates toward me and I can smell his incredible, earthy scent. My heart starts beating faster and my hands feel unsteady. I adjust my grip on the papers to stop them from shaking.

I try to play it cool. "So, uh, this is the one for the front face of the house. The garden beds there..." I say, showing him the first drawing. "And this"—I pull out the second one—"is for the... what did you call it? The *too far gone area*?" I risk looking up at him with a grin.

Mistake. His green eyes lock on mine and my smile falters, my mouth opening slightly as my gaze drops to his lips. I quickly tear my eyes away, forcing my attention back to the sketches.

He must *have seen that*, I think to myself, shame rising up. My cheeks feel flushed. When I shuffle the papers to show him the third sketch, I swear I hear him take a long, slow breath.

His voice rumbles low beside me. "Is that a fire pit at the center of a... sunken garden?" He points to the drawing, his arm brushing against mine slightly and making my eyes flutter shut. Even this accidental touch is electric, and I am quickly losing my battle to stay in professional mode.

"Uh, yeah, and these—" I start to say.

"Olena! Jude!" Charles' voice snaps me back to reality and we both whirl around to greet him. I'm both grateful for the interruption and genuinely happy to see him again.

"Hi, Charles, good morning." I force myself to break the spell cast by Jude being so close to me. "I was just showing Jude the initial sketches." I don't dare look at him directly, but I can see in my peripheral vision that he's put some distance between us since Charles arrived.

"Oh, excellent, I can't wait to take a look, myself." Charles beams. "Would you two like to come inside for a cup of coffee? We can look them over together at the dining room table. And I can introduce you to Carol."

❦

Carol, I learn, is a hugger. In the vaulted foyer of the old house, she comes at me with wide open arms, a broad grin splitting her round face. A hug feels like a bit much for our first meeting, but she has such a loving, motherly smile that there's no denying her. Reminded of how my mom is with Nat and Wyatt—she's practically adopted them into the family—I let Carol scoop me into a tight embrace. The scent of roses envelops me.

"It's so great to finally meet you!" She pulls back, holding my shoulders to study my face. "Goodness, my dear, aren't you just *lovely*. Look at you!" She beams, looking me up and down.

"Thank you, Mrs. Faulkner," I say sheepishly, surprised by her sudden familiarity. She's Wyatt's aunt so I guess it's not that weird. Or is it weird? I'm overthinking again.

"Ah ah ah, none of this *Mrs. Faulkner* business," she says, smoothing down her short gray hair and looking at me over her glasses. She shakes her head, then points a finger at me and Jude. "Carol. Just Carol."

We nod dutifully.

"And you must be Jude."

He extends a hand for Carol to shake and gets yanked forcefully into an equally tight embrace, looking both alarmed and amused.

I smirk at him, suppressing a chuckle.

"Oh, and this one's built like a mountain!" she exclaims jovially, still hugging him.

Jude awkwardly pats her on the back, his eyes wide. "Nice to meet you, Carol," he says, smiling at me over her shoulder.

She releases him and steps back, clapping her hands together decisively. "Come on, you two. Let's get the coffee going." She practically trots along the hallway ahead of us, motioning for us to follow.

Charles, who hasn't said much other than the most basic of introductions, smiles knowingly and trails us down the hall.

Carol's enthusiasm is contagious and I find myself pulled into her cheerful and slightly sassy orbit as we take our seats at the dining room table. The view overlooking Black Bear River is beautiful from here, framed by the large picture window. Carol sits beside me. Jude and Charles take the seats across from us while I lay the sketches out in the center of the table.

She perches her glasses on the end of her nose, peering through them at one of my sketches.

"Let's see, now..." She pauses to take in the details. "Oh, my goodness, is this the cliff-side view here?" She turns to look at me and I nod. "Oh, what a great idea to have a seating area right there. Don't you think that will be beautiful, Charles?" She passes the sketch over to him.

"I think it's perfect. The view will be great, looking out over the river." He smiles at me.

Carol looks at Jude over the rim of her glasses, leaning in. "Don't you think it would be romantic? Looking out over that stunning view while you share a glass of wine with your sweetie?"

Jude rubs the back of his neck, smiling awkwardly. "I uh—"

Cutting him off before he can answer, Carol swivels to look at me with a conspiratorial expression. "Oh, I'll bet he's got himself a girlfriend, a handsome devil like him." She pats my knee with a wink and reaches for another sketch to inspect.

My eyes snap over to meet Jude's gaze across the table, but I can't bear the eye contact; I look away immediately, my cheeks burning with sudden self-consciousness. I'm doing everything in my power not to let my face show that I'm both desperate to know if he's single and determined not to care.

We are coworkers, I remind myself for the thousandth time. *Focus, Olena.*

"No, I don't, actually." Jude's words pull my eyes back to his against my will. His unflinching gaze is intense, and for a moment, I can't breathe.

"Oh, my goodness, I almost forgot about the coffee!" Carol pushes up from the table and heads to the kitchen.

I swallow and force myself to return my eyes to the sketches in front of me, glancing up and smiling politely at Charles. Carol returns with four steaming mugs on a tray, little ceramic containers of sugar and cream alongside them.

"Oh, Charles, look at this one!" Carol croons as she sets down the tray next to the sketches. "A bench swing at the bottom of the chestnut tree, with a little platform to climb up to it!" She reaches over my shoulder and passes the sketch to Charles.

Taking a careful breath, I point out, "It's hard to see in the sketch, but the swing will be surrounded by little fairy lights, so it will be a beautiful place to sit at night." I'm surprised at how eloquent I manage to sound.

Effusive praise keeps coming from both Carol and Charles, and with the designs roundly approved, we finish our coffee and head back outside.

Standing outside the front door, I zip up my jacket.

"Jude, darling, aren't you freezing in just a t-shirt?" Carol intones, leaning on the doorframe and rubbing her arms.

My traitorous eyes rake over his chest, his arms.

He glances at me, catching me staring. "Not at all; I run hot," he says to Carol with a barely suppressed smirk.

Um, tell me about it, I think to myself, biting the inside of my cheek and fixing my eyes on the ground.

When the Faulkners finally close the door, Jude and I stand there looking at each other in stunned silence for a moment. I'm dying to know what he's thinking about Carol's unexpected hugs —nevermind what she *said*. We both break into grins at the same time before cracking up into hushed laughter, the tension of keeping it together in front of the Faulkners finally snapping. We turn from the house, still laughing.

As we make our way along the path, Jude lets out a long sigh.

"Well, that was... interesting." He raises an eyebrow and smoothes a hand over his beard.

"Right? Oh my God." I look up at the sky and try to settle my nervous laughter, inhaling a steadying breath with my hand on my stomach.

"Tell me something..." Jude's low voice stirs electricity in me again and goosebumps prickle over my arms, my demeanor suddenly more serious—on alert. "Why haven't I worked with you before?"

His question takes me by surprise.

Watching my expression, he continues. "This is a pretty small town and we work in the same industry. So, where have you been hiding?" We reach the driveway and he hops onto the open tailgate of his truck, those intense green eyes locked on me.

I let out a breath and look out across the river at the mountains, as if a palatable answer will reveal itself there. "Well, I grew up here," I begin, weighing how to explain, glancing back at him. "I went to college in Seattle and then ended up staying for a few years. Got my business started there. It seemed like the thing to do." I smile at him, shrugging. "I just moved back home recently." I stop there, hoping that's enough detail.

He furrows his brow slightly. "What brought you back here?"

My smile falters, not wanting to go into what really pushed me to move home.

When I don't respond right away, he continues. "I mean, it must've been hard to leave after getting your business up and running in a big city."

The universe sends me a lifeline when Jude's phone rings. He gives me a regretful look and answers. I gather from his side of the conversation that Teddy's not coming into work today, after all.

Jude hangs up.

I throw him a quizzical look.

"Well, it appears Teddy's dentist gave him the good drugs for his procedure and he can't drive. So we're down one more person." Jude ponders a moment, then curses softly under his breath, slipping his phone into his back pocket.

"Did you need him today?" I ask, noting his furrowed brow.

"Yeah, actually."

"Well, I can stay to help." The words come out before I realize what I've said.

Jude gives me an uncertain look, then smiles. "I'm not going to ask you to do that."

Instead of backtracking, I double down. "What, you don't think I can do manual labor?" I tease. "Come on, I'm up for some hard work." My eyes challenge him to argue.

He smiles, lowering his eyes briefly before meeting my gaze and hopping down off the truck. "Okay, but... you're gonna get dirty."

❧

STEPH FINDS a hoodie in her car to lend to me. "Trust me, you're not gonna want to get dirt all over your clothes," she says with a knowing look.

I'm grateful for the heads up. I hadn't thought about what I was wearing before impulsively offering to help. I tie my hair up in a quick ponytail and she hands me a pair of work gloves. I'm suddenly feeling out of my element. *Why did I offer to do this again?* I think wistfully about being home in my cozy bedroom, working on the renderings in front of my laptop. They'll have to wait until tomorrow.

A dump truck full of fresh, black soil beeps a warning as it backs down the driveway. At Jude's direction, the driver unloads the dark earth onto a few tarps laid out on the grass.

Jude and Steph shovel the soil from the pile into two wheelbarrows for me and Dimitri to move over to various marked areas on the property. Jude tells Dimitri to top up the soil along the garden beds around the house; he tells me to wheel my barrow over to the *too far gone area*, which Teddy had dug out on Monday.

When I return to the pile of soil after several trips with the wheelbarrow, I discover Jude and I are alone, Steph having moved on to help Dimitri with the garden beds.

Jude gives me a once-over. "How're you doing so far?" he asks, leaning on the handle of the shovel.

"Oh, fine." I'm breathing a little hard and can feel sweat trickling down my neck. "I just... I don't normally do this much heavy lifting." I sigh and smile at him bravely.

He tilts his head at me, smirking. "Must be hard being stuck behind your desk all day," he teases as he plunges his shovel into the pile of dirt.

I nod. "It is brutal," I deadpan, putting my gloved hands on my hips, my breathing slowing down.

"Sounds pretty rough." He scoops a shovelful of soil and turns it into the wheelbarrow, the muscles of his tattooed forearms shining with a hint of sweat. "I bet your fingers cramp up from typing so much."

"They really do," I say, playing along innocently.

"You probably have to readjust your reading glasses from time to time too," he continues, then adds sarcastically, "How do you manage it all?" He smirks as he lets another scoop of soil fall.

I smile sheepishly and lower my eyes, laughing softly. "I actually do have reading glasses." I meet his gaze again and don't look away.

Fire flashes in Jude's eyes and he pauses his digging. His expression turns darker than before.

I smirk at him with a raised eyebrow. "What, you wanna see them?" I ask, openly flirting. It looks like some of Carol's audacity has rubbed off on me, because I'm failing miserably at keeping this professional.

He blows out a hard breath, looking away from me. I catch a hint of a smile as he turns.

I grab Steph's abandoned shovel and drive it into the pile of soil beside him. "Focus up, Jude. Back to work."

I'M off the hook by mid-afternoon when Jude assures me he, Steph, and Dimitri can handle the rest of the day's tasks.

He leans against the side of his truck. "Thanks again for your help. You really didn't have to stay."

The look on his face tells me he's glad I did. I am too. "It was fun," I reply honestly.

"Hey, listen, I should get your number." Jude pulls off his work gloves and reaches into his back pocket for his phone.

What?

"My—uh, you want my number?" I ask uneasily, not knowing how to respond.

Is he asking me out? I know we've been flirting a bit, but...

"Uh, yeah," he says slowly. "I mean, I gave you my business card, but I didn't get yours." He's looking at me with an unreadable expression.

My eyes widen as I realize what he means. *Oh my God. For work, you jackass. He needs your number so he can contact you for work.*

"Oh! Of course! Yes!" I'm stumbling over how to minimize the way I epically misread his intentions. I busy myself digging for my phone in the abyss that is my purse, taking longer than necessary to find it.

We go through the motions of saving each other's numbers while I internally eviscerate myself for misunderstanding the situation so badly. I thought we were past the part where I make a fool of myself. I don't know what to say as he fixes his eyes on me intently.

He looks like he wants to say something but then changes his mind. "Will I see you here tomorrow?" he asks instead.

"Um, yes, actually." I tuck a wisp of hair behind my ear. "I'll be putting an initial order in with the nursery when I get home and I'll be coming back here to direct the delivery. Probably late morning?"

He nods.

"Oh, speaking of which, did you hear about the oak tree? Do we get to keep it, or what?"

"Yeah, the arborist gave us the all clear; just the branch removal for now." He smiles.

"That's great news; it's a beautiful old tree," I say, glancing over to where it stands near the house.

"Agreed." He pauses and looks at me for a moment. "Hey, and Mitch is still off tomorrow so, if you feel like pitching in again, I won't say no." He gives me a half-smile.

I let his implied invitation hang between us for a moment, his eyes searching mine for an answer. "Sounds like a plan," I say.

13

OLENA

With the temperature having dropped significantly overnight, my breath fogs in front of me as I step out of my car at the Faulkner property. Threatening rain, the morning sky is an overcast, pale gray gloom that is so typical in Lennox as late winter gives way to early spring.

I shrug on a coat over my hoodie. This morning, remembering how ill-prepared I had been for moving soil yesterday, I dressed for physical work in warm leggings and hiking boots with thick socks. Along with my layered t-shirt and sweatshirt combo, it helps to keep out the chill. Zipping my coat, I'm grateful for each cozy layer hugging my body. *I could get used to this*, I think to myself. *It's like wearing pajamas at work.*

I sweep my hair up into an organized mess that will stay out of my face, squinting at my reflection in the side window of my car. I open the back door to grab my bag and notebook.

"I thought you weren't coming until late morning," Jude's voice rumbles from over my shoulder.

I'm smiling before I've even finished turning around to face him. It's nine o'clock. "Yeah, I finished the design renderings last night and figured there was no reason to wait to come out and help."

I don't tell him I was also pacing in my bedroom for the better part of an hour this morning, trying to shake off the desperate urge to see him before eventually giving up and driving here.

"Well, I'm glad you did, because Steph called in sick," he says, shaking his head.

Dimitri walks by, carrying a heavy piece of lumber. "Morning, Olena." He adjusts the wood on his shoulder with a grimace. I look in the direction he's walking and see he and Teddy are busy framing out the pathway from the cliff-side to the sunken garden stairs.

"Good morning," I say to him, throwing Teddy a wave, which he returns. "Looking good so far with the pathway."

"Thanks," Dimitri nods at me over his shoulder.

I turn my eyes back to Jude. "Well, *boss*?" I smirk. "What's the plan?"

He smiles and turns to the truck, digging out a pair of thick gloves and a set of safety glasses for me. "Got any carpentry experience?"

I shake my head, take the gloves, then scrunch my nose and shrug. "High school shop class, I guess. And I watched my dad a bit, growing up."

He nods.

I raise a curious eyebrow. "You do carpentry?"

He smirks. "One of my many talents." He cocks his head toward the chestnut tree. "Follow me."

We spend the morning cutting deck planks and stair stringers on a portable table saw to build the stairs that will sit under the bench swing. By late morning, sawdust covers everything I'm wearing and clings to the outside of my safety glasses. I feel like I can taste it.

"I'm gonna go get a drink," I say to Jude, coughing lightly and gesturing at my mouth.

He looks up from where he's drilling a plank into the stair frame. "Sure."

I jog over to where I left my bag near the car. I take off my jacket, shaking it roughly, and try to jostle the sawdust out of my hair. As I lean forward and shake my head, a deluge of it rains down in front of my eyes.

Teddy walks up to me, grinning, and rummages through the tools in Jude's truck. "Well, looks like you're one of us now," he jokes, watching me struggle.

I smile at him, taking off the glasses and trying to wipe them on my sawdust-covered hoodie. "God, it's *everywhere*," I say to him with a grimace, laughing at the futility of trying to clean myself up.

"Just become one with the sawdust. Let it be," Teddy jokes, putting on a serene tone.

"I don't think I have a choice," I reply with a throaty laugh.

"You'll get used to it," he calls out over his shoulder as he walks back to join Dimitri, tools in hand.

A truck from the local nursery pulls into the driveway, and I realize I need to get my head in the game to direct where these plants are going to go. I open my bag to pull out my plans and my copy of the plant order. Jude walks over and grabs his water bottle as I'm looking them over. I realize I look like a sawdust monster yet need to talk to the driver like a professional in a minute. I wipe a sleeve across my forehead self-consciously. More sawdust.

"Jude, tell me the truth," I say, and he turns to look at me. "Do I look vaguely passable as a professional?" I turn around in front of him, holding out my arms. "How bad is it?" I feel a twinge of anxiety when the driver hops out of his truck.

His eyes rake over my body, taking his time. *Hurry up,* I think to myself, but can't help but smile.

"I think you need more, to be honest." He takes a swig from his water bottle, smirking.

I roll my eyes. "No, seriously. How bad do I look? And tell me quick 'cause the guy's coming to talk to me right now." My words drop to a rushed whisper when I notice the driver quickly approaching.

"Olena. You look perfect," he says quietly, holding my gaze.

My joking demeanor falters at the sincerity in his eyes and my breath catches.

"Hi there, I'm looking for Olena MacMillan?"

The driver's voice from behind me wrenches me away from Jude's gaze and I turn, heat rising to my cheeks. *What just happened?*

"Hi, uh, yes, that's me," I say slowly.

I glance over my shoulder to where Jude was, but he's already walking away. I turn back to the driver and smile, following him to the truck.

By the time I wrap things up with the delivery and make my way back to the platform, Jude's installing the last plank.

"This is pretty much ready to stain," he says. He looks up at the sky, considering the clouds, then shakes his head. "I don't like the look of them. We should wait."

I look up too. The gray from this morning has deepened; the clouds look like they'll open up on us any second. Unsurprising. Lennox Valley is known for its quick weather changes.

"Listen, I need to run to the hardware store for a part. I'll be back in a bit," says Jude, pulling off his gloves and stuffing them in his back pocket. He pulls off his safety glasses and tousles his hair, letting loose a miniature cloud of sawdust. He smiles at me and wipes his face. "Teddy and Dimitri can show you what to do while I'm gone."

"Okay, I'll check in with them." I'm slightly disappointed but try not to let on.

A curious expression crosses Jude's brow for a moment and he walks directly toward me, narrowing his eyes, looking at something on the top of my head.

"Hold still," he says in a low voice.

"What?" I freeze, my heartbeat hammering faster as he comes so close.

With an eyebrow raised, he slowly reaches up to my hair. I can feel the heat of his chest in front of me and want to bury my face in his warmth. The impulse is so strong I have to clench my hands at my sides to stop myself from doing exactly that. My eyes lift to his, searching. As he pulls his arm back down, he lowers his eyes to meet mine, holding a small leaf in his hand. He twists the stem between his fingers, making it twirl between us, then drops it.

"You had something in your hair." He grins at me, eyes shining with amusement, then walks away to his truck without looking back.

It takes me a few seconds to remember to breathe.

AFTER I EAT the lunch Wyatt packed for me with Teddy and Dimitri, they show me their progress on the path trim. They've dug the edges of the pathway out on either side for rows of alternating perennials and shrubs. The arbor has been installed near the sunken garden entrance, so we chat about the timing of planting what the nursery just delivered.

Dimitri crouches down to point out the channel where the strip lighting will be installed to light the path at night. He grimaces suddenly, squeezing two fingers hard against his forehead.

"Hey, are you okay?" I ask.

"Ah, it's my head. It's been killing me all day. Feels worse when I bend over. But I'll be fine." He looks like he's putting on a brave face.

I frown.

"I dunno, man," says Teddy. "It's been hours now. It's still not better?"

Dimitri stands. "No, but I've had worse." He smiles grimly at us. I suspect he's in more pain than he's letting on. "It's just a migraine."

"Wait, a migraine?" I ask. I had them as a teenager; I know they're horrid. "Why don't you head home and rest? You shouldn't be trying to muscle through a migraine. I'm sure we can handle things. Go take care of yourself."

"Really?" He looks relieved enough at the possibility of going home that I know he needs to go.

"Yes, really." I nod. "Please, go rest; I'll explain to Jude when he gets back," I say reassuringly.

Dimitri gratefully shuffles off to his car and I turn to Teddy.

"Everyone's dropping like flies," he says. "We might have to promote Murphy from mascot to packhorse."

I laugh. I eye Murphy dozing in his dog bed on the grass. He looks enviably cozy there, despite the cold day. "I don't know if he can be convinced."

Teddy's phone rings. He answers and, after a series of clipped responses, he hangs up. "Well, this is terrible timing," he says. "You're not gonna believe this..."

෫෨

Jude pulls up and hops out of his truck, jogging over to me with a crease in his brow. "Where is everybody?"

"I sent them home." I stand up from where I've been laying sheets of landscaping fabric between the timbers that will line the pathway. Teddy gave me instructions about what to do before he left.

He looks a bit taken aback. "Uh, bold of you to manage my team for me," he says, crossing his arms with his eyebrows raised, a mixture of confusion and amusement in his expression. "Care to give me a little more detail?"

"Dimitri had a migraine and Teddy's kid is sick and needed to be picked up from school. His wife isn't off work for another couple of hours, so I said he should go," I explain.

"You realize this means we are down to just the two of us and there's a truckload of gravel arriving any minute, right?" He screws up his eyebrows incredulously.

"I figured we could handle it," I say, shrugging defensively. "I mean, would you have done things any differently?"

He considers for a moment, his expression softening slightly as he looks at the ground, then back up at me. "Okay, probably not."

"Well, then, we'll have to figure it out." I give him a slightly smug smile.

He tilts his chin at me. "Hey, weren't you supposed to be the brains and I was supposed to be the muscle?" he teases.

My eyes can't help but slide over his muscular chest and arms and I vividly remember the heat of his body close to me earlier. I force myself to shake off the memory and take a breath, meeting his eyes. "Yeah, well, I'm stronger than I look."

THE FIRST WHEELBARROW full of gravel doesn't budge when I push it.

Jude watches me, clearly enjoying himself.

"What's wrong with the wheel? Is it stuck on something?" I lower the handles and look at the side to see if there's anything in the way.

He chuckles, his arms resting on the shovel. "Nope. It's just that damned heavy."

"Are you kidding me?" I heave the handles up again and throw my body into it with a grunt. It shifts the slightest bit forward, then back into place. I huff out a frustrated breath.

"Here, switch with me." Jude moves to take the wheelbarrow and holds out the shovel.

Sighing, I give in. "Fine." I take the shovel from his hands.

He gets the wheelbarrow going on the first try, and I squint at him resentfully. He walks off with the load, smiling smugly, though my eyes can't help but linger on his arms and back as he goes. His muscles strain under the weight. Dumping the load between the pieces of wooden trim lining the pathway, he quickly returns for a refill.

I drive the shovel into the pile of gravel and my eyes widen as I try to lift the handle, realizing it, too, will take far more effort than the soil did yesterday.

Again, Jude watches me. "Yeah, you're gonna want to lift with your legs."

"You're just loving this, aren't you?" I grouse at him with a frown.

"Oh, don't worry," Jude paints on an innocent expression. "We're in this together. We can handle it, right? At this rate, we'll be done by the time it's dark." He looks at the sky, then lifts an eyebrow at me pointedly.

Raindrops start to hit our faces and we both look up at the clouds, frowning, then back at each other.

"Okay, look... I'm sorry," I admit. "This is obviously not... ideal. But those guys had to leave, and we're stuck here, so let's just get on with it." I brace my hands in a better position on the shovel handle. This time, I lift it with a little more grace and carefully pivot to the wheelbarrow, dumping the gravel inside. I blink as more raindrops hit my face.

We shovel and haul load after load until we're both sweating despite the cool rain. I take off my hoodie and throw it on the grass. It's already wet and dirty enough that I don't care if it gets any worse; I'm too exhausted to put it anywhere else. Standing in my t-shirt, the rain feels cool against my bare arms. I turn my face up to the sky with my eyes closed for a moment, appreciating the brief pause to breathe before getting back to work.

When the pathway is filled, we move on to the area around what will be the firepit in the middle of the sunken garden. The work is hard; we have to bring the gravel down a small hill, and the wet grass is slippery. By the time we're done, we both collapse on the ground, exhausted and sodden from head to toe.

"Oh, my God," I pant. "Are we done yet?"

"You wish." Jude grins at me between breaths. "We have to level out the gravel before we go."

I groan and fall backward, closing my eyes and feeling the rain beating against my skin. I hear Jude moving at my side but don't open my eyes.

"Here. Drink."

I crack an eye open to see him holding out my water bottle. I push myself up and he sits back down beside me, drinking from his own.

"Thanks," I say gratefully. We sit in silence for a few minutes, looking out over the cliff at the river. The rain clouds drape the mountains across from us in mist.

"Okay, champ. Break's over." He slaps my knee and jumps up,

holding out his hand. Looking up at him with a frown, I take it and he hauls me to my feet in one strong pull. "You gonna survive?" he asks, his voice rough. He's standing close enough again that I can't think.

I step back to clear my head, avoiding eye contact. "Yeah. Let's get this over with. It's getting dark."

As we crouch down and get to work leveling the gravel path, rain collects in the trenches next to it, huge muddy drops splashing up beside us.

I notice Jude watching me, smiling. "What?" I ask, feeling self-conscious. I probably look like a drowned rat.

"Nothing." He looks away.

"No, tell me," I challenge him, stopping what I'm doing.

"Just remembering the first time I saw you soaked in the rain," he answers quietly, smiling to himself.

The memory of that day crashes over me and I wrinkle my nose. "I acted like a jackass."

"Yeah, you did," he deadpans.

"Hey!" I laugh. Dipping my fingers in the mud beside me, I flick them at him, spattering his face.

He flinches, his eyes wide. "Oh, it's like that?" Challenge gleams in his eyes. He flicks muddy fingers back at me, and a small splat hits my cheek.

I recoil, blinking. "Oh, yuck!" I exclaim, my mouth agape as I wipe my face with my wrist. "How dare you!" Narrowing my eyes, I pull off my gloves. Holding Jude's stare, I reach back into the mud, covering one of my fingers in muck. I stand.

Eyeing me carefully, he gets to his feet, slowly removing his own gloves.

I walk over to him, a grin spreading across my lips, and reach up. Without breaking eye contact, I bite my lip as I draw a line of mud slowly down the ridge of his nose. He watches me, frozen in place under my touch, his breath mingling with my own as the rain pelts us. Several breathless seconds hang heavy and an intense energy thrums in the air between us. The energy of anticipation—of recklessness.

We break into a run at the same moment. I cackle and screech, giddy with exhaustion as he sprints after me. I push my tired limbs to their limits with only adrenaline for fuel. I run as fast as I can, leaping over equipment and piles of dirt, laughing wildly. Our steps splash through the saturated grass, Jude's close behind mine.

Suddenly, his hand grips my arm and I'm spun around to a stop as his chest slams into mine, almost knocking us both down. My breasts heave against his chest, both of us breathing hard and fast from the chase.

Jude watches my expression as he reaches his hand up to my face, brushing wet hair out of my eyes. Then he slowly wipes a muddy finger down the middle of my cheek and traces my jawline, a half-smile tugging at the corner of his mouth.

My eyes close at the intimacy of his touch and at the heat radiating from his body pressed against mine. A warm, tingling sensation pulls low in my belly, my senses tuned to the places he's touching me.

Opening my eyes, I search his expression.

His gaze is dark and flaring with intensity. The pull between us feels electric. He runs his hand down my arm as his gaze drops to my lips. I'm shivering from the rain and from sheer exhaustion. A drop of water from his hair drips onto my cheek and I lift my face, giving in to this—giving in to him. My eyes flutter shut when I feel his breath against my mouth.

Murphy's sharp bark jars us and my eyes snap open. Jude's wide eyes match my own, and for a moment, we're frozen. More barking. His grip on my arm releases and he breaks eye contact, looking over at his truck, where Murphy has been sheltering from the rain on the passenger seat.

I follow his gaze. Headlights from another vehicle emerge from the trees at the end of the driveway, and he steps away from me, my body suddenly chilled by the cold air filling the space between us. I slowly rub my arms, watching in stunned silence as Jude glancces at me one last time before walking over to the driveway, rubbing his hands down his face.

Oh my God. What just happened? Or... almost happened? I put my hands to my chest, trying to steady myself.

"Teddy! I thought you went home!" Jude calls out, sounding surprisingly normal.

I turn and watch them.

Teddy turns off his truck and steps out to talk to him.

I can't hear their conversation. I realize I'm still standing in a daze where Jude left me. I don't know what to do with myself. Exhausted, I walk back to the gravel path where we'd been working. I pick up my sodden hoodie and look around in bewilderment.

I hear Teddy's truck engine again, and Jude walks back over, rubbing his arms.

"Hey," he says quietly. "Teddy just forgot his phone." His eyes linger on mine.

I nod, unsure of what to say.

"We should probably pack up; it's getting cold." He looks at me cautiously and rubs the back of his neck.

I sense something like regret in his eyes and my heart sinks. He doesn't want this. He doesn't want me.

I push down the sting of rejection, my cheeks burning. "Yeah, I need..." I gather up my water bottle and gloves, trying not to look at him. "I need to go. Yeah. And this..." I force myself to meet his eyes, gesturing to the path.

"This can wait," he says quickly.

"Good. Okay." I turn and walk back to my car.

"Olena."

My eyes close the moment he says my name and I stop, a tightness burning in the back of my throat. I inhale to fight off the tears and turn back to face him. "Yeah?"

"Thanks for your help."

My brows pinch together and I turn away, not trusting myself to respond.

14

JUDE

Thanks for your help.

The words weigh me down like an anvil on my chest as I push open my front door. Regret doesn't begin to touch how I feel about the way I left things with Olena tonight. The pain in her eyes as she turned away from me haunts my thoughts. I can't believe I've been such an asshole.

I had her in my arms, could feel her body against mine, had those beautiful brown eyes staring up at me... and I blew it. I balked at the first tiny interruption and pushed her away. I should have run straight back to her and finished what we started. I should have kissed her right there in the rain the minute Teddy drove off.

But no. I had to drive an ice cold wedge between us and *thank her for her help?* I had treated her like any other colleague, making it seem like that's all she was to me.

Nothing could be further from the truth. The reality is, no matter how hard I've tried to fight this attraction, I haven't been able to get Olena out of my mind since the first time I laid eyes on her. I should have told her as much tonight, while we were alone and I had the chance. Now she'll probably never look at me with anything other than hurt and resentment.

And I'll deserve it.

Fuck, she felt so good up against me.

I shake my head and drop my keys on the table inside the door, plodding to the fireplace with Murphy at my heels. I grimace and curse under my breath when I see I'm out of firewood.

No, this is good, I realize. Even though I'm soaked to the bone, filthy, and exhausted, I need to work off this energy if I want to sleep tonight. Murphy settles on his bed in the living room and I head out the back door, flicking on the light outside the shed. Its yellow pallor casts a grim glow around me.

Under the overhanging shelter between my house and the shed, I pull my axe out of the chopping block and set up a log to split. The hiss of the rain surrounds me as it hits the roof, gutters, and ground. I exhale harshly, my breath a cloud of fog, then raise the handle above my head. I slice down and strike the wood, grunting loudly in frustration. Over and over again, I raise the axe and strike down hard until the log gives way, splitting into two pieces that tumble at my feet. The burn in my muscles from the hard work feels like far less pain than I deserve for pushing Olena away. Shaking my head, I set up another piece to split. Her hurt expression flashes in front of my eyes once more. Grimacing with renewed anger at myself, I slam the blade down. Again and again, I slice downward with everything I've got left.

Breathing hard now, I'm reminded of how her body felt pressed against mine, our breaths fast and hot after I chased her across the property. *Fuck.* I can't push the memories away. In frustration, I hammer down one last time, splitting the second piece in two, before throwing the axe to the ground. Pacing a few steps to let my breathing settle, I collect enough of the wood to make a fire, stack the rest, and head inside.

Murphy raises his head as I come in, lifting a quizzical eyebrow in the way only dogs like him can.

"We need to talk about your timing, bud," I say to him, ruffling his head as I pass by. "*That's* when you decide to bark?"

Murphy yawns and lays his head back down on his paws.

I peel off my soaked hoodie and t-shirt and hang them across the rack above the wood stove to dry, then crouch down to build the fire. My legs are chafed and burning from the wet denim against my skin. I need a shower—and badly.

Once the fire has started, I peel off my jeans and hang them above the stove as well, heading to the bathroom.

The hot water feels like the second best thing to touch my skin tonight. I wash slowly, watching all the dirt, bits of grass, and sawdust sliding down the drain at my feet. When I'm finally clean, I stand under the water, steam billowing up around me, tormented by my memories.

Olena smiling at me. Olena covered in sawdust with the leaf in her hair. Olena's eyes as she painted me with mud. Olena's shrieking laughter as she ran from me. Olena's lips inches from mine.

I close my eyes and frown, trying hopelessly to shake the images from my mind.

I can't get involved with Olena. But I can't get her out of my head...

I'm rock hard at the mere thought of her and I know chopping wood wasn't enough; I need the release I've been craving every day since I met her. I take my cock in hand, stroking gently at first. I so badly wish tonight had ended differently; that, somehow, she was here with me. Picturing her here in my shower—the water running over her breasts, down her back, over her ass—has me pumping harder. My body aches for her and my cock pulses beneath my hand. I close my eyes as I stroke faster, imagination running wild as I picture her naked body pressed against me; a feast for my senses, a sweet indulgence for my lips and tongue to devour. My release builds quickly and the thought of tasting her is enough to send me over the edge. With a groan, I come hard and long, shuddering under the running water.

It takes me nearly a minute to get my bearings. After I turn off the water, the steam begins to clear—both in the bathroom and in my head.

I dry off and put on a clean t-shirt and sweatpants. Grabbing some leftovers from the fridge, I return to the living room and sit in front of the fire with Murphy, who wanders over to the couch and drops his head in my lap. As I eat dinner and stare through the glass door at the flames, an awful but inevitable realization settles over me.

Teddy came close to catching me and Olena in a very compromising position tonight. If he'd caught us doing what we were about to do, the project at the Faulkner property could have been jeopardized. It could have undermined his trust in me as the leader of our team.

This is my business, the company I built. The reputation I've made for myself in Lennox Valley is strong. And this is a small town; people talk. I almost unwittingly sabotaged my career tonight; almost threw away everything I've built for a lustful moment with a beautiful woman.

Running a hand down my face, I kick myself for letting it get that close. I'm supposed to be the boss, the decision-maker, the steady hand guiding the ship. I'm sure as shit not supposed to be behaving like some hormone-addled teenager.

Hadn't I spent the last week vowing to be professional around Olena for just this reason? The scope of my failure to keep my feelings in check rests heavily on me now. No matter how attracted I am to her, I can't let this happen again. I need to protect the life and career I've made for myself. Getting close to her would be short-sighted, anyway; I can't risk another loss—another heartbreak.

It's better this way. She can't leave you if you don't let her in in the first place.

Looking down at Murphy, I see things in a new light. His barking was the warning I needed to stop things with Olena before they went too far. Before we got caught. Before everything got complicated.

I pat Murphy's head gratefully, absentmindedly letting my fingers rest on his soft fur. I needed his warning as a wake-up call to see tonight for what it was: a huge mistake.

And yet, doubt prickles. There's something about this whole thing niggling at the back of my mind, something I can't name, but I'm mentally and physically out of steam and I've got nothing left in me to chase the thought down. Finishing my food, I can't be bothered to get up, so I rest my head back on the couch and close my eyes. I'm out like a light.

15

OLENA

Pouring my guts out to Wyatt is an old tradition. He knows my protocol, which was the brainchild of our boy-obsessed teenage selves: tissue box, ice cream, and warm blankets. While probably the most cliché girly thing I'm associated with, it always works to help me feel better, so I don't question it.

So, when he sees me come in the front door of our apartment —sopping wet, exhausted, and with a tearful expression on my grime-caked face—he launches into action.

"Oh, honey." He stands in front of me and tentatively reaches out a hand, then pulls it back, taking in the full head-to-toe picture of exactly how wet and dirty I am. "Can I... run you a bath?"

"No." I sniff, my expression flat. "It'll be like sitting in a dirt soup. I need a shower."

"Okay, I'll get it started for you, and then I'll make you a blanket nest on the couch with a hot water bottle." He walks toward the bathroom, then stops, looking back at me. "What flavor of ice cream?"

I level him with a look. My brain is not available for decisions right now.

"Any ice cream; got it. Let's go." He waves me along to the bathroom and helps me peel off my t-shirt, throwing it in the sink. I sit on the closed toilet lid and pull off my socks, adding them in with the shirt.

"You got the rest, babe?" he asks softly, turning on the shower for me.

"Yeah," I sigh, then blow my nose on a wad of toilet paper.

Why am I so upset about this? I think to myself, scowling. *I shouldn't have been touching Jude in the first place, especially not at work. Murphy probably did us a favor by interrupting.*

"Have you eaten dinner?" Wyatt asks.

"I had the Meal of Shame on the way home," I say with a nod. I remember the concerned look on the drive-thru worker's face as she handed me my order. I'm sure I looked like I had been auditioning for a horror movie and then had taken a swim in a swamp.

"I thought we agreed to stop calling it that," he says with a soft half-smile.

"Old habits." I wave a hand dismissively at him.

Without saying any more, Wyatt steps out and closes the door behind him.

When I emerge in a towel half an hour later, he looks up from his phone and gives me a kind smile, patting the couch next to him. "When you're ready. No rush."

I smile weakly back.

WYATT CONVINCES me to tag along with him to the grocery store the next day; he hardly ever has Saturdays off work and, even though food isn't my area of expertise, he says he wants my input for some dish he's cooking up for Sam. We both know full well that I won't contribute one useful opinion about the ingredients and instead will probably end up impulse-buying a box of overpriced, semi-palatable protein bars for myself. But I think he knows I need the distraction.

"Do you think arugula or something milder for the salad? Maybe romaine?" Wyatt holds two bundles of leafy greens, looking pensive.

I look at him in a daze. "Whatever you think makes sense?"

He nods, dropping one of them into his basket, before moving on to squeeze an avocado from a nearby display.

I stuff my hands deep in the pockets of my sweater and follow him. The grocery store's fluorescent lighting is too bright; the aisles of vibrant products are upsettingly cheerful, and I squint.

My stomach rumbles. On the way past the deli, I grab a pre-made sandwich and fiddle with the plastic edge of the clear container as we make our way through the store. Wyatt picks up a can of white beans and a bottle of sauce with a name I can't pronounce on the label.

We queue up behind a few other customers at the front of the store. To pass the time, I read the headlines on the terrible magazine covers near the checkout. "Wyatt, look, a celebrity has had a relationship development!" I say in a jaded deadpan, pointing at one of them.

"No way, that is shocking information," he replies dryly, then picks up a different magazine from the display. "Oh, look, this celebrity has a different sized body than previously!"

"Oooh," I intone sarcastically. "What's their secret?"

"Oh, wow, handsome man alert," he says in a hushed tone.

I'm still looking down at the magazine I've picked up, flipping through the pages with distant interest. "Yeah, I mean, but they're celebrities. Is that really shocking?" My eyes linger on the glossy pages in front of me.

"No, Olena, real life." He tugs at my sleeve. "Real life hot guy.

In the floral department." He's still speaking quietly so the other customers won't hear us.

I look up and Wyatt dramatically jerks his eyes over my right shoulder. I turn around and my stomach drops.

Jude is standing at the floral counter, putting his wallet into the back pocket of his jeans.

Frozen, I watch as he picks up a bouquet of flowers and heads for the door. When my body finally clues in that he might see me, I duck down behind the magazines so I'm hidden from view. My mind and heart are both racing and my face flushes.

Wyatt's voice sounds confused. "Wait, do you know him?" Then realization lands. "Wait, is *that* him? That's your hunky lumberjack?" He pulls me up to standing, his eyes shifting between a few nearby customers with an apologetic smile; people are starting to stare.

A glance at the door confirms Jude is gone. I hug my arms over my chest protectively and Wyatt puts an arm around me, pressing a kiss to my head.

"More ice cream when we get home?" he asks softly.

I close my eyes.

I SPEND Sunday in a numbed state, scrolling on my phone and trying not to fixate on who those flowers were for.

It doesn't matter, I remind myself. *He's clearly got some other woman in his life.* Even though he said he didn't have a girlfriend, he could be dating someone casually. Or maybe he lied. I barely know him, after all. I have no right to be jealous or hurt. Still, the sting of seeing him buying flowers for someone else leaves an ache in my gut that I can't shake.

The image of Jude's regretful look after Teddy drove away on

Friday flashes into my mind and I wince. *We should probably pack up,* he'd said.

More like wrap it up. Shut it down. We're done here.

It's late when I finally shuffle to my bedroom and take stock of what I need to deal with before work tomorrow. I try to push down the dread of seeing Jude again and focus on my job. Standing in my sweats with my hair in a sloppy bun that falls halfway off my head, I rifle through my work bag. I pull out my notebook and a bundle of paperwork, and settle onto my bed to look through it all. I remind myself about the deliveries coming in this week, including the swing and furniture for the seating areas, stones for the fire pit, and the ceramic planters. Listing the items and their delivery dates in the notebook so I can keep track in one place, I remember I'll also need to be there to speak with the electrician and the irrigation company...

My thoughts swim together and I find it hard to keep everything straight. The emotions of Friday curl their claws into me, sapping my mental energy. I put down my pen and sigh deeply, rubbing my face with both hands. I'm so exhausted and frustrated... and I hate that I can't stop thinking about Jude. I cringe again, remembering those moments when I flirted with him so blatantly, thinking he felt what I felt. I was so wrong.

My phone rings and I jump, whipping my head to look at the screen with resentment. Frustration quickly boils into anger when the words *"withheld number"* pop up on my screen.

Fuck it. I answer. "Hello?"

"Olena, finally." Sean's voice pulls me back in time and I feel ill.

"What do you want, Sean?" I'm agitated. I stand and start pacing.

"I just want to talk to you. Why haven't you been answering my texts?"

"Look, we broke up. I moved home. I need you to stop trying to contact me." *We agreed he wouldn't.*

"Olena, I'm sorry. I'm sorry about everything. I had no idea things would get that bad. Those guys... look, I've handled it now and they won't come after us again. I promise."

I grimace at the reference to the robbery, remembering with visceral revulsion the feeling of that man's hand covering my mouth and pulling me backward, my head wrenched into his chest.

"Sean, there is no *us*. I'm living here now, and I'm not coming back."

"Why won't you listen to me?" He sounds frustrated.

"I'm listening to you just fine." *And what I'm hearing is garbage.*

"No, you're not. I'm saying we can work on things. We can be together. I've got it under control now. I'll be better. Come on, Olena. Come home."

"Sean," I say, rubbing my temple, "you're not getting it. I don't want to be together. I'm done. I've moved on. I've got a job here now and—"

He cuts me off. "So, what? You think you can run away from the life we had together for three years? You're just throwing that away? Like none of it matters? Like *I* don't matter?"

"Sean, calm down." He's making me nervous. The phone slips against my sweaty palm. I readjust my grip and try to breathe slowly.

"No, fuck calming down. Fuck that. *I love you*, Olena. I'll always love you. You can't just ignore that and pretend I don't mean anything to you."

Feeling numb, I take a deep breath. I need to make him understand. "Listen. It wasn't just the robbery. You'd been using for a while before that even happened and... things changed, okay? I don't feel... I can't be with you. You changed..."

I'm scrambling. I'm not making sense.

"I *changed?* What the fuck does that mean? How did I change? I know you didn't like the drugs, but I thought... Are you saying you don't love me anymore?" His voice is incredulous.

I close my eyes, bracing for impact. "Yes," I say softly.

The line goes quiet. For a moment, I'm not sure if he's still there.

"You know what, Olena? Fuck you. I gave you everything and you just... *Fuck you.* I can't believe this."

The call disconnects.

16

JUDE

"Happy birthday, Mom," I say quietly, standing at the foot of the joint burial plot, cellophane crinkling under my grasp.

I lay the bouquet against the headstone and straighten up, rubbing my jaw. I've never been any good at talking to her—talking to them—when I'm here.

My eyes drift to my father's headstone. "Hey, Dad. Happy... Saturday, I guess." I shove my hands in my pockets and look around me. I feel awkward, like I'm talking to myself. Or talking to no one.

When I first started seeing my grief counselor, she had encouraged talking to them out loud. I tried to speak to them when I came to visit the cemetery in the beginning, but it never felt natural or comfortable, so, eventually, I stopped. Unless my brother, Miles, is with me, I usually prefer to visit in silence, remembering them quietly in my own way. I don't believe in God or an afterlife but, if anything like that does exist, they'd know I was here. That I visited. That I tried.

Today, however, I've got more on my mind than usual. I find myself wishing I could ask my parents for advice. They were happily married for twenty-five years before the accident took them from us a decade ago; I'd bet money they could steer me in the right direction with Olena.

Just get over yourself and talk. I look around me, glancing over my shoulders to make sure I'm alone here. Finding the coast is clear, I take a deep breath.

"Well," I start uncertainly, "I guess I wanted to tell you… I met someone. At work."

I take another quick look around. Still alone. *Just talk, man.*

"She's…" I trail off and smile to myself, realizing I don't know where to begin. I know Mom and Dad would have liked Olena. I try again. "She's beautiful. And smart. And funny. And possibly a little quirky."

I smile again, looking down at my feet. *Quirky in a good way.*

"Steph says she's *got me good*, which I guess is true. Anyway, I kind of fucked things up," I admit quietly, furrowing my brow.

I try to think about how my parents had handled their disagreements and misunderstandings. They had their share, for sure, but they usually found a way to communicate and forgive each other. I don't remember any ugly fights or insults thrown; they always stayed respectful enough to talk things out.

"We… almost kissed," I add, feeling a little extra self-conscious. "But then we got interrupted and I ended up worrying we shouldn't be doing that at work. So I kind of shut it down— shut *her* down." I grimace at the memory. "She was obviously hurt," I say with a sigh. "So… now I don't know what to do."

What I do know is we can't be chasing each other through rainstorms, having mud fights, and nearly kissing on the job site; that was a step too far and totally unprofessional. Even if I haven't been able to stop thinking about her body pressed against mine ever since. Or imagining what would have happened if Teddy had arrived even one minute later. Or fantasizing about what those lips would have tasted like.

Christ, I can't stop thinking about her. I clear my throat. *Not here, man.*

"Anyway, I really like her. She makes me feel... well, it probably doesn't matter. I mean, nothing can happen, right?" I wait for a beat as if I'll hear someone agree with me. The graveyard is silent, save for a few birds chirping nearby. "It's too complicated—us working together." I kick gently at a twig on the ground. "Even after this project. I have to think about my reputation, you know? Professionally speaking." I smooth a hand over my beard.

Fuck. She already has this hold on me, though.

The idea of having my heart ripped out of my chest again scares the shit out of me. After losing Mom and Dad, and then Alexis leaving... How can I risk letting Olena get close when she might not stay?

I rub the back of my neck and let out a long sigh, looking up at the nearby trees.

I get why Alexis left. We were so young, and I wasn't in a good place after Mom and Dad's death. The grief consumed me. I get it, but... *fuck,* it hurt. Jesus, even Miles didn't want to stick around and moved away the first chance he got.

I rub at the tightness in my chest and nod, telling myself that keeping my distance is the safest choice. Not just for now—for the foreseeable future.

Almost immediately, the thought settles like lead in my stomach, the weight creating a sinking feeling deep inside my gut.

"Oh, Christ. I don't know," I say, looking up at the sky. *Never being more than colleagues? Could I just... do that? Could she?*

I rub my forehead, realizing I don't even know how she feels or what she wants. The fact that she wanted that kiss as much as I did on Friday night was pretty clear, but... beyond a kiss? Maybe I'm reading too much into it.

The look on her face that night swims back into my memory, and I'm almost certain there's more than just pure attraction between us. She must feel it too.

So, if being colleagues is impossible... could we be more than that? How?

The thought is both terrifying and exhilarating. *Shit.*

"I guess this project with the Faulkners will only be another few weeks, at most," I say out loud, raising my eyebrows as I dare to let a seed of hope creep in. "Maybe we could wait?"

Could we cool our jets until the project wraps up? Even this thought creates an urgency that tugs at the back of my mind. *Or... could we keep things professional on-site and see each other outside of work?*

"Would dating really be *that* scandalous?"

It's not like she works *for* me. And we're grown adults; we can control ourselves at work. We'd have to.

Could I open myself up enough to try with her? I know I can't hold on to this idea that everyone will leave me forever.

The tension leaves my shoulders at the thought of taking a chance with Olena. I rub a hand down my face, a smile tugging at my lips.

My eyes fall on my mother's headstone. *What would Mom tell me to do?*

Standing at my parents' graves—my parents, who died so young—I can't help but think they'd encourage me to go for it. They wouldn't want me to deny myself something that could be good. No one on their deathbed wishes they'd worked more. Relationships are always what they wish they'd made time for. Life is too fucking short.

"What was that thing you always used to say, Mom?" I smile

to myself. "That you just wanted us to be happy and healthy and the rest was gravy?"

Could Olena make me happy?

I don't know the answer, but the warmth in my chest at the thought of her makes one thing clear: I want to find out.

17

OLENA

Braiding my hair over one shoulder, I make an effort to shove down any thoughts about Sean's unsettling phone call and focus on work. I mentally check over my plans before I step out of the car, not wanting to risk getting cornered by Jude in the driveway to talk about what happened on Friday; I just want to get to work.

I step out with my bag over one shoulder and my notebooks and papers in my arms. Without stopping to look around, I make a beeline for Steph.

"Steph! Great to see you're feeling better."

She turns and smiles. "Hey, yeah, thanks, much better now. What's up?"

There must be a look of wild determination on my face because Steph looks hesitant. I relax my shoulders and plaster on a pleasant smile, trying to appear more casual. "I was wondering if you had time this morning to help me get that wisteria planted and attached to the arbor; we want to get the branches training along the frame as soon as possible."

"Oh, sure, yeah, I can do that..." My overeager facial expression must betray me because she raises her eyebrows slightly, looking surprised. "Right now? Oh, okay, yes, right now works."

"Great!" I sound overly enthusiastic. *Rein in the unhinged vibes, Olena.*

"Okay, let me grab my gloves." Steph motions that she'll be right back.

Bless you, Steph.

I need to keep my head down and focus on concrete tasks. And, while I'm tempted to look around to find out where Jude is, I'm determined to ignore him today.

Putting my stuff down on a nearby tarp, I tug on my gloves and walk over to the arbor. The wisteria tree sits in a large nursery pot on the ground beside it. I grab the roll of garden twine sitting nearby and look around for a pair of scissors. I notice Teddy and Dimitri leveling the last of the gravel path, finishing the job Jude and I abandoned Friday night. I frown to myself as I remember tracing his nose with mud.

"Olena." Jude's voice stirs up the pain of rejection all over again. *Damn it.*

"Hi," I reply, turning but barely meeting his eyes, and return to my search for the scissors.

"Look, I wanted to—" he starts.

"Morning, Jude." Steph rescues me, returning with her gloves with perfect timing.

"Hi, Steph," Jude says politely. "Listen, Olena, I was hoping we could talk when you have a minute."

"Um, I don't, actually... have a minute. I mean, Steph and I were just going to get this wisteria planted." I meet his eyes with carefully controlled calm.

Steph glances between us and gives me a questioning look. She appears slightly uncomfortable. I smile at her reassuringly.

"Olena," she says carefully, "did you want to leave that with me, or—? Like, if you two need to talk..." Her eyes dart between us again.

"No, it's fine," I blurt out. "I want to get this done. Let's do this." I clap my hands together. I can feel my forced cheerfulness hitting all the wrong notes, but I can't stand the feeling of Jude's eyes on me.

Steph raises her eyebrows but seems to accept she's stuck with me in this awkward situation. She drags the pot over to where we can both lift the plant.

"Okay, uh, maybe later, then." Jude sounds confused but I don't look at him. In my peripheral vision, I see him turn, then pause. A pair of scissors lands beside my feet in the grass. He says nothing and walks off.

"Everything okay between you two?" Steph asks quietly when he's out of earshot.

Having loosened the root ball and soil from the pot, we lift the wisteria up and place it on the ground near the arbor.

"Absolutely." I smile. *Absolutely fucking awful.*

Steph glances over at Jude and turns back to me, giving me a skeptical look, but says nothing more.

I SPEND most of the day fixating on any task that means I don't have to think about or be anywhere near Jude. The site is busy with deliveries and decisions for me to make, so staying occupied is not as hard as I'd expected. I quickly become an expert on monitoring his location out of the corner of my eye and make sure to walk in the other direction, finding any excuse to check on progress or inspect supplies. I even snap a few photos on my phone just to create the illusion I'm thoroughly engrossed in the project at all times.

Even by colleague standards, I know my behavior toward Jude

is poor form, but I can't seem to snap out of it. The pain weighing heavily in my chest won't allow me to be the bigger person. Not yet. *God, why do I have to be so overdramatic about this?*

Walking over to the sunken garden, I take my time inspecting the benches and cushioned seating that were just delivered. Alone in this corner of the property, out of view of the others, I can drop the pretense of being cheerful and professional. Relieved to finally have a moment to myself, I stand at the edge that overlooks the cliff-side and try to take a deep breath. The air enters my body jaggedly, catching on every surface on its way into my lungs. I frown to myself and try again.

"There you are." Jude sounds fed up.

Shit.

"I was just leaving." I paste on a fake smile and move to walk past him. As I pass, he catches my arm, the memory of how he grabbed me after our chase instantly vivid in my mind. I can feel the same magnetic pull from his body now, but this time I'm hell-bent on fighting it. I sigh, rolling my eyes. "Please let go. I've got work to do."

"Olena. Please stop running away from me. I've been trying to talk to you all day." His voice is low; he sounds tired.

I yank my arm out of his grip and we turn to face each other, my aloof facade finally dropping away. "Why should I? You made it perfectly clear you don't want anything to do with me the other night." *So much for playing it cool.*

His brow creases and he rubs his forehead. "Shit."

"Yeah. I got the message loud and clear." I raise my eyebrows.

"Olena—" he starts.

"No, you know what? Don't. I thought... I thought you might've... felt what I felt." I grimace at the vulnerability of the admission. "I don't know why. Clearly, I was a fool for trusting you." I cross my arms in front of me.

A look I can't place crosses his face. "Wait, what does this have to do with trust?" His eyes search mine.

My anger and hurt is boiling over. "Don't do that... Don't play innocent!" I realize I'm raising my voice and drop it down a notch. "I saw you on Saturday," I say more quietly.

"Saturday?" The wheels turn behind his eyes.

"At the grocery store. Buying flowers."

His brow smooths out suddenly and I know I've hit my mark.

I narrow my eyes at him. "As if it wasn't humiliating enough for you to reject me after Teddy showed up... then I find out you're seeing someone else?" Tears threaten behind my eyes and I blink rapidly, trying to steady my breathing. I refuse to cry.

"Olena." He looks at the ground.

"No, don't bother." I move to walk past him again and he grabs me by both arms, pulling me back to face him. His eyes are flaring with some emotion I can't read.

"Olena, stop." He takes a deep breath. His face is unusually calm, almost patient.

"*What?*" I'm the opposite of patient. My brow furrows as I watch his expression change, like he's wrestling with something. "You know what? Nevermind, I don't care."

The lie is bitter on my tongue, but I need to get out of here. I break away from his grasp and walk a few paces toward the newly built steps leading up to the path.

His voice comes from behind me. "The flowers were for my mother."

I freeze. Realization hits me like a wave crashing into a wall. I squeeze my eyes shut.

"For her grave, actually. Saturday was her birthday."

The humiliation stabs deeper and I wince. I slowly turn around to face him.

He's watching me with dark intensity.

"Oh, my God, I'm so sorry. I shouldn't have said... I made an assumption. And I... I didn't know." I wince. "I'm such an asshole. And, oh, God... your mother died? I'm so sorry for your loss too." I'm burning with shame. I put my palm to my forehead, realizing I'm blathering again but can't stop. "Sorry, I know I should... I should just shut up. It's just whenever..." I look at my feet. I can't bear this. I squeeze my hands into tight fists as I look up at him, my eyes pleading for forgiveness as he watches me flounder under his silent gaze. "Ugh, I always do this. I just go on and on whenever I'm—"

Jude crosses the distance between us before I can react, sweeping my face up in his hands, the kiss desperate and devastating.

My eyes flutter shut. My body melts against his, all the tension and emotion rushing between us and out of me. His lips are searching, his tongue sweeping softly against mine as his hands at the nape of my neck pull me closer, deeper. My hands are pinned between us, pressing against his heaving chest.

Jude slows, softening, and breaks the kiss, pressing his forehead against mine. "I thought you'd never shut up," he says, smiling.

I can't help but smile too.

He kisses my forehead and my eyes close again as I exhale a shuddering breath, not trusting myself to speak. Jude sweeps a thumb over my cheek. "Look at me."

I shake my head. I can't; the shame of my accusation is unbearable.

"Olena," he tries again. This man's patience is impressive. He lifts my chin with a finger and I force myself to meet his gaze.

I almost look away again; the emotion in his eyes is so potent. "Jude, I—"

He cuts me off, his voice rough. "*Of course* I want you."

I inhale sharply.

"You're all I think about." He leans down to kiss my cheek.

My heart hammers in my chest as he brushes his lips against my skin.

"I can't get my head straight when you're around me," he says softly against my cheek. "I want you every moment of every day. I can't sleep because I'm thinking about you." His hands run down my arms and I shiver.

I want to fall into his chest and lose myself. But something nags at me. I remember the regret in his eyes from Friday and I pull back, searching his expression. "Then what happened the other night? Why didn't you just kiss me after Teddy left?"

A pained look crosses Jude's face. He blows out a breath. "I got scared. Scared we almost got caught. Scared about what that would mean for"—he gestures around us—"*this*. My business. My team."

My brow creases with worry. "Well, are you still worried about that? Have we screwed everything up?"

He looks away and smiles. "I hope not," he chuckles, meeting my gaze again. "Or, at least, I don't think so. Not yet, anyway." He tucks a loose wisp of hair behind my ear.

I look down and smile.

"I realized..." He pauses, looking for the words. "I realized some things are worth the risk. You're worth the risk."

I inhale a breath, my eyes meeting his. "Jude..." I don't know what to say. I don't know how to take all of this in.

He furrows his brow. "I can't believe I acted like such an ass." He shakes his head, looking pained. "I should never have pushed you away like that." He runs his thumb over my jawline, his fingertips in the hair at the nape of my neck. "God, even the *idea* of rejecting you is absurd. I mean, *have you seen you?*" He raises his eyebrows at me, his green eyes shining.

I snort out an awkward laugh. I must look awful—all flushed and distraught. "I'm a mess, sorry..."

"No." He looks at me seriously. "Now, *that* I do reject." He kisses my forehead again.

I can't help but smile, but I'm still feeling cautious. I look up at him. "So, what now?"

"Well, we have to stop messing around like that on the job site, for one," he says with a grimace. "That wasn't very..."

"Professional?" I offer.

"Right." He smiles down at me. "And I know I didn't handle it very smoothly, either. With you, I mean. After you left that night... I instantly regretted hurting you." His brow furrows as he looks at me. "I'm so sorry, Olena. For making you think, even for a moment, that I didn't want this..." It looks like the idea hurts him physically. His eyes drop to my mouth and I'm drawn in again. "That I didn't want *you*." He pulls me in to him, pressing a soft kiss to my lips. The kiss is slow and gentle, but, as our lips part, the heat in his eyes promises more.

Oh, God, I want this too.

"I'm sorry too," I say quietly. "For jumping to conclusions like that. And for avoiding you all day." I roll my eyes as I start in on the long list of things I'm sorry for. "And for putting my foot in my mouth and for not being able to shut up when I—"

His finger covers my lips, stopping me. The corner of his mouth quirks up into a half-smile.

"I was doing it again, wasn't I?" I ask, grimacing.

He nods with a sober expression and drops his hand, both of us breaking into a soft laugh.

He glances at the path that leads to the reality we have to face. "Speaking of being professional, though, we should probably..." He trails off, meeting my eyes.

I realize we are still, very much currently, at work.

We take a reluctant step apart and my chest already aches with that space between us.

He reaches out and smoothes my hair, taking a deep breath. "Can we try this properly?"

I nod, holding his gaze.

"Have dinner with me. Tonight. I'll cook."

18

OLENA

Nestled in the woods, perched on a hill overlooking the river's edge, Jude's place has a kind of dreamy, rustic log cabin vibe. I can't help thinking it suits him perfectly. *Hunky lumberjack is fucking right*, I think with a smirk. Standing on the covered front porch, I knock on his door and wait, my insides fluttering with nervous anticipation.

Jude answers the door looking freshly showered, his hair slightly damp. He's wearing a fitted navy blue henley shirt and clean jeans. His sleeves are pushed up, showing the tattoos on his arms. He slowly wipes his hands on a tea towel, regarding me with a lazy grin.

I take a moment to catch my breath. Neither of us speaks as he steps aside to let me in the door. As he shuts it gently behind us, his hand slides down my arm, pulling me close.

I wrap my arms around his waist and close my eyes, my face in his chest, breathing in deeply. He smells so good.

Burying his face in my hair, he presses a kiss to the top of my head and softly rubs my back. "You smell amazing," he murmurs into my hair.

I rushed home after work to shower too. I've never gotten ready so fast in my life.

"I was just thinking the same about you. Beats mud by a mile." I smile up at him. "Although that does have a certain... appeal." I raise an eyebrow and he smirks.

He leans down, pressing a gentle, lingering kiss to my cheek. Releasing our embrace, I quickly shrug off my coat and kick off my shoes, leaving them near the front door.

Murphy lumbers over to greet me, tail wagging lazily, and I stoop to ruffle him around the neck. When he's had his fill of affection, he plods away, settling down in his dog bed nearby.

"Come with me." Jude takes my hand and leads me into the kitchen, where a pot of water simmers quietly on the stove. The kitchen is simple, a small island in the center.

"Your house suits you," I say as my eyes travel the room. Across from the kitchen is a small living room with a wood-burning stove. The back of the couch, draped in a plaid blanket, is all that separates the two rooms, which are otherwise one big space. There's a small hallway opposite where I stand, presumably leading to Jude's bedroom at the back of the house.

"Suits me? How so?"

I turn to him, stepping in close as he runs his hands up and down my arms.

My hands find his waist. "Well, it's quiet. And rugged." I raise an eyebrow and see him smile, dropping his gaze briefly. "And sturdy, I guess... like it's been here for ages. Weathered some storms."

"Well, you're right about the house being old," he replies, smiling. "My grandfather built this place. It was our family's summer cabin when we were growing up."

"We?" I ask, tilting my head.

"Me and my little brother, Miles."

I nod.

"He lived here with me for a while, but he works in construction in Seattle now. So now it's just me here."

Just me, I repeat to myself in my head. Like there's anything *just* about Jude.

His eyes pass over the room. "I've had to fix the house up quite a bit to make it comfortable for living here year-round but... it works." He gives a small shrug.

"Well, I love it. Very cozy," I say, smiling up at him as he brushes a thumb over my cheek. My eyes dip down to his lips.

"Glad you like it." He sounds almost sheepish. "I do too. It's quiet, like you said—for the most part. Miles shows up to crash once in a while. Keeps me on my toes."

"Seems pretty quiet right now," I say suggestively. I love that we're in this isolated, private place together. Just us. We've never been alone like this.

He grins and pulls away, squeezing my fingers before motioning for me to sit on one of the stools at the island.

As I take my seat, he moves behind me and I hold my breath as he gathers my long hair in his hands and sweeps it forward over one of my shoulders. I close my eyes and lean my head to the side, baring my neck to him.

Dear God, I'm not going to make it through dinner if he keeps touching me like this.

Jude's hands slide over my shoulders and he bends to kiss my neck. "I can't believe I get you all to myself," he breathes against my skin.

I turn my face up to meet his eyes as he straightens, then squeezes my arms. "You're gonna need to pace yourself."

He grins guiltily at me.

"I seem to remember you saying you wanted to do this *properly*." I arch an eyebrow and he pushes away, looking pained but smiling.

"I do, I do," he says, almost to himself. He blows out a breath and walks into the kitchen, running a hand down his face.

"Plus, I want to watch you cook." I lean my chin on my fist, propping my elbows on the surface of the island in front of me. "You promised me dinner."

"Dinner. Yes." He points at me with one hand while opening the fridge with the other. He pulls out carrots, an onion, and a red bell pepper. I shamelessly watch his arm muscles working as he runs them under water at the sink.

He is so fucking hot. I love that I can openly stare at him now that we're not at work.

He pauses, turning off the tap and shaking out the vegetables before placing them on the cutting board. Drying his hands, he turns away from me to open a cupboard above the counter.

I let my eyes slide down his back, admiring his ass and blowing out a soft breath.

He pulls down two wine glasses. "What kind of wine do you like?" he asks.

"I uh..." I start, tearing my eyes away from his body and blinking. "I don't actually know." I look down, a bit embarrassed to admit my lack of fancy-person knowledge. "I usually just order whatever other people are having. Or I pick a random one."

"Well, okay... red or white? Should we start there?"

"White." *No wine stains for me this time.*

He nods and pulls a bottle out of the fridge. Placing it on the counter between us, he unwraps the top and twists the corkscrew into place, pulling the cork with ease as he watches me.

"How am I going to do this?" he asks, looking pensive as his eyes rove over my face. His gaze pauses for a moment on my lips before he looks away to pour the wine.

"What do you mean?" I ask warily, accepting the glass of wine he hands me.

"How am I going to manage being with you at work every day?"

I smile and lower my eyes.

"Even now, you're three feet away from me and I want to jump over the counter just to be closer to you."

I set down my glass and hop off the stool, walking around the edge of the island. He goes still as I come closer, looking down at me with heat in his eyes. Reaching for his hips, I hook my fingers into his belt loops on both sides and pull him against me, our faces inches apart.

"There. One problem solved." I arch up and give him an inviting look.

He lifts my face gently with both hands and brings my mouth to his. I feel his breath on my lips, the pull between us filling my senses.

"Temptress," he whispers against my aching lips. A slow grin spreads across his features and he lets go of me, turning back to the cutting board. "Someone's got to make this meal."

My jaw hanging open, I stand there and remind myself to breathe—his sudden absence almost painful. I slowly return to my stool and Jude glances at me over his shoulder, smiling. I look up at the ceiling as I take a long sip of my wine, lifting my hair off my neck with my other hand; suddenly, it feels too warm in here.

"Oh my God, this is incredible," I mumble around a bite of stir-fry.

"You're incredible." Jude smiles and drains his glass.

I roll my eyes. "You're a shameless flirt."

"*Me?*" He sets the glass down, leaning forward. "Are you kidding me? You've been trying to destroy my self-control for over a week." At my confused expression, he goes on. "The reading glasses?" A hint of heat returns to his eyes and he shakes his head.

I smile and look down at my food, fidgeting with the handle of my fork. "I couldn't help myself." My eyes lift to meet his. "It was too perfect."

He narrows his eyes with a rueful smile.

I rest my chin on my hand and tilt my head. "You should've seen your face," I say, grinning with delight.

"I probably looked like a man about to have a heart attack."

"You did," I laugh softly.

"Careful how you wield that power, MacMillan." He raises an eyebrow and his green eyes flicker with desire.

We finish eating and Jude stands to clear our plates. He walks to the sink, and I let my eyes devour his body from behind. Again. *I will never get sick of this view.*

He turns, catching me in the act.

I grin and bite my lip.

"Hold on, were you just... objectifying me?" he asks with mock incredulity.

"Yuh-huh. One hundred percent," I tease, finishing the last of my wine. "As you were." I motion for him to turn back around.

"Alright, I'll allow it." He smiles, turning back to the sink.

"How generous of you." I stand and walk to the kitchen, approaching him slowly, making a point of placing my empty glass next to the sink beside him.

He watches me over his shoulder, letting out a breath when my breasts graze against his back as I reach past him. He dries his hands, then turns to face me, sliding them around my waist.

Kissing my forehead, then my nose, Jude's hands slip under the hem of my shirt behind me. He traces the bones of my spine with a finger, sliding his other hand down over my ass, a low sound of satisfaction rumbling from his throat.

My arms circle his neck, resting on his strong shoulders, and our lips meet in a slow kiss. My fingers drift through his hair to the back of his neck, then travel slowly down his muscled arms. Pulling away, I twine my fingers with his and lead him by the hand to the living room. I bite my lip as I guide him to the couch, seeing the heat in his gaze. He sits and I climb over him, straddling him on my knees.

Cupping my face in both hands, he pulls me down, kissing me deeply, fiercely, like he's been holding back all night before unleashing himself like this. He shifts his hips forward to meet mine and grabs me from behind to crush me into him, letting out a soft growl against my mouth as his hardness presses against me.

My eyes flutter at his sudden intensity and I can't help but move my hips against the delicious heat pressing between my legs.

His tongue sweeps into my mouth, searching, tasting, and sliding against mine. He bites my lower lip softly before he kisses his way along my jawline, then down my neck. Reaching my collarbone, he sweeps my hair back and I arch my neck as he licks me there, causing my entire body to shiver, all my senses firing at once.

I roll my hips as he grips onto my ass, pressing me closer, and trail my tongue along the arc of his ear.

He hisses a sharp inhale and softly groans, sliding his hands over my thighs.

Dipping my head down to kiss his neck, I'm desperate to feel more of him. I pull his shirt up between us, raking my fingers over his stomach muscles.

Fucking hell.

"Olena..." He takes my jaw in his hands and pulls me to face him. His eyes are hooded, his expression dark. "I want you in my bed."

Yes, please. I smile, leaning in to kiss him again, craving him so badly I feel almost drunk with need. His cock pulses against me, straining behind the fly of his jeans. I run a hand down his chest between us, fisting his shirt, and crush my lips to his. His hands are in my hair, his tongue tangled with mine. The kiss deepens, getting wilder, like we've been starved of each other's taste and can't get enough.

He tears his mouth away again, breathing hard. "But we have to stop."

I tense. "What?" I ask quietly, pulling back, the sting of rejection threatening once again. "Why?" I search his eyes.

He kisses my cheek. His voice is low and rough. "Because... we were supposed to do this properly." He gives me a lazy grin, his eyes lingering on my mouth. I can tell he wants more, too, but is trying to control himself.

"But..." I start to say.

He leans in close, his cheek against mine, his lips next to my ear. "Because... when I make you come," he breathes, and I inhale sharply at his words, closing my eyes for a moment, "I want to take my time." He kisses my neck, his voice a low rasp. "I want to watch you. I want to see the look on your face when you go over the edge."

My cheeks blaze with heat. I can't look at him. I bite my lip as he brushes his mouth against my neck and a pulse of soft pleasure courses through my body.

"And I want you to spend the night so we can do it all over again in the morning."

My eyes shutter as I exhale. *Holy fuck.* I move my hips against him in response, almost involuntarily.

His hands stop me gently, and he continues with his infuriating, sexy logic. "I want to enjoy every minute of it. Of *you*. I don't want to be worrying about waking up for work the next day."

Right. It's Monday night. We have work in the morning. I let out a groan of frustration and he chuckles softly against my cheek, kissing me there. I reluctantly shift my hips back from him in an effort to help me concentrate. I pull back and meet his eyes.

"How do you have this much self-control?" I ask with a teasing prod to his chest. "It's very unfair of you to show off like that."

He laughs. "Well, someone responsible had to step in." His gaze drops to my mouth and he looks away, taking a steadying breath. He meets my eyes again as he runs his hands down my back, leaning back on the couch. "Friday night."

"*Friday?*" I groan again, throwing my head back. "I have to work with you all week. I'm going to lose my mind." Leaning in again, I kiss him softly.

"The suffering will be mutual, I promise you." He smirks.

"Okay," I say regretfully, "but only so long as you promise to suffer."

He puts his hand to his heart. "Promise."

19

JUDE

Seeing Olena Tuesday morning is almost painful.

After she left my house last night, I stood with my forehead pressed to the door for several minutes, trying to fight the urge to run after her and pull her back into my arms. I only let myself move after I heard her car leaving the driveway. I cleaned up dinner, smiling to myself the entire time, then took a cold shower. Still, I barely slept.

This morning, she texted me.

OLENA

let the suffering begin

ME

way ahead of you.

As she steps out of her car in the Faulkners' driveway, I blow out a breath. She's done nothing to ease my pain. Her hair is in two French braids... aaaaaaannnd the grown man in me is suddenly nowhere to be found. It takes all my willpower not to reach out and tug on them like a boy in a schoolyard. Except, unlike a schoolboy, I wouldn't run away.

My eyes lock on her. She meets my gaze.

"Morning, Jude," says Mitch as he walks past us.

My eyes barely leave Olena's. "Hey, Mitch, good to have you back."

She smiles as she adjusts the strap of her shoulder bag. I want to tear off her clothes.

"Morning, Olena," Mitch says to her.

"Good morning," she says, glancing at him, then back at me with a hint of heat in her eyes. The look on her face tells me she's drowning in this just as much as I am.

The memory of her on my lap last night flashes into my mind and I stare at her lips. I'm desperate to finish what we started; I don't know how I'm going to get through this week at work. But we promised to act like professionals. I can't let my inner Tarzan take her right here on the ground—however much I may want to. I take a deep breath to make sure I don't embarrass myself.

We are going to have our work cut out for us here. *Work. I'm at work.*

I tear my eyes away and find my gloves in the truck, then head across the property to get started on the stone firepit in the center of the sunken garden. Out of the corner of my eye, I see Olena shaking hands with the electrician who just arrived. I breathe a sigh of relief that she'll be busy and, hopefully, far enough away from me that I can think straight.

Dimitri joins me and we haul paving stones from a nearby pile, arranging them into a circular pattern around the dug-out area on the ground. The basic structure only takes us about fifteen minutes. Assuring him I can finish the rest myself, I send Dimitri to install the swing while I do the finishing touches here.

I'm hauling up a bag of decorative river rock when Olena and the electrician walk down the steps, deep in conversation about lighting.

She stops short when she sees me.

"Jude, hi," she says, looking surprised and a little flushed. "I didn't know you were over here."

"Hey," I say, not able to help staring at her. With effort, I remember there's another person with us. "Jude Sharpe. Nice to meet you." I smile at the electrician, an older man with a red nose and thick gray eyebrows. I put the bag of rocks down beside the fire pit and take off my glove to shake his hand.

"Peter Sparling," he says.

I nod.

"We were just looking over all the areas that will need electrical installed," Olena explains, holding my gaze.

"Go for it, by all means." I smile at Peter politely and gesture for them to come into the secluded garden space.

As they walk in, Olena continues talking to Peter, somehow forming complete sentences like a pro.

My mouth only wants to be doing one thing right now—and it's definitely not talking.

"So, around the fire pit there will be six posts in a hexagon shape; we'll have string lighting hung between those. So we'll need a plug at the base of one of them."

She must feel my eyes raking over her.

Peter considers. "So, the question is, where are those going in the ground and which one you want hooked up to power."

"I was thinking the one that makes the most sense is the..." Olena's eyes find mine and she falters. "The uh..."

I wink at her, then turn away to open a bag of sand with my pocket knife.

I hear her recover behind me. "Sorry. What was I saying? Right. The one closest to the path is probably best, since I assume the line will be coming from that direction."

My back is to them both, but I'm smiling to myself as I pour the sand into the pit.

§.

THE ARBORIST CREW descends on us midday Wednesday to take out the two sick maples, so our lunch break is not remotely enjoyable; the sound of chainsaws ripping through branches ruins any chance of conversation or rest. My crew piles into Teddy's truck to pick up lunch in town and escape the noise. I stay behind to manage the carnage from the tree removal.

Olena stays behind, too, and sits in her car with the doors and windows shut, ear protection on, eating snacks while she looks over some paperwork. I'm glad she packed food today, because I'm fresh out of protein bars.

My phone buzzes in my pocket.

OLENA
is it Friday yet?

ME
is there something you're looking forward to in particular?

OLENA
well I just started seeing this guy at work…

ME
oh, do tell

OLENA
he's very handsome

ME
yeah? go on

OLENA

and kind of quiet and mysterious sometimes

ME

he sounds dreamy.

OLENA

you have no idea.

ME

so what's happening Friday?

OLENA

I'm not sure but he promised to show me a good time.

ME

like a gentleman

OLENA

oh that remains to be seen.

ME

I'm actually seeing someone at work too

OLENA

oh?

ME

yeah but she's driving me up the wall

OLENA

how so?

ME

yesterday she showed up wearing her hair in two braids

OLENA

what's wrong with braids?

ME

they are very... distracting

OLENA

why's that?

ME

I kept imagining pulling them.

OLENA

that's very immature of you

ME

trust me, my thoughts in this area were very much mature in nature.

OLENA

scandalous

ME

oh, have I offended you?

OLENA

oh it takes a lot more than that to offend me.

ME

I'll have to work harder then.

OLENA

you seem like the imaginative type. I'm sure you'll find a way.

I smirk to myself and shake my head, pocketing my phone.

I walk over to the Faulkners' front door to ask them what to do with the firewood, passing her car on my way. Unable to resist, I stop to tap on her window, pulling off my ear protection. She rolls the window down and pulls one side of her earmuff away from her ear, wincing at the noise. I brace my hands over the door frame, leaning in.

"How goes the suffering?" I shout over the roaring noise.

"Oh, it's pure hell. You?" she shouts back, squinting up at me.

"Same." I grin, staring at her mouth. I want to kiss her.

"Good." She smiles wickedly... and rolls up her window in my face.

I give her a rueful smile as I rub my jaw, shaking my head, and continue walking to the house.

STEPH and I are crouched beside one another on Thursday afternoon, a stack of empty nursery pots between us. We've been planting ornamental grasses and shrubs along the garden beds edging the cliff-side. I pat the soil around the base of the azalea I've just put in the ground and stand to take stock of our progress. The day is sunny and Murphy stretches out nearby, soaking it in. I walk over to give him a scratch. When I straighten, I stretch my arms back, feeling the pull in my chest muscles. I've been hunched over all morning and my body is feeling it.

"Jude!" Carol's voice comes from over my shoulder.

I turn around and see her walking quickly along the cobble-stone path toward me. "Hey, Carol. Nice to see you again," I say with a smile.

"I came out to admire your progress." She places her hands on her hips and scans the property. "My goodness! It's looking fantastic out here!" She beams at me.

It's true; we've made a huge impact on this property in a short time.

"Thanks. I think it's all coming together." I smile at her. "The lighting should be going in tomorrow too," I explain, scanning the property. My eyes catch on Olena across the yard, talking to a man with a clipboard as he gestures at the ground. An irrigation truck sits in the driveway.

"Oh, wonderful!" Carol clasps her hands together.

My gaze lingers on Olena, watching her easy manner, the way she tucks her hair behind her ear. I am vaguely aware of Carol strolling around the area where we've been working, looking at all the plants.

Her voice gushes from nearby. "Oh, I love this seating area, especially with the flowers framing each side. It's going to be stunning. Well done!"

When I don't respond, she evidently catches the source of my distraction. She appears at my side, pulling my attention back. She gives me a knowing smile, squeezing my arm. "I remember when Charles used to look at me like that," she says quietly, a warm, wistful tone in her voice.

Caught off guard, I chuckle good-naturedly, trying to cover up my embarrassment at being caught staring at Olena while at work. "Like what? I was just... uh..." I trail off, unable to come up with a good excuse.

"Admiring the view?" Carol pats my shoulder. "It's okay, darling. We were all young once."

I stare at Carol, speechless.

She winks at me.

I don't know how to respond. "I—"

"Just treat her well." She raises her eyebrows, challenging me with a protective look in her eye.

"Of course," is all I can say.

Another delivery from the nursery arrives on Friday, most of the plants destined for the sunken garden. Unloading and carrying them there, my team's energy is buzzing.

"Big plans this weekend, Teddy?" Steph asks, placing a heavy pot down beside a line of others and wiping her hands on her cargo pants.

"I have little kids. Surviving the weekend is the only big plan." Teddy laughs, descending the stairs heavily as he carries a sprawling blueberry bush and tries not to get poked in the face by the branches. He bends, grimacing as he puts the pot down with the rest.

Mitch and Dimitri navigate the steps carefully, balancing a larger rose bush between them. "I remember those days," Mitch notes gruffly. "You're in the trenches, Ted."

Teddy raises his eyebrows and nods; he looks tired.

"What about you, Jude?" Steph asks.

"Oh, I think we know." Teddy pumps his eyebrows, smiling, and the others snicker.

"What does that mean?" I ask defensively.

"Oh, come on, Jude." Steph throws me a knowing look.

"What?" I press.

She rolls her eyes. "You and Olena were tense as fuck around each other on Monday and, ever since then, you've been ogling each other like damn teenagers." Steph raises her eyebrows at me, smirking.

I scoff, folding my arms over my chest with a frown.

"Yeah, it's been hard to miss," Dimitri adds with a chuckle.

I raise my eyebrows at him, then turn to Mitch, hoping he'll come to my defense. He says nothing, just raises his hands in front of him like he doesn't want to get involved.

"Teddy?" I look at him hopefully.

"Hey, I don't know, man," he hedges. He looks like he has more to say.

"Out with it." I narrow my eyes at him.

"Okay, I'm just saying... last time I had that look on my face, Lisa ended up pregnant."

The team erupts in laughter.

"Okay." I roll my eyes. "Laugh it up, guys."

"No, but seriously, boss," Teddy says, slapping me on the shoulder as he leaves for another load, "you guys make a cute couple."

"Yeah, and she's a good egg," Steph adds. "If you don't go for it, I will." She winks at me, spinning her ball cap backwards as she turns to climb the steps.

Mitch and Dimitri both smile knowingly at me, evidently agreeing with the others. They retreat up the stairs and head back to the truck for more plants.

Left alone for the moment, I run my hands through my hair and blow out a long breath. I feel a strange mixture of embarrassment and relief.

Smiling to myself, I pull out my phone.

ME

The others are onto us. I don't think we've been as stealthy as planned.

OLENA

Oops. Everything okay?

ME

Yes and apparently we have their blessing.

OLENA

Aww. Well good because I don't know if you noticed, but it's Friday.

ME

How could I forget?

20

OLENA

J ude's hand runs lazily along my thigh as he drives us into town. He told me our plans were a surprise, so I dressed simply in nice jeans and a fitted, button-up silk top. Remembering Jude's promise from Monday, I told Wyatt not to expect me home tonight.

Wearing a black t-shirt and jeans, Jude looks... edible. I can't stop staring at him. The setting sun casts a golden glow on his face as he drives, a hint of auburn shining in his dark beard. He glances over at me and smiles. Returning his eyes to the road, he slides his hand higher. My eyes roll involuntarily and I exhale; I'm having a hard time keeping my composure as electricity spreads up my leg from his touch.

"That is a very dangerous move," I say, leaning back against the headrest and turning to look at him. He grins. "Unless you're planning to find somewhere to pull over, you'd better keep those hands in check." I raise an eyebrow at him.

He pulls his hand away, feigning innocence. "My sincere apologies," he says solemnly, then smiles at me, his green eyes shining with mischief. He pulls into the parking lot of a place I don't remember from before I'd moved to Seattle. In the front window, a sign reading *"The Battle Axe"* sits above a logo of a wooden target. I look inside and my eyes widen.

"We're going *axe throwing?*" I ask, beaming at him. I've always wanted to try it.

"I thought we could work through some of this... *tension*," he says, his eyes traveling over my body and shamelessly lingering on my breasts. Shutting off the truck, he leans over, reaches a hand to the back of my neck, and pulls me in for a kiss.

Our lips part and I smile up at him. "We'll have to leave the truck first."

Reluctantly, we climb out. As we walk in the door of The Battle Axe, the sound of Celtic punk music fills my ears. I peer past the front desk to see paired throwing lanes with wooden targets mounted on the walls, each pair separated from the lanes next to it by a section of chain-link fence. There's a mural behind the front desk of a badass Viking woman holding two axes across her chest.

A muscular woman with pink hair and full sleeve tattoos greets us as we step up to the desk. She taps a pen against her palm and smiles at us.

"Jude, welcome back," she smiles at him with a nod. "Same as usual? Or...?" She looks at me, inquiring.

"Ooh, do you come here often?" I tease, leaning forward on the desk and twisting up to look at him.

"I've been here a few times, yeah," he smiles over at me.

"So, you're really leaning into that whole axe-wielding lumberjack vibe, huh?" I let my gaze travel up and down over his body and grin at him.

He rolls his eyes at me then turns back to her. "Yeah, axes for both of us, thanks. An hour." She nods and turns to collect our equipment.

Jude leans in close to me. "Keep it in your pants, MacMillan," he teases quietly, whispering against my cheek.

"You started it," I say, straight-faced.

He raises an eyebrow, shaking his head.

The woman with pink hair walks us over to our throwing lanes and leads us through a quick safety demonstration, showing me the correct technique. Jude stands by, silently watching us. Watching *me*. He's distracting me and I find I'm not taking in what the woman is saying. When she leaves, I hold the axe in my hands cautiously.

Jude leans against the fence nearby with his arms folded and his own axe propped up beside him at his feet.

"I have to admit, *for some reason,* I had a hard time focusing on what she was saying just now." I give him a playfully confused look.

He smiles at me, raising his eyebrows. "Is that right?"

"Yeah, it was so weird," I say, smiling as I sweep my hair over my shoulder with one hand, axe in the other. "I think something was distracting me." I arch an eyebrow at him.

"Come on, I'll show you." Jude pushes off the fence and picks up his axe, then steps into his throwing lane. He stands behind the red tape on the floor in the split stance I remember the woman demonstrating. Holding the handle in both fists, he raises it over his head, aiming for the target. His muscular arms swing slightly backward, then smoothly forward as he releases his grip. The blade lodges in the target with a thud.

"The trick is not throwing too hard, or it'll over-rotate," he explains.

"Hmm, I dunno. I might need to see that again," I say with a frown.

He gives me a look but indulges me and goes to retrieve his axe. He demonstrates for me once more. I watch his muscles working, my eyes devouring his incredible body.

I might be drooling.

"Your turn," he says, jolting me back to reality. He leans over and kisses my cheek, then reaches behind me and gives my ass a quick slap.

Um, yes, please.

"Come on, this ain't a spectator sport," he adds quietly in my ear.

"Oh?" I feign surprise. "Well, it should be. Because that was… chef's kiss, really. No notes." I reach behind him and grab his ass.

He inhales sharply.

I let go and hold his gaze, my mouth slightly open. As I pull back, his eyes dip down and linger, and I realize he can see down my top at this angle.

I give him a half-smile, lift my axe again, and walk back to my throwing lane.

"Olena," he says in a low voice.

"Yeah?" I position my feet behind the red line in my lane, then arch a brow and look at him.

His jaw clenches. "Remember that woman at work I've been seeing?"

"Oh, that's *right*." I play along, lining up my hands on the handle. I focus on the target.

"Remember how I said she was driving me up the wall?"

I glance over and catch the clench of his hands on the axe handle. "Uh-huh…" I raise an eyebrow and lift my eyes to his.

"She's doing it again."

I drop my gaze, smiling, then meet his eyes again with a pout. "Aw, poor baby," I say, lifting my axe over my head. Turning back to focus on the target, I pull back and swing it forward, letting go in front of me. The blade lands with a crack on the bullseye.

Jude gapes at me as I pull my hair up in a quick ponytail, grinning, and turn to retrieve my axe.

❦

AN HOUR LATER, we step out of The Battle Axe in a more wound-up state than when we went in. Searching out some quick dinner, we walk half a block to a nearby food truck and order burgers, which we eat outside as the sun goes down.

I'm still finishing the last of my fries as we stroll back to the truck, flirting harder than ever now that we can do it openly.

A voice comes from behind me. "Olena?"

At the sound of my name, I whirl around to find Bradley standing across from me. Art gallery Bradley. Humiliating, awful date Bradley. Cue the inward cringe, outward smile combo.

"Bradley? Hi." It takes me a few beats to get my bearings. *What is he doing here?* I can feel the heat of Jude's massive body standing behind me as I watch Bradley take him in, his eyes shifting between us as if he's trying to figure out how Jude fits into my life.

"I thought that was you. I haven't seen you since, well... since that night at the gallery, I guess," he says with a rueful smirk.

I'd much rather bypass that memory altogether. "Yeah, uh, we're just... finishing up dinner," I say with what I hope is nonchalance. I hold up my remaining fries by way of explanation. *This is so awkward.* I'd rather not visit the museum of my poor decisions. With Jude. In public.

"Aren't you going to introduce me?" Bradley asks, lifting his chin at Jude.

"Yes, sorry, Jude, this is Bradley, Bradley, this is Jude," I say with a frown of concentration.

Jude steps out from behind me to shake Bradley's hand. Eyeing Bradley, he doesn't speak, just gives a polite smile and nods his head in a silent greeting.

"He doesn't say much, does he?" Bradley raises his eyebrows at me.

Jude tenses at my side and I glance up at him. His eyes narrow ever so slightly.

"Uh, Bradley and I know each other from…" I trail off, my mind scrambling to explain our ill-advised date.

"We dated a while back," Bradley offers, looking at Jude and straightening slightly.

Ugh, does he look proud? I want to smack his smug face. It was *one* date. And it was a disaster.

"Olena, that reminds me. My friend Dale is hosting a fundraiser for wildlife conservation next week at the Gareth Mason Gallery. It'll coincide with the Basilio Domínguez exhibition. You know, the Cuban street art photographer?" He raises his eyebrows inquisitively, as if to confirm I know what he's talking about.

I don't. "Sounds… interesting," I say weakly. *Why is he telling me this?* I must look visibly confused.

"You do something environmental for work, isn't that right?"

I fight the urge to roll my eyes. "Yes, landscape design."

"Right, right, the little gardens," he laughs softly. "I remember now." He smiles, looking satisfied.

Once again, I feel Jude tense at my side.

I don't know what to say to escape this interaction; I just know I want to ejector-seat myself out of here to avoid enduring another second of looking at Bradley's smug face and his condescending gaze. Or hearing anything more about modern art—especially the windbags who stand around talking about it.

"Well, thanks for the info. We'd better get going." I grab Jude by the arm, making to pull him toward the truck.

"Okay. Nice to see you, Olena," Bradley offers politely. "I'll send you the details. I've still got your number."

Gross.

"And nice to meet you, Jude."

Jude lifts his chin at Bradley. "Brad, was it?"

"Bradley, actually," he corrects him, insufferable pride oozing from his face.

This time I do roll my eyes, but I turn away first—just barely. I can't face looking at Jude yet, knowing I'm flushing with embarrassment.

We make our hasty departure and I exhale with relief, but an awkward silence has crept in between us.

21

OLENA

The tension is palpable as we climb into our seats. I search Jude's face for signs of the fun and flirty energy, but that seems to have suddenly evaporated. His expression is dark and pensive as he starts the truck and pulls out of the parking lot. I want to apologize and explain about Bradley and his vapid art gallery friends, but I don't know where to begin.

Fuck.

In an attempt at lightening the mood, I try to channel some of the flirtatious vibe we had going earlier.

"So, do you think that was just beginner's luck, or have I discovered a new superpower?" I venture with a wry smile, remembering all the delicious touching and teasing we shared while throwing axes. Spurred on by Jude's approving gaze, I'd felt like a badass at The Battle Axe—like an invincible sex bomb with a blade. I desperately want those moments back.

Jude glances at me out of the corner of his eye and grunts softly in response, my efforts falling epically flat.

I exhale a breath, not sure how to get back to where we were before Bradley showed up and soured everything. The dreadful weight of rejection twists in my stomach. I pick at the rough edges of my fingernails, shifting in my seat.

"I had a lot of fun tonight," I say, trying again. "And those burgers were amazing."

"Yeah," he replies quietly. "They were good."

More silence. *Ugh.*

"Running into Bradley was..."

"Awkward?" Jude offers, smirking slightly.

"Yeah, that's one word for it." I laugh nervously. *And now we're all awkward. Fucking Bradley.* "Is something on your mind?"

"Just thinking."

"About what?" I ask. *Come on, I'm dying here.*

"You," he says simply, glancing my way.

"Oh." I can tell he doesn't want to say more, so I drop it.

The truck rumbles along the dark road as we sit in silence, the streetlamps rhythmically illuminating my legs, the dashboard, and Jude's hands, in sweeping orange swaths of light. *I don't know how to fix this.*

After what feels like an eternity, Jude finally speaks. "You really went out with that guy?" His voice is low and quiet. He keeps his eyes on the road.

A pang of humiliation hits me in the gut, both at the memory of that awful date and at how Jude must think differently of me now by association. A pained expression crosses my face. "Yes, but only once. I don't know why he made it sound like more than that. That date did not go well." I look out the window.

"Is that what you want?" he asks.

"What do you mean?" I almost laugh. I'm flabbergasted he'd assume anything about that pompous display would appeal to me.

"You know, the art gallery, the fancy dates, the fundraisers? Is that your scene?" he asks as he pulls the truck into his driveway and kills the engine. He shifts in his seat to look at me. It's dark, but, even in the shadows, I can tell his expression is serious.

"Oh, God, no," I reply quickly. "I mean, clearly I wouldn't fit in with art gallery people."

"He seemed to think you did. He invited you to that fundraiser," he replies.

I can't tell what he's getting at. "He doesn't even know me." I shrug, a bit defensively. "Obviously, going out with him was a huge mistake. That experience... the people there made it clear I didn't belong. They were... not my people." I cringe at the memory of everyone staring at me as I almost had a very public panic attack.

"Then why'd you agree to go out with him in the first place?" he presses.

"Does that matter? I told you it was a mistake. Can we just forget about it?" *I know I wish I could.*

"Just humor me." His voice is calm. He doesn't sound jealous or territorial, but curious, like he's found a puzzle piece that doesn't fit.

"Okay..." I breathe and pause to reflect. "I guess I didn't know what I wanted. I felt like I should get out there and try dating after I moved back here... and he offered, so I said yes. He seemed nice enough when we were chatting online. I thought maybe an art gallery could be interesting... that maybe I could blend in with the fancy crowd. I don't know. Obviously, I was naïve to think that." I look down at my hands.

Jude scoffs. "You don't have to do that, you know." He pulls the keys out of the ignition and turns away from me, climbing out of the truck.

Confused by his reaction, I don't immediately follow. *What the hell?* Then, realizing I'm sitting in his truck alone in the dark, I cautiously climb out of the passenger seat.

He unlocks the front door for Murphy, who's been lounging on one of the porch benches. Murphy briefly raises his head to look at Jude before pushing up and slowly stretching. He hops down from the bench and heads into the house, apparently content to avoid the human drama unfolding outside.

Jude paces on the front porch.

I walk over to him, hugging my arms across my chest. "What do you mean I 'don't have to do that'? Do what?" I ask, thoroughly bewildered.

He runs his hands through his hair and lets out a breath. "You don't have to shrink yourself to fit into someone else's story, Olena. You don't have to keep apologizing for existing."

His words hit me in the gut. "I'm not apologizing for existing. I don't know. I just make bad choices, I guess. I'm not fancy or put-together or successful. I don't have my shit together, okay?"

He looks almost angry.

"Why does it matter?" I ask again, frustrated. "It was just one date." I don't understand why he's stuck on this.

Jude puts his hands on his hips. "That prick didn't deserve *one* date with you."

"I don't know about that, I mean, I'm not perfect either, I—"

In a few strides, Jude is in front of me, grabbing me by the shoulders, pulling me in close. "Bullshit," he whispers, silhouetted by the dim porch light behind him.

I can feel his breath on my face and the heat from his body pressing against mine. I turn my head away, trying to avoid his words.

He slides his hands up the sides of my neck and gently raises my face to look up into the darkness of his own. "You're incredible. It kills me that you can't see how brilliant you are."

I look down. "No, I'm not. I'm a total mess."

"Stop it," he says abruptly.

I meet his eyes. "Stop what?"

"Talking about yourself like that!" He releases me from his

grasp and turns back to the porch, looking exasperated. He circles back to me, looking as if he's weighing what to say next. "Do you know why I left in such a hurry that first day at the property?"

I shake my head, confused, watching him closely.

"Because I looked at your portfolio, Olena, and it blew me away. Your work was..." He looks like he can't find the words. "You're an incredible designer."

"I don't understand." I watch him warily.

"Look. Even from the moment I first saw you, when you were shouting at me on the side of the road, soaking wet, calling me an asshole..."

I look down in shame and he steps closer.

"You were beautiful."

I close my eyes.

He reaches a hand to my cheek. "Olena."

I blink back the tears that threaten to fall. No one has ever said anything like this to me.

"Look at me, Olena."

I draw a shaky breath and meet his shadowed eyes.

"When I asked for your portfolio... I was hoping it'd be mediocre."

My brows furrow in confusion.

"I was hoping I'd find some problem with you—with your work. Some flaw... because, I guess, if you were average... if you were *boring*..." He inhales. "I could find some way to ignore how you made me feel."

I exhale a messy breath, my heart twisting.

Jude draws me in close and presses his forehead to mine. For a moment, he just breathes with me. "But, as it turns out," he adds quietly, brushing a stray lock of hair away from my face, "you're both gorgeous *and* talented."

My cheeks redden, though he can't see me blush in the darkness.

His voice is low now, the deep rumble vibrating against my body. "And that scared the hell out of me. So I ran."

Understanding clicks and I pull back to stare at him in disbelief. "Wait, I intimidated you? *I* intimidated *you?*" I let out a cynical laugh as I shove his chest gently, but he doesn't let me push him away, his strong hands gripping my lower back.

His face is serious.

My teasing smile fades.

"Yes. You did," he admits, holding my gaze intensely. "And that time Teddy interrupted us... I ran then too. I pushed you away because I was scared again."

"About getting caught," I remember.

He pauses. "It was more than that." His words are quiet, his voice a low rasp in his throat.

"What do you mean?"

He looks up at the night sky like he's searching for the words. "I was worried that if..." He takes a breath, looking back at me. "That if I let you into my life..." He's struggling to go on. The vulnerability he's showing is breaking my heart.

I stand on my toes and kiss his cheek softly, then pull back to meet his eyes again.

"I had my heart broken pretty badly. Years ago. She left me when I was going through something really rough and..." He takes a steadying breath. "It was awful. And now... I'm just used to being on my own here. It's familiar. Predictable. Uncomplicated..."

"Safe," I add quietly.

He pauses. "Yeah." He sighs. "You're changing all of that."

"I'm sorry," I say sincerely, then realize the irony. I feel Jude suppress a groan at the fact that I'm apologizing yet again.

"Don't you start with that," he smiles ruefully at me. He reaches up and wipes a tear from my cheek with his thumb, then slowly traces my jawline with a finger.

Heat flushes through my body, my eyelids fluttering at the

sensation. When I open them, something in his expression darkens; even in the dim light, I sense a shift in him.

"Though, yes, how *very* unfair of you," he teases as his lips brush mine softly, his hot breath filling my senses, need gripping me deep in my core.

I slide my hands around his neck as he runs his hands down my back, over my ass.

"But Olena..." he rasps.

I hold my breath.

"I'm done running." He lifts me up, wrapping my legs around his waist as he carries me into the house. The front door bangs loudly as we crash through the entryway and he kicks it shut.

22

OLENA

Jude's chest crushes against mine, pinning me against the inside of the front door. One of his huge hands grips my ass while the other cradles the back of my neck, angling my head to press our lips together in a burning kiss.

I wrap my arms around his shoulders, pulling him closer, and trail my fingers through his dark hair. My tongue flicks against his, teasing him. Tasting him. His beard scratches lightly against my face; the contrasting sensations of soft and rough are delicious. I want more.

I sweep my tongue into his mouth and Jude responds by deepening the kiss, his mouth opening and taking more of me, claiming me. A responding heat pulses low in my belly, and I trace his lips with my tongue, pulling a rumble of pleasure from deep in his throat. Desperation building, our lips crush together again with need. Jude's chest heaves against me, his hips pushing into me against the door.

I squeeze his waist between my thighs. Kissing me deeply, he pulls off one of my shoes, then the other. He slides a hand between us and exhales a sharp breath when he grazes my breast.

He grins, pressing his forehead against mine, and we breathe together as his fingers work the buttons of my shirt.

"I'm on the pill," I say quietly.

His eyes flick up to mine and his hands stop.

I let my gaze fall and slide my palms over his muscled shoulders. "Tested and all clear too." I bite my lip and look up, meeting his eyes again.

"Presumptuous," he teases, giving me a lazy half-smile before his lips meet mine in a slow, enticing kiss.

I smile, my cheeks heating. "I just thought—" I start, looking away.

He gently pulls my chin back to face him. "You thought correctly," he whispers against my lips, his fingers now tugging and tearing at my shirt until the last of the buttons give way. "Because I've been fucking you in my mind for the last two weeks."

I suck in a breath and close my eyes. His nose brushes my cheek, then his lips find my mouth and I melt into him.

"I'm clear too," he adds when our lips part, pulling my shirt down over my shoulder. "But..." His mouth is on my neck and I can't think straight.

Wait... but? I open my eyes, confused again.

"That'll have to wait one more night." He flicks his tongue over my earlobe before brushing his lips against my cheek. "Because tonight is all about you."

My jaw drops open as I exhale hard. Pulling back, I search his eyes. "What do you mean?" I whisper, barely breathing.

A slow grin spreads over his face. "I think you know what I mean."

Our lips press together again with desperate hunger. I struggle to free myself from one sleeve, then wrap my arms around his neck, dragging my fingernails over his skin. He tears my shirt away from the other arm and lets it fall.

His need strains under his jeans, pressing hard between my legs. The heat against me is intense, and my own response is hot, damp, and aching. I roll my hips slowly, grinding into his hardness, chasing the friction of the fabric between us. He groans against my lips and his tongue slides over mine, drawing it into his mouth.

Grasping handfuls of his t-shirt, I tug the fabric up, needing to feel all of him. He reaches behind his neck and yanks the shirt over his head, pressing me up against the door with his full weight while he extracts his arms from the shirt one at a time, his heated gaze never straying from mine. He lets the shirt fall to the floor and I run my hands over his muscled back and chest, relishing the feel of his bare skin. His warmth is incredible.

He lifts me away from the door and I cling to him, my legs and arms wrapped around tight. He carries me to his bedroom and, as we move through the house, he gently kisses and licks my neck. I tilt my head, closing my eyes with pleasure. He stops us at the foot of the bed. A small, dim lamp on the bedside table is the only light, casting a soft glow on Jude's features. His eyes dark with need, he leans in, kissing the sensitive corner of my mouth.

"Olena," he breathes against my cheek, nipping at my earlobe. "Can I show you?"

"Show me what?" I pull back, my eyes searching his.

One of his calloused hands roves over my bare shoulder and he drags his fingers down my spine. He swiftly unhooks my bra and I shiver with pleasure at the feeling of him kissing his way along my collarbone, then sliding my bra strap off my shoulder. He kisses his way back up to my neck, licking and tasting my skin.

"Can I show you how incredible I think you are?" he asks in a low, husky voice.

My breath is coming in soft gasps at the sensation of Jude's mouth on my skin and his breath on my neck. I inhale deeply to steady myself, but his delicious scent is overpowering and my eyes roll with hunger. I scrape my teeth over the ridge of his ear, my arms gripping tight around his strong shoulders. He grabs my ass hard with both hands, hefting me up against him.

"Can I show you how you deserve to be treated?" He practically growls the words.

My fingernails dig into the muscles of his back and I let out a soft whimper, my legs tightening around his waist.

He quickly frees my arm from the other bra strap. Smiling against my mouth, he wrenches the bra from between us in one rough movement, tossing it across the room. A deep growl of satisfaction rumbles from his throat as my breasts press into his bare chest. Stroking the fingers of one hand up the side of my waist, he takes my breast in his palm, circling my peaked nipple with his thumb.

"Jesus, Olena," he groans into my neck, trailing his tongue up under my ear. "Answer me."

I smile with pleasure. "Yes," I breathe. I arch my neck and he sweeps my hair aside, his teeth scraping the spot where my pulse is hammering. "Yes, please."

A pause. "Good girl."

I gasp as my back slams into the bed.

Jude quickly kicks off his boots and climbs over me, his knees between my legs. A sensuous smile tugging at his lips, he bends down to kiss me hard, his tongue exploring, tangling with mine. He lowers onto me and pushes up between my legs, grinding his length against me again, the fabric of our pants an infuriating barrier.

My fingers drift down his chest, needing to feel all of him. I squirm under him, pushing my hips up, needing more. When he thrusts against me again, I let out a moan and throw my arms around his neck, rocking my hips while I nip at his lower lip with my teeth.

He shifts and trails kisses down my chest, flicking his tongue over one nipple before sucking it into his mouth, rolling my other nipple between his fingers. When he switches sides, the hard draw of his tongue has me gasping and my back arching. I clench my fingers, digging them into his strong shoulders, my body begging him for more.

Moving lower, he runs his tongue slowly down my stomach. When he gets to my waistband, he sits up overtop of me and straddles me, pinning me to the bed. He looks down at me with hooded lids and a half-smile, his eyes and hands drifting lazily over my exposed flesh as if he's drinking in the sight of me.

"You're so fucking beautiful."

This time, I don't look away. I surprise myself when I realize I believe him, that those green eyes on my body make me feel incredible, like a sexy goddess.

He doesn't break his gaze with mine as he undoes my jeans. Sweeping his fingers under my waistband, he teases me. I shudder at how close he comes to grazing where I'm desperate to feel his touch. My core clenches, pulsing with anticipation. Jude smiles and drags his palm between my legs, his fingertips finding my clit through the fabric of my jeans. I inhale sharply, catching the look of satisfaction on his face.

My eyes drop down, drinking in his muscled chest and arms, his carved stomach, and the trail of dark hair that disappears under his waistband. My gaze lands on the outline of his cock pushing against his jeans and my eyes widen at the size of him. *Oh, fuck.*

I'm suddenly desperate to feel him: in my hands, my mouth—I don't care. Propping myself up on an elbow, I reach out and grip him through his jeans. He's rock-hard and hot under my touch, even through the fabric. His eyes shutter and a deep groan escapes his lips as my palm rubs over his straining hardness, my fingers stroking his length through the denim.

I'm craving the taste of him, the heat of him in my mouth.

Pushing up, I start to unbutton his jeans, kissing his chest. But he quickly grips my wrist, stopping me.

Confused, I look up.

"This isn't about me, remember?" he rasps, steadying himself.

I collapse back onto the bed and let out a frustrated groan.

He chuckles softly. With a devilish grin, he grasps the waistband of my jeans with both hands and jerks them down to my thighs, looking almost pained. He lets out a hissed breath, curling down into me, and presses soft kisses to my stomach.

My fingers trace the angle of his square jaw and slide over his upper back. I squirm and make a small gasping noise when his hair tickles my skin, my stomach hollowing as I suck in a sharp breath.

He lifts his head to look at me, one dark eyebrow raised.

Holding his gaze and biting my lip, I let my hands drift up to my breasts, my fingers gently pinching my nipples while he watches.

Jude exhales hard, looking like he's going to come undone at the sight, and rises to his knees. He pulls my jeans off the rest of the way before throwing them on the floor, slipping my socks off quickly as well. With his palm sliding up my bare thigh, he looks down at me, those intense green eyes blazing with desire. With a steadying breath, he hooks a finger into the narrow strip of fabric that runs between my legs, grazing the sensitive flesh beneath and making me gasp.

"*Fuck*," he breathes and closes his eyes when he finds the wetness pooled there.

I lift my hips as he slides my panties down and off my legs.

Climbing up over me once again, Jude rakes his gaze over my body, now laid totally bare in front of him. With a lazy smile, he leans down and takes one of my nipples between his teeth, his tongue flicking and his breath heating my sensitive flesh. I writhe beneath him and claw lightly at his back, coaxing him to continue. He moves to my other nipple, licking and nibbling, then trails one hand slowly down my stomach, lower and lower, stopping just short of where I want his fingers. Releasing my breast, he moves up to claim my mouth in a heated kiss, then fixes his dark eyes on mine. His voice is low when he speaks.

"Where do you want me to touch you?"

My lips part but no sound comes out.

He leans down close, his lips against my cheek. "Tell me what makes you melt, Olena." He kisses my flushed skin, his breath dancing across the slope of my jaw. "What makes you scream." He trails a finger from one of my hip bones to the other, tracing a line across the bottom of my stomach. "What makes you come so hard you lose the ability to walk."

Pleasure blazes through my core at his words, the air leaving my lungs as my eyes shutter once again. *Am I still breathing?*

"Fuck, Olena. Tell me," he nips at my lower lip, "so I can do it *all*. I need to show you that's *exactly* what you deserve."

He kisses me slowly, torturously, and I feel him smile against my lips as he lightly grazes one hand up my arm and over my shoulder, then traces a thumb down the center of my throat.

I inhale sharply as I arch up, my eyes flying open and locked on his.

His brow twinges, a look of animalistic need passing across his expression. "You'd better tell me quick what to do with these hands," he breathes, "because they're gonna get a mind of their own if you keep looking at me like that." He slides his thumb across my lower lip, then takes my mouth in a drugging kiss.

Unable to answer, heat flares in my cheeks and I slide my arms up around the back of his neck, as if part of me knows I will have to hold on to this man for dear life. The intimate muscles of my core are quivering. *Quivering. That's a first.*

"Hmm, you seem to be... unable to speak for some reason," Jude says, smirking down at me again.

Cheeky bastard. I can't help but grin and roll my eyes, because the look on his face tells me he's enjoying every moment of winding me up tight.

"Maybe you can show me, instead." His hand slides down to cup my breast.

I can only nod and swallow. Holding his gaze, I lift his hand to my lips. I kiss his fingertips softly before sucking his middle finger deep into my mouth.

He lets out a rough breath and those green eyes almost roll as I swirl my tongue over his finger, then slide it out, guiding his hand down between my legs.

"Jesus…" he breathes. He drags his fingers up through the wetness pooled at my entrance. "Right here?"

"Yes," I say on a breathy exhale.

"Oh, fuck," he whispers as he slips his fingers to my clit, circling softly.

I squirm, inching myself down, seeking the pressure of his fingers, but he pulls back ever so slightly, drawing out the anticipation.

He nips at the shell of my ear. "Do you want my mouth on you, gorgeous?"

"Yes." I close my eyes. *I want everything.*

"Oh, thank fuck," he chuckles quietly. Walking backward on his knees, his strong hands grip my hips and he tugs me firmly down the mattress, letting out a soft grunt. Backing off the foot of the bed, he settles himself on the floor, kneeling between my legs. He drags his hands along my inner thighs, squeezing once, before pushing my legs further apart.

He curses under his breath. "Tell me something…" His voice is deep in a way that makes my core clench. He kisses my upper thigh right next to where I'm desperate to feel his tongue. "Do you like it… slow and gentle?" He slides a finger inside me and I softly cry out as he slowly—so slowly—pushes in and out, curling his finger just enough to send shivers of soft pleasure through my body. I grasp at the sheets above my head, my fingers tangling in my hair.

Oh, God. More.

"Or do you like it... fast and hard?" At this, he adds another finger and I cry out again, louder, clenching around his fingers. He pumps harder, sending waves of dizzying sensation all over my body, and I moan with pleasure. He pauses and withdraws, waiting for my response with an eyebrow raised, his thumb working lazy circles on my most sensitive spot. His lips graze against my inner thigh, his teeth biting softly at my skin.

Oh, fuck. I can't think straight, let alone speak. All I know is I want his fingers inside me again so badly that I feel on the edge of madness.

"Olena..." he rasps, still teasing my clit, waiting for me to answer.

I can't believe he's somehow expecting me to say words while he touches me this way. While he melts my senses.

He kisses my upper thigh again.

I can feel his breath right *there*. So close. I whimper at the feeling of emptiness. I want him filling me, licking me, slamming into me until I'm senseless.

Say words. Tell him what you want.

"I—"

Before I can say any more, he's thrusting his magic fingers into me again, strong and fast, while desperate pleasure rips through me. He slows once more and I hear him chuckle against me, his beard brushing my sensitive skin. He has his answer.

"Jude, please..." I beg, needing to feel his mouth on me too.

My body arches up at the first touch of his tongue.

"Oh, God..." I breathe, clawing at the bedsheets, all my muscles tightening. His touch is disorienting, his tongue so warm and wet, his fingers still pumping inside me. Sucking on my most sensitive bundle of nerves, Jude takes his time, slowly making me lose my mind until release is just out of reach. I writhe, grinding my hips, pushing into his mouth, his face, his fingers. Harder. I want him closer. Faster. *More.*

I can feel my pleasure building, gathering in my core. I throw my head back onto the bed and clench around his fingers, my hands curling into his hair.

As if reading my mind, he deepens the pressure. Thrusting his fingers harder and faster inside me, sucking and licking me madly, he brings me closer and closer to the edge.

With his fingers still pumping fast, he breaks his mouth away just long enough to say, in a deep rumble, his lips grazing against the burning heat of my center, "You taste fucking amazing, Olena."

His words are the end of any control I had been holding onto. Release crashes over me, shattering my senses. With my core clenching and my muscles gripping tightly around his fingers, he quickly sucks my swollen clit back into his mouth, flicking his tongue rapidly back and forth, drawing out my pleasure as long as possible. I cry out in a ragged moan as the waves of overwhelming ecstasy thrum and pulsate through my entire body.

When my breathing finally calms, my ears ring and sparkles dance across my vision. As I try to piece together my grip on reality, I look down to see those green eyes gazing up at me, smiling.

I'm done for.

No one has ever made me feel like that.

I exhale.

"Again," he growls, pushing his fingers into me once more.

23

OLENA

My phone buzzes beside me on the nightstand. With some effort, I crack one eye open, quickly taking in my surroundings and remembering where I am with a smile. Noticing Jude's not beside me, I roll over and reach for my phone. His text reads:

JUDE

good morning, beautiful. went to get breakfast.
stay put. x

He must have found my phone and put it here for me. I let it fall against my chest and smile, biting my lip as the memories of last night wash over me in flashes. *Oh my God.* Jude's lips brushing mine on the porch. Crashing through the doorway in his arms. His head between my legs. '*Again,*' his throaty growl echoes in my mind.

I put my hands over my face, the memories enough to bring back the heat in a wave of delicious pleasure. Curling into the pillow, I'm grinning so hard I might pull a muscle. I let out a long breath to steady myself.

I decide to get dressed, though my shirt is nowhere in sight. I see a flannel shirt of Jude's hanging on the back of a chair across the room and go to pick it up, bringing the fabric to my face to breathe in his scent. *Dear God, this man smells so good*, I think to myself as my eyes flutter shut. I slip the shirt on. Buttoning it up halfway, I notice it's enormous on me and hangs down below my ass. Loving the feeling of the fabric swishing against my bare skin, I pad through the house to locate my own clothes.

I find my panties and jeans near the bedroom door and put them back on, the cold fabric chilling me slightly. I scrunch the sleeves of Jude's flannel over my hands like makeshift mittens and hug my arms tight to my chest. My nipples are hard from the morning chill and I relish how sensitive they feel rubbing against Jude's shirt. Another flash of memory hits me: Jude's tongue flicking and sucking, sending ripples of pleasure through me... I flush at the thought and continue smiling like a fool all by myself.

The house is quiet; *Jude must have taken Murphy with him when he left.* I flick on the bathroom light, taking in my rumpled reflection in the mirror. I wet my hands and use them to comb down the most unruly sections of my hair.

After hunting around for my purse and realizing I'd left it in Jude's truck, I locate a chopstick in one of the kitchen drawers and use it to twist my hair up into a messy bun. Pleased at my resourcefulness, I renew the search for my shirt, remembering with a smile that we were near the front door when Jude ripped it off me. My eyes land on it and I walk over to pick it up.

Shirt in hand, I've barely stood up when someone suddenly pounds on the front door and my head snaps up, eyes wide. My heart leaps into my throat. Another loud pounding sound has me stumbling backward several steps.

Jude? Why would Jude be knocking on the door? This is his house... Surely, he has keys... Doubt crawls over my skin as I realize someone else must be out there and my pulse quickens. Stepping back another few paces, I bump into the edge of the kitchen counter and stop.

"Jude!" a rough, deep voice calls from outside.

My stomach drops and I freeze, my shirt clutched tightly in my fist.

"Jude, man, you home? I just came to see if you—"

I hear a stumble and a crash outside.

"Oh, shit," the voice exclaims, then there's a rough, strange laugh.

Something's not right. This guy sounds drunk. *Why is some drunk guy banging on Jude's door at 9am on a Saturday?*

Three more loud bangs. He mutters something I can't quite hear.

"Jude, buddy, I need to talk to you!" the voice shouts.

I flinch as he rattles the door handle roughly. The memories rush back: me in my Seattle apartment, hiding behind the couch as two men shout outside our window, Sean's terrified, wide eyes watching mine as the glass shatters.

My breath comes fast now and my ears start to ring. *This isn't happening. Not again.*

I try to focus on finding somewhere to hide but can't move my feet. I'm breathing hard now, my heart racing in my chest and pounding in my ears. My muscles start to feel weak and I crumple toward the floor in slow motion, landing in a heap between the kitchen cabinets. I scramble backward until my back crashes against a cupboard door.

I flinch at each pounding sound on the door and cover my ears, hiding my face in my knees. My hands grasp at the sides of my head and my fingers dig into my hair, knocking the chopstick loose. I don't even hear it clatter to the floor, my desperate gasps and the ringing in my ears drowning out the sound. The pounding at the door sounds farther away now, as if I'm deep under water.

I gasp for breath as I sit there, shaking, my stomach roiling and sweat gathering on my forehead. The room spins around me. I feel like I'm going to die.

24

JUDE

I glance at the bag of groceries on the front seat and smile to myself, running a hand over my beard. I've been gone maybe twenty minutes and I'm already desperate to get back to her. Memories from last night flood me: Olena's incredible body writhing in my bed, her moans of pleasure as she came over and over again, the taste of her... I have to take a deep breath to keep concentrating on the road. I can't wait to wake her up with breakfast, then spend a lazy day together in bed.

I glance in the rear-view mirror as Murphy pushes up from the back seat, turns around, and lies back down. I smirk to myself; it's like he wrote the damned instruction manual for how to nap.

As I pull into the driveway, I see a familiar car parked at a strange angle and my thoughts ice over. I'm instantly on alert.

He can't be here. What's he doing here? A sinking sensation hits me when the front porch comes into view. Miles is pounding hard on the door. I slam on the brakes and turn off the truck—forgetting the groceries, forgetting my plans for breakfast with Olena—and leap out to face my brother. I jog to the porch as he beats his fist on the door again, calling my name, the booming racket he's making cutting through the quiet of the forest that surrounds us.

"Miles!"

He doesn't seem to hear me over his pounding and hollering. I stop at the foot of the porch steps as he bends down, pulling up the doormat, presumably hunting for the spare key our parents used to keep hidden there.

"Miles!" I try again as I climb the steps. "What the fuck are you doing here?"

He looks up at me and staggers to a standing position, swaying a bit as he catches his balance. His glassy eyes and the smell of his breath tell me what I already know: he's drunk.

"Juuuuuude! My bro!" He looks happy to see me, spreading his arms and coming at me for a hug.

I shove him back. "Dude, no."

He looks surprised by my reaction. "Whoa, man, what the fuck?"

"What are you doing here? When did you get back into town?" I pin him with a glare.

"I'm here to see my best brother, of course!" He chucks a light punch at my shoulder, trying to play it off like a joke that he's shown up here unannounced. Again.

"You're wasted. It's nine in the morning, Miles, Jesus." I rub my head.

"Wasted? Nah! Okay, maybe I had a little fancy breakfast coffee this morning..." His eyes are smiling but he looks pitiful. He looks older than he should, the bags under his eyes revealing this likely isn't a one-off slip.

Then, I realize: Olena's been inside this whole time, with a stranger practically beating down the door. *Shit.*

Kicking myself, I unlock the door as fast as I can and swing it open with a crash. I find her huddled in a corner of the kitchen, her head in her hands, sobbing and gasping for breath. I drop to the floor and pull her into my arms.

"Shhh," I say, stroking her hair and squeezing her tight against me. "I'm so sorry. I should've been here. I'm here now. You're safe."

"Ohhh, shit, I didn't know you had a lady friend here. Niiiice," says Miles from the open doorway.

I turn and scowl at him, hoping he's not too drunk to read the *I will end you* look on my face. "Get the fuck back outside. I'll deal with you later," I bark at him.

He raises his arms and mouths a dramatic *yikes*, then turns and staggers back onto the porch. I watch through the window as he collapses onto the bench outside, resting his head against the glass.

Olena is still gasping in my arms, so I pull back and try to get her to focus on me. Her eyes are squeezed shut and she's shaking. I rack my brain, trying to think of what to do. Miles used to have panic attacks when we were younger, after Mom and Dad died. I try to remember what was helpful for him all those years ago.

"I'm going to pick you up and take you back to my room," I tell her. I scoop her up and carry her there, sitting her down on the edge of the bed. Crouching in front of her, I squeeze her hands.

"Olena," I say softly. "Olena, look at me." I brush my thumbs over her flushed, wet cheeks and try again. "Olena. Look at me. Breathe with me." She raises her tear-streaked face to mine and meets my gaze, breath shuddering. "Breathe. Just breathe." I breathe slow and steady, pulling her forehead against mine, until her breath evens out to match my own. We stay like that for another minute until I'm sure she's coming down the other side of it. I pull the rumpled blanket from behind her and wrap it around her shoulders like a cocoon.

She's wearing my shirt, I notice with a small smile. A warmth settles in my chest at the thought of her scent on it.

"I'm so sorry," I say again, kissing her tears on one cheek, then the other. "Miles is my brother. He's got a drinking problem. I thought he was doing better, but..." I trail off. There's so much to explain, and this is not how I imagined explaining it. "I didn't even know he was in town."

She inhales a shaky breath. "It was... I was..." She tries to speak between jagged gasps, but the tears well up in her eyes once again.

I kneel and pull her into my chest, stroking her hair. "Don't. You don't need to explain. Not now. Just breathe." I'm gutted I wasn't here to protect her. My heart wrenches when I think about the panic that Miles' sudden appearance clearly caused. *I know he's harmless. But* she *doesn't.*

I pull back and kiss the bridge of her nose, promising to be back quickly with a glass of water.

When I return, she's lying down on the bed, still wrapped in my blanket, curled up on her side and turned away from me. I place the glass on the bedside table and kick off my boots, then climb in behind her, wrapping my arm over her and pulling her into me. We lie there for a few minutes in silence, and I breathe in the sweet smell of her hair, flashes of our night together coming to mind unbidden.

Now's not the time, I remind myself. There's a serious problem still waiting for me on the porch.

"I'm gonna have to go deal with him," I whisper into her ear, nosing her hair out of the way. She smells amazing and I don't want to leave her. *Fucking Miles and his fucking timing.*

She says nothing but gives me a small nod. I kiss the back of her head, wishing this morning had gone much differently. It takes all my willpower to extract myself from her.

Shoving my boots back on, I storm outside to confront Miles, pausing when I notice he's now passed out, sitting up, on the porch bench.

Cursing under my breath, I leave him and return to the truck. I let Murphy out. He stretches awake and hops down out of the cab, lumbering toward the front porch to his next napping location, familiar enough with Miles to have been unperturbed by the commotion he made earlier. Pulling the bag of groceries off the front seat, I return to the kitchen and pull out the paper bag of chocolate croissants I bought to share with Olena. I put one on a plate and flick the switch on the coffee maker with agitation, before taking the croissant back to my bedroom for her.

I stop short in the doorway, plate in hand. My flannel shirt is laying on the bed and she's buttoning her own shirt, having apparently located her clothes somewhere in the chaos. My eyes land briefly on her bra and the curve of her breast. *God, she's beautiful.*

"Olena?" I ask carefully. She doesn't meet my gaze, just stuffs her phone in the back pocket of her jeans and sniffs, wiping at her eyes with her other hand.

"I need to go." Her eyes are still on the floor, looking for more of her belongings, no doubt.

I step back silently as she hurries into the hallway, then comes back into the room. She finds one sock, then the other, and slips them on her feet, stumbling awkwardly in her hurry to leave.

"Are you sure? I have breakfast. And coffee's brewing." The words feel trite as they come out, as if breakfast is enough to repair what's just happened to her.

Don't leave, I silently beg. But I can't ask her to stay.

"No, I need to go," she says again. "I can't... I'm sorry." Her pained eyes don't meet mine.

She pushes past me, her delicious scent reminding me of everything we shared last night, making it even harder to watch her walk out of here. She finds her shoes near the front door and shoves them on quickly, not looking back as she leaves.

I follow her at a distance, giving her space so she doesn't feel cornered. Standing in the front doorway helplessly, I watch her open my truck to retrieve her purse, then climb into her own car and drive away.

She barely looks back at me.

It takes me a moment to tear my eyes away. I exhale a breath. *Fuck.* I'm still holding the damned plate.

I turn to look at Miles, still sleeping on the porch, and give a hard kick to the leg of the bench he's sleeping on.

The jerking motion jostles him awake. His eyes fly open and he squints at me with a frown. "What the hell, Jude?" he asks, like he hasn't just scared Olena off and ruined my morning.

"Wake the fuck up, Miles." I'm pacing in front of him.

"Okay, okay," he relents as I pause and offer a reluctant hand to pull him up. He takes it and stands with a wobble.

"You good?" I ask.

"Yeah, man, I'm good. I'm good," he assures me.

I don't believe him.

"Well, that makes one of us. Get your ass inside. I'll get you some coffee," I grumble.

STANDING AT THE KITCHEN ISLAND, I resentfully fill two mugs with coffee. I glance at the croissant meant for Olena and frown, shoving the plate across the counter to my brother, who perches unsteadily on a stool on the other side.

"How much did you have to drink this morning, Miles?" I ask, although I don't really want to know. What I want is for him to get his shit together.

"I dunno, man, not that much. I'm fine, really." He looks tired.

"You don't smell fine." I frown, placing a mug in front of him. "Drink this; it'll sober you up."

"That's a myth, you know. That coffee helps you sober up. I saw it in a magazine," he says unhelpfully.

My eyes narrow as I look at him. I brace both hands on the counter across from him, leaning close. "It's coffee or a slap in the face, Miles. You got a preference? Because after this morning, I'm thinking I know which one I'd choose." My lips are tight in a grim expression.

"Okay, geez, coffee it is. Sorry," he says, taking a dutiful sip.

"I thought you were doing better lately." I take a bite of my croissant. It's fucking delicious. I inwardly groan again at the morning's events. This is not who I was supposed to be sharing decadent baked goods with.

"Well, things changed," he says, averting his gaze.

"When?" I press.

"I dunno, dude, they just did." He clearly doesn't want to talk about it.

Too bad.

"When did you start drinking again, Miles?" I'm not letting him off the hook. Not after he gave Olena a goddamned panic attack.

He shrugs, as if being fuzzy on the details will help soften the reality that he's relapsed. "I dunno. Maybe a few weeks ago. Or months?" He squints up at me.

"Months?" My voice is louder than expected, eyebrows raised in surprise.

"Okay, probably not months. Not months." I can tell he's trying to ease my obvious alarm.

"Have you called your sponsor?"

He leans back in his seat, grimacing. "Barry is a killjoy, Jude. I'm not calling him."

"Barry keeps you sober. Barry is good. You've gotta follow the program, man," I remind him and he looks away with guilt in his eyes. He doesn't respond. "Fine, I'll call him then," I say. I move to pick up my phone.

Then, I remember: "Wait, Miles, your car's out front. You drove here?" My big brother disappointment is on full display. "That's so fucking dangerous." I'm shaking my head as I scroll through my phone for Barry's number.

"Hey, man, I got here safe and sound. It all worked out," he says casually.

I level him with a look that says *you're fucking lucky you did*.

"Why are you here, anyway? What's happening in Seattle?"

"Aw, you know, I'm fine. Don't worry about it."

He's lying. He's always been a shitty liar. I don't know why he bothers trying this crap with me. "Bullshit. Out with it." I put the phone down.

He meets my eyes reluctantly. "Okay, so, that power-tripping foreman I told you about... kinda laid me off."

"You lost your job?" My hands grip the edge of the counter. I look at the ceiling, searching for patience. "Miles..." I rub my face, exhausted. "When are you gonna get it through your head that you can't keep going like this?"

He frowns, then takes a bite of Olena's croissant. "Who was that girl, anyway?" he asks, pumping his eyebrows suggestively. He's trying to change the subject. I let him; I'm too tired to do this again right now.

"Don't worry about it." I turn and grab a glass from the cupboard and fill it at the sink. I put the water in front of him and pull out a second glass for myself.

"I don't know, man, she didn't look like a *don't worry about it* kind of girl," he says with a knowing look. "Looked to me like you were doing a lot of *worrying about it*, in fact." He raises his eyebrows with a smirk.

I roll my eyes.

"What's her name?" He tries again.

"None of your business."

"Okay, cool, cool. I can take a hint." He gets up and walks over to the couch, then falls heavily into his usual seat with a sigh before he seems to have a better idea and moves to lie down. "Say no more," he says as he adjusts into a comfortable position. He closes his eyes.

I grab a spare blanket and pillow from the hall closet, then walk back to the couch, dropping them heavily onto his stomach. A satisfying *oof* noise escapes his mouth in surprise. His eyes fly open, then he narrows them to look at me.

"How long do you need to stay this time?" I ask, looking down at him, both of us knowing I won't kick him to the curb.

"I dunno... two, three days, max?"

"Great," I say, puffing out a breath before I walk away. I don't bother to ask why this time.

I pick up my phone and dial Barry's number.

25

OLENA

I'm still shaking as I pull into the parking lot of my apartment complex. The events of last night run laps in my head and this morning's humiliation colors everything that felt beautiful with a sickly hue of regret.

I can't believe I thought I could be with him. I'm in no state to be with *anyone*. No one should be saddled with the ugly emotional baggage that's clearly still weighing me down, drowning me at every opportunity. My trauma from the robbery is obviously not something I can escape with time and space—or even with the distraction of a gorgeous man who literally makes me see stars.

Oh, God, but it was so good. He *was so good.*

I lean my head back on the headrest and close my eyes at the memory of Jude's deep voice against my skin, then his green eyes smiling up at me after my first brain-melting orgasm. A shiver passes over my body, just thinking of it.

I squeeze my eyes shut and a tear runs down my jaw. I swipe at it with a finger. *Everything's ruined.* Now he's not going to want anything to do with me. I've shown him the truth: that I'm an unstable mess who collapses into a helpless, sobbing heap the moment any vaguely alarming misunderstanding crops up. It was just his brother visiting. Sure, he was drunk and loud, but...

I flinch again at the memory of Miles pounding on the front door.

Oh, God. I behaved like such a chaotic, walking disaster. I'm sure I scared Jude off with my overreaction.

Some small, naïve part of my brain remembers his words from last night: *I'm done running.* But no. That was before. Who wouldn't want to run from a broken train wreck like me?

I pull out my phone and text Nat.

ME

> Still up for our usual run? I'm home earlier than expected and need to blow off steam. Long story.

She writes back a minute later.

NAT

> Oh no! Big hugs. Yes to the run. On my way asap.

I go upstairs to change. When Wyatt sees my face, he looks concerned. "You're home early."

"I'm... not ready to talk about it yet," is all I can manage in a shaky voice. I walk most of the way to my room, then stop and come back a few steps to where he's sitting at the table. "I'm going running with Nat. I need to... move my body." I blow out a breath, fighting off the tears that threaten to spill out, and he nods in understanding.

I know exercise, wretched as it may feel right now, will help me process my intense emotions. *Wretched exercise,* I think with resentment. *The most wretched part is that it fucking works.*

"Okay, sweetie." He nods again. "I love you," he calls out as I go into my room. "Whatever you need. Let's talk when you're ready."

I change quickly and leave the apartment, avoiding Wyatt's concerned glances on the way out. I'm already outside waiting for Nat when she pulls up.

Driving in silence to the river, Nat gives my knee a squeeze. She can tell I need more time to feel my feelings before talking it out. Unlike me with my usual anxious blathering, Nat has the ability to be patient in these situations. As she parks her car beside Lyons Park, I push away the memory of running into Jude here. That was before everything went to shit. *Before I ruined everything with my drama.*

We get out and stretch. I try to breathe deeply and slowly to settle my nerves. Nat waits for me to talk and breaks off a piece of her granola bar to share with me. I accept the food gratefully; I haven't eaten anything yet today.

Right. Jude brought me breakfast and then I just... Fuck.

I swallow the bite and take a deep breath. When I speak, the story comes out in a jumbled rush. Through shuddering sobs, I tell her everything while we sit on the park bench. Being the boss-level best friend that she is, Nat listens with rapt attention.

"That sounds like it was really fucking hard, Olena," she says when I'm finished.

"It was pretty brutal, yeah." I take a deep breath and meet her eyes. "I haven't been that scared in... a long time."

"No shit. I'm so sorry."

"Thanks. And like... the *timing.*" I let out a soft whimper and drop my face into my hands.

"Yup. Shit timing."

"*Such* shit. After the night we'd just had?" I drag my hands down my face, then sit up and look at her. "It was just so beautiful and perfect... and *hot,* Nat," I say, pressing my fingers against my forehead. "Oh, my God, it was *so hot,* you have no idea..." I take a deep breath and wipe my eyes on my hoodie sleeve.

She smiles at me sadly.

"And I just... freaked out and fucked everything up." I shrug helplessly. "He's never gonna want to see me again."

Nat levels a look at me. "Len, my beautiful, amazing friend..." She reaches out to touch my hand. "Remember when we agreed to call bullshit on each other?"

I look at her warily. "Yeah."

"Well, I hate to be *that person* but... what I'm hearing is bullshit."

"What?" I'm not sure how to respond.

Nat smiles at me. She brushes a wayward braid back from her forehead and tucks it into her hair elastic. "Here's how I'm seeing things. You had a panic attack, and he saw that. Now, is that *ideal* right after a sexy date and an even sexier sleepover? No. But... he stayed with you, held you, and helped you calm down. He showed concern for your well-being."

I give her a look and frown.

She goes on more quietly. "Sounds like he didn't know this jerk brother of his was coming over and he was just as surprised as you were."

I tilt my head, considering.

"And... it sounds like this guy has real feelings for you." She raises her eyebrows at me. "Like, don't tell me you didn't swoon right out of your shoes when he said that stuff about being *done running*. Because," she says as she widens her eyes, "Olena. Come on." She fans her face with her hand and rolls her eyes dramatically.

I laugh, blinking the tears away.

"He didn't run away. You had a hard time in his presence, and he reacted with kindness and care. He didn't run."

I meet her eyes.

She pauses a moment before continuing. "You know who ran, though?"

Realization slams into me. "Oh, fuck." I drop my face into my hands. "Me."

"Ding ding ding!"

"Hey, shut up." I sit up and slug her in the arm lightly.

"It's okay; you have legit reasons. Reasons you're still working on." She squeezes my shoulder. "But girl, listen to me. You are *allowed* to have a hard time. He can give you the grace to be a human being with complex emotions and experiences. If he isn't willing to do that... *that's* the red flag. You having a panic attack? That ain't a red flag. His response is a big-ass green flag. Huge."

I take a moment to let her words sink in as I look out at the river. Jude was incredible last night—and this morning, if I'm honest with myself. My spiral of shame made *me* push *him* away and I couldn't see it. I couldn't see *him.*

"Shit, Nat." I look at her, frowning.

"Yeah," is all she says with an apologetic look on her face.

I pull out my phone to text him, then pause. I'm not ready. Not yet. I tuck it back in my pocket.

I look at Nat again, needing more reassurance. "But are we sure *I'm* not a gigantic red flag, though?" I ask, still feeling like one.

"I'm sure," she says simply.

The love in her eyes soothes my self-doubt.

"And, in the spirit of calling out bullshit," Nat says, eyeing me, "I'm going to be *that friend* again, and remind you to make an appointment with that therapist." She holds my gaze with her eyebrows raised.

I let out a big, long breath, then press my lips together and nod. She's right. I've been procrastinating about taking that step.

"I still really think talking to someone could help." She quirks her mouth up in a hopeful smile.

"I know." I lean my head on her shoulder and sniff. "I'll call to make an appointment tomorrow."

"Atta girl." She gives me a squeeze.

"I love you." I cast my eyes up at her. "Thank you."

She smiles. "And hey, congrats. You've found yourself a unicorn."

"What?" I lift my head and look at her.

"Len, you found a man who's gorgeous, kind, *and* single. Do you know how rare that is?"

I raise my eyebrows. She's not wrong.

"What can I say," Nat sighs, looking out over the river, "they just make men better in Lennox." She gives me a teasing grin, then raises her eyebrows seriously. "Trust me, I moved here for one."

I smile thinking about Nat and Graham's sweet relationship. "Speaking of which, your anniversary trip is next week, right?"

"Yeah," she says, "I can't wait."

"Hold on, will you be back in time for Marchmas at my parents' house?" I ask, a bit worried. We have this tradition where, every year on the 25th of March, we have a big dinner. It's something to look forward to at the end of a long, cold, and rainy winter season. My friends always come to celebrate with us. My parents love them like they're my honorary adopted siblings.

"Yup. We get back earlier that day. I made sure of it!" Nat grins at me proudly. "You know I wouldn't miss that shit! I love your mom and dad."

"Oh, I'm so glad," I say. "And I'm excited for you guys. I promise not to have another major life crisis while you're away."

"Minor ones are allowed. You can always text," she reassures me.

"Okay, deal." I smile.

Nat stands and turns to me, holding out her hand. "Now, let's get up and move before my ass falls asleep on this bench."

26

OLENA

I take the rest of Saturday to rest and am impressed by my self-control in not texting Jude to over-explain everything. Well, *self-control* may be overstating things. I've drafted about twenty texts trying to explain my behavior and I've deleted them all, too nervous to actually hit send. The reality is I don't know how to explain or where to start, so not saying anything is easier. But by late morning on Sunday, I feel like I should try. I can't just avoid Jude indefinitely.

Once again, I type into my phone:

Hey. Sorry for running off yesterday. I will explain in person soon. I had an incredible time with you and I hope I didn't ruin it by fleeing in tears like a drama queen. You free this afternoon?

I stare at the screen, biting my thumbnail as I try to work up the courage to hit send.

My phone rings and I jump. *Withheld number. Fuck.*

Sean hasn't contacted me in a week; I thought he'd gotten the message that we're done.

Reluctantly, I answer. "Sean, you need to stop calling me. I mean it. This isn't okay." I try to make my voice sound stern but I'm feeling anything but strong and confident.

"Baby, I miss you," Sean breathes heavily into the phone.

I clench my free hand into a fist. "I told you I'm done. You need to leave me alone."

"Aw, fuck, I can't. You know that," he says. He sounds weird.

"Are you high?" I know the answer but I ask anyway.

"Olena, fuck, I just want you back, okay? Everything is so fucked up right now. Please, just come home."

He's definitely high.

"You're still using. I can hear it in your voice right now." *Jesus.* I sigh. "Look, you need to get some help. Start going to that program again, maybe. I don't know. But I can't be the one to help you anymore."

"I'm not... look, I'm fine. I've got it under control, like I told you last time."

"You're calling me *high,* to beg me to come back? Fuck off, Sean. I don't want to be with you. Stop calling me. Stop texting me. It's over."

He's quiet for a moment. Then I hear a sniff and he clears his throat. *Is he crying?*

"What's the point?" he finally asks, his voice shaking.

I don't answer.

"What's the fucking point of getting clean if I don't have you? Huh?" He's getting progressively more aggressive. "What's the *fucking point?*" He's yelling into the phone now, so loudly I have to pull it away from my ear.

"Sean..." My voice is high-pitched and nervous.

"No. Take me back. I can't do this without you. You have to. I need to make you see..." He's raising his voice again.

"Sean, you can't change my mind. Stop calling."

"Olena. Baby, please—"

I cut him off. "No! Stop contacting me. We're done!" Tears well in my eyes and I'm shaking, but somehow my voice comes out sounding stronger than I feel.

A pause on the line. Then, a guttural sound of frustration. "You fucking bitch!" Sean screams into the phone and I recoil.

I hang up, my heart hammering in my throat. I sit on my bed in stunned silence.

He never used to talk to me like that. Not when we were together and he got high. Not even at the end when things were going badly between us. But the tone in his voice now was threatening. My hands shake and I squeeze them into fists, letting the phone drop onto my bedspread. I've never heard him like that.

Staring at the dark screen in front of me, my mind reels. *How can I block a withheld number? Shit.* I'm still trying to process Sean's phone call when Jude's text lights up my phone.

JUDE

Hey, beautiful. So sorry about my brother. Are you okay? Miles is harmless but I could see you were scared and I'm so sorry that happened. Can I see you? x

I don't touch the phone, letting the screen darken. Slowly, I hug my knees to my chest. *I can't do this.* Obviously, Sean is still a very real, very toxic presence in my life. I need to figure out how to get rid of him for good. Whatever I feel for Jude, he doesn't deserve to get wrapped up in the personal drama of a traumatized disaster with a drug-addicted, angry ex who won't leave her alone.

I pick up my phone and delete the draft from earlier, the words looking strangely cheerful and optimistic considering what just happened.

Instead, I type out a new text. My heart breaks as I hit send.

ME

I'm sorry. I can't. I need time.

Squeezing my eyes shut, I crumple into the fetal position on my bed. When my eyes open a minute later, a frozen numbness has descended over me and I stare at the wall.

27

JUDE

Reading Olena's text is like getting slugged in the chest. Sitting in my parked truck on Riverside Avenue, I stare at my phone, reeling, unable to understand how we went from falling asleep in each other's arms Friday night to... *this.*

She needs time? Why? What's going on with her? Everything was so easy between us last week, then I opened up to her and she spent the night with me and... *What the fuck happened?*

"So, you good to buy the sandwiches this time, bro?" Miles looks at me from the passenger seat with a hopeful expression. "I'll pay you back when I get a new job. I'm good for it."

I narrow my eyes at him. *Oh, right. Miles happened.*

"Yeah, Miles, I'll buy your fucking lunch," I say in a resigned tone, turning and climbing out of the truck.

Wisely, he doesn't follow me in.

I was too on edge at home, unable to stop thinking about Olena's tearful departure Saturday morning. My pacing was irritating Miles, so he suggested we pick up lunch. I haven't been to

Riverside Deli before, but I remember Teddy raving about their sandwiches.

The deli is busy and I get in line. The smell of freshly baked bread and savory meats mingles in the air and my stomach rumbles in response. Two teenagers stand at the helm of the sandwich station. A kid with braces who can't be over fifteen stands at the cash register taking payments, looking *"all knees and elbows,"* as my mom used to say about me that summer when I grew three inches. A lanky blond who looks closer to my age weaves between them behind the counter, restocking supplies and giving them instructions here and there. He meets my eyes for a moment, then looks away, continuing with his work.

I don't think much of it until my turn comes up and he cuts in front of the girl who's about to take my order.

"I'll take this one, Mia," he says to her over his shoulder.

She looks caught off guard but backs away, busying herself by wiping the coffee machine with a wet cloth.

"What can I get you?" He tilts his chin at me.

I give him the order: a club sandwich for Miles and a Reuben for me. I check my phone again, hoping Olena might have texted me something more. Nothing. I put my phone in my back pocket with a frown.

I wait while he makes the sandwiches, stuffing my hands in my front pockets and feeling restless. I notice him look up at me, then back at what he's doing.

Pulling bread slices out of a bag, he places them in the toaster behind him and turns back to me. Glancing outside at my truck, he gives me a look. "You're Jude, right?"

My brow furrows. "Uh, yeah. Sorry, do I know you?"

"Wyatt. Olena's roommate." He raises an eyebrow.

I straighten at the mention of her name. He's got my attention.

"Hi," I say carefully. I remember Olena telling me about Wyatt over burgers on Friday night.

"So, you wanna tell me why she came home yesterday morning in tears?" He holds my gaze confidently, like he's got no patience for bullshit.

"Uh..." I glance around me. "Is this where you wanna talk about this?"

He shrugs. "It's as good a place as any," he says, then glances over his shoulder at the timer on the toaster. "You've got ninety seconds."

I pause for a moment. "Look, I don't know exactly what happened—for her, I mean. We had a great night." I shrug, then run a hand through my hair. "But I left to get us breakfast and my brother showed up while I was gone."

He leans on the sandwich counter, waiting for me to continue with his eyebrows raised.

I lower my voice and lean in slightly. "He was drunk and didn't have a key." I look around, uncomfortable talking about this in a public place with a line of customers waiting behind me. "He pounded on the door, and I guess he scared her pretty badly. She left after that."

He puts his hands on his hips and squeezes his eyes shut for a moment, not saying anything.

"Listen," I say, "do you know what's going on? She wouldn't..." I stop, correcting myself. "She *couldn't* talk to me. And now..." I trail off, remembering her text. I shake my head.

He presses his lips together, considering me. He seems to decide something. "It's not my story to tell, man. She'll do that when she's ready."

I look at him, confused.

"Let's just say... what you described? That would be"—he pauses, as if searching for the right words—"very triggering for her."

I let out a breath, frowning. *Shit. Olena's been through something major and fucking Miles had to stir it up. And I wasn't there.*

I look down at the floor, rubbing the back of my neck, and curse under my breath. I try to explain. "The thing with my brother... It's complicated. But he's harmless. He was just looking for me. He didn't know she was there."

He looks at me skeptically. "Yeah, well, just don't..." He takes a breath. "Don't fucking hurt her, okay?" The emotion behind his words hangs between us for a moment.

My chest tightens at the implication. "I would never hurt her. I tried to help her..." My words feel useless and small trying to defend myself against Wyatt's concern for Olena, which seems to be absolutely warranted.

Wyatt glances at the line behind me. "Look, man, I've got other customers waiting. I'll get Mia to call you when your sandwiches are ready." He lifts his chin to Mia, now wiping the counter to his left, openly eavesdropping on us. He unties his apron and turns to walk to the back.

"Hey, Wyatt," I call out before he can get too far.

He turns back to me, crossing his arms over his chest, and lifts his chin expectantly.

"What can I do? To help?"

He considers a moment. "Just listen. Listen to her. She'll tell you what she needs."

28

OLENA

C harles catches me early Monday morning and asks if I'd like to join him and Carol for a cup of coffee inside to discuss something. I haven't seen Jude yet, although his truck is parked in the driveway; even the knowledge that he's here is weighing on my heart. Grateful for any reason to avoid facing him for a little longer, I agree and head inside.

As I walk toward the front door behind Charles, I look up to see a crew of roofers removing moss from the shingles and washing and suctioning out the gutters. Along the path, Teddy cuts through the weeds with a pressure washer, turning the machine off as we walk past and throwing me a quick wave. A delivery truck beeps, backing into the driveway. Collectively, it all feels a bit much and I'm relieved to step inside the quiet house and sit down at Charles' invitation.

"Olena, my darling, you've done absolute wonders out there!" Carol beams as she pokes her head into the dining room from the kitchen.

Charles sits across from me at the table, smiling in agreement.

"Thank you; it's starting to look great, I think." I squeeze my hands together, looking away. "It's been such a wonderful project to work on. You have a beautiful property here. And a beautiful home too." I gesture at the house around us. Several areas are still under renovation but the home itself retains its classic beauty.

"Well, glad to hear that, actually, because we wanted to talk to you about the house," Charles says.

I look at him with confusion; my area is the outside stuff. "I don't understand." I smile politely.

"Well, Wyatt was telling us a while back that he and Sam have some trouble getting time for just the two of them," Charles explains.

Carol joins us with coffees on a tray, reminding me of the last time I sat at this table. I glance briefly at the empty chair where Jude had sat that day, remembering how my cheeks flushed when he let it be known he was single.

"I guess, between Sam living at his parents' house and Wyatt living with you, they don't have their own space," says Carol, settling down into her seat beside me.

"Oh..." I nod, then chuckle in an effort to cover up my staggering confusion. "Sorry, I'm not following. What does this have to do with me?"

"Oh, Charles, we've gone and explained it all back to front!" Carol laughs and waves a hand in front of her face as if to dismiss the confusion. "See, the noise here with all the construction is getting to be a bit much for us." She glances at Charles. "And we've got a chance to stay in Seattle for a week with friends."

Charles cuts in. "We were hoping you might consider house-sitting for us while we're away." He gives me a hopeful look.

"Oh!" I take a moment to consider the unexpected offer.

"We thought it was perfect, didn't we, Charles?" Carol asks. He nods as she carries on, turning to me. "If you could come stay here, Wyatt and Sam could have some time at your apartment for the week, and you would have a very short commute to work. You could take care of the plants, bring in the mail... all that usual stuff. You know, keep an eye on things." Carol pats my arm and I smile.

"Oh, wow, well, that's a very generous offer!" I say with gratitude. This house is beautiful. I look around the dining room, trying to imagine staying here on my own. Their home is enormous for just one person.

"Zero pressure, of course," Charles adds. "We could always ask Wyatt and Sam to stay, but we thought it would work better for you, since you're already driving out here every day, anyway."

"We'd just love to help Wyatt out and give him some special time together with Sam. They remind me of when Charles and I were dating when we were younger. It was so hard to find time alone." Carol looks wistful.

"Well, that's because your overprotective parents never let us out of their sight whenever I came around," Charles says with raised eyebrows.

Carol turns to me with delight shining in her eyes. "It's true, they thought he was a..." She looks at Charles. "What was my father's word for you? A *scoundrel*. Oh goodness, they were old-fashioned!" Carol laughs melodically as Charles shrugs, chuckling.

I smile, struggling to picture any version of reality in which Charles could be a scoundrel.

"Anyway, darling, let us know what you think. We leave on Wednesday, back the following Wednesday night." Carol smiles as she and Charles observe me for any sign of my reaction to their offer.

"Wow, that's pretty soon. Okay. Well, yeah. I mean, sure! I'd love to!" I say, feeling cautiously optimistic about the arrangement. Not having to drive here every day would be pretty convenient. I could even sleep in. I can't think of a reason to say no.

"Oh, fabulous, well, that's settled, then!" Carol pats my arm again. "This all worked out well, didn't it? Come on, I'll show you around the house."

LEAVING THE FAULKNERS' home, I'm feeling a little unsure about the commitment I've just made. Teddy has finished power washing the path and, as my feet travel along the wet cobblestones, I turn around to look up at the house, walking backwards a few steps to get the full view. It's beautiful—ladders, scaffolding, and all.

I let my gaze drop and turn back toward the driveway, heading to my car to grab my notebook. Then I stop short. Jude stands a few feet ahead of me on the path. My contemplative smile falls from my face as I take in the concern etched into his features.

"Hey," he says, searching my eyes.

"Hi," I reply softly.

We stand there looking at each other for a moment. The silence between us feels heavy.

"Look," he says, "you don't owe me anything. You don't owe me an explanation."

I inhale, my brow creasing.

He goes on. "But just tell me you're okay. Tell me I haven't fucked this all up."

"Jude..." I don't know what to say. I shake my head. "It's not... It's not you. You were..." I look up at the sky, blinking, trying to keep my composure and find the words. *How can I express how incredible this man is?*

Memories of Friday night threaten to flood my mind.

My eyes lower back to his. "There are just... things from my past I'm still working through."

He looks down at the ground, nodding gravely, and puts his hands in his pockets.

"I told you, I'm a mess."

He snaps his head up to meet my eyes, his expression almost a warning. "Olena, listen." He takes a step toward me, his voice low. "Take whatever time you need."

My eyes close. When I open them again, his expression is pained.

"I'll wait." He says the words so simply.

"Jude," I say in disbelief.

"I meant what I said. I'm done running. I'm not scared off by this, Olena."

I look away.

"I may not know what happened, but I know what matters."

My eyes meet his.

"I know this," he gestures between us, "is worth waiting for. *You're* worth waiting for."

The tears threaten to fall once again. I can't speak. *He doesn't know what he's getting into.*

"You say the word..." He levels me with a look. "You tell me when you're ready," he says, his green eyes burning with intensity, "and I'm all in."

At that, he walks away, leaving me standing on the path, speechless. He crosses the lawn, running a hand through his hair.

࣭

JUDE KEEPS a respectful distance from me for the rest of the day. I try to forget what he said and concentrate on work; letting it in is too painful. I know I can't let him get tangled up in my baggage, so I can't dwell on his promise to wait.

Wait for *what*, exactly, anyway? How much time do I need to sort this out? What do I do about Sean?

Unable to focus, and noticing we're ahead of schedule with the necessary tasks on-site, I head home earlier than usual. I change into my sweats and snuggle into the couch under a blanket, tucking it up under my chin and down over my toes.

I need to figure out what to do about Sean. He won't listen to me when I tell him to leave me alone *and* he's still using drugs, which makes everything more complicated. He's more persistent in his attempts to talk me into moving back to Seattle, which worries me. *I wish he'd accept we broke up and just go away.*

With no solution, my thoughts inevitably drift back to Jude. He really wants to wait for me? Why is he so sure about me? He doesn't know about the robbery or about Sean. Should I tell him about Sean's recent calls? Would he still want to wait for me then?

Probably not. No one wants someone with a dumpster-fire of an ex that won't go away.

The tears start falling as I wrestle with the grip Jude has on me already. I must be kidding myself to think I can back away from what we started. To think I can avoid him. That I can work alongside him.

Keys turn in the door and Wyatt comes in to find me sobbing on the couch. Hanging up his keys and kicking off his shoes, he hurries over to me and sits down. He pulls me into a hug and strokes my hair.

"Wanna talk about it?" he asks softly.

I look up at him, wiping my nose with the crumpled tissue in my hand. Without thinking, I launch right in, consumed by my swirling thoughts. "He just keeps texting me and calling me and he won't leave me alone, Wyatt, no matter what I say! I don't know what to do!" I fall into his embrace again. "He's scaring me..."

"*What?*" Wyatt pulls himself away to face me, looking angry. "That fucking asshole! I told him not to hurt you." He shakes his head ruefully.

I freeze. "What?"

"I told him! Oh, man, I could kill him." Wyatt rubs his forehead with his palms.

"Wait. When did you talk to him?" I have no idea what's happening.

"Yesterday. He came into the deli."

My stomach lurches. "Oh my God. Sean is in Lennox?"

"Sean? What do you mean? No. Jude. I was gonna say... he didn't seem like... Wait... You were talking about Sean? *Sean* has been calling you?"

I nod nervously.

"What the fuck! Since when?" Wyatt's clearly pissed I didn't tell him.

Guilt twists my stomach. "I don't know... he's texted a couple of times in the last few weeks... And when he started to call, I tried to ignore him, but he kept calling, and—"

"What has he been saying to you, Olena?" Wyatt searches my eyes.

"He keeps asking me to come home even though I told him I won't, that I don't want to be with him, and he won't take no for an answer. And then he gets angry... and I know last time he called he was high, and... Wyatt, what do I do? He's freaking me out!"

He puffs his cheeks as he blows out a long, frustrated breath. When he speaks again, his voice is calmer. "That fucking prick. I thought you were talking about *Jude.*" He runs a hand through his hair and sinks back into the couch, placing his other hand on his stomach. "Thank God. I was trying to figure out how to kick his ass."

I sniff. "You were gonna kick Jude's ass for me?" I can't help but smile at the mental image.

"Well, obviously. I have to defend my best girl." He squeezes my knee and smiles at me sadly. "Oh, thank God, babe, honestly... I put on my best butch attitude yesterday to warn him not to fuck with you. But I don't have it in me long-term." He chuckles, putting his arm around me again.

I turn and smile up at him. "You went all butch in front of Jude? To defend my honor?" I'm having a hard time picturing it, but what I can imagine is both sweet and hilarious. "Thank you." I wrap my arm around his waist and squeeze him.

Wyatt sits up again to look at me. "Okay, so, wait... Sean's been giving you shit for weeks? Why didn't you tell me? Does Nat know?" he asks, his eyes searching mine.

"I told her about the first text," I admit. "But after that... I don't know. I guess I just wanted him to get the hint and go away, and kept hoping he would. But then he'd call again... Maybe I didn't want to admit to myself that Sean was still in my life. Things were going so well with Jude, and I wanted to just shut Sean out of my mind. Obviously, that didn't work, though..." I trail off. I still don't know what to do.

"Hey. It's okay." Wyatt smoothes back my hair, sighing. "I'm glad you told me now. We'll figure something out. And good news about Jude, I guess." He exhales. "Man, he's even prettier up close."

"*I know,*" I say, my eyes wide.

"He told me what happened on Saturday morning."

I close my eyes and grimace, not wanting to remember. "Yeah?"

"Sounds like a shitty situation. You okay?"

"I think so. *Now*, anyway. I had a panic attack at his place. He was really good about it, though." I look down at my hands. "He helped me. It was *me* who ended up being a jerk and running off." I grimace at the memory. "I was just so embarrassed he saw that."

"Oh, babe. It's not your fault. Trauma fucks with you pretty hard sometimes. If it's any consolation, he did seem genuinely concerned about you."

"Yeah. I know." I pick at a rough fingernail. "I saw him this morning. I told him I need time to figure my shit out."

"What did he say?" Wyatt asks.

"That he'll wait for me," I say in a small voice, with an even smaller smile.

He grabs his chest dramatically, his hand clutching at his heart. He grimaces, then crunches forward, laughing softly and looking pained. "Agh, it hurts so good."

"I know," I say, wiping my tears and laughing with him. "How do you think *I* feel?"

29

OLENA

I pick up the keys Charles and Carol left for me in the mailbox when I finish work on Wednesday. While the crew packs up, I head to my hatchback and pull out a few bags, shutting the trunk with a bang. Jude is loading up his truck beside me and seems to notice I've stayed behind longer than I have the last couple of days. He pauses as he lifts his toolbox, bracing the weight against his hips, and looks at me with slight confusion.

I feel the need to explain. "Carol and Charles are away for the week and asked me to house-sit for them." I smile awkwardly and nod over my shoulder at the massive house.

Jude looks unsure. The situation must sound odd to him.

"That way," I continue, "Wyatt gets time alone with his boyfriend and… I guess I get to sleep in? No commute, right?" I scrunch my nose and give him a small smile, shrugging. I shiver as a cool breeze gusts past.

"Okay." His voice is flat. He looks contemplatively at the house, then continues loading bags into his truck. As he closes the tailgate, he eyes me with a furrowed brow. "You gonna be okay here all by yourself?"

"Oh, yeah, I'll be fine," I say reassuringly. "I mean, when we're not all here working, I think it'll be pretty quiet." I look at the house again, as if I can consult it for confirmation.

"Okay," he says again. He looks at me for a long moment, like he wants to say more, but turns away, throwing the last odds and ends into the truck bed, and dusts his hands on his jeans. "See you tomorrow," is all he says.

My eyes follow the strong planes of his body as he climbs into the truck and drives away. My chest tightens when his truck disappears around the bend in the driveway.

I pick up my bags and head inside to get settled.

Walking up the staircase, I find the guest bedroom set up for me and put my bags on the floor next to the bed. I look around at the large room. A king sized bed sits in the center against the far wall, covered in beautiful burgundy linens with white pillows. To my left, facing the cliff-side and overlooking the river, a large window pulls in the early evening light. White curtains hang from either side and, drawn open, they make the room look even more spacious.

In the far right corner is the ensuite bathroom. I walk over and flick on the light, illuminating the spacious bathroom and its large, surprisingly modern rainwater-style shower. I run my hand over the small, lush towel hanging from a ring near the sink and catch my reflection in the mirror. I look strangely tiny in this enormous house.

I snap a selfie in the mirror and text it to Nat, flicking off the light as I leave the ensuite.

ME

Hope you're having fun in Portland with G

FYI you're not the only one staying in luxurious accommodations. (House-sitting at the jobsite this week. Sent you a photo!)

A sudden metallic bang makes me jump and turn around, searching for the source; I exhale and take a steadying breath when I remember Carol mentioning the old radiator pipes can get noisy as the heat of the day fades.

A dresser and desk sit in the far corner of the bedroom, opposite the bed. I dig out my laptop from one of my bags and place it on the desk. *Maybe I'll be able to get some work done here in the peace and quiet*, I think to myself, remembering the spreadsheet of expenses I need to finalize.

AFTER TAKING myself on a leisurely tour of the house, I realize that, without Wyatt, I'll need to make myself dinner. Snooping in the fridge, I find a plastic container of something that looks like stew and another of rice, both labeled with my name. The stew has a note attached that reads: *"Olena: Thank you for taking care of our home. Enjoy the stew! - Carol & Charles."*

How did they know I can't cook?

I sigh, relieved at not having to prepare something for myself. Smiling at their generosity, I pull out the containers and close the fridge, opening the lid of the stew. My stomach rumbles when I breathe in the smell; even cold, the aroma is incredible. I know it will be delicious. Thinking about the bag of trail mix I brought for emergency food, I'm even more thankful that I get to eat this instead.

Waiting for the stew and rice to heat up, I turn to look out the kitchen window. Dense gray clouds are gathering over the mountains across the river. I frown. It's been cold lately and the wind is already picking up, the branches of the trees outside bending in the erratic gusts. I hope the rain holds off; I was looking forward to turning on the new garden lighting after dark.

I eat in silence, scrolling social media on my phone. My news feed shows a sweet selfie of Wyatt and Sam snuggling on our couch and I smile; I'm glad they're having a great date night together. Scrolling further, I see Nat has posted a photo of a beaming Graham holding up an enormous zucchini at the Portland Farmers Market. I sigh. My friends look so happy.

Setting my phone down, my eyes drift to the window again. Outside, the light is fading. I can no longer see the river; only my reflection in the glass stares back at me. Deciding to treat myself to a luxurious shower, I put my bowls in the sink and switch off the kitchen light, heading back up to my room. I stand for a long time, letting the hot water rain down on my skin. I try to relax, but my brain is still puzzling over the problem with Sean—and the solution I don't yet have.

After my shower, I sit down at the desk in a towel and open my laptop with one hand as I comb out my wet hair with the other. I go through my social media and email accounts, setting up restrictions and blocking Sean any way I can. Taking this step feels like something is finally within my control.

But it also feels so inadequate. With my business here, my website has to have my name and phone number posted so clients can reach me. I purse my lips, knowing I can't erase all the ways Sean can get to me.

A whooshing howl drones through the house and I spin around in my seat, eyes wide, my fingers gripping tightly to the comb. *What the hell was that?*

Sitting very still, I wait to hear if the sound will happen again, my eyes shifting left and right as I hone in on what I can hear around me. The wind is blowing hard outside and a distant tapping sound is coming from somewhere downstairs. I put down the comb and gather my towel around me tightly, pulling my knees up to my chest in the chair. A crack sounds at the bedroom window, jolting me once again. *What are all these sounds?*

My phone lights up with a text from Carol.

CAROL

Just saw on the news about the windstorm.
Hope all is well. Just wanted you to know the
chimney howls like an old wolf when it's stormy.
Lots of popping and cracking noises too. Don't
be alarmed. x

Too late.

I try to shake off the anxiety. *It's just an old house.*

Warily, I push up from the desk. Getting dressed in clean leggings and a sweater, I grab my phone and walk downstairs. I find the den with the TV and, luckily, Charles and Carol have a bunch of old movies on the shelf nearby. I pick *Dirty Dancing* because I've seen the movie enough times to have memorized every line between Johnny and Baby; it's perfect for background noise. *Maybe it'll help me feel less alone in this weird house.*

I watch the movie with semi-detached interest for a while, getting as far as the part where Baby puts her foot in her mouth, nervously declaring she carried a watermelon. I've always loved that scene. Fidgety and restless, I leave the movie playing and get up to explore more of the house again. I nervously rake my hands through my damp hair; I don't know what to do with myself.

Another howl rips through the house as I walk down the hall and my breath catches in my throat, my heart racing despite myself. More howling and, then, a repetitive banging noise seems to come from the ceiling. I close my eyes. *I don't know if I can do this.* I try to relax and breathe.

When another sudden bang sounds from the pipes, I've got my phone in my hand, about to text Nat to come stay with me— that is, until I remember she can't rescue me right now.

Scrolling to Wyatt's name, I pause again and chew on my lower lip. *Fuck.* I can't interrupt his night with Sam. The whole point of me coming here was to leave them alone. I squeeze my free hand into a fist. The thought of calling my parents crosses my mind, but I need to show them I can land on my own two feet like a grown-up. Calling them because of scary noises in a house doesn't exactly scream *capable adult.*

Rolling my shoulders, I go to the front door and check it's locked. Looking behind me to reassure myself there's no one else here, I head back to the den and park my butt on the couch—determined to distract myself by watching the movie—but I can't seem to relax my rigid limbs into the soft cushions.

The sound of shattering glass from down the hall a few minutes later is what sends my shoulders into my neck and my pulse threatening at the edge of full-blown panic. *I can't do this. I can't be alone here.*

My breaths shallow and rapid, I reach for my phone. Heart hammering, I press the call button beside his name and squeeze my eyes shut as it rings.

"Olena?"

"Jude. I need you."

30

OLENA

Grabbing a throw from the couch, I stuff my feet into my shoes and race out the front door, gulping in breaths of fresh night air. Wrapping the blanket around my shoulders, my still-damp hair whips around my face in the wind. The chilly night takes the heat from my cheeks and I close my eyes, grateful for the sensation. Outside feels safer. My breathing slows. The rain hasn't hit yet. With a glance at the dark driveway, I shuffle over to the newly installed switch near the front porch and turn on the garden lighting.

Twinkling fairy lights dance to life in the chestnut tree across the clearing from where I stand. The lights for the cliff-side seating area flick on, their soft yellow glow illuminating the table and chairs. Along the garden borders and among the new plants, staked lanterns glow low to the ground, bringing the yard into focus like a stage. The lit edges of the cobblestone and gravel paths in front of my feet glow a soft pinkish white, snaking along the ground. From where I'm standing, I can see the top of the lights hovering over the firepit in the sunken garden. It's beautiful.

Pulling the blanket tighter around my shoulders, I take a

steadying breath. Walking carefully across the grass to the bench swing in the sparkling chestnut tree, the warmly lit property feels ethereal and hushed despite the howling wind. I slowly climb the steps to the swing—the steps Jude and I built. The wind around me is somewhat lessened under the shelter of the branches. I sit down on the swing, tentatively leaning back, and look up. The soft glow cast by the twinkling tree is stunning; the lights look like stars.

I hear the engine before I see the lights. Jude's truck roars into the driveway and I watch, frozen and heart racing, as he gets out and jogs to the front door.

He knocks hard. "Olena!" he calls out.

"Over here!" I have to shout to be heard over the sound of the wind whipping between us.

Jude spins around. His eyes find mine in the soft glow around us.

I stand, shakily descending the steps, and his eyes lock on mine as he starts to cross the yard. Still hugging the blanket around my shoulders, I move to meet him, my pace quickening. The relieved expression on his face wrenches something in my heart and tears well in my eyes. I break into a run, the blanket falling from my hands and fluttering to the grass. I slam into his body, burying my face in his chest and squeezing my arms around him. His strong arms envelop me.

"I'm sorry. I'm so sorry," I murmur into his shirt, clinging to him tightly. "I just can't be here alone. The house—" My pulse is racing again and I'm shaking. "There are all these banging noises, and the wind is making a howling sound inside the chimney somehow, and I heard glass break... I got scared. I just... I needed to see you." I take a breath. "I need you."

Jude pulls back and lifts my chin to look at him. "Hey, hey. It's okay, I'm here." He slowly rubs my back with one hand, and smoothes my hair away from my face with the other, searching my eyes. "I'm here," he says again. His hands on me again feel so... *right.*

My breath catches at the concern in his expression. *This man.* He's been nothing but incredible to me. All this time, I've been convinced I didn't deserve him, but what if he's exactly what I need? Not later. Right now. Everything I've been holding back— everything I've been trying to push down—suddenly becomes clear to me. I can't deny my feelings any longer. The words come rushing out.

"I don't want space or time, okay? I don't. I hate being away from you so much; it's making me feel sick and I can't stand it anymore."

Jude lets out a breath.

I wipe my eyes with my sweater sleeve, my voice shaking. "You said you weren't going to run. Well, *I* was running. And I don't want to run anymore either, Jude." I exhale an exhausted breath and close my eyes. I feel his fingers slide into the hair at the back of my neck, his thumbs brushing my cheeks. The warmth of his hands feels like home. When I look back at him, it takes me a moment to steady myself. "I want you. I've wanted you all this time. I just—"

Jude's lips meet mine and I crumble. Tears run down my cheeks as I grasp at him, my hands at his neck, pulling him closer. I've missed his touch so desperately; feeling his lips on mine soothes a deep ache inside me. My eyes are still closed when our lips part, my breathing shallow.

"Are you sure?" he asks.

"Yes," I breathe.

He kisses me again, deeply and tenderly. "Olena..."

I look up.

"It's about fucking time." He smiles with relief and meets my eyes. "I was losing my goddamned mind."

I let out a messy, breathy laugh. "I'm so sorry," I say again as he kisses my nose, then hugs me tight to his chest.

I feel the first raindrops fall on my forehead, my hands, and my cheeks.

I pull back to look at him. "Jude, I need to tell you about what happened." I wipe my eyes again, taking a deep breath. "About why I get so scared—why I have panic attacks and nightmares."

"Are you sure?" he asks again. He furrows his brow, looking cautious.

"Yes." I nod. *He needs to know.*

"Okay," he says softly, rubbing his hands over my arms. "Come on, let's go sit down." He offers me his hand.

We walk back to the swing in silence, his thumb brushing rhythmic strokes over the back of my hand. On our way, Jude bends to retrieve the blanket from the grass. He settles in close beside me on the swing and wraps an arm around my shoulders, pressing a warm kiss to the side of my head.

Steeling myself, I take a deep breath. "Back in Seattle, I lived with my ex, Sean. We were together for a few years, but he started using drugs and things got... complicated."

The rain picks up, filtering through the still-bare branches above us that only bear the first buds of early spring. We don't move. He waits for me to continue.

"Our relationship got really stressful." I brush the stray hairs from my face. "I kept trying to help him—to make us work—but it was bad. Things got kind of messy." I drop my gaze and play with the hem of my sweater.

Jude listens silently, reaching for my hand. He intertwines his fingers with mine in his lap. I glance up and see the worry written across his furrowed brow.

I take another breath, looking back down at our interconnected fingers. "Last fall, these two guys..." The tears well up again; the pain of this memory is visceral, even now.

"It's okay, take your time," he says in a low voice.

I exhale a shaky breath into his shoulder. "Two guys came banging on our door, shouting about some money that I guess Sean owed them—I don't know. We were home. We hid behind the couch. They broke our window to get in." I lift my eyes to meet his.

Understanding blooms in Jude's expression, his brow smoothing out. "I'm so sorry, Olena." Releasing my hand, he pulls me gently into his chest.

"I was so terrified." My voice breaks as I say the words. "They had knives and they—"

He pulls back suddenly, searching my eyes with worry. "Did they hurt you?"

"No," I say, sitting up, and he looks relieved. "But one guy held a knife to Sean's throat. And the other one..." I trail off, dropping my gaze. "He put his hand over my mouth so I couldn't scream. I couldn't breathe." I take an uneven breath, fighting against the suffocating sensation the memory brings. My face feels hot, and there's a dull buzzing at the back of my skull. I lift my eyes back to meet his, the tears spilling over.

Jude's expression is pained; he presses his lips together, his anger palpable. He wipes the tears from my cheeks.

My chest feels tight, and a faint nausea roils in my stomach. Taking another deep breath, I continue. "They took the money we had and threatened us. They said they were gonna come back, said they might have to be less *friendly* the next time." I grimace hard at the memory of how that threat haunted me. "But they eventually left. And no one was hurt. Not physically, at least."

Jude exhales a breath, his brow creased with concern. "Fuck."

"Yeah. It was fucked up." I look down, an ache spreading across my collarbone and up into my jaw.

Rain pelts the ground around us. I briefly consider with a

detached sort of amusement that this seems to be our thing—getting caught in the rain.

I lift my gaze.

Jude's hair is dripping wet, raindrops gathering on his skin and running down his face. He kisses my forehead, then pulls back to face me.

"God, I'm *so* sorry you had to go through that," he says with quiet intensity, his eyes searching mine.

I nod. "I broke up with him and moved home soon after that," I explain quietly, frowning. "I couldn't be in that apartment or be around him any longer. I was always scared. Always."

Jude's brow knits together as he closes his eyes and exhales. He opens them again and brushes my cheek with his thumb. "Olena..."

"I still am," I admit quietly. "The panic attacks... the nightmares... and tonight..." I glance over at the house.

Jude nods and pulls me into him again. He says nothing for a while, just rubs my back gently with one hand. Eventually, he speaks. "Thank you for telling me."

"Thank *you* for..." I look up at him, my eyes burning. "Everything. Seriously. Everything." I tuck my head back under his chin and squeeze him tight.

The sound of the rain changes, and my gaze lands on the ground, my face still pressed against his warm chest. Tiny balls of hail bounce off the grass.

Jude sees it, too, and pulls back to face me, lifting my chin with a finger.

"Hey, I know we've done the rain thing a couple of times now." He kisses my forehead. "But this is..." He trails off as the sound around us intensifies. We watch as the hail bouncing up from the ground becomes larger, the sound louder.

We meet each other's eyes before jumping up, then scrambling down the steps to make a break for the house. I grip tightly to Jude's hand as I shield my face from the frozen onslaught with the other arm. The hail is the size of peas and stings where it hits my skin. Jude tries to hold the blanket above us until we get to the covered porch and stop, breathing hard. We stand there without speaking, listening to the cacophony.

"I forgot how quickly the weather changes here," I say, giving him a small smile. My clothes and hair are wet from the rain, and I can see his are too. The chill is seeping into me quickly and I feel drained and cold.

"You okay to go inside again?" he asks gently, squeezing my hand.

"As long as you stay with me." I meet his eyes, feeling unsteady.

"Olena, I'm not leaving," he says with heartbreaking sincerity. And I know he means it.

31

OLENA

"It was just a vase," Jude says, returning from the downstairs hallway to where I'm waiting in the foyer. "Looks like someone left a window open in the bathroom down here." He shrugs. "Guess the wind knocked it over. The floor tiles showed no mercy." He gives me a lazy half-smile.

I exhale with relief and make a mental note to tell Charles and Carol about the vase tomorrow.

Jude smiles and reaches for me, pulling me into his chest. "I cleaned it up. And the window's shut now." He rests his chin on my head and rubs my back gently.

"Thank you," I murmur against his damp shirt. "I feel silly for getting so freaked out. It's just... that sound." I squeeze my eyes shut, trying to shake off the memory once more.

He pulls back and lifts my face to his, looking into my eyes. "Hey. You're not silly. It makes sense that sounds like that would be scary." He kisses my cheek softly. "What do you need?"

"What do you mean?" I ask, searching his expression.

"To feel safe right now. What can I do to help you?" His gaze drops to my lips for a moment, lingering there before he kisses me.

"I feel safe with you here." Seeking the warmth of his body, I slide my chilled hands under the back of his soaked shirt and smile apologetically when he sucks in a breath. "But I think I need to warm up," I add, standing on tiptoes and brushing my lips against his cheek. "Come on."

We climb the staircase in silence, Jude trailing behind me with his hand in mine. At the top, I pause to look around the sitting room in front of us. I'm shivering in my soaked clothes. Jude wraps his strong arms around my waist from behind, warming me. Over my shoulder, I see him lift his chin toward the fireplace. "Do you think we should make a fire or...?"

I turn in his arms and lift my eyes to his. "No." I bite my lip and slide my hands over his muscled chest.

"No?" he asks, giving me a crooked smile.

"I had something else in mind," I say quietly.

His dark gaze simmers with heat as his strong hands pull my body against his. His forehead grazes mine, his eyes lingering on my mouth, and an electric current surges from my core through my body in anticipation.

I lift my chin, my lips slightly parted.

Reaching between us, he slowly, achingly, traces the outline of my lips with his thumb, sending shivers of pleasure through me as he watches the soft flesh of my lips yield under his touch.

My breath catches. I'm waiting for more, not daring to move a muscle.

He doesn't kiss me.

"Show me your room." His lips are nearly touching mine. I'm dizzy with the desire already coursing through me.

I take a breath and reach a hand to his chest, grabbing a handful of his shirt and pulling him in the direction of my room.

Before we get to the bedroom door, Jude stops me from

behind, slipping his hands around my waist and up under my sweater. He presses his hips into my back, his delicious hardness pushing against me. I lean into him, inviting more.

I grin with pleasure at the low rumbling sound from his throat.

His hands travel higher, palms cupping my breasts over my bra as he exhales against my neck. I tilt my head back against his shoulder as he traces his fingers down my stomach. He presses a soft kiss to my neck. I let out a breath, my eyelids fluttering.

"I thought you wanted to see my room," I manage to say, still not turning as his hands rove over my skin, his fingertips dipping under the waistband of my leggings.

"Watching you from behind was too much," he replies, pushing his hands lower still, his grazing touch stopping just short of where I know I'm already wet—and not from the rain. As he pulls his hands back up, I spin around to face him.

Dragging my hands down his chest, I smile. His eyes close as I run a palm slowly and firmly down his length. I love watching him react to my touch.

"Come on." I pull on his belt loops and drag him the last few feet into my room. "Let's warm up." I arch an eyebrow as I lead him into the bathroom. The hunger in his eyes follows my every move.

I lean into the shower stall and turn the handle, the water hissing to life. When I turn around to face Jude, I can't help but stare. He pulls off his soaked sweater, then his t-shirt, dropping them both on the floor at his feet as he steps into my arms. I let out a sigh at the sight of his impressive bare chest, the smooth planes of defined muscle I find my hands sliding over, exploring greedily.

God, he's incredible.

He pulls me against him and I sweep my arms around his strong shoulders, softly moaning at the heat from his bare skin.

With heavy-lidded eyes, he gives me a hungry smile before he claims my mouth in a kiss.

Jude's hands slip under my sweater. I lift my arms when he pulls the damp fabric over my head, tossing it aside. As his eyes drink in the sight of me in my bra and leggings, desire blazes in his gaze and his self-control slips.

With a growl, he pushes us inside the shower stall, still half-dressed. The hot water hits us as he shoves me up against the cold tile wall, and I gasp at the chill on my back. His lips crush against mine, his tongue sweeping deeply into my mouth. He rips my bra straps down to hang slack at my elbows, shoving the rest down to my waist. I hear him let out a harsh breath as he looks down at my breasts. Palming them in both hands, he groans with pleasure and takes my mouth in another burning kiss as he gently squeezes me, teasing my nipples into tight peaks under his thumbs. Water runs down us in rivulets, collecting in the places we are pressed together, spilling over our flesh.

Jude bends to kiss his way down my body, kneeling on the floor of the shower in his soaking wet jeans. Looking up at me with dark, ravenous eyes, he slides his hands up the backs of my legs and over my ass, then peels my drenched leggings and panties down slowly, exhaling hard. He rests his forehead on my stomach as I step out of my soaked clothes.

I reach behind me, quickly unfastening my bra and letting it drop to the shower floor, bare before him now.

With his arms wrapped around my thighs and my hands tangling in his dripping hair, he presses reverent kisses to my legs and hips, looking up at me with water running down his face. He slowly climbs back up to standing, his huge frame towering above me.

I gasp when he trails a single, teasing finger up between my legs, sending shivers through my entire body.

I can't wait any longer to feel him in my hands. Watching his eyes, I roughly work the fly of his jeans open and slip a hand under his waistband.

"Oh my God..." I moan softly at the feeling of him, at how incredible the heat of his shaft feels in my hand as I stroke gently down his length.

Breathing raggedly, his mouth ravages mine. His tongue desperately sweeps against my own, his fingers rubbing my nipples and pinching hard.

Freeing him fully from his jeans and underwear, I work both hands up and down, gently squeezing the sensitive head of his glorious cock and marveling at the size of him.

Jude growls against me, pressing into my hands. I release him, letting his hard length rub against the slick skin of my stomach as he thrusts up, our bodies and lips crushing together like we can't get close enough.

My hands claw at his lower back, pulling him against me, and he groans. I run my hands down over his muscled ass, then pull back from his intense kiss to turn us around in the shower. A flicker of understanding shines in his eyes and he gives me a searing look.

Working his wet jeans the rest of the way down, I slowly kneel at his feet, sliding my hands down his strong thighs, then calves, as he steps out of the last of his clothes. Looking up and seeing his smooth, hard shaft before my eyes, I'm suddenly desperate to taste him. Locking eyes with him, I smile suggestively and hold his gaze as I slowly drag my tongue all the way up his entire length, flicking it teasingly when I get to the top.

His groan is guttural and his hands tense in my wet hair, his eyes rolling. "Fuck," he breathes out slowly, wiping a hand over his face. Rivers of water trace winding paths down his chiseled chest. He's exquisite. I feel him shudder as I take the head of his cock into my mouth, swirling my tongue in a tight circle over the sensitive tip, my teeth lightly scraping over him.

"Olena..."

The sound of my name on his lips has me craving more, and I take more of him into my mouth. As I pull him deeper, he lets out a resounding groan, as if he's struggling for self-control. I tighten my hand and lips around him, sliding back up. His hands grip at my hair. Letting him guide my movement, he pushes me down again, filling my mouth with his thickness as I moan against his skin. He pulls me back up, then down again, pumping inside my mouth slowly. Too slowly.

I reach my free hand around to grab him from behind, pulling him into my mouth, encouraging him.

Jude's hands tense in my hair, as if he's trying to hold himself back to avoid hurting me.

Releasing my grip, I grab his ass hard with both hands. I dig my fingers into his flesh, driving him deeper still, showing him what I want: *all of him.* My lips are tight, my tongue sweeping against him, drawing him in. A pulse of need thrums between my legs as he thrusts harder, deeper, faster into my mouth. He slides hot and wet against the roof of my mouth, the back of my throat opening to take all of him.

He lets out a deep groan of satisfaction. Out of the corner of my eye, I see his hand slam into the glass of the shower wall, bracing himself, as he barely holds onto control.

With obvious effort, he stops and lets out a rough breath, his hands leaving my hair to graze my cheeks. I pause.

"You..." he says, his voice a low rumble.

I pull back, licking and flicking my tongue against the tip of his cock as I look up at him through my wet lashes.

"You are going to destroy me," he rasps, smiling darkly and shaking his head.

I stand slowly, pushing my chest in, arching my back to feel his rock-hard length sliding slowly between my slick breasts and down my stomach. As I rise to meet him, I press my breasts hard against his chest.

His eyes shutter and his hands slide over my ass, pulling me against him.

Water spills over us, streaming down from my hair. Jude reaches up and lifts my face to his, pressing a burning kiss to my lips, pushing his hips into me. His cock pulses against my stomach.

"I think I'm warm now," he says, smiling against my lips. Reaching for the tap, he shuts off the water. For a moment, we just stand there, pressed together, dripping wet, our breathing shallow and rapid. He slowly gathers my hair, peeling it off my neck and shoulders. He squeezes it gently, releasing the excess water as he kisses my neck. My fingers drift between us, sliding down his chest and stomach.

"I want to fuck you," he says, his voice rumbling deeply below my ear.

Hearing him say the words, my fingers tense against his skin as pleasure ignites all over my body.

"Do you want that, Olena?" He runs his tongue along my collarbone, licking up the droplets of water. "For me to fuck you?"

My eyes close and the ache between my legs intensifies. I've never wanted anything more. I let out a soft groan; I need him inside me.

"Yes," I breathe.

We stumble out of the shower and into the bedroom, not bothering to dry off. My back hits the bed and Jude climbs over me, my hands sliding down his chest. I grasp his rock-hard cock once more, and he exhales roughly when I start working my fist over him slowly. With one hand, he reaches down between my legs. I open for him and he inhales sharply as his fingertips graze my entrance, dipping in slightly, slowly dragging a slick finger up and over my clit.

"Oh, my God," he groans, "you're so fucking wet."

I laugh softly, meeting his hungry eyes with an innocent look. "Yeah, we just got out of the—"

He slides a finger inside me.

I arch up with a gasp, my eyes closing, the words lost.

"Don't give me those doe eyes, gorgeous," he growls, pumping his finger, curling it to hit the spot that makes me throw my head back and groan. He leans down, his face beside mine. "You and I both know you're wet for me."

My cheeks flush with heat as I slide my free hand around the back of his neck, gingerly scratching my fingernails over his skin. Tightening my grip with my other hand, I work my fist over the sensitive head of his cock, relishing the way his breath skitters in response.

"Jude," I breathe. I can't take this any longer.

"Uh-huh?" He's nipping at my neck, scraping my skin with his teeth. His finger slides in and out of me in a slow, teasing rhythm.

"Please," is all I can say. I'm breathing hard. My hand slides over his length faster now.

"Please what?" He is kissing underneath my ear, his voice a hoarse whisper. He plunges two fingers inside me, pushing in deeper and faster. "I want to hear you say it," he breathes.

I can only whimper in response.

His fingers slide out of me and he shifts to line up the head of his cock, torturing me by sliding it up and down against my slick opening. Its warmth against me makes me feel desperate. I want him inside me. *Now.*

"Please," I say again, my head spinning.

Jude slowly presses the tip of his cock into me, letting loose a ragged breath with the effort of his self-control, then pauses.

I whimper again, writhing to feel more of him, but he doesn't let me. I'm losing my mind. My hands clench at the bed in frustration, my eyes squeezing shut, my breath heaving.

"Look at me, beautiful." His voice is a deep rumble. My eyes open and meet his gaze, his lips inches from mine. "Say it." The need flares in his eyes.

"Fuck me," I breathe, and he plunges in hard with a throaty growl. I gasp, muscles clenching, as his delicious length buries deep.

Pulling back, he slams into me again, deeper, harder this time.

"Olena," he groans, his chest radiating heat, the smooth skin grazing the peaks of my nipples as I arch up into him. "You feel..." His hips crush into me with each thrust and I pull my knees up around his torso to let him in deeper; he lets out a harsh breath as he meets me in a powerful thrust that buries his shaft to the hilt. "You feel fucking incredible," he rasps.

I smile at his words, reveling in the feeling of him filling me so completely.

But it's not enough.

I grip his ass with both hands and pull him in with each thrust. Jude quickens his pace, the grip on his control wavering.

I slide a hand down between us and tease the base of his cock with my fingers each time he withdraws, gently coaxing, watching his response. My fingers find my clit, swollen with desire, and work small circles there. I clench hard around him as he pounds into me. Chasing my pleasure, I hold my muscles tight and reach my free hand up to his neck, pulling his face down to mine. I tangle my tongue with his, nipping at his lower lip.

"Harder," I breathe against his mouth.

The word barely escapes my lips before he unleashes himself fully, plunging into me hard and fast as I throw my head back against the bed, crying out with pleasure.

The bed shifts under us with each of Jude's driving thrusts. My fingers work in fast circles over my clit, my other hand clawing at Jude's rippling back. I feel my release building, delicious sensation gathering inside me.

"Come for me," he bites out between thrusts.

I'm losing myself rapidly, giving myself over to the mind-melting pleasure of being fucked this hard. As I tighten around him, both chasing and intensifying the sensation, I moan, then cry out raggedly as the first wave of pleasure cascades over my senses, the muscles of my center clamping tightly over Jude's length.

He exhales harshly and plunges into me repeatedly, even harder than before, his control completely lost.

I clench and writhe, my body bucking as a fresh wave of pleasure rolls over me, more intense than the last.

Jude slams into me again and again, finding his own release, thrusting hard until he's shuddering, completely spent. Still sheathed inside me, he slowly lowers himself until our chests are touching, his eyes glazed. His lips find mine and he kisses me slowly and softly. With my breasts pressed into his chest and my legs wrapped around his waist, he collapses completely into our embrace, his face buried in my neck. Our breathing slowly settles as we hold each other. The echoes of my orgasm make my muscles jump against him and he makes a low sound of satisfaction into the pillow beside my head, flexing his cock with a pulse inside me. I smile in a daze and sweep my hands through his damp hair and down his neck, softly tracing along his heated skin. I want to remember everything about this moment. I close my eyes and inhale deeply, drinking in his incredible scent.

Jude shifts to get up and I pull him back to me, my arms around his neck. "Don't go. Not yet," I whisper against his cheek, kissing him softly there. I don't want this moment to be over.

He smiles down at me. "I won't," he replies. Rolling himself under me, he shifts me above him, curling up from the bed to take my nipple in his mouth, licking and sucking lightly. I brace my hands on the headboard above him, arching my back. He moves to the other nipple, sliding his hands down my back and over my ass, squeezing gently. Releasing my breast, he flops back down on the bed, watching me with a sleepy, satisfied gaze. My hands push off the headboard and I sit up, resting on my knees. He pulses again, still inside of me, and my eyes close with soft pleasure.

"I might've blacked out for a minute there," he grins, reaching up to palm my breasts, his thumbs lazily circling my tight nipples as I arch into his touch.

"Me too," I breathe. I smile and bite my lip, exhaling a long breath.

Jude sits up again and gently takes my face in his hands, kissing me softly, slowly. His cock pulses, hardening again.

"Mmm, see what you do to me?" His eyes flare as need returns to his gaze. He kisses me again, more deeply. I rock my hips, encouraging him, and he groans, biting my bottom lip.

The wind howls through the old house once more but, this time, I don't care.

32

JUDE

The sun cuts in through the open curtains, waking me with its bright glare. Lying on my back, I feel the soft weight of Olena's hand draped over my bare chest, her body tucked into mine under my outstretched arm. I turn my head to look at her sleeping face beside me. Her hair is a tangled mess, reminding me of everything that messed it up last night: the rain, the hail, the shower... the sex.

She's gorgeous. Remembering our night together, I smile and run a hand down my face. It was more intense than I could have ever imagined.

Unable to stop myself from touching her, I reach out and gently sweep the hair away from her cheek. She murmurs softly as she pushes her face into my hand, her eyes still closed. She cracks one eye open, squinting in the bright morning light, grinning a delighted, sleepy grin and scrunching up her nose when she sees me watching her. I pull her into me, breathing in the scent of her hair as she nuzzles into my chest. *God, this feels so right.*

"Morning," I whisper into her hair. My cock is already responding to her.

"Mmm, the cold light of day." She chuckles against my skin, tucking her forehead down into my chest.

"You'd better not be hiding," I say. "Come here." I lift her chin to face me.

She pulls the sheet up under her nose. "Ugh, no, I've got morning breath and eye goops! Don't look!" She giggles and then spins to face away from me. "I'll breathe this way so I don't scare you off."

"Impossible." Reaching under the sheet, I slide my arm around her stomach and pull her in tight, my cock twitching to attention against her ass. I trace the slope of her waist with a lazy finger. "I actually think I might never be able to leave this bed," I say, kissing her soft shoulder. "Plus, I'm pretty sure all my clothes are still soaked." The image of Olena on her knees in the shower last night floods me. It had taken everything I had in me to stop myself from coming right then and there. I'm instantly hard again from the memory.

Olena obviously feels it because she presses her hips back into me, her fingers interlacing with mine against her stomach. "Mmm, so we might have to stay here forever?" she asks innocently.

"I think so." I kiss the back of her neck. "Real shame."

"Imagine if Charles and Carol come home in a week to discover we've just starved to death, naked, in their guest room," she laughs, turning up to look at me.

"We'd make the news for sure," I chuckle, sliding a hand over her breast, her nipple hard under my palm. I inhale sharply. "Let's call that plan B," I mumble, nipping at her shoulder with my teeth.

"And what's plan A?" She twists onto her stomach to arch an eyebrow at me, her lips pressed into the pillow.

"Well," I say, craning my neck to squint at the clock on the bedside table, "I hate to say it, but we have work in about an hour and a half."

She whimpers and buries her face in the pillow while I trace her back lightly between her shoulder blades.

"You know, it's kind of funny staying here with you," she says, her voice muffled as she peeks up at me from the pillow.

"How so?" I look at her curiously.

"Well, it's not your house... and it's not my house." She pauses. "It's like we're on some kind of wild sex vacation." She laughs as she says it and I chuckle with her.

"Well, when you put it like that..." I say, deadpanning. "Let's never fucking leave." I grab her ass and smile suggestively before sliding my hand around her waist. I'm about to pull her into me again when I stop suddenly. "Wait, shit..." I roll onto my back and press my fist to my forehead.

"What?"

"I need to go get Murphy. I left in a rush last night and didn't bring him."

"Oh, no, is he okay?" She looks concerned. I remember with a smile how much she liked him when they first met. And how much he liked her.

"Oh, he's fine. There's a dog flap on the back door. He'll just need breakfast and a lift back here," I reassure her.

"Can I come with you?" The vulnerability in her expression is mystifying to me; I can't imagine letting her out of my arms.

I smile back at her as I run my hand down the length of her spine and over the curve of her ass, squeezing. "You'd better."

She smiles softly. "Okay."

"Think we can make it to the shower first?" My eyes flick to the bathroom doorway, my eyebrows raised.

She turns her head to contemplate the distance. "Let's hope so... Although that ten feet might be a struggle." She looks back at me, smiling shyly. "But I need my toothbrush."

I press a quick kiss to her nose and she pushes up, swinging her legs over the side of the bed. She reaches down to rummage through something on the floor, then turns to me with a bag of trail mix in her hand.

"Breakfast," she announces with a grin, her eyes gleaming.

"Aw, you cooked?" I chuckle and slide my arm around her waist, pulling her into me. She laughs softly as I kiss her temple.

"Ugh, I also need my hairbrush, apparently." She tries to tease the tangles out of her hair with her fingers. As she stands, my eyes trace the length of her back, the dip of her spine, then linger on the curve of her gorgeous ass. Suddenly, I'm seriously contemplating pulling her back to bed.

Turning and clocking my gaze, she throws me a suggestive smile and disappears around the corner into the bathroom.

I lie back on the bed and exhale a breath.

"Jude," she calls out from around the corner. "Not to alarm you, but someone seems to have trashed this bathroom last night."

33

OLENA

"Tell me about your tattoos," I say from my perch at Jude's kitchen island.

Work had wrapped up early, so we came here to grab dinner and a few of Jude's things. I admire him from behind as he stands at the sink, cleaning up our plates.

He pauses, looking over his shoulder at me as he reaches for a towel to dry his hands. Turning to face me across the island, he pushes his sleeves up further, laying his forearms out between us. I graze my fingers over his skin, looking at them in detail for the first time. On his right arm, in black ink, is a dandelion; the roots twine around his wrist and the leaves and stem travel up his forearm. At the top, the petals have gone to seed. Some of them float away, carried by the wind.

"So, obviously, in my line of work," he glances up at me and smirks, "*our* line of work, plants are kind of the thing. The dandelion is because it's ordinary but strong." He runs his other hand down over his beard. "My mom also always had a soft spot for dandelions; she said the bees liked them." He smiles as he remembers her. "She'd always give my dad shit for ripping them out."

"It's beautiful." I meet his eyes again, then look back down to his other arm. "What about this one?"

I touch the dark outline of what looks like a woodworking tool I vaguely remember from a high school wood shop class.

"The hand planer—" he starts, his vision clouding slightly. "That's for my dad."

I look up at him, remembering what he told me about his mother. Searching his eyes, I know before I even ask.

"Are they both—" I start, and he drops his gaze with a small nod. "Jude, I'm so sorry." The words feel so inadequate; a long silence stretches between us. "Tell me about what happened?" I ask quietly, rubbing his arms again. "If you want to. You don't have to."

"No, I can. I should." He smiles sadly at me. "It's been ten years."

"Ten years?" I'm floored. They were so young. *He* was so young.

He takes a breath. "Yeah. Car accident." His brow creases.

I close my eyes. I can't imagine the pain he went through losing them both like that. He would have been about twenty when it happened. I look up at him again. Reaching for his face with both hands, I pull him toward me, pressing my forehead to his. "I'm so sorry," I say again. I kiss him softly, then sit back in my seat.

We stay silent for a few moments as I let it sink in.

Jude's voice is quiet when he speaks again. "After they died," he begins, "Miles and I moved out here." He looks around the kitchen before his eyes meet mine. "We grew up in town, not far from Riverside, but we spent every summer out here."

I squeeze his hands, waiting for him to continue.

He takes another breath. "The house... I had to sell it. It was too hard to live there after—without them, I mean." He rubs his jaw, smoothing down his beard. "And Miles was seventeen when it happened, still in high school. I got a job to take care of us while he finished senior year... but the mortgage was too much." His shoulders drop and he rubs his thumbs over the backs of my hands, taking a moment to collect himself. "The memories were too."

I nod. I can only imagine how alone they must have felt living there.

He clears his throat. "Anyway, that's why we moved out here. Living here worked for us for a couple of years before Miles left for Seattle. I think he needed to get away from town, you know? Too many difficult memories." He pauses as I nod again and looks down at where I'm rubbing his hands softly. "He really struggled after the accident."

My eyes fall to the countertop next to our hands as I turn Jude's words over in my mind. *Miles...* a dull ache spreads across my chest, my heart breaking for him too. *Maybe that explains why he was drunk that morning.* I inhale an unsteady breath before lifting my eyes to meet his.

"What was your dad like?" I ask gently, remembering the emotion in his eyes when he mentioned him earlier.

Jude blows out a breath and stands, coming around the island to face me. "Come with me," he says, holding out his hand.

"This is amazing." I stare at the inside of Jude's shed, which is large; it's almost the size of a full garage. A well-stocked wood shop with an enormous wooden workbench takes up most of the space. I spin around slowly to take in everything around me. A collection of vintage woodworking tools is hung and meticulously organized on a huge, wall-mounted pegboard above the work-bench. In the far corner is a simple home gym setup and, on the wall opposite the workbench, an expansive set of cabinets fills the space from the floor to the ceiling. Everything here has been well taken care of, almost reverently preserved. I think I understand why it was hard for Jude to talk about his dad. Some things you just need to see... and feel.

The room smells of fresh cedar and I close my eyes, inhaling deeply; instantly, I'm transported back to watching my own dad working in his garage. In the center of the room, a table saw sits atop a weathered wood table with a lathe, used for carving the rounded legs of furniture beside it. Dad had always made me do a safety check before he turned on those big machines—hair tied back, safety goggles on, earmuffs in place—to calm my unease about the roaring noise.

"Most of this was my dad's," Jude says quietly, stepping inside and leaning against the workbench.

I turn toward him. A small, half-finished table sits at one end of the bench, next to a can of oil stain and a paintbrush. The surface is otherwise spotless.

Jude rubs the back of his neck. "We used to work in his shop at our house every weekend when I was growing up. He didn't talk much, but spending that time with him was a huge part of my childhood." He crosses his arms over his broad chest and smiles. "I loved it."

I smile softly and rub my arms in the chill air of the shed.

"I still do—love this stuff, I mean." He looks down for a moment, then back at me. "After they died, we got rid of a lot from the old house... but I couldn't bring myself to get rid of all this." He flicks his eyes to the wall of tools. "So I moved it out here."

I look around again. "I bet your dad would be happy," I turn back to him, "knowing you held onto something you love so much."

He holds my gaze with a sad smile, and something I can't decipher flickers in his eyes.

I wander over to the cabinet. Touching the wood surface of one door gently, I look back at him. "Can I ask—what's in here?"

"Open it." He smiles, lifting his chin.

Grasping the handle, I pull it open. Inside is another cabinet, this one with a handle at the top and a hinge at the base. I quirk my eyebrows at Jude. He's still smiling.

"Is this, like, a trick cabinet or something?" I grasp the second handle and pull it down. It swings open and rests on the floor, revealing a smallish mattress with a tufted, plush dog bed on top. I laugh, then gasp when I get the joke. I spin to Jude, who's grinning now. "A Murphy bed!"

"Had to do it." He shrugs. "He likes hanging out here while I work."

I smile, reflecting fondly on how Murphy is never too far from Jude on the job-site. It's easy to imagine him curled up here. I close up both cabinets and walk toward Jude, rubbing my arms again.

"You cold?" he asks, stepping toward me.

"A little," I admit. "I'm sure you don't relate, Mr. *I Run Hot.*" I widen my eyes and poke him in the chest. He smiles and looks away, sliding his warm hands over my arms. "Honestly, I still can't believe you said that in front of Charles and Carol." I shake my head and give him a rueful smile. "But you knew what you were doing to me, didn't you?" I arch an eyebrow at him, wrapping my arms around his waist.

He meets my eyes again and lazily rubs my back. "Mmm, hard to say." His lips twitch up in amusement. "What did it do to you?" His voice is low. I hear the change in his breathing as he slides his hands down over my ass, grasping lightly. He leans in. "I think I'm gonna need more information," he breathes against my cheek.

My eyes close and I press my body into his, my fingers gently gripping the back of his shirt. I nuzzle into his neck, kissing him below his ear, and pull my hands up over his shoulders. My fingers play with the back of his hair as I breathe him in. *God, this man's body is my new happy place.*

"It made me want to touch you," I say, sliding my hands down his chest. Gripping his shirt in my fists, I rise on my tiptoes to whisper in his ear. "And later, when I was alone and I was thinking about you..." He inhales at my words. "It made me a little...wet." I flick my tongue against his earlobe.

He exhales raggedly, his hardness pressing against my stomach through his jeans.

I pull back to meet his eyes, seeing the fire in his gaze.

Crushing me into him, he kisses me deeply, his tongue sweeping into my mouth with surprising intensity as a low sound of pleasure rumbles from his throat. My breath catches when he reaches down between us and quickly undoes my jeans, plunging his hand inside my panties. He breaks the kiss, cursing softly, sliding his fingertips through the wetness pooled at my entrance.

"Fuck, Olena. Wet like this?"

His voice is a deep rumble that makes my core clench. I meet his eyes and nod, my breath shallow.

He exhales and slides two fingers into me as I cry out, gripping his shoulders. His sudden urgency takes me by surprise.

He pulls away. "Turn around," he rasps.

"Here?" I breathe, glancing around us, unsure. I look back at him.

"Here."

I slowly turn to face the workbench and Jude wrenches my jeans and panties down to my thighs. My eyes close at the sound of him unzipping his jeans and I flush with heat, anticipating his touch. When he lays his hard, hot length against the center of my ass, I inhale sharply.

"Feel how hard you make me?" he rasps.

"Yes," I breathe.

His hands dip under my shirt, my skin burning under his

heated touch. He pulls me back against him, pressing my back into his chest. His tongue flicks at the ridge of my ear and I shiver. Working his hands under the band of my bra, he squeezes my breasts and pinches my nipples hard, making me whimper from the wave of intense sensation that spreads to my core.

"Oh God," I moan when he crushes me harder into his body, pulling my hips back. His cock presses warm and eager against my ass and I tilt my hips back against him.

"You want this?" he asks, thrusting against my ass.

"Uh-huh," I breathe, nodding.

Jude's lips and teeth are on the back of my neck, one hand roughly sweeping my hair to the side to bare my skin as he kisses me there. I lean my head back under his chin, reaching up to his cheek as he traces his fingers down my stomach, dipping low, brushing over that aching place between my thighs. Circling them over my most sensitive spot, he slides his fingers inside me, pushing them against the place that makes me cry out.

I let out another groan of pleasure when he suddenly pushes me forward onto the bench, my elbows bracing against the cool, wooden surface. A brief chill fills the space between our bodies as he steps back, positioning himself, before the delicious warmth of his cock slides softly against my entrance. I moan and collapse slightly into my arms, the strength in my shoulders buckling at the wave of heat that pulses through me. Every fiber of my being is suddenly attuned to that place—the one place he's touching me.

I feel vulnerable under his gaze, knowing he's staring at me from behind with those intense green eyes, readying himself to plunge inside me at any moment.

"Oh, fuck, Olena..."

"What?" I breathe, turning to glance over my shoulder.

"I wish you could see how fucking perfect you look like this."

His hands slide slowly over my hips, gripping me in a moment of stillness.

Anticipation floods me and I close my eyes, bracing my hands on the workbench. I moan as he slowly, excruciatingly, pushes all the way inside me. A deep groan escapes his throat as he buries himself deep, then stops again, sliding his hand around to rub my aching clit.

"I want to watch you come," he rasps from behind me and I shudder, his fingers circling my clit as he withdraws his cock just as slowly as he entered. "And then I want to watch you do it again." He slams into me and I cry out. He quickly withdraws. "And again." Slam. "And again." Slam.

Oh my God.

My mind and body reel as he pumps inside me, swirling his fingers fast, almost growling with effort and pleasure. With each thrust, my release gets closer, surprising me with how quickly it's building—how ready I am for him.

I reach behind me, grasping at his hips, pulling him in hard, wanting him deeper inside me still.

He groans his approval and speeds up, pounding into me until it hurts in the most delicious way. I clench around him, tightening as the aching desperation builds.

The wave crests and my release wrecks me; the pleasure pulsates through my body, my cries and gasps uncontrolled as Jude pounds into me over and over with his long, slick cock. As I come down the other side, shuddering ragged breaths, he pulls out.

Grabbing my arm, he pulls me up and spins me around to face him, smiling with blazing heat in his eyes.

My lips are parted, my breaths heavy.

"We're not done here."

His rock-hard shaft gleaming between us, he slides his hands under the backs of my thighs and lifts me up, sitting me on the edge of the workbench. He pulls me into a rough kiss before yanking my jeans all the way off, taking my shoes and socks with them. When he spreads my legs open wide in front of him, he curses softly under his breath.

"God. Look at you," he says, his voice rough, then drags his fingers roughly up my soaking wet center.

He dips his fingers inside me, softly at first, then increasing the pressure. The firm, pulsing rhythm of his touch pulls jagged breaths into my lungs. My hips rock involuntarily and I grind into his hand, chasing the pleasure that's already building.

I wrap my fingers around his thick shaft, working him with long, firm strokes. A moan escapes from Jude's lips and he claims my mouth in another drugging kiss. Our hands work each other frantically, the exquisite tension building to an unbearable, heady peak. With his fingers pumping relentlessly, his thumb rubbing over my clit, I explode with pleasure as I come again, fast and hard, my voice ragged as I cry out. I stroke him harder.

"Shit, Olena," he rasps, leaning close, his breath against my cheek. "You're sexy as hell when you come."

His hips kick forward and my grip tightens. My eyes fly open when his hands grasp my hips, and he suddenly jerks me against him.

"Do it again for me." He plunges his hard length deep inside me once more. "Come all over my cock."

I moan and close my eyes again, lost in the pleasure. Senseless, I wrap my arms around his shoulders and hold on as he repeatedly thrusts into me, his lips crushing against mine, his tongue ravaging my mouth in a deep, primal kiss.

"Fuck!" I tear my mouth from his and cry out as I come again, another wave of intense, burning heat crashing over me. My muscles convulse and shudder around him.

I've barely caught my breath when he kisses me hard, then leans me back onto the workbench. Resting on my elbows, I draw my legs up on either side of him, the angle sending fresh waves of blissful sensation through me. He grasps at my breasts under my shirt, working my nipples. I reach down to touch myself. When I slip a finger inside myself next to his cock, pulling everything tighter, fire blazes in his eyes.

"Olena!" My name rips from his lips as his control starts to waver.

I clench around his hard length as he fucks me. Shifting my hand, I hold two fingers over my entrance, squeezing him there. He falls forward slightly, groaning against my raised knee. His eyes close as he loses his grip on control, crying out in a ragged growl as he starts to come. As he slams into me, I slip my fingers back to my clit, working it faster, tightening with everything I have left as another release builds.

He's still pounding into me relentlessly, riding the tail end of his orgasm as mine crashes over me, and I drench where our bodies meet, spilling over him hot and wet.

Aftershocks of pleasure still pulsing through my core, Jude shudders down over me. He lowers himself, bracing his elbows on either side of my body.

Collapsing onto my back, I let out a jagged breath then close my eyes as a grin spreads over my lips. I bring my hands up to cover my face, laughing a shaky, dark, and throaty laugh, my whole body senseless and twitching. I feel delirious.

"Oh, fuck," is all Jude can manage.

"Uh-huh," is all I can say in reply. I bring my hands down from my face and look at him, biting my lip. I wince slightly as he withdraws from me.

He lets out a low curse and shakes his head with a smirk. Sweat glistens on his forehead.

Our breathing is still ragged as we look at one another, slow smiles spreading over our faces, both of us completely shattered.

34

JUDE

Olena's gasping breath cuts through my exhausted haze and, for a moment, I think I'm dreaming. I open my eyes to the darkness, blinking in confusion as I take a beat to remember where I am. A dim light shines in on us from a lamp down the hallway, but it's enough that I can make out her silhouette sitting up in the bed beside me. Immediately on alert, I sit up beside her and rub her back. Worry churns in my stomach.

"Hey... hey, what's wrong?" I ask softly.

She's breathing hard and fast, shaking and hugging her knees to her chest with her eyes squeezed shut. She looks terrified.

I put my arms around her and she crumples into my chest, heavy sobs spilling out of her.

"It's okay, you're safe," I say quietly, smoothing her hair, touching her cheek. "You're safe. I've got you."

She shudders, quickly sliding her arms around my waist and squeezing hard like she's scared I'll let go.

"I've got you," I say again, hoping I can bring her back from this. "It was just a bad dream."

She squeezes me again, still breathing rapidly. I gingerly ease us back down on the bed. I hug her shoulders protectively, only letting go to pull the blanket up over us, tucking it snugly around her.

"Just a dream," I reassure her again. "I'm here." I rub my hands over her arms rhythmically, trying to soothe her as I wait for her breathing to slow down. Wet tears gather on my skin as she blinks against my chest, sniffling, and takes a long, deep breath.

"That's it," I say, "just breathe."

I hear Murphy get up from his dog bed near the door and walk over to her side of our bed and sit down, keeping watch. He's worried about her. He's not the only one.

Her voice is small when she finally speaks.

"I was dreaming about," she starts, then takes another deep breath to steady herself, "the robbery." Her arms tighten around me again, the memories clearly still too close to bear. "The guy had his hand over my mouth and I couldn't..."

My heart breaks for her. I take a deep breath. "Shhh," I whisper. "Hey, it's okay..." I smooth her hair away from her face again. "It's over now. It's all over." I twist to kiss her forehead, then pull her back into a tight hug.

My thumb grazes small circles on her shoulder as we lie there in the darkness.

"I've got you," I whisper into her hair.

Safe in my arms, her breathing slows. I stare up at the dark ceiling, an ache settling inside my chest.

OLENA IS QUIET AT WORK, contrasting the easy, flirtatious vibe we've had going lately. Her silence concerns me, especially after her nightmare last night. The tension I sense in her today feels worryingly different.

I work with Dimitri to spread loads of mulch over the new

garden beds and keep a cautious eye on her, silently begging her not to shut me out again.

A rare moment of privacy presents itself when the crew breaks for lunch and we find ourselves alone again in the sunken garden.

"Hey, you okay today?" I ask, taking off my gloves and walking over to hug her. She's standing next to the fire pit, where she's been quietly peeling the protective plastic coverings off the new bench cushions. I run my hands down her back, playing with the ends of her hair.

She puts her arms around me and squeezes, then pulls back to look up at me. "I'm fine. Don't worry about me, okay?" She stands on her tiptoes and kisses me on the cheek, then drifts back to her work.

Something isn't right. "Have you had nightmares like that before?" I ask, eyeing her.

"Jude, it's okay, honestly."

She gives me what looks like an attempt at a reassuring smile. I can tell she doesn't want to get into it.

"Okay," I say, narrowing my eyes slightly at her as I watch her work. I don't buy that this is no big deal. It seemed like a pretty big deal last night. *It felt like a big deal to me.* "I guess... just let me know if you wanna talk about it."

"I'm good. Really." She smiles bravely at me.

There's something she's not telling me.

35

OLENA

"These stairs are gonna be killer to walk back up." I turn to look up at Jude and squint in the bright light.

He tromps down the steep wooden steps close behind me, descending the stairs that zig-zag down the hillside near where his home is perched.

My hand slides along the wooden railing as I look out across the river. The day is overcast, but it's warmer than it's been in a while. Below us, the river burbles along the rocky shore. Birch and arbutus trees with peeling bark shoot up along the bank between the mix of boulders and smaller, smooth stones.

"You get used to it." He exhales the words with a smile as we descend at last to a small cement landing surrounded by rocks.

I step off and climb over them, balancing with my hands as I teeter on precarious footing. I grab the low branch of an arbutus and pivot to the next boulder. Jude clambers after me, following my lead.

"God, it's beautiful here. I didn't know this spot existed," I say, stopping to admire the view. The breeze loosens strands from my messy bun and they whip around my face and neck; with effort, I pull them away from my mouth with my fingers. I turn and grin at Jude, who squints back at me, a half-smile on his lips. "What?" I ask, seeing his amused expression.

"I was just remembering that day I saw you beside Lyons Park in Nat's car."

I roll my eyes and throw my head back, cringing. "No! Erase it! Erase it from your memory! That was so embarrassing; I could've crawled into a hole."

He laughs as my cheeks flush and I shake my arms, trying to shrug off the memory of how foolish I must have looked.

He moves toward me, pulling me into a tight hug. "Sorry to say, but that one's already burned into long-term memory," he says with a chuckle, pressing a kiss to my head.

I wrinkle my nose.

"Come on." He pulls away and offers his hand. He leads me over several more rocks and around a corner to a small floating dock. We sit down at the end, hanging our feet over the edge. The river laps at the posts not far below us. Jude puts his arm around me and squeezes my shoulder, kissing my cheek.

"I can't believe we're almost done with the Faulkner property," I say, twisting to look at him as I wrap my arms loosely around his waist.

"Yeah," he agrees with raised eyebrows, his gaze resting on the river in front of us. "It's gone by fast."

I pause. "What happens next?"

"What do you mean?" he asks.

"Like, are we supposed to just go on to other projects?"

"I think so, yeah," he chuckles, glancing at me with a hint of confusion. "Why? What did you imagine?"

"I don't know," I sigh, looking out across the river, watching as a few tiny white boats slowly float along with the current near the distant shore. "I mean…" I look down at my hands. "I like working with you." My eyes lift to meet his.

"I should hope so!" He arches an eyebrow at me and I smile.

"We've made a pretty good team, I think."

He smiles. "Yeah, Charles and Carol seem pretty happy so far."

I sigh. "I'm so glad. And I really needed this job. They did me a huge favor, hiring me."

"Agh, you're killing me with that," he says, pulling his arm away and shifting back a bit to look at me.

My arms drop from his waist. "What?"

"You never give yourself any credit." He looks exasperated. "They hired you because you're *good*. Full stop."

"I dunno," I say, shrugging. "They only hired me because they're Wyatt's aunt and uncle..."

I trail off as he pushes himself to a stand. "Where are you going?" I ask, my brow creasing. I twist around as he walks back to the other end of the small dock, toward the rocks.

He runs a hand over his beard and turns to me. "Repeat after me." He looks serious.

"What?" I shift my eyes with a nervous laugh.

"Repeat after me," he says impatiently, his voice louder.

I tilt my head, my expression flat. *Is he kidding me with this?*

"I am a *brilliant* and *capable* landscape designer." He looks at me expectantly, eyebrows raised.

I roll my eyes and turn back to the river.

"Olena!" he calls out.

I say nothing.

After a beat, his footsteps shake the dock behind me as he approaches. I turn to look up at him towering over me.

"Get up," he says.

Again, rolling my eyes, I reluctantly push up to standing, brushing the fly-away hairs away from my face.

"I am a brilliant and capable landscape designer," he repeats with total seriousness.

"Jude, this is silly." I frown as I look around us, checking for onlookers.

"Say it." He ducks his head to get in front of my face, making me look at him.

I roll my eyes again. "I am a brilliant and capable landscape designer," I mumble quietly, looking away from his intense gaze.

"Yes, you fucking are."

I look up, meeting his eyes, a small smile tugging at my mouth.

He smiles encouragingly at me. "Now say... I deserve to be successful and happy."

"Ugh, Jude..." I frown at him. I hate this.

"Say it!" He lifts his eyebrows, not backing off.

I blow out a breath. "I deserve to be successful and happy," I say quietly.

He backs up a few feet. "Louder for the people in the cheap seats!" He's grinning at me, gesturing for me to try again.

I chuckle, feeling ridiculous, although his enthusiasm is starting to work its magic.

I squeeze my eyes shut. "I deserve to be successful and happy!" I call out, then wrinkle my nose. The words feel so phony.

"Sorry! Still can't hear you!" Jude calls back to me, cupping his ear with one hand as he walks backward toward the far end of the dock.

I ball my hands into fists at my sides, narrowing my eyes at him, then take a deep breath. "I deserve to be successful and happy!" I shout loudly, throwing my head back, my voice bouncing off the rocky hillside. I laugh and cover my face with my hands.

Jude whoops from across the dock, cupping his hands over his mouth. He drops them to his sides and walks back to me with a grin, his eyes gleaming.

"Well, that was fucking painful," I say, laughing softly. I fall into his chest and wrap my arms around him.

His hands rub gently between my shoulder blades. "The truth hurts—or so I hear," he replies dryly, squeezing me.

I close my eyes as I nuzzle into him, still feeling like a cheeseball. "That was really corny, you know," I say against his chest.

The deep sound of his laugh rumbles against my ear. "I know. Brutal. But I had to take one for the team."

I smile to myself. *We do make a good team.*

My eyes widen as an idea occurs to me. "What are you doing tomorrow night?" I look up at him.

"After work?" He rubs my shoulders.

"Yeah."

"Uh... You?" He grins down at me with a devilish expression, chuckling.

I smack his ass hard and he flinches, still smiling. "No, come on, for real." I give him a rueful smile.

"Nothing planned. Why?" He's still smirking at me.

"Would you like to meet my parents?"

His expression gets more serious for a moment.

When he doesn't answer right away, I continue. "They have this big dinner every year on March 25th. We call it Marchmas." I look down. "It's silly, but we've been doing it since I was a kid. Wyatt and Sam and Nat and Graham all come and it's a lot of fun; I just thought if you wanted to come, too, it could—"

He lifts my chin with a finger. His kiss is soft and slow, his arms around my shoulders. Our lips part and he kisses the tip of my nose, wrapping his arms around me in a tight hug.

"Is that a yes or...?" I pull back, looking up at him with a hopeful expression.

"That's an absolutely, yes." He holds my face in his hands and kisses me again.

36

JUDE

I trim my beard in the bathroom mirror while Olena gets dressed in my room. I just got out of the shower, having taken extra care to wash off the work grime so I look presentable for her parents.

"So, where'd Marchmas come from, anyway? Christmas in March, right?" I call out to her over the buzzing sound of my clippers.

She appears in the doorway to my right wearing only a bra and thong, running a wide-toothed comb through her wet hair.

I shut off the clippers, taking in her beautiful figure in the mirror. My eyes linger on her breasts.

"Yeah, kind of. Winter is so cold and wet here, plus there aren't any good holidays this time of year. So we made one up. Well, I did," she explains, throwing her hair over one shoulder as she looks in the mirror. "It's sort of like a Christmas in July thing, but earlier. I came up with the idea when I was little and we just... kept doing it." She shrugs, putting down the comb. "It kind of turned into a whole thing."

I turn to her, unable to stop my eyes from roving over her

body. "You're going to..." I trail off, exhaling, then force myself to shake it off and meet her eyes. I clear my throat. "You're going to have to put some clothes on, or I'm not going to be able to hear a thing you say." I arch my eyebrow and tilt my chin at the door.

"Um, the same goes for you." She quirks an eyebrow at me, looking for a long moment at my bare chest. She catches herself and wags a finger at me, making a throaty noise and shaking her head like she's trying to shake off temptation.

I know the feeling.

She turns to leave and I smile, returning to look in the mirror. I'm about to start the clippers again when she reappears, wearing a short black dress.

Christ. My willpower is fading fast.

She turns her back to me and lifts her damp hair away from her neck. "Zip me up?"

I put the clippers down and shake my head ruefully. I slide my hands around her waist, dipping down to kiss her neck. "See, now you've got me touching you again. Very dangerous." I pull her between me and the sink, meeting her eyes in the mirror. She leans back against my chest and her eyelids flutter slightly as she sucks in a breath.

"We're going to be late," she chastises me gently, arching an eyebrow. With visible effort, she pulls away from my chest. My hands slide down to her hips. "Come on, zip me up." She leans forward slightly over the sink, eyeing me suggestively in the mirror.

I curse softly to myself. "You should know you are making this *very* difficult for me." I pull up the zipper, snugging the dress tight against her chest, then run a hand up the back of her thigh, under her skirt, as I watch her reflection.

She lets her hair fall, bracing both hands against the edge of the counter as she exhales.

I slide my fingers up between her legs, grazing the tip of my middle finger over that small triangle of fabric separating us, and hear her breath hitch. Her eyes close and she arches her back, lifting her hips. The feeling of her, warm and damp, through the fabric of her thong, almost has me taking her right then and there.

But I stop myself. I blow out a breath as I pull my hand away, finding willpower in some distant recess of my mind.

Her eyes open and she inhales, as if suddenly snapping back to the same reality.

I force myself to pick up the clippers again, shaking my head.

She turns, smiling, and kisses my cheek, making my breath catch. *She's so fucking tempting, but—no. Being late would make a shitty first impression.* She walks out of the room, slightly flushed, and I adjust myself in my jeans, heaving a deep sigh at my reflection.

Dear God, this woman does *things to me.*

"Jude, darling, you're so tall... Can you reach to attach this corner?" Lynn hands me a strand of twisted silver garland and gestures to one corner of the kitchen ceiling. "You'll save me from having to get the stepladder out." She smooths down her chin-length gray hair; the salt and pepper color still carries a hint of dark brown. My eyes shift between the two MacMillan women and I smile. Lynn looks like an older, shorter version of Olena.

"Sure, no problem," I say, easily reaching up to tack the decoration in place.

Olena watches from Lynn's side with a smirk, waiting to hand me a paper flamingo decoration next.

"Sorry we didn't get these up ahead of time, sweetheart," Lynn says to Olena. "I've been running around all day trying to get the food ready, and your dad lost track of time fixing the back fence all afternoon."

"Well, you've pulled it off, Lynn," I say. "The food smells amazing."

She waves a dismissive hand at the compliment. "Ah, it's nothing fancy."

"So, what's the deal with all the flamingos, anyway?" I ask, securing the pink paper bird to the corner of the ceiling where the garland ends.

"I know they're really kitschy," Olena explains, wrinkling her nose. "But when I was little, I went through this phase of being *obsessed* with flamingos. I can't remember which came first—Marchmas or the flamingos—but eventually they were just... part of the holiday." She shrugs. "Like a mascot, I guess."

"I think they're fun!" Lynn exclaims, smoothing her hands over the front of her novelty apron, on which a pair of flamingos pose with heads bent together in a heart shape.

Olena's father, David, opens the back door onto the patio and looks up at the sky, squinting at the fading evening light. "You know, I think it might rain on us," he says, stepping back into the kitchen and running a hand over his graying beard. "Jude, do you mind handing me the meat and veg there?" He gestures at the counter next to me.

I pass him the tray of skewered chicken and vegetables, then return to my decorating duties.

"Shoot, really?" Lynn asks. "Do you think we should cook them in the oven instead?" She places her hands on her hips and frowns, considering the options.

"Nah, Lynn. What kind of West Coast wimp would I be to shy away from a little sprinkle?" David grins proudly. "The show must go on!" He winks at his wife and heads outside to the barbecue.

This is nice. I've missed the organized chaos of family get-togethers. It feels good to help out—and to be included. And I'm definitely not complaining about getting a home-cooked meal that I don't have to prepare myself.

Standing near the kitchen sink, Olena untangles another strand of garland and rolls her eyes at her father. "Dad takes his barbecue duties very seriously," she explains quietly, handing it to me to hang up.

I chuckle to myself, remembering that my dad was the same way. I bet Dad would have gotten along with David. *Damn, I miss him.*

"They'll taste better barbecued anyway," Wyatt chimes in from the stove, where he's whisking a sauce in a small pan. He fell right into step with Olena's parents the moment he'd arrived, joining them in the kitchen to get the food ready.

I tack up another flamingo, then move to Olena's side and jerk my head toward the door. "So, does the rain thing run in the family or...?" I ask under my breath so only she can hear me. I quirk an eyebrow at her as I reach for another flamingo from the counter beside her.

"Jude!" She gives me a gentle swat on the arm, and I recoil with a quiet laugh.

"Is there anything else I can help with?" I offer, turning to Lynn as I tack up the last of the decorations.

"Not at all, darling!" she replies with a kind smile. "Just relax and enjoy."

"You sure? Because I can chop a mean potato, and I'm not afraid to do it." I rub my hands together and she laughs.

"Oh? Well, I'm glad to hear that," Lynn says, her eyebrows rising above the frames of her dark-rimmed glasses. "Someone's got to feed this girl." She gestures with a serving spoon in Olena's direction.

"Mom!" Olena laughs and flushes slightly.

I smile and reach for my beer on the counter behind her, then lean against the sink, my arm brushing against hers.

The evening has been going smoothly so far. Being here with Olena's parents is soothing in a way I didn't know I needed. I've missed this—feeling like part of a family. The only slightly awkward moment was seeing Wyatt again after our encounter at the deli. After a stoic handshake, he now seems to have settled into a cautiously optimistic opinion of me. I'll take it.

My eyes drift to the dining room where Natalie and her boyfriend, Graham, are sitting at the table drinking wine with Wyatt's boyfriend, Sam. The couple evidently just arrived back from a week in Portland. They look both rested and tired, somehow. They show Sam their vacation photos on Nat's phone, laughing.

Graham squeezes Nat's shoulder as he gets up and walks into the kitchen to grab a beer from the fridge.

"I'm glad you could make it, Graham." Lynn pauses as she removes a stack of plates from the cupboard to raise her eyebrows at him. "I guess that office of yours finally let you escape?"

"Hey, Lynn, I haven't given you a proper hug yet," he says to her warmly as he closes the fridge, beer in hand. Graham crosses the kitchen to slip an arm around Lynn's shoulders. She pats his hand and looks up at him, smiling; he's probably half a foot taller than she is, with red hair and freckles.

"Graham works too much," Lynn explains to me and then ducks away to continue setting the table.

"What do you do for work?" I ask him.

"I'm an accountant."

"He works at that big property management company in town," Olena explains.

"Sitka Properties, yeah," he says, popping the lid off his beer with a bottle opener. "We just got this big contract with a new developer and we've been slammed lately."

I nod.

David pokes his head in from the patio and asks Lynn for his raincoat, which she retrieves for him from the front hall.

Watching him zip it up, I can see raindrops have already collected on his glasses.

"How's the big landscaping project going?" Graham asks. "Up on Dogwood, right?" He takes a sip of his beer. "Nat told me a bit about it. Sounds like quite the place."

"Yeah, we're almost finished, actually," I say. "And it's looking great. Olena's design was perfect for the property." I extend a finger from around the beer bottle and brush it against her upper arm, smiling down at her.

"Well, it's been a team effort," Olena hedges, blushing slightly.

I give her a look.

She straightens. "I mean... thank you."

I smile and pull her in to kiss her cheek. *That's right.*

Despite the rain, the food is soon declared ready and we all move to the dining room to eat. Alongside the barbecued skewers, there's a bowl of steaming rice, an enormous green salad, roasted potatoes, spicy garlic green beans, fried mushrooms, and fresh bread rolls.

"Everything looks so good," Olena says. "Thanks for having us, Mom and Dad."

Murmurs from around the table confirm everyone agrees.

"Oh my goodness," Lynn says. "Our pleasure. We're just so glad you're back from Seattle, Olena." She takes a sip of her wine.

Olena gives a small smile at the mention of Seattle.

"Yes, honey, we are so happy to have you home safe and sound," David adds, reaching for the potatoes. "Marchmas wouldn't be the same without you."

"Thanks, Dad," she replies quietly, her eyes lingering on her plate as she sets down a chicken skewer. Knowing what happened to her before she left, I'm inclined to agree with her parents, but I can't help but notice she looks uncomfortable. I put a hand on her thigh under the table, hoping to reassure her.

She gives me a quick, brave smile, then reaches for the salad.

"I tell you, I never liked that Sean," David goes on, oblivious to her reaction. He drops a spoonful of mushrooms over the small pile of rice on his plate.

"Dad." Olena gives him a wide-eyed stare.

Nat pauses as she puts down the bowl of green beans. She shifts uncomfortably in her seat, smiling at the others. The silence hangs.

Wyatt's eyes are wide, his fork hovering midair. He gives Sam a loaded look.

David continues, apparently picking up on the pregnant pause. "What? It's true! There was always something a bit *off* about him. So I'm glad he's out of your life now. Onto better times, I say." He pries open a bread roll to butter it.

"David." Lynn gives him a serious look. He misses it.

"Best to cut those ties, I think. Start fresh." David smiles, oblivious to the reaction of his daughter and, increasingly, everyone else. He looks at Olena, finally noticing her unease at what he's said. "What, you're not still in touch with him, are you?"

"No, Dad, of course not!" Olena looks bewildered at being put on the spot.

Nat makes a face at Olena that I can't discern. I frown slightly, not sure what's happening.

"These rolls are amazing. Have you tried them?" Wyatt's sudden change of topic is jarring, but we all turn our gaze to him. He chews, wide-eyed, and holds out the basket of buns.

I pull my hand away from Olena's leg and nod politely at Wyatt, taking one.

37

OLENA

My phone rings late Tuesday afternoon as Teddy waves goodbye from his truck on his way home. I wave back distractedly and peer down at my phone screen. It's hard to see in the bright daylight, but I have a sinking feeling I know who's calling. I finally manage to shade the screen to see the call display. My stomach sinks.

Not again. Not now.

Jude is packing up his truck so, before I answer, I quickly motion to him that I'm going inside the house to take the call.

He nods.

Closing the door behind me, I accept the call, taking a deep breath. "Hello?"

"Who the fuck do you think you are, anyway?" Sean's voice is rough and unsteady.

Shit.

"Sean, I need you to leave me alone."

"Oh, you need me to leave you alone? Like you're the only person in this relationship? The one who gets to call the shots?"

His voice cracks, his words stumbling out unnaturally. He sounds unstable.

Worry prickles across the back of my neck. "I've told you a million times, there *is* no relationship! It's over! Get it through your head!" I'm losing my patience. He can't keep calling me like this. He can't keep intruding on my life. I look over my shoulder, making sure the door is closed.

"Fuck that, Olena. Fuck that. This isn't over. If you won't listen to me, I'll..." He trails off.

"You'll what, Sean? You'll *what?*" I'm fuming with anger. I just want to move on. I'm trying to be happy here. With my friends. With Jude. "Look... I'm seeing someone now. Just leave me alone."

The silence is heavy on the line. My heart races with instant regret. *Shit. I shouldn't have said that.*

His voice is scarily quiet when he speaks. "What did you just say?"

I falter a moment, but there's no turning back now. I take a deep breath. "I said... I'm seeing someone."

"Fuck you. No, you're not."

"Yes, I am. You need to understand I'm not coming back, Sean. Stop calling me."

"Who is he?" He sounds worryingly calm.

"That's none of your—"

"*Who is he, Olena?*" He's shouting at me now.

My hands are shaking. "Look, I'm not—" My voice shakes now too.

"Fuck this. I'm coming to see you. I need to talk some sense into you. I'll make you understand that you can't do this."

The line goes dead. I've made a horrible mistake. I squeeze my eyes shut, trying to steady my breathing.

I walk slowly to the bathroom and splash some cold water on my face. My cheeks are flushed, but I take several deep breaths to regain some composure before returning outside.

As I step out the door, I avoid Jude's eyes for a moment, focusing instead on the equipment left to load into the truck. When I finally meet his gaze, he looks concerned.

"You okay? What was that about?" he asks, tilting his chin at the house. He walks over and rubs my shoulders, giving me a kiss on the forehead.

"Oh, nothing," I lie and force a smile. I hate myself for it, but I can't tell him. The thought of him knowing about how I'd let myself get into this situation with Sean... The shame of it chokes me, trapping the words in my throat.

"You sure?" His brow creases, searching my expression.

"Yes, totally fine. Let's finish packing up." I move to lift a few buckets and bags into the truck for him. Murphy wanders over and I give him a scratch on the head, grateful to have the distraction—and an excuse to avoid Jude's attention. I take my time giving the dog extra love, focusing on breathing like a calm person.

"Do you want me to stay again tonight?" he asks carefully. "Last night in the big house." He flicks his eyes to the windows on the upper floor, raising an eyebrow at me.

I turn to look at him and smile. *Yes, please. Always.* It's not a hard question to answer.

He lifts a wheelbarrow into the bed of the truck, then wipes his brow with the back of his gloved hand.

"I want you to stay every night."

The corner of his mouth tugs up in a soft smile. "Deal."

38

OLENA

*S*ean's terrified eyes bore into mine from across the room, the man's knife pressed against his throat. I struggle against the other man's hand over my mouth, desperately trying to breathe. Or scream. I can't do either. My hands scratch at his forearms and my feet slide uselessly against the cold floor. He's so much stronger than I am; I can feel his breath on my face.

"Where's our money, asshole?" the guy holding onto Sean spits in anger, pressing the knife deeper into Sean's skin. Sean is barely breathing, petrified.

"Did you think we wouldn't find you?" the guy holding me shouts, his voice booming in my ear, echoing as I struggle to get free. "Did you think we wouldn't fucking find you?"

I'm thrashing against Jude's arms when his voice cuts through the terror and reaches me at last.

"Olena!" he pleads with me, trying to catch my flailing limbs. "Olena!"

My last couple of swings soften when I finally realize where I am. The tension leaves my arms and I crumple forward. He scoops me into his chest as I heave racking sobs of fear, of relief, of exhaustion.

"Shh, you're okay, it's me. I'm here. I'm here." He whispers the soothing words against my sweat-slicked hair.

My face feels both hot and cold and the damp sheets tangle my legs, restraining me. I kick them away in a panic, the restriction on my movements intolerable, then retreat once again into the safety of his arms. I gulp breaths of air against his bare chest, my own chest heaving as my pulse hammers hard.

"Just breathe," he reminds me.

I try. My breaths are ragged but slowing. I squeeze my arms around him.

"I'm—" I try to speak, but my voice is hoarse. "I'm sorry." Hot tears spill over my cheeks.

"Don't be sorry," he says. He rubs my back and holds me until I can breathe more steadily.

I glance at the clock and see it's just after five in the morning. I doubt we'll get back to sleep.

Jude follows my gaze, seeing the time too. He brushes my damp hair out of my face and kisses me gently. "I'm gonna make us some coffee, okay?"

I can only nod. I curl up in the fetal position on the bed while he's gone and try to forget about the nightmare—and about Sean's threat to come to Lennox. He can't show up here. He can't.

Realizing I'm shivering, I pull the blanket over me. *What am I going to do?*

Jude eventually comes back with coffee and sets the mug on the nightstand. I sit up slowly as he pulls on his jeans. He sits down on the bed next to me.

"That was a smart move," I manage to joke through my tears, raising an eyebrow at him as I glance down at his pants.

He smiles softly. "Can't have you distracted." He pauses, handing me the coffee. "You gonna tell me what's going on?"

My brow furrows and I look away.

"Olena." He gently pulls my face to his. "Look, I know something's up. This isn't normal. The nightmares..." He trails off.

I take a deep breath and look at him, tears falling again as I consider what I'm about to tell him. "Okay." I try to blink away the tears. "You're right."

"Okay," he says, a flicker of concern settling over his features. He watches me closely.

I put the coffee down again and wipe at my eyes, hugging my knees to my chest. "Sean has been texting me. And calling me, more recently." I hesitate a moment before meeting his eyes.

He straightens and I see his jaw clench in the dim light. He doesn't speak.

"He's... I think he's high sometimes when he calls. He thinks he can convince me to go back to Seattle. To get back together with him. I keep telling him no, but he..." I turn my head and breathe out a long, shaky breath. I don't know how to explain the way Sean's been acting—the way he's been scaring me.

Jude looks at the floor, then back to me. "How long has this been happening?" he asks quietly.

"I don't know, a few weeks? It's not like it's been all the time—"

"He's been harassing you this entire time?" He stands, rubbing a hand down his face. "The entire time we've been... the entire time since I met you," he says, gesturing between us, "this guy's been bothering you? And you didn't say anything?" A deep crease forms in his brow.

"Jude, I just... I kept thinking he'd stop, that he'd finally hear me saying no." My shoulders drop at the obvious futility of wishing Sean away.

A pause. "Did he say anything else?"

I grimace. I can't look at him.

Jude scoffs. "Is there more? What else, Olena?" His intense gaze bores into me.

My eyes meet his, pleading. "Look, please don't be mad."

He folds his arms over his chest, waiting, and I take a breath.

"Yesterday, when I came inside to take that call, that was him." My voice is quiet, the shame that I'd lied eating me up.

He raises his eyebrows and a muscle ticks in his jaw.

"He... he got really angry." I look down at my hands, grimacing. "And loud. And he said he was going to come see me, and talk sense into me... make me understand." I can barely get the words out through uneven breaths.

Jude backs up a pace from the bed. He lets loose a breath and rakes a hand roughly through his hair. He's silent for a moment, pressing his lips together. When he speaks, his deep voice is calm. "Why didn't you tell me?"

I exhale hard. "I don't know. I was scared... I just want him to go away, and I didn't know how to make him stop." My eyes widen, looking down at the bed. "I tried blocking him every way I could think of, but he just keeps..." I let my forehead rest on my knees as fresh tears spill out.

"So, let me get this straight, you've got some dirtbag ex harassing you and *fucking threatening you*? And you didn't think you could share that with me?" Jude gestures toward his chest, his disappointment palpable. "And when your dad asked the other night... you just lied to him?"

I look up at him, pleading. "I don't want them to worry about me. I don't want *you* to worry about me." I push my fingers into my hair, letting my head fall into my hands.

"Olena..." Jude paces in front of me. "Don't you realize there are people in your life who want to worry about you? Who care about you? Who—" He cuts himself off, shaking his head with a grim look.

I lift my head at his words. "I thought I could handle it, that I could make him understand."

"So, you were hoping, what, that this guy just wouldn't show up here?" he asks, shaking his head in disbelief.

"I didn't think he would ever hurt me." *Am I that naïve?*

"But he's all fucked up on drugs now and scaring you? Have I got that right?" He raises his eyebrows in an exhausted kind of frustration.

"Yes, but—"

"Olena," he starts, his shoulders pulling up, "I don't know what this guy is capable of. But this doesn't sound good." He rubs a hand down over his beard.

"Look, I didn't know what to do, okay? I still don't know what to do. What can I do?" I feel desperate.

He drops his shoulders, throwing his hands out at his sides. "You could've told me! I can help you. Protect you."

I can tell he's hurt that I didn't trust him with this. But I didn't want to make my baggage his problem. "That's not fair to ask of you. You're not my bodyguard, Jude." I hold his gaze, my vision blurring.

He levels me with a look, his voice low and even. "So, what am I to you?"

I can't answer. *How can I find the words to tell him what he means to me?* I let my eyes drop away from his. When I look back up at him, I see the flicker of pain in his expression.

"What is this, Olena? Is this just sex?" His expression is raw with emotion.

"No! That's not what I'm saying..." Tears spill over. I can see in his eyes that he doesn't understand, but I can't find the words to fix this.

"What *are* you saying, then? Do you even know?" His words sting and I wince. His voice is distant now. "Sounds like you need some time to think, after all."

My heart feels like it's been hit by a freight train when he turns away from me, grabs his things, and walks out.

I hear Jude call Murphy's name, followed moments later by the sound of the front door shutting firmly behind him.

39

JUDE

I've chopped all the wood I have, I've worked out hard, and I'm still crawling out of my skin two hours after leaving Olena. I can't believe she didn't tell me about her ex-boyfriend threatening her. Dishonesty gets deep under my skin. The years of managing Miles as he tried to hide his drinking have burned me, and I can't handle someone who isn't honest. It never occurred to me that Olena would lie to me.

Cool your jets, man. This is more about Miles, I realize, and that's not fair to put on her. We've only known each other a few weeks, after all. But still. She pushed me away. Again.

I feel sick. I thought we were...

I don't know what I thought we were. But it wasn't this.

I shower and get ready for work in a daze. I barely eat breakfast; my appetite is non-existent, replaced by a nausea I can't shake. Murphy watches me closely as I dump my untouched food into the trash. He can sense something isn't right.

Buried under my disappointment and hurt is worry. What if this unhinged asshole does something dangerous? What if he shows up in Lennox and tracks her down? What is he capable of? Would he hurt her?

She's made it clear she doesn't want my help protecting her. *You're not my bodyguard, Jude.* The sentence echoes in my head.

How can she not see how I feel about her? That I want to care for her and keep her safe?

Because you haven't told her.

I sit down heavily on the couch and rub my hands over my face. I don't even know how she feels about me. Everything's happened so quickly between us. We've never even talked about what we wanted from each other. Maybe she'd never intended for this to be anything more than a bit of fun.

The sex *has* been incredible. Mind-blowing. *Is that all she wants?*

The thought makes me feel ill. I swear I sense in her that it's so much more than that... I can feel it in how she looks at me. She even took me to meet her parents.

So why didn't she tell me about Sean?

Fucking Sean. I don't even know this guy and I want to punch his face in. How could anyone scare Olena? Threaten Olena? Anger simmers and nearly boils over at the thought of anyone hurting her. The impulse to get into my truck and run back to her—to be there to protect her—is intense, but I shut it down. She doesn't want me to rescue her.

Unable to sit still any longer, I head outside with Murphy and lock up.

Settling us into the truck, I buckle my seatbelt and a small, petty part of my brain reminds me none of this would have happened if Olena and I had managed not to get involved in the first place. *See? You put your heart on the line again, and this is what you get.* I blow out a long breath. This is exactly the kind of compli- cated mess I was hoping to avoid. But this thing with Olena... I shake my head and look up at the sky through the dirt-dusted windshield. I must have been fucking kidding myself for thinking there had ever been a hope in hell of us keeping things professional.

My mind circles around from worry to anger and back again until I can't put off going to work any longer and I reluctantly start the truck. Knowing I will have to face her at the job-site pulls at me, twisting my stomach into a tight knot.

I drive there in a fog, pulling in only to see that her car—for the first time in a week—isn't parked in the driveway. I look at the house. Murphy's dog bed sits neatly at one corner of the porch.

An emptiness I wasn't expecting descends over me. *Where is she?*

40

OLENA

My hand slips on the rocks and my elbow scrapes against the rough boulder as I jerk down, almost losing my grip.

"Ow, shit," I mutter under my breath as the pain from my elbow reaches my awareness. I shift my weight so I can shake out my hand. *Maybe rock climbing today wasn't the best idea.* I dig my toes in and try again, the fingers of my other hand white with the strain of holding on. My arms feel weak. I'm not doing great up here.

Nat calls up from the ground, tightening up the slack in the top rope. "You good, Len?"

The late afternoon sun shines on my back, but there's not much warmth to it at this hour. I managed to convince Nat to blow off work a bit early so we could climb together. I needed to get out of my head and out of the house after spending most of the day shut in my bedroom. I'd cried a good long while before it slowly dawned on me that beating myself up wasn't making any sense. I realized with painful clarity that this isn't just me messing everything up. The problem isn't *me*. No, the real problem here... is Sean.

Sure, I should have told Jude what was going on sooner, but was I that unreasonable for expecting Sean to leave me alone? My relationship with Jude is—or *was*—still pretty new, even if it had been toe-curlingly intense in that short time. Sean had started contacting me before I'd even met Jude, after all.

Realizing Sean has wrecked my life yet again fills me with nothing but cold, festering resentment. I can't believe he weaseled himself between me and Jude like this. I can't believe he's had the nerve to harass and threaten me, and to get into my head in a way that's ruined something that could have been beautiful with Jude.

I still haven't told Nat everything because I'm worried I'll fall apart if I try to voice how I'm feeling. I want to punch something. Or someone.

Heaving myself at last to the top of the climbing route, I exhale harshly. I feel like I've been hit by a bus. My arms are shaking and my legs are heavy with exhaustion. Nat tightens the rope again.

I call down to make sure Nat is ready for me, then push off the edge, repelling off the rocks as she belays me back down.

"Hey, are you sure you're up for this?" she asks as I land on the ground beside her. She glances at me as she unclips the belay device from her harness. "You looked a bit shaky."

"That's because I am *a bit fucking shaky*," I grouse at her, clenching my fists.

She raises her eyebrows at me.

I sigh. "Sorry, I've been up since five," I explain, softening my tone. "And that was just the beginning," I add, shaking my head, getting irritated all over again. "Then Jude walked out on me and I blew off work like an asshole." Seeing her eyes widen with caution, I apologize again, scowling. "I'm all over the place, sorry. I'm just pissed."

"You still haven't told me what happened with Jude. And, I

don't know if you've noticed, I've been patiently waiting for the story." Nat raises her eyebrows at me, the unspoken *out with it* painted on her face.

"Ugh, fine." I untie my rope and drop the end, letting it dangle from the anchor point above us. "I had another nightmare this morning."

"That explains the five am thing, okay..." Nat narrows her eyes in partial understanding.

"And Jude was with me and..." I look away from her, feeling the tears threatening again. I take a deep breath, feeling sick of my own shit. I refuse to keep blubbering pathetically at every turn. Again, the anger at Sean rises in my throat. I fight it down, struggling for composure.

"It's okay. Take your time." She reaches out and rubs my shoulder.

"I told him about Sean contacting me," I say finally, looking back at her.

"Yeah. Okay, so... wait, Sean texted you a while back, right? Am I missing something? Why did Jude walk out?"

I wrinkle my nose, cringing. Nat doesn't know about the phone calls. "There's been more than that one text," I confess, frowning.

"What the *fuck*?" Nat's incredulous voice comes out loudly.

I tell her about Sean's angry phone calls—and his threat yesterday. I relay Jude's reaction when he'd found out: how he'd left early this morning, how I'd cleaned up the Faulkners' place alone, how I'd poured the coffee he had made me down the sink in tears. How I'd dropped Carol and Charles' keys in the mailbox before driving home, gutted and afraid. And, finally, about how I'd realized the obvious: that Sean had caused all of this.

"Oof. Okay." Nat rubs her forehead, frowning. "This isn't good."

"Of course this isn't good!" I throw up my hands, feeling helpless. "What can I do? How do I deal with Sean? He's not in his right mind. I don't even know what drugs he's using." I drag both hands over my hair, blowing out a breath.

"I mean... I think we need to go to the police. He threatened you," she says carefully.

"I don't know if the police will take this seriously. He said he was going to come see me. Does that count as a threat?" I hug my arms tightly around my waist. "I feel sick thinking about him showing up here but... I don't think that's an actual threat. Legally, I mean."

"Yeah, good point. Shit." Nat puts her hands on her hips, looking at the ground and frowning.

"So, like, what can I do? He doesn't know where I live... or where I work, which is good. But beyond that?"

We stand there in silence.

"I hate this," Nat says.

"Yeah, me too." I rub at my forehead, my brows knit with tension.

Nat looks up at the climbing rope for a moment, then back at me. "Okay. You promise me if he contacts you again... or if anything else happens with Sean, you'll tell me right away?" She raises her eyebrows, searching for confirmation that I won't hide anything more from her. "And, if he makes a tangible threat, we'll get you a restraining order or something."

I relent. "Okay, yes, I promise. I'm sorry. I know I should've told you." I shrug. "But, like I said to Jude, I was just hoping each time was the last time. That's not delusional, right? Or naïve? A reasonable person would listen to the word *no*, right?"

"No, you were not delusional or naïve." Nat gives me a serious look. "There's no manual for this stuff, Len." Hearing her confirm that gives me a sense of relief. I look up at the sky and take another deep breath.

I look back at her, shaking my head. "I'm so pissed."

"You have every right to be," she replies simply.

"Because what I had with Jude…" I try to keep my voice steady. "You should've seen his face, Nat. I don't know if he'll ever forgive me."

"Hey, look. You're a human being. You're allowed to make mistakes. And you're allowed to be going through some complicated shit, remember?" She raises her eyebrows at me.

I nod, looking at my feet.

"If Jude truly cares about you… if he's your person? He'll find a way to understand where you're coming from."

I give her a dubious look. The memory of Jude's pained expression this morning haunts me.

"But Len," Nat adds gently, "Jude isn't wrong."

I frown. "What?"

"You should have told him. Just like you should have told *me*." Nat pauses. "Sean's a fucking asshole, don't get me wrong, but he's not the only reason Jude walked out. Getting threatened… That's a pretty high-stakes thing to keep from someone. Shit, I'm a bit pissed at you too!" She gives me a pointed look.

I squeeze my eyes shut. "I know." She's right; I've fucked up too. "I'm sorry I didn't tell you. And Jude." *Probably something to unpack with that therapist…*

"Look, there's no shame in asking for help. And you have to tell your people when scary shit happens to you." She gives me a little shrug. "That's what we're here for."

"I'm sorry, okay?" *I hate this. It was easier when I could just blame Sean for everything.*

"Hey, I forgive you. Just doing my bullshit-calling duty." She pauses, rolling her eyes. "Again," she adds with a cheeky smile.

I narrow my eyes at her. "You're annoyingly good at it."

"You're welcome," she says, smiling with her eyebrows raised.

"Thank you." I roll my eyes.

"That's more like it." She gathers me in for a tight hug, then pulls back, reaching for the climbing rope. "Okay, my turn."

41

OLENA

S ettling onto the couch at home with my laptop, I open my email and attempt to get caught up. The window above me is open, letting in a cool breeze. It's been warm again and the fresh air feels nice. *Not much else feels nice right now.* I take a breath and try to be present, noticing how the air feels on my neck.

When welcoming Charles and Carol home from Seattle earlier today, I told them I had some administrative things to do and would be heading home early so I could focus here. The truth is, I couldn't stomach staying any longer than necessary with Jude nearby, even with both of us dodging each other; the change in his body language around me was too painful. As I got into my car, I couldn't help but feel his eyes on me. But, when I turned to meet his gaze, he looked away.

I start to sort through invoices from the nursery when the sounds of angry shouting suddenly drift in from outside. My fingers freeze over the keyboard, hovering in midair as I listen. I hastily set down my laptop when I hear more shouts and I recognize Wyatt's voice. Scrambling up on the couch to see if I can get a better look, I crane my neck to see the front entrance of our building. I can just make out Wyatt standing in his work clothes, gesturing angrily at...

Oh, shit. A wave of nausea churns in my stomach. *He actually showed up.* How did Sean find out where we lived? I pause another moment, feeling a mixture of panic and anger before realizing I need to go down there. This is my life and my mess; I can't leave Wyatt—or Jude or anyone else—to fight this battle alone for me. My heart races as I jam my feet into my shoes and snatch up my coat. I run down the two flights of stairs to the main floor, pushing out the door that leads to the lobby. Sean spots me as I shove open the glass door at the main entrance.

"Olena, baby..." Sean says, looking relieved to see me.

I'm anything but relieved to see him.

"Olena, don't come out here. I'm handling this," Wyatt says, holding a hand out in front of me. "You should stay inside."

"No, Wyatt, you shouldn't need to deal with him," I say, though I'm grateful he's here and willing to stand up for me.

"Deal with me?" Sean throws his arms out at his sides, his shoulders pulled up. "What the fuck, Olena? I'm just here to talk to you. Don't be so dramatic." He shoves his hands in his jacket pockets, looking away.

I monitor his movements carefully, looking for signs that he might be high.

Wyatt cuts in. "What's fucking *dramatic*, Sean, is you showing up here after Olena specifically, and repeatedly, told you it was over." His wide eyes are filled with resentment. He's pissed.

"Wyatt, I've got this." My voice is firm and I put my hand on his arm. "Go back inside." I flick my eyes to the door.

"I'm not leaving you with this prick!" Wyatt says, frowning as he lifts his chin at Sean.

Sean pulls his head back, recoiling. "Who are you calling a prick, Wyatt? Jesus Christ..." He shakes his head.

"*Wyatt*," I say again, my eyes wide. "I can handle this. I'm okay for now." I tilt my head toward the door. "I'd tell you if I wasn't, I promise."

"Okay, fine, but I'm waiting in the lobby for you." Wyatt looks at me with wide eyes.

Then he narrows his eyes at Sean once more, shaking his head. He flicks his gaze to me, pointing at Sean. "You know this asshole actually went online to find out where I worked and then fucking followed me home to find you?"

I whirl to face Sean, wide-eyed, my arms out at my sides. "What the hell, Sean? What the fuck is wrong with you?" This violation reignites the anger that's been smoldering in me since yesterday. I pin him with a look of disgust.

Wyatt shakes his head again and turns away. "You're a fucking piece of shit, Sean."

I glance over my shoulder as he opens the main entrance door and steps inside the lobby.

Sean steps toward me and I quickly take a step back. He lets out a breath, looking frustrated. "Baby, I had to find out where you were. You said you were gonna stay with Wyatt when you came back here, so... Listen, I had to find you!" He reaches out his hand, pleading with me.

I frown, repulsed.

He looks unwell. He has dark circles under his eyes. His hair is shaved in an unflattering buzz cut, shorter than how he used to wear it. The old brown leather jacket and jeans he's wearing look a size too big for him and hang off his frame. He's lost weight. While he doesn't appear to be high currently, he must still be using regularly. I'd feel sad for him if I wasn't so angry.

"No, you did *not* have to find me. I told you *not* to contact me," I shout at Sean, swiping both hands across the space between us to emphasize the point. "I don't want anything to do with you!"

He scoffs and rolls his eyes.

"You need to turn around and go home. Stay out of my fucking life."

"I can't, baby." He shrugs. "I need you to see that I can get clean. I can be better." He straightens. "Look, I'm not high right now. I can do it. Just take me back. I'll be good. Fuck... I miss you so much." He tries to approach me with his arms outstretched and I recoil, holding my palms out in front of me. He stops, looking hurt.

"I can't believe you did this," I say to him, seething. I hope he can see the hatred in my eyes. "Such a gross move. You know this makes me feel *more* unsafe about you, right?"

"Unsafe? What've I done that's unsafe?" He looks genuinely confused.

I let loose an exasperated breath. I hate him. "*Um,* harassing me when I kept begging you to stop, for one. Stalking me? Stalking Wyatt to find me?" My brow knits together in a deep glare, my jaw hanging open at his willful ignorance. I'm baffled that I even have to explain this.

"Stalking? Are you kidding me?" He scoffs as he looks away, wiping a hand down his jaw.

I widen my eyes to show I am deadly serious. "What the fuck did you think this would accomplish?" I can't believe he's got his head so far up his own ass that he doesn't get it.

"What other choice did I have?" He throws his arms out at his sides. "You wouldn't fucking listen to me!"

"Because the answer is fucking *no,* Sean. It's *you* who isn't listening."

He puts his hands on his hips and turns to pace the entryway, shaking his head.

"I told you I was with someone else, anyway." I neglect to mention this drama with Sean has put an end to that.

"Don't." He stops in his tracks, lifting his chin like I've hurt his pride.

I don't care.

"What do you mean, '*don't*'? How else can I make you see it's over?" I throw my arms out at my sides in frustration. "Why can't you just accept that I've moved on?" My voice is getting louder as my anger takes over.

"No, you haven't." He smiles ruefully and shakes his head. "I don't believe you. There's no other guy."

"Yes, there is. And he's *incredible*. And he would *never* treat me like this." There's fire in my eyes as I needle him with the comparison.

"Fuck!" Sean shouts, grabbing his head with both hands, like he can't bear to imagine me with anyone else.

I'm beyond caring about his feelings. I will hit him where it hurts if I have to. "You need to leave." I point at the road.

People on the sidewalk nearby are stopping to watch us. Some are whispering.

"Why would you do this?" Sean asks with a sneer.

"We're done, we've *been done*, and even if we hadn't? You'd have put a nail in that fucking coffin with this shit, Sean." I cup my hands around my mouth. "Go home," I say, projecting my voice in a loud monotone as if that'll help get the message through.

"You can't do this to me." When I don't respond, he gets louder. "I said you can't fucking do this to me!"

I flinch as his face comes closer to mine, his eyes bulging in anger in a way I've never seen. I don't recognize the man I used to live with.

Wyatt opens the door behind me. "Sean! Fuck off! Leave her alone!"

Glancing at Wyatt, Sean breathes hard in his rage. He looks back at me once more, stepping closer still, his jaw clenching as he reins himself in. He keeps his voice low, seething with righteous anger. "I won't let you leave me. I'm gonna fucking *make* you see we belong together. You"—he places a fingertip on my sternum and I flinch—"belong to *me* and no one else."

I quickly swat his hand away as Wyatt comes up beside me.

Sean glances at him, then turns and stalks out of the entryway.

The gathered onlookers move aside to give him a wide berth as he turns down the sidewalk, disappearing from view.

My hands are shaking. Wyatt touches my shoulder. I turn to him and he searches my eyes. He sees the tears welling up and moves to give me a hug.

"No." I back up a step as I brush him off. "I don't want a hug. I don't want to cry anymore." Balling my hands into fists at my sides, I pace in the entryway in front of him. "I'm sick of this bullshit."

Wyatt watches me with an empathetic crease in his brow.

I stop, turning back to him, my anger burning. "I'm sick of being afraid all the time!" A tear spills down my cheek.

He only nods.

When I can trust myself to speak again, I swipe at my eyes and look up at him. "This has to stop." Suddenly cold, I hug my arms tight to my chest. "Can you come with me to the police station?"

42

OLENA

N at meets us at the courthouse after the police direct us there. It turns out that filing the paperwork for any kind of restraining order is a three hour administrative ordeal and, even before I start, I'm already shattered from everything that's happened in the past couple of days—most notably, Sean's ominous threat before he left. To say this situation is unfair would be a brutal understatement. This situation is *hot garbage.*

I watch the dust dance in a late afternoon sunbeam from the stuffy third floor of the Lennox County Courthouse, Wyatt and Nat in matching chairs on either side of me. The sickly orange walls somehow match the earthy scent of old books and papers that permeates the stale air around us; it smells like a library in here. The sound of squeaking metal drawers being pulled and pushed occasionally interrupts the intolerable quiet, and we intermittently look up from scrolling on our phones with disinterest.

Wyatt leaves and returns with coffee that I barely touch. I take occasional sips of the too-sweet, lukewarm drink, but it only fuels the queasy feeling in my stomach. Several other people wait along with us, pressed into the uncomfortable plastic seats. No one here looks like they're having a good day. I sit with my arms folded across my chest, my leg bouncing with impatience.

After about half an hour, the clerk calls my name and hands me a stack of six forms. Flipping quickly through them, I see the first form alone is twenty-four pages long, including multiple appendices, one of which depicts various firearms. The fine print is already swimming in front of my eyes. I take a deep breath.

After an administrative eternity and a slew of clarifying questions put to Nat, Wyatt, and the long-suffering clerk, my forms are complete and we're directed to a courtroom. The judge reviews my paperwork and signs the order without issue, reminding me in a well-practiced, droning monotone that no arrests can be made if Sean's in violation of the order before being served these papers in person. His words sound distant and detached. I let them wash over me as I stand there in a daze, my irritation having been crushed by the tedious paperwork into something more like dissociation.

I can't believe my relationship with Sean has come to this— talking with a judge about how and when he can get arrested for contacting me. I don't even know where he is right now. How will he get served with the paperwork if they can't find him? And if Sean's still here in Lennox Valley and he tries to find me again... what then?

Sean's final words to me drift through my head. *"I'm gonna fucking make you see we belong together. You belong to* me *and no one else."*

I shudder. What did he mean by that? What's he going to do? Jude was right. I don't know what he's capable of. I feel uneasy again but, holding my copy of the restraining order, I also feel like I've finally done something to protect myself. This boundary between me and Sean was long-overdue. As we file out of the courthouse to head home—and through the fog of my weary exhaustion—I feel proud of myself.

"Olena, you did good, girl." Nat reaches over and squeezes my arm as we stand together on the sidewalk out front. "This was the right step to take."

"Thanks," I say. "I'm still feeling twitchy, though. Like I keep having to watch over my shoulder in case Sean's following me."

"Understandable." Wyatt slings his arm around my shoulder and gives me a squeeze. "What a prick. I'm so sorry you're dealing with this."

"Yeah," I say, looking at the ground, "but... I'm almost feeling like I want to celebrate this." I hold up the restraining order in my hand. "I mean, I took legal action to get Sean out of my life. That deserves gold stars, right?" I glance up at Wyatt, then over to Nat, who's smiling proudly at me.

"Did I just hear you say you want to celebrate? Um, yes please," she says.

"Fuck Sean drinks at our place?" Wyatt arches an eyebrow.

"Fuck Sean drinks!" Nat nods, smiling.

"Fuck Sean drinks, it is," I say.

"And all the gold stars, of course," Nat adds, giving my hand a squeeze as we head to the parking lot.

I smile at my friends, knowing I have to get through this even though it's hard. I refuse to be a victim to Sean's delusions. I am going to handle this. I *am* handling this.

43

OLENA

The final touches at the Faulkners' property wrap up Friday afternoon. The fertilizer is spread, the grass mowed one last time, and the irrigation system is turned on. I spend the afternoon with my camera, taking the pictures that will be the *after* photos of my before-and-after set for the project—at least until I can get a final set done later in the spring when all the plants have settled and the new flowers are blooming.

Wyatt and Nat text me throughout the day to check in, likely a team effort on their part to ensure I'm safe. They help distract me from the ball of dread and anxiety that's taken up residence in my stomach. Holed up with my camera in the sunken garden, I'm grateful to have a private place to linger. Finding I need a break from the constant, chirping text notifications, I set my phone on silent and toss it onto one of the benches. I take my last photos of the firepit and the view over the river.

I'm reviewing the images on the camera's screen when the sound of approaching voices has my eyes snapping up to the pathway. *Shit.*

Jude's been taking Charles and Carol on a walk-through, making sure there are no last steps that need to be flagged for completion before we pack up the equipment. Unable to stomach the possibility of being cornered into joining them, I hurry to leave.

"Excuse me," I mutter as I rush past the three of them on the path. "Sorry, just have to..." I trail off, holding up my camera and smiling apologetically like I've got more work to do. I barely meet Jude's eyes.

Once I've safely escaped the sunken garden, I realize I've also finished all that I need to do. I take a deep breath and exhale slowly, looking around at this beautiful property. Spotting Jude's team chatting across the yard, I head over to say my goodbyes. I thank them for their hard work and tell them I hope to work with them all again—which I do. As awkward as things have been with Jude on and off throughout this project, this group has been unfalteringly professional and kind to me.

With Jude still busy touring the Faulkners around, I decide to leave without saying goodbye to them. *Probably for the best,* I think, pushing down the twinge of regret I feel about sneaking off. I'll need to call Charles next week to follow up, anyway.

I drive home feeling vaguely numb. I get as far as my apartment door before I realize I left my phone behind. *Shit.* I know exactly where I left it. I can picture where I tossed it down on the bench in the sunken garden.

I groan at the thought of driving all the way back out there to get my phone. I briefly consider texting Carol to ask her to look for it, but then realize I'd need a phone to do that. Laughing joylessly at my dependence on modern technology, I unlock the door to my apartment.

Still holding my keys in my hand, the sudden realization I may never see Jude again descends over me and a wave of grief twists at my insides.

Whoa. Where did that come from?

Sinking slowly onto the chair beside the door, a weight settles deep in my gut at the idea of losing him for good. And I slunk away from work today like a fucking coward. How can I let that be *it?*

I shake my head. *No.* I can't just let him go, especially not when I know I hurt him and never had the courage to apologize. Or to at least tell him how I feel.

Oh God. A sudden, gut-wrenching need to see him claws at me, threatening to swallow me whole. I already know in my bones I'm going back. And not just for my phone.

Sifting through the clutter in my room, it takes me several tries to find a pen that works so I can write Wyatt a note so he doesn't worry about me when he gets off work and finds me gone. With a drug-addicted stalker ex potentially on the loose, he'd obviously assume the worst. But, when even the ink of my one working pen runs out a few words into my message, I crumple the paper in anger and stuff my shoes back on. It'll be faster to just jog down to the deli.

Pulling open the door, I see the usual late afternoon crowd of high school students and seniors gathered inside, the savory smell of sandwich meats tempting me to grab an early dinner. But I don't have time to eat.

Wyatt walks out of the back office, through the kitchen, and looks up; seeing my stricken face, his eyes are instantly on alert and he rushes to the counter to speak with me.

"Everything okay? What are you doing here?" he asks, his eyes shifting around behind me, probably scanning for Sean.

"I'm fine; everything's fine," I reassure him, still panting a bit from running there. "I just left my phone at work," I explain. "And... I need to go back. To see Jude. I need to talk to him. I want to tell him I'm sorry."

Wyatt tilts his head at me, unsure. "Okay..."

"I need to... I need to see him." I'm getting impatient now, wishing I could just teleport myself there. "I need to apologize and explain. About Sean and about... Look, I just need to see him again, Wyatt!" I'm getting emotional and loud. That twisting feeling in my stomach is back.

"Okay, okay, it's alright," Wyatt says reassuringly, trying to calm me down so I don't make a scene in front of his customers. He smiles politely at one of the deli patrons who's staring at us while grabbing napkins from the nearby dispenser.

"I just needed to tell you where I was going," I say quickly. "If I hurry, I can get back to work before he goes home."

My anxiety is building; I need to get a move on.

"Okay," Wyatt says, taking everything in. "Well, I guess... go get your man, babe." He smiles and winks at me.

I smile nervously at him and rush back to the door. Before I push my way outside, I turn back and call out to him, grinning. "I will! And don't call me *babe!*"

44

JUDE

I'm packing up the last of our gear into my truck, so I can take a final look around the property before we leave. Teddy hops into his truck, which is parked beside mine, and pauses to ask if I need a hand doing a last pass before he takes off.

I wave him off. "Nah, I got this, Ted. Thanks, though."

He smiles and lifts a hand from the steering wheel. "See ya, boss!" he calls from the open window.

I wave back, heading off to do a full walk of the property. There's almost always some small tool or stash of scrap materials we've left behind, even when we're sure we've got everything.

My phone rings in my back pocket and I pull it out.

"Miles, what's up?" I answer, wondering what my brother wants. I spot a pair of pliers in the grass and stoop to pick them up.

"Hey, man, not much," Miles replies. "Just calling 'cause I... Well, I've been thinking about some things. And I wanted to say thanks."

I pause. I'm listening for any signs he's been drinking, and so far, nothing. "Uh, thanks for what?" I reply dubiously.

"For letting me crash a couple weeks back." He sounds unusually steady.

I'm skeptical. "Miles, you've crashed here plenty and you've never called to say thanks." I chuckle in my confusion and keep walking. "What's up?" I ask again, scanning along the cliff-side, down the line of all the plants. All clear.

"I just want you to know I appreciate you. You've taken care of me a lot when I've been in pretty rough shape. Look, I've been talking with Barry. I'm getting back on track with AA."

"That's great, Miles." I sigh with relief; it's about time. "You getting all sappy on me, now or..." I smirk to myself.

He laughs. "Hey, no, sorry, just wanted you to know I'm doing better."

"Seriously, that's great news. Keep it up." I turn, walking down the gravel path to the sunken garden.

I hear him scoff on the other end of the line, then laugh. "*Keep it up?*" he repeats, mocking me. "No *congratulations?* Just keep it up? Like, don't fuck it up?"

I switch my phone to my other ear, smiling to myself. "Yeah. Don't fuck it up." Gotta keep that big brother thing going.

"Alright, alright, message received," he laughs. I can almost hear him rolling his eyes. "Well, that's the plan, anyway."

"Good."

He pauses. "Hey, about that girl you had over. Sorry again for freaking her out, by the way. Everything okay with her?" He sounds concerned.

I hesitate. "Uh, not really, actually. Long story." I've been trying my hardest not to think about Olena for the last three days.

"Sorry, man," he says, "I hope I didn't... I mean, I hope it wasn't me."

"No, it wasn't you. Don't worry about it." Looking around the sunken garden, my eyes land on one of the benches around the fire pit. Something black sits tucked between the cushion and the frame.

"So, what happened with her? What was her name, anyway? I don't think you ever told me."

I walk over to take a closer look. It's a phone.

"Olena."

Turning it over in my hand, I recognize the case. I press my lips together and close my eyes, shaking my head.

"Alanna?"

"No, *Olena*." I sigh. "Nevermind. Uh, well..." I pause, rubbing my forehead with the back of my knuckles, Olena's phone still in my hand. I contemplate how to explain everything without it taking hours. "Her ex was bothering her—scaring her. He's from out of town and apparently he threatened to come see her here." I look at the phone once more and slide it into my pocket, then continue walking.

"Shit, man. That's grim," Miles says.

"Yeah, not great. Anyway, she didn't tell me about it... but then I found out. And I got... upset. We haven't really been talking since." Memories of a tearful Olena hugging her knees sweep into my mind. I'm not proud of how I left things with her on Wednesday morning.

"That's rough."

"Yeah." I sigh. It has been.

"So, wait a sec, she's got some unstable ex-boyfriend who might show up in Lennox?"

"Yeah." I frown.

"And you got pissed and split?"

"Uh, yeah." I'm uncomfortable with where this is heading.

"This is the same girl you were falling all over yourself about when I showed up there last time?" He chuckles incredulously.

"Get to the point, Miles." I wasn't prepared for my little brother calling me out like this.

"Okay, okay, I'm just saying... I could see you were a goner that first day, man." He pauses. "Even though my memory's a bit fuzzy, that much was clear."

"Yeah, well—" I start, feeling the need to defend myself.

He cuts me off. "And I mean... finding out some dude is threatening your girl and then leaving her alone... That doesn't really sound like your thing, man."

I grimace. "Hold on. My *thing*?"

"Yeah, Jude." I hear him scoff. "You're the guy who takes care of people. You know, like how you took care of me after Mom and Dad died. How you took care of Grandpa when he got sick, remember? And how you've been taking care of me all this time, you know, with my drinking and shit. It's what you do."

The silence hangs on the line for a moment as I take this in.

"Fuck." I squeeze the bridge of my nose between my fingers. He's right. I hate that he's right. I've up and abandoned Olena to fend for herself when she's got a potentially dangerous man trying to track her down. And, to make matters worse, I've gone back on my word and run away from her. I let my pride and my own hang-ups get in the way of being there for her when she was in crisis.

How the hell did I not see this?

"Look, I don't know what her deal is," Miles says. "I could be talking outta my ass here, but... from what I saw? It looked like you cared about her."

"Yeah, Miles, I—"

"Like, *a lot*."

"Yes, Miles," I say again. "Point made. Thank you." I shake my head.

"What?" He sounds like he's smiling on the other end of the line.

I realize what I have to do. "Miles, I gotta go."

Realizing that I've never been to Olena's house and I have no way of calling her, I head to find Wyatt. I pull open the door of the deli about two minutes before closing time and let out a breath of relief. Wyatt is wiping down the sandwich station countertop. He looks up and frowns in confusion and surprise when he sees me.

"Jude, hi…" He tilts his head at me. "Is Olena with you?"

"What?" I frown. That's not what I was expecting to hear. "Why would she be with me?"

"She was just here. She left to drive back to the job site—said she left her phone there. And she said she wanted to talk to you…" he says, trailing off, both of us realizing at the same time what's happened.

"Fuck." I reach into my pocket and pull out Olena's phone, holding it in front of me. "I've got her phone."

"And she…" Wyatt starts slowly.

"And she just drove back to see me while I was driving here to see her." I press my lips together and grimace.

Wyatt looks apologetic. "You probably passed each other."

"Shit." I look up at the ceiling.

"I know she wasn't sure she'd make it before you went home. I mean, obviously, she didn't get there before you left," he says with a half-smile.

Connecting the dots, I tap the top of the sneeze guard and point at Wyatt. She would have gone to my house after seeing I'd left. "I think I know where she is. Thank you!"

"Jude!" Wyatt calls out before I'm fully out the door. I pop my head back inside, my hand on the door handle. "Sean showed up here. At our place."

My eyes widen as anger swells inside me.

"She's fine," he quickly adds, and I exhale. "She gave him hell.

You'd be proud." He smiles sadly. "But just... watch out for her. I don't trust that asshole. He might still be in town."

I nod, frowning, suddenly feeling uneasy that she's alone right now. Not only do I want to find her—now I *need* to find her. I turn to leave again.

"And Jude..." Wyatt calls out again. Again, I pause, almost out the door. "Hear her out." He levels me with a look. "This isn't all on her."

I pause, holding his gaze, then nod again before leaving the deli. Hopping back into my truck, I quickly pull a U-turn out of my parking spot and speed toward home.

45

OLENA

Driving back to the property is torturous as I navigate the rush hour traffic. I dart my eyes between the road and the digital clock on my dashboard, sending fervent wishes to the universe that Jude won't leave before I get there. The drone of traffic all around me is a continuous backdrop to my buzzing anxiety. It's not until I get onto the quieter roads closer to the Faulkners' that I can think a bit more clearly.

I realize I don't even know what I'll say to him. Attempting to formulate a plan in my mind is like wrangling the flailing tentacles of an octopus. *What if I drive all this way and then can't pull a coherent sentence together?*

My thoughts are so complicated and swirling in all directions. There's a good chance I could make this worse with my babbling. If I even get the chance. My heart sinks at the thought. *What if he doesn't want to talk to me?*

Pulling into the Faulkners' driveway, I let out a curse. I'm too late; Jude's truck is already gone. *Fucking traffic.* I park anyway and run to the sunken garden, hoping, at the very least, to find my phone. It's gone. *Damn it!* Someone must have found it before everyone left for the day.

I run back to my car and quickly throw it into reverse. Smiling with renewed resolve, I back onto the roadway and drive the short distance to Jude's house. He likely went home after work. I can talk to him there in private—and, right now, that's more important than my phone.

My heart is in my throat when I finally pull into his driveway and his log cabin house comes into view. I deflate with a shaking exhalation when I see his truck isn't here either.

Not knowing where else he'd go, I get out of my car and pace in the driveway for a moment. I need to talk to him. It suddenly feels so urgent. Maybe he'll come home soon; I can wait here until then. Looking at his house, all the memories of being here with Jude come into focus. That emotional night out here on his front porch, getting dressed in his bathroom, my back pressed up against his front door, that time in the shed... *Oh my God, the shed...* I let out a long breath.

Standing here alone now, a fresh ache forms in my gut as I realize how much I miss him. I walk up to the porch and knock on the door, although I know in my heart he's not home. I adjust my purse on my shoulder and wait for the answer that doesn't come.

"Well, looks like I finally got you alone," a familiar voice comes from behind me, and I freeze.

No.

I spin around to see Sean standing near my car, his hands in the pockets of his brown leather jacket.

"What are you doing here?" I ask in shock. "How did you know where..." I trail off, shaking my head at him. I already know the answer. The asshole followed me here, just like he followed Wyatt. I had been so caught up in my own thoughts and my plan to talk to Jude that I hadn't been paying attention to the other cars around me. I *know* I didn't hear him drive up and I don't see his car anywhere. I bet he parked it on the road and walked down the driveway *specifically* to arrive undetected. I feel sick looking at him.

"This your new boyfriend's place?" Sean lifts his chin, indicating the front door. His eyes look glassy and heavy-lidded.

I consider how to get out of here. I can't call the police without my phone.

"Fuck you, Sean." Anger rises up through my panic.

"Aw, I just wanted to meet him, that's all." His expression is hateful.

"He's not here," I say, stalling, trying to think of something, mentally mapping my exits. *There aren't any.* Not unless I want to run down all those steps and jump in the river. Right now, that ice cold water might not be my worst option.

"Well, that worked out, I guess." Sean sniffs harshly. He raises his eyebrows, his eyes still squinting slightly. "I get some time with my baby."

Ugh, stop calling me that. It feels so vile.

He looks deranged. He takes a step toward me.

"Stay away from me," I say, my heart hammering. I don't step back, though my instincts scream at me to get away.

He stops. "Aw, now, why would you act like that, Olena? I'm not gonna hurt you." He smiles in a way that gives me zero reassurance.

"You already have, you fucking asshole." I spit out the words. He's ruined so much for me that he doesn't even realize. My cheeks feel flushed. I grip the strap of my purse.

He smiles ruefully and shakes his head. "You need to stop talking to me like that."

"You deserve it," I say quietly. Too quietly for him to hear.

"What did you just say?" His eyebrows draw together and he raises his chin.

"I said you fucking deserve it, Sean!" I don't know where this confidence is coming from, but I'm embracing it because I'm sick of his shit.

He raises his eyebrows and laughs an ugly laugh, then runs his tongue over his teeth, shrugging. His movements are jerky and jarring. "That's rich. You're the one who deserves to suffer, Olena." He blinks a few times. "You're the one who abandoned me and broke my heart."

"Because you were high every single night!" I throw my hands out at my sides, infuriated. "And you wasted all our money on drugs, and got us fucking robbed... at *knifepoint*!" I take a breath, trying to steady myself—without much success. "Do you know what that did to me?" I hiss, jabbing a finger into my chest. "I couldn't sleep or eat or go to work without having a panic attack."

He rolls his eyes. "See, you're being dramatic again."

"No." I straighten. "You destroyed my sense of safety," I seethe, clenching my hands into fists. "My *sanity*. And now you're doing it again!"

He scoffs.

"You won't leave me alone, and now you're following me? *Threatening* me?" I look at him with disgust, shaking my head. "You colossal, selfish asshole."

His expression hardens at the insult. "I told you, baby," Sean says, pulling his hands out of his pockets with eerie calm. "You need to stop talking to me like that."

In the fading light, I catch a glint of metal. My heart lurches, my eyes laser focused on the knife. I can't speak; my pulse is pounding in my ears.

"See, baby... the problem with you is you're not showing me the respect I deserve." He starts to walk toward me slowly. My gaze is locked on the hand holding the knife. He scratches his head. "I gave you everything. For three fucking years. Everything. And this is the thanks I get?"

I retreat a few steps on the porch until my back is against Jude's front door. I try the handle behind me but it's locked.

Some part of my brain goes into survival mode and I find my voice. Maybe I can talk my way out of this. "Sean, hey, look, we can talk this out. Please. Put the knife away." My voice is thin and strained. The only thing keeping me from a panic attack right now is some primal instinct to stay alive.

He sneers at me with disgust. "Oh, yeah? *Now* you're suddenly willing to talk? Now you see you can't just ignore me? Huh? Is that it?" He's at the bottom of the porch steps.

I inhale, holding my breath. "Yes, I see that now." I swallow hard. "Sean, just... please. Don't do this. Don't. You don't have to." I reach a shaking hand into my purse. "Look, I think there's a spare set of keys somewhere in here..." I'm bluffing, stalling for time. "We could go inside and sit down, talk things out..."

My hand grasps around in the bottomless pit of my bag, my fingers frantically trying to identify what I'm touching while my eyes stay trained on the threat in front of me.

"Yeah?" Sean says warily, climbing the steps. He sniffs again and blinks hard. "Okay, let's talk." His eyes are wild and blood-shot. He keeps using his free hand to scratch at his jaw. Whatever he's taken tonight has him in a bad way.

And then I feel it. My hand grasps the cool metal canister. I set my jaw. Praying for good aim, I extend my arm between us.

"Fuck no." My voice is tight as I pull the trigger.

I unload a cloud of bear spray directly into Sean's face, shielding my eyes with my other arm. I duck around him and run. Behind me, I hear the knife clatter against the wooden boards of the porch. A second later, Sean's guttural cry of pain rips through the woods around us.

His shouting recedes behind me as I run to my car. I pull open the door and glance back to see him clawing at his face, screaming in agony. *Good,* I think to myself. *That'll make it worse—rubbing only spreads it around.*

He stumbles, quickly losing his footing on the stairs. Flailing blindly and in incredible pain, he can do nothing to protect himself as he falls. The crack of his head against the hard steps makes me wince. Crumpled on the ground on his side, Sean's jarring screams give way to groans, the blow to his head having made his movements slower, groggier.

I'm ready to make a break for it when I stop, my hand still on the door handle. I realize he could get away with this if I run. *What if he recovers enough to make it back to his car before I can find a way to call the police?*

I look down at my climbing bag on the front seat and snatch it toward me, ripping it open. My heart hammering, I pull out the rope and quickly untie the two ends from the coil.

You can still run, my survival-brain reminds me. I ignore all my instincts. Clutching the rope and bear spray tightly, I tentatively walk back to Sean. His eyes are squeezed shut, the lids red and swollen, his brow clenched in a painful-looking grimace. He coughs and sputters, gasping in wheezing, labored breaths, his lungs no doubt on fire. He seems disoriented—and maybe blinded. For now.

Carefully setting down the canister and rope in arm's reach, my heartbeat whooshes in my ears. Adrenaline kicking through my veins, the *fight* part of fight-or-flight takes control. I dart forward, grasping tight onto one of Sean's wrists, wrenching it away from his face and behind his back as he cries out in pain. He yanks back, shouting in agony and confusion, but I somehow hold on. Sean's bigger than me—but not by a lot.

I think I might be able to pin him when he suddenly jerks his body and rips his wrist from my grip. He twists onto his back, clawing blindly, snagging my hair in a clenched fist. He kicks out hard, connecting with my right shin, and I cry out in pain, landing heavily on my knees in the gravel.

"Fuck you, you bitch!" Sean slurs in a rough wheeze, spittle flying from his mouth.

I bite down hard on his forearm and he screams, letting go of my hair just long enough for me to scramble out of reach. My shin throbs, no doubt already starting to swell.

"No, Sean, fuck *you*," I seethe. I lunge for his hand again and crank it behind his back, using my body weight to force him down onto his stomach. He shouts when I kneel on his lower back and yank his arm up sharply. I snag the rope from the gravel beside us and shove one end between my teeth, tasting dirt. Scrambling, I manage to wrap a length of it around his wrist several times.

He wheezes out another groan and claws at my injured shin with his free hand, his fingers gouging into the tender flesh through my jeans. Despite the screaming pain from my leg, I stomp with everything I've got on his elbow, his guttural cry telling me I hit my mark. Jarring pain zings up my leg and I hiss out a curse. With his arm having gone limp, I grab hold of his free wrist, clawing to hold on as he tries to pull away. Pulling hard on the rope and hooking my leg around his, I roll him onto his side, pinning his free arm under his own weight. I quickly loop both his wrists together, keeping tension on the rope, and let the end drop from my teeth. With another few wraps of his wrists for good measure, I quickly tie it. *Thank God for mastering those fucking climbing knots.*

Shoving away from Sean, I scramble on my hands and knees to grab the bear spray, spinning around onto my ass and holding it out between us, heart hammering. Sean thrashes but it's clear he's not getting out of that rope anytime soon, so I slowly push myself to a stand. I'm still holding the canister in front of me with shaking arms when I hear the roar of a familiar engine tearing down the driveway toward us. I look up, wincing, as a set of blinding headlights lights us up.

46

JUDE

The only thing more alarming than seeing a car I don't recognize parked near my driveway is the scene illuminated in front of me when I pull up to the house.

Time seems to slow as I process what I'm seeing. Olena stands at the foot of the porch steps, stiff and trembling. She's got a vise grip on something I can't quite see—*a canister of something?*—in her outstretched arms, aiming it at a man on the ground. His hands are tied behind his back as he writhes and struggles in front of her, his eyes swollen, red, and squeezed shut, in obvious pain. She turns and squints as I drive up, blinking repeatedly. I'm out of the truck in an instant, running to her. Murphy follows at my heels, barking and growling at the man, who must be Sean.

"Olena!" I say, my eyes wide. I stop in front of them. "Oh my God..."

"Call 9-1-1," she grits out. She's breathing hard, her voice strained.

Of course. No phone, so she couldn't call for help. I reach into my back pocket for my phone. Murphy's still barking and I call him to my side, quieting him, and dial 9-1-1.

Taking in the knot, which would put any boy scout to shame, it doesn't look like Sean's got a hope in hell of wriggling out. My eyes widen when they settle on Olena's hands, and I realize the canister in her shaking grasp is bear spray. *Holy shit.*

Sean jerks on the ground, groaning with the strain of fighting to get free. "I can't fucking see!" he wheezes out, angry and desperate.

Her eyes snap down to him. "Shut the fuck up, Sean," she snaps, her voice ragged. She coughs, looking like she's struggling to take a deep breath. *Probably from the bear spray. That shit gets everywhere.*

My mind reels as I wait for the 9-1-1 operator. "Jesus, Olena..." I press a fist to my forehead. *Where'd she even* get *bear spray? What just happened here?*

Relaying what I can to the operator, I'm soon assured the police and ambulance are on their way and am told to stay on the line. Putting the call on speakerphone, I place my phone down on the porch and slowly approach Olena. Meeting her tearful, red eyes is like a punch to the stomach. *She looks terrified.*

"Let me," I say gently.

She holds my gaze without moving, still pointing the bear spray at Sean, her breathing ragged. She's frozen.

I try again. "It's gonna be okay. Let me help." I reach a hand toward the canister. "Take my phone and go wait by your car, okay?"

"Olena!" Sean groans, wheezing. "Untie my fucking hands!"

His words seem to snap her into action and she hands me the bear spray, backing away in an unsteady stumble. She grabs my phone and hurries toward her car, looking grateful to put some distance between herself and Sean. *Is she limping? What the fuck did this prick do to her?* My jaw clenches.

"Fucking let me go!" he wheezes.

When I see Olena reach her car, I turn my attention to the asshole on the ground.

"Not a fucking chance, dickhead," I grit out at him through clenched teeth. *He hurt her. I could kill him.* My concern for Olena is the only thing stopping me from plunging headfirst into a blind rage and taking it out on Sean. Well, that and knowing that I'll have to keep it reined in if I don't want to get hauled away for assault too.

"Fuck you, asshole!" he grinds out hoarsely.

I speak in a deadly calm. "This ends here. You're never gonna see her again."

He groans again, wheezing from the bear spray's inflammatory effects on his airway.

The ambulance arrives in minutes, followed closely by the police, who quickly take over. They handcuff Sean and cut the rope restraint. While one paramedic assesses Sean, the other checks over Olena.

"You're gonna want to wash up after touching that stuff," an officer says to me, tilting her chin at the canister of bear spray in my hand.

I nod, then place it on the porch, numbly wiping my hands on my jeans. Seeing that Olena is busy speaking to another officer, I duck into the house. I quickly change my clothes, then wash my hands thoroughly to remove any residue.

It's only when I come back outside that I spot the knife; the gleaming edge of the blade is just visible from under one of the benches, lit up by the red and blue police lights. My stomach drops and my eyes snap to Olena, who is rubbing her arms in the chill of the evening air as she relays her statement to the officer.

He pulled a fucking knife on her. A weight descends heavily over me as I watch her.

She glances over and meets my eyes before she looks back to the officer in front of her.

He motions to yet another officer, who confers with him quickly before coming up to search the porch.

Standing there in a state of shock, I numbly point out the knife. He quickly bags it, then places the bear spray in a separate bag before walking away.

I can't take my eyes off Olena, marveling at what she pulled off. The relief I feel knowing she got the upper hand with Sean mixes with a thick, hot nausea. Bile rises in my throat when I think of what could have happened to her. *If Sean had hurt her—or worse, if he'd taken her from me—and on my own front porch...* The idea of losing her claws at the inside of my ribs, threatening to deflate my lungs.

She looks cold and exhausted. I go into the house and find a spare blanket, bringing it outside. Walking over to her, I silently wrap it around her shoulders. The gesture feels small and inconsequential; I wish I could wrap her up in safety—take away the trauma of fighting for her life against someone she never should have had to face at all, let alone by herself.

She looks up at me gratefully, clutching the corners of the blanket into her chest.

The officer finishes taking her statement and hands over his business card so she can get in touch later. With a nod at me, he plods away, leaving us alone.

We turn to face each other. For a moment, neither of us speaks.

"Did he hurt you?" is all I can think to ask. "You were limping..."

"I'm okay." She looks at the ground.

I exhale a long breath. "I'm so sorry. I should've been here."

"No, it's okay." She lifts her eyes to look at me.

"No. It's not fucking okay. He had a knife, Olena." I step toward her. "He could've—"

"I know." She closes her eyes, looking exhausted.

My brow creases as I realize how badass Olena had to have been to bear spray her knife-wielding ex in the face and then single-handedly tie him up. I look over at the porch, rubbing my jaw.

"But this was my mess to clean up," she says.

When my gaze meets hers, her eyes are filled with heart-breaking emotion.

"Look, I know I should've told you about this—about Sean." Her voice wavers. I can tell she's trying hard to keep it together. "I'm gutted that I hurt you."

I grimace, the pain all too close to the surface, and cross my arms over my chest.

"I know I can't fix that," she continues. "But I came here because I need you to know I'm sorry." She closes her eyes, almost wincing. "I know I apologize constantly for every little thing." She meets my gaze and takes a breath. "But this was a big thing. And I'm devastated every single day when I think about how I hurt you. How you looked when you left that morning." Fresh tears slide down her cheek. "It's been eating me up inside ever since."

I say nothing—a knot growing in my throat—and wait, watching her.

Her hair is a mess from the struggle with Sean, backlit by the flashing red and blue police lights. Tears streak through the dirt on her face and her eyes blaze, lit with a newfound courage that looks both daring and fragile.

"I don't expect you to forgive me." She pauses. "But I need you to know I'll be okay. Even if you never forgive me. Even if you never want to see me again."

"Olena..." I uncross my arms, my stomach twisting.

"Hold on, I'm not done." She takes another steadying breath.

I put my hands in my pockets and shut my mouth. Wyatt's words float through my mind: *Hear her out.*

"Look, I know I suck at being an adult in a lot of ways," she says. "But I needed to do this myself. I needed to prove..." Her eyes well up again and she looks away, blowing out a slow breath. When she steadies, she turns back to me. "I needed to prove to myself that I could handle this. And I did. I *did* handle this. I got a restraining order against Sean. And then today... well, you saw..."

My eyes fall to the ground between us and I nod, knowing I'll never forget the sight that greeted me when I pulled up.

"Everything Sean did... it made me feel so fucking *powerless*, like I didn't have control of my own life." She pauses, taking a steadying breath. "I had to take that control back. Take my *power* back. That's why I needed to do this myself. And I didn't tell you because I was scared." Her voice wavers with emotion. "Scared you'd think I was too much, too messy, that I had too much baggage, or that I wasn't worth the trouble. And you're so..."

I look up.

"You're so... *fucking wonderful*," she says, her eyes widening, "that I couldn't stomach the idea of you thinking that about me."

I slant a small smile at her words. How could I ever see her as anything less than incredible? Especially after what she's just done.

"But you know what I realized? I'm so fucking *sick* of being scared all the time. And I'm sick of that script. I'm done, Jude. I am done trying to hide and shrink and mold myself into what other people want from me. Or what I *think* they want, anyway. I'm allowed to have baggage and I'm allowed to fuck up..." She looks away, taking a deep breath, before meeting my gaze again. "And I don't need you, or Nat, or Wyatt, or anyone else to save me." She stops, looking like she's carefully guarding against what I'll say in response.

I look at her for a long moment. "Good," I say simply, exhaling hard around the obstruction in my throat.

She startles at my unexpected response. "What do you mean, *good?* I thought—"

"I don't want you to need me." I look up at the sky and shake my head.

"What?" she breathes, furrowing her brow.

I meet her tearful eyes. "I don't want you to *need me*, Olena," I say again, quieter this time. I take a step closer. "I want you to *want me*."

She shudders out a breath, her eyes searching mine.

I reach out, sliding my hands over her arms.

She closes her eyes at my touch and takes a deep breath before meeting my gaze again.

I continue, moving in closer, my voice low. "The way I want *you*. So badly it's killing me. Seeing you at work and knowing you'll leave without me at the end of the day. Knowing I won't have you in my bed at night. Or wake up next to you in the morning." I blink back my own emotion as my eyes dip down to her lips. I look back at her tear-filled eyes. "Olena, it feels like there's this gaping hole in my life where you used to fit." I take a deep, steadying breath.

She looks at me in disbelief. "Jude..."

The police cruiser pulls slowly out of the driveway with Sean locked in the backseat. As it disappears from view, I meet her gaze again. "Olena, you don't owe me every detail about your past. We've known each other, what, a month?" I smooth a hand over my chin and laugh wryly at the realization: how quickly things have moved between us in that short time.

A hint of a smile tugs at her lips.

"And I can see that you don't need my help. *Clearly*. You were... fucking incredible today." I shake my head, still in awe of what she did. "Messy baggage and all—and God knows I've got my own— that shit doesn't scare me, okay?"

She nods, and the last of the police cars pulls onto the road, leaving us in the quiet of the night.

"So, you might not need my help, but it's here if you want it.

I'm here. For you." My brows knit together as I try to get the words out. "I want to know these things about you." I reach a hand to her face, brushing my thumb over her cheek.

Her eyes close and she exhales softly.

I brush the hair back from her forehead and she looks up at me again. "I want to know *everything* about you." I smile down at her. "Even the hard stuff. Even the scary stuff. *Especially* the scary stuff." I raise my eyebrows.

A slight grimace crosses her features at the reminder of what she didn't tell me. She nods again.

"And speaking of scary stuff... I owe you an apology too." I take a deep breath. "I should never have walked out on you when you were in danger." My voice is low in my throat. "That's not what you do when you love somebody."

She sucks in a breath and her eyes widen, searching mine. "What?" Her voice is barely more than a whisper.

"Olena..." My heart aches looking at her: this beautiful, strong, incredible woman. I reach up to cradle her face in my hands, my fingers in her hair at the nape of her neck. I lean down, my lips inches from hers. "I love you," I breathe, smiling.

Her brown eyes brim with tears once again.

The blanket falls to the ground as she rises up to kiss me hard, her hands clutching at my shirt, pulling me close. As our kiss softens and she pulls back, her expression is a mixture of relief and pain. The emotion of everything that's happened between us spills over her features and she slides her arms around my waist, sagging into my embrace.

I hold her as she cries softly against my chest. The feeling of my arms around her again brings me such relief; I close my eyes and try to keep it together.

"I love you too," she says against my chest.

I exhale a jagged breath and smile. Rubbing her arms, I rest my chin on her head. "Come on. Let's get cleaned up."

47

OLENA

"Bad news," I call out over the sound of the washing machine. I'm skimming an article on my phone, the screen's bluish glow and the dim bedside lamp providing the only light in Jude's bedroom.

He pops his head around the corner, his eyebrows raised.

"It says here it might take multiple wash cycles to get rid of all the bear spray residue." I'm lying in his bed, naked under the warm blankets. My hair is still damp from the shower.

"So, no clothes for a few hours? I don't hear any bad news," he deadpans, arching an eyebrow at me.

I grin back at him, scrunching my nose. "Scoundrel."

He chuckles, looking satisfied.

"I guess you'll have to keep me for a while longer," I say with a coy smile.

Jude walks slowly into the room, shirtless, and crawls over me on the bed, taking care not to bump my injured shin. I drop my phone beside me and shift my leg out of the way with a small wince. I slide my hands over his shoulders.

"Oh, no," he says, kissing my neck softly, "what will we do to pass the time?"

A slow grin spreads over my face and I bite my lip as his mouth brushes under my ear, my eyes closing at the warmth of his lips. I gently drag my fingernails over his back.

"Gosh, I can't think of anything," I say, playing along innocently. He smells so good. I missed him.

A yawn takes me by surprise and I try unsuccessfully to stifle it. The adrenaline crash after the ordeal with Sean must be finally catching up to me.

Hearing my exhaustion, Jude lies down beside me, sliding under the blankets.

I turn onto my side to face him, tucking my hands between my cheek and the pillow.

"Do you wanna talk about it?" he asks gently.

"Not now," I say, dropping my gaze away from his. "I don't think it's really hit me yet." I meet his eyes again.

He nods, his thumb brushing the curve of my waist. "What do you need right now?"

"I think just to be here... with you." I pause as he smiles softly. "To have this little slice of normalcy to distract me—just for tonight, at least."

"Distraction." He grins. "I think I can manage that."

"Plus—" I raise an eyebrow at him. "I could get used to watching you do my laundry."

His eyebrows quirk up in amusement. "Is that like a domestic porn thing or something? Have we discovered your secret fetish?" He gives me a crooked smile.

I grin and bite my lip. "If it features you? One hundred percent yes."

"Well, alright, but you might have a tough time convincing me to let you have your clothes back," he says, his deep voice rumbling as his fingers graze lower on my bare stomach.

I suck in a quick breath and lean closer to kiss him.

"And hey," he says, reaching up to trace my jawline with a finger, "I know you don't want me to play bodyguard or swoop in to save you—you can clearly fight your own monsters." He raises his eyebrows pointedly. "But maybe we can *both* take care of you."

I smile at him, pressing a quick kiss to his cheek. "Yeah? Is that 'cause you *looooove* me?" I grin a huge, cheesy grin.

"Damn right. C'mere." He kisses me. "But seriously. Just because you *can* handle hard things all on your own doesn't mean you *have to*," he adds. "My brother pointed out to me earlier..." He pauses, frowning. "Oh, God, was that just *today*?" He shakes his head in disbelief. "Feels like a lifetime ago."

I make a soft sound of agreement. So much has happened in the last few hours.

"Anyway, Miles was saying it's kind of *my thing* to take care of people." He cups my face with his hand, rubbing his thumb over my cheek. "So, how about this: I won't jump in to save you, and you won't pretend to be fine when you're not." He raises an eyebrow. "Deal?"

"Well, I suppose you could be my faithful sidekick." I smile softly.

"Ooh, sidekick? How generous," he says, chuckling.

"I mean, I could use someone like you on my team. Because— and I hate to stereotype you, but—you do kind of have that whole *big strong man* thing down," I say, gesturing to his incredible body with a grin.

Jude smiles, arching an eyebrow. "Yeah? And you like that, don't you?" He chuckles softly, his fingers grazing my lower back.

I nod. "Mmm, like, one thousand sexy lumberjack points to you, sir, seriously." I laugh and kiss him, tracing a finger over his chest.

"I *do* chop my own wood," he replies dryly, putting on an air of aloofness.

I throw my head back, a joyful sound escaping my throat. "Oh, please let me watch you. Pleasepleaseplease." I kiss his nose and wiggle closer.

"Wow. First laundry, now chopping wood?" He chuckles again and shakes his head.

"Mm-hmm," I say, nodding enthusiastically.

He sucks in a slow breath, as if thoughtfully pondering my request. "Okay. I *guess* I'll let you watch. But only if you're well-behaved," he teases, narrowing his eyes at me, then quirks a half-smile.

"No promises," I say, smiling, as I unbutton his jeans.

48

OLENA

"Jude! Come on, I can't wait! Carol said she'd turn the lights on for us at eight thirty!" I pull him by the hand down the dark forest trail, using my phone as a flashlight so we don't trip. My camera thumps into my chest as it swings around my neck. I feel like a kid on Christmas morning, getting to see the property from across the river for the first time.

The night is warm for early April and I'm *so* ready to be outside. After spending hours stuck indoors this afternoon while we waited for my lawyer to call, Jude and I had finally heard: unable to afford bail, Sean will be held in jail until his court date. Facing felony stalking and misdemeanor harassment charges, he's looking at jail time, hefty fines, *and* court-mandated rehab, plus a court order is being drawn up to prevent him from contacting me for at least five years. The feeling of relief is immense. All I want to do right now is let this sense of freedom wash over me.

A light breeze ruffles my floral print dress against my bare legs. I shiver, pulling the collar of my jean jacket tighter around me with one hand. I'll probably regret the mosquito bites coming my way, but there's a lightness in my step and, right now, I don't care.

"I'm going as fast as I can, Olena!" Jude laughs behind me, gripping my hand. "You've got the light in front of you. I can't see a damned thing."

"Sorry! I'm just excited," I say quickly. "Oh, I think I can almost see it!" I catch a glimpse of golden light between the dark mass of trees.

After winding our way around another sharp bend in the trail, the trees clear and the river—and the Faulkners' property across it —comes into view. I stop short and inhale, bringing my hands to my mouth as Jude comes to a stop beside me.

"Look!" I breathe.

Taking off again, I clamber down the small set of stairs that takes us to the floating dock. Completely out of the forest now, I have an uninterrupted view.

I'm speechless. My vision for this place has finally come to life and it's more beautiful than I could have hoped for. It's glowing. The lights, woven through the trees and strung between posts, twinkle a soft yellow, like a beacon of calm perched up on the cliff across from where we stand.

Jude slips his arms around my waist. "Gold stars, MacMillan," he whispers in my ear. "You did good." He presses a kiss to the side of my head.

I break into a huge grin. "Actual gold stars." I laugh, sliding my hands over his. I pause, almost mesmerized by the view. "I did, didn't I?" I say quietly.

I still feel uncomfortable giving myself credit. When I catch myself wondering if we should have put more lights closer to the house, I push down the familiar whisper of self-doubt, and embrace my new mantra: *good enough is good enough*. My new therapist will be proud.

I pull up my camera and snap a few photos of the property.

"It's perfect," Jude says, kissing my cheek as I reach back to touch his face. "I told you, you're excellent at your job."

I finally tear my eyes away from the sparkling lights and turn to him. "So are you."

He scoffs. "I was just the muscle, remember?" He leans in and kisses me, his lips smiling against mine. "This was all your vision."

"Hey, well, thank you." I tuck my hair behind my ear. "For your muscle." I arch an eyebrow as I run my hands down his strong arms.

He smiles. "Here," he says in a low voice, taking my hand and sitting down on the wooden dock. He sits with his legs bent in front of him, forearms around his knees. I sit down beside him, sloping my knees toward him, my ankles crossed. I tug down the hem of my dress. We look out again at the sparkling gold light in the distance as he slips an arm around my shoulders.

"I think the property is gonna need a new name," I say, turning to Jude.

"What do you mean?"

"Well, Charles and Carol want the place to be like a bed-and-breakfast type of retreat, right? A romantic getaway," I explain.

"Right," he says. "I guess... mission accomplished?" He chuckles and squeezes my arm.

I kiss his cheek, smiling as I remember our time staying in the house. "I think they need something better than *The Faulkner Property*, right?"

"Yeah, I guess so. Any ideas?" He takes my hand and twines his fingers between mine.

I look again at the twinkling lights across the river, considering. "Something *stars* or *golden... Starlight*? I don't know; I'll have to think about it. And talk to Carol and Charles, of course."

Jude turns to me and smiles softly. He brushes a thumb across my cheek, then lowers his hand, carefully removing my camera from around my neck and placing it beside us on the dock.

The moonlight casts a dim glow on his square jaw and I can't tear my eyes away. *God, he's sexy.*

"I was just wondering"—he places his hand on my knee, sliding it up a little—"what it would take for *me* to earn some gold stars." He leans in to brush his lips over my cheek.

"Oh, I think we can come up with something," I say with a coy smile.

"Fuck, this dress is..." he says, moving his hand farther up my thigh, fingering the hem, "... distracting me." His voice drops to a low rasp. He kisses the spot right beside my lips.

"Oh?" I lean in, my lips finding his, my tongue flicking once into his mouth.

"Mm-hmm." He slips his hand up under the hem of my dress and runs a fingertip under the lace edging of my panties, slowly tracing an arc around the top of my thigh.

I shiver at the sensation, kissing him more deeply. I eagerly sweep my tongue into his mouth, my breathing getting shallower. He pulls away. I look up at him.

"Stand up."

"What? Why?" I ask softly, confused.

His expression is dark. "Just stand up. Trust me."

Puzzled, I slowly push up until I'm standing next to him.

He looks up at me. Holding my gaze, he reaches up under my dress, pinching the fabric of my panties and sliding them down my legs.

My breath hitches.

He presses soft kisses to my thighs as he helps me step out of them, carefully pulling the fabric off over my ankle boots.

I bite my lip, feeling nervous, and look around us to make sure we're alone. "Jude, I don't know... what if someone sees us?" I whisper.

"There's no one here," he replies in a deep rumble.

"But what if—"

"Then I guess they'd have a story to tell," he says simply. He reaches up and holds my waist, bringing us face-to-face, as I lower onto my knees over his lap.

Feeling the cool air against my bare skin as I straddle his outstretched legs, arousal washes over me. I know he can sense it. I can't deny I want this too.

Now. Here.

I suddenly feel desperate for his touch. Taking one of his hands in mine, I kiss his fingertips, then pull it down between us, guiding his fingers, placing them exactly where I want them. Hearing his low sound of need, I sharply inhale as he slides his fingertips up and down the length of my center, then slips a finger inside me. I stifle a moan, trying to keep my voice down.

"Don't..." he says, kissing me softly. "Don't hold back." He works his finger slowly as my eyelids flutter shut. "I want to hear every sound you make." His lips claim mine in a scorching kiss as he slips two fingers inside me and pumps them harder.

Soft sounds of pleasure escape my throat. I rock my hips, riding his hand and nipping at his lips with my teeth.

Jude's free hand works the top buttons of my dress, then tugs my bra down, my nipples instantly hard in the night air. Lifting and squeezing one breast, he sucks my nipple hard, flicking it with his tongue, then scraping lightly with his teeth.

I arch up into him as an aching pleasure rolls down through my core, whimpering as Jude's fingers speed up.

He moves to the other nipple and slips his fingers out, finding my clit and rubbing quick circles over it, covering me in my own wetness.

Suddenly overcome by need, I grab his face and pull him into a crushing kiss, my tongue desperately sweeping against his. His free hand reaches up to my breast and strokes my nipple with his thumb. I tear my mouth away from him, breathing fast, and press my forehead to his.

Placing a hand on Jude's chest, I pull back to meet his eyes. With a dark smile, I shove him back firmly and he catches himself on both elbows behind him.

He looks at me with raised eyebrows, surprised and amused.

My mouth is slightly open as I look back at him, quickly releasing him from his jeans. He is hard as steel in my hands. A groan escapes from his lips as I stroke him with one hand, twisting my fist at the top just to hear his breath hitch.

I shift myself down his body, leaning close as he watches me. Teasing, I run the side of his shaft over my cheek, kissing and licking his hip bones, first on one side, then the other. His skin is soft and smooth, the heat of his arousal radiating against my face and hand. I tighten my fingers around him and stroke faster.

Sliding my tongue up one side of him from base to tip, I let out a soft moan at the feeling of his cock. I relish the taste of him as I reach the top and slide my tongue along the small slit at the tip, licking up the bead of moisture there. Jude's responding groan urges me on, and I do it again on the other side, coating him. His thick heat pulses in my hand, his need intensifying. I feel my own desire pooling between my legs. I flick my tongue over the sensitive head, then wrap my lips around him and plunge down, filling my mouth with his slick, smooth shaft.

His hips buck up from the dock, thrusting up hard into my mouth and throat, and I take him with a moan. *I love it when he does that.* I push my free hand up under his shirt, raking my fingernails across his stomach.

With a growl, he thrusts again, fucking my mouth as I squeeze tight.

My core pulses with need. I slowly pull back and sit up, eyes locked on his, then crawl forward on my knees, lining his cock up with my wet, aching entrance.

He sits up to kiss me desperately, his tongue plunging into my mouth. His hands grip my head, twining and tensing in my hair.

I reach my hand between us to guide the head of his cock, rubbing it through my slick center before pushing down onto him slightly. Then I pause.

He breaks the kiss and meets my eyes. He groans loudly as I lower down all the way, so slowly, and I moan against his lips at the delicious sensation of him filling me.

Holding onto the back of his neck, I grind my hips, feeling his length hitting that spot of pleasure deep within me. My tongue sweeps into his mouth, sliding against his teeth, and he bites my lower lip with a growl.

He moves his hands to my hips, encouraging me, pushing and pulling along with my movements as I grind against him, my clit rubbing against his skin.

"Fuck, yes, Olena," he grits out, his breath hot against my burning lips.

Aching for more, I rise on my knees, only just keeping him inside me, then I crash back down with a gasp of pleasure. Clinging to his shoulders, I do it again, relishing his low groan in response. Working my hips up and down in a steady rhythm, the scraping of my knees and the burning of my thigh muscles is a small price to pay for every delicious stroke. The up is torture. The down is worth it.

Not able to hold off any longer, Jude's grip tenses on my hips and he slams me down onto him, his cock plunging deep into me in a primal stroke that has me crying out, and loudly this time. A feral smile spreads over his face at the sound of my pleasure. He lifts me up, then pulls me down eagerly again, watching me, listening, devouring my reaction with his eyes. Again and again, he lifts me up and pulls me down, my cries of pleasure piercing the quiet night.

Oh, fuck, yes.

I gasp as Jude suddenly rolls me under him with a growl, my back crashing into the planks of the dock, my dress pulled up to my stomach. He doesn't miss a beat fucking me. Now under his own power, his strong muscles drive his rock-hard cock down into me deeply, the slight pain feeling incredible mixed with the intense pleasure. I grasp and scratch at his back as he braces his arms on either side of me, pounding into my aching center.

He reaches between us to swirl his fingers over my slick clit. I feel my release building, just out of reach.

I tighten around him, hearing his growl of approval as he fucks me harder and faster still, his breaths heaving, matching my own. His fingers speed up and I clench my muscles tighter. My eyes squeeze shut as my release gets closer. Thrusting into me with renewed vigor, Jude groans and his slamming strokes push me over the edge. I cry out into the night as I come, Jude's body tensing along with mine. I hear his breath catch before his shuddering release is unleashed, spurting hot and hard inside me. He fills me, spilling out over us both, as his last few powerful strokes give way to slower ones. His chest sagging slightly over me, he lowers his head to press his damp cheek against mine.

"Fuck, you're incredible," Jude whispers into my ear, breathing heavily.

"The feeling is... very mutual," I reply, trying to catch my breath.

"I love you." He presses a quick kiss to my lips and brushes the hair out of my face as he smiles down at me.

I tighten my muscles around him and grin at the surprised sound that escapes his lips. Biting my lip, I lift my head to kiss him softly.

"I love you too."

49

OLENA

"Shut up!" I shout, my eyes wide as I search Wyatt's face, squeezing his hands. "You did not!" My jaw hangs open, then my mouth quickly spreads into an excited grin.

"I very much did, babe." He winks, grinning back at me. He shows me the ring he's wearing, and we do a little jumping hug, squealing like teenagers. "Sam's got a matching one."

"How long were you planning this? Why didn't you tell me? Ahh! I have so many questions!" I put my hands up to my cheeks, my eyes wide in disbelief and joy for my oldest friend.

Wyatt smiles and rolls his eyes, shrugging. "You were going through some shit. It's all good."

"Jude, come out here!" I yell toward my bedroom door.

He emerges, pulling on a t-shirt and squinting in the bright light of the kitchen. He leans against the doorframe.

"Wyatt proposed! He and Sam are getting married!" I wrap my arms around Wyatt's waist and squeeze him tight, smiling at Jude, then Wyatt. I can't stop beaming.

"I gathered," he smirks at us. "You guys... aren't quiet." He chuckles and I give him a guilty look. It's eight in the morning.

"Hey, congrats, man," he says, walking over. "That's awesome news." Jude extends a hand and Wyatt shakes it.

I turn to Wyatt, still hugging him. "When's the wedding? Do you know yet?"

"Haven't quite figured that out," he says. "Probably next year, sometime. But we are going to throw a killer engagement party soon, that's for sure." He unwraps my arms from his waist and goes to get a glass of water. He fills it and leans against the counter, smiling at me.

I don't know what to do with myself.

Jude puts his arm around my shoulders and I squeeze him so hard he makes a sound. "Oof, easy, now." He smiles down at me and kisses my cheek.

I suddenly freeze. "Wait, Wyatt... the apartment. Should Sam move in with us? It would be a bit weird for him to keep living with his parents while he's engaged, right?" I think for another moment. "Or... should I, like... should I move out? Is it weird to be engaged and have a roommate? I don't want to be a third wheel for you guys. I mean, I'd need to find another apartment... or I guess I could move back in with my folks..."

"Uh..." Wyatt looks unsure. He meets Jude's eyes. Some unspoken understanding passes between them.

"Guys, what am I missing?" I ask, looking between them, a bit worried.

Wyatt smiles as Jude turns to me.

"What's going on?" I ask, my brow creasing with concern.

"Olena," Jude starts, "how do you feel about living in the woods?"

My eyes widen. I wrap my arms around his neck and jump on him. He catches me, pulling my legs around his waist.

He has his answer.

50

JUDE

I finish buttoning my shirt in the mirror and pull out my phone, checking the time. Olena should be back home any minute from Nat's house, where they've been getting ready for Sam and Wyatt's engagement party... for hours. A notification catches my eye: Miles has posted some new photos. Killing time, I tap the screen and scroll through, stopping on one photo in particular. Miles is grinning at the camera, his arm wrapped around his new girlfriend. They're each holding one side of a homemade sign bearing the text *"100 days sober."* I smile to myself, proud of my little brother.

"Jude! Are you ready?" Olena calls out from the kitchen. My head snaps up and I slip my phone into my pocket. "Come on, we're going to be late! We're supposed to be at Carnival at seven!"

"Yeah, coming!" I call back.

"Are you wearing them?" she calls out to me. "Please tell me you're wearing them."

I walk out of the bedroom and our eyes meet. I let out a breath; she looks stunning, like some kind of Viking punk pin-up girl, all smoky eyes and bare shoulders. Most of her hair is swept over to one side, two tight braids criss-crossing from her temple, and back over her ear. *Fuck,* I think, fighting the urge to cross the room and sink my hands into that hair. I can feel my pupils dilating at the sight of her. I'm suddenly not sure we're leaving here anytime soon.

"Dear God," I say, my voice low. "Turn around." She indulges me and does a little spin. Her silky-looking, sleeveless top plunges down in a deep vee between her breasts and she's got on this glittering miniskirt that is entirely too short for me to avoid staring at. I clutch at my chest, blowing out a breath when I see her stockings are the kind with the seam straight up the back of the leg. *I'm not going to survive tonight.*

She chuckles softly at my reaction, sweeping a hand through her hair as she walks toward me.

I move to meet her, my eyes roving over her body. I'm speechless.

"Um, you look fucking amazing in those," she says, taking in what I'm wearing. Reaching for me, she runs a finger underneath the edge of my suspenders, taking a good long look.

I roll my eyes, smiling.

She grins as she pulls the elastic back a little and lets it go with a snap.

I flinch but my eyes don't leave hers.

"Lumberjack fantasy *majorly* leveled up." She gives me a giddy smile.

I adjust the collar of my white button-up shirt and she bites her lip, watching me with hunger in her eyes as she drags a hand down my chest. Running my hands up the backs of her thighs, I lift the hem of her tiny skirt and squeeze her ass. I want to ravage her right this second, but I know if I kiss her even once, it'll be my undoing.

"Come on," I say, shaking my head and taking a deep breath. Using all my willpower to pull away, I take her hand and we head out to the truck.

※

AS WE ARRIVE, the bass music is pounding and spills out into the warm summer air. Wyatt and Sam's families have reserved the entire restaurant and bar for the party. Olena walks in ahead of me; I can't take my eyes off her and need to remind myself we're in public since openly ogling a woman like a Neanderthal—even the woman you're dating—is frowned-upon. Nonetheless, I still have to resist the urge to push her into the coat check and do unspeakable things to her.

As she leads me by the hand through the crowded room, Olena is lit up in pulsing blues, purples, reds, and greens that throb along to the beat of the music. She turns to me. "I wanna find Wyatt!" she shouts over the noise.

I nod.

"Can you go get us drinks?" she asks, miming drinking from a cup.

I nod again, letting go of her hand, and walk backward a step or two, running my hand down my face. I let out a breath as she disappears into the crowd. As I turn toward the bar, I bump lightly into someone and immediately move to apologize for not looking where I was going.

"Jude!" Carol pulls me into a tight hug before I can get my bearings.

Pulling away, I falter a moment. "Sorry. Hi. Wow, Carol! It's great to see you." I lean in so she can hear me. I had forgotten she and Charles were part of Wyatt's family.

"What are you doing here?" she asks, searching my eyes.

"Um..." I trail off, unsure how to explain. "Olena and I—"

"Say no more, darling," she interrupts with a cheeky smile. "Saw that one coming a mile away."

I smile, looking at my feet. She did. Everyone did.

"Well, I'm glad to see *you*. Goodness, you clean up nice!" She winks at me and taps my chest with a finger. I smile awkwardly and thank her for the compliment.

Charles appears at her side and hands her a glass of some dark amber drink. He reaches out and shakes my hand.

"Hello again!" he says, smiling. "I was just thinking about calling you," he shouts over the music.

My brow furrows. "Is anything wrong with the property?"

"Oh, no, it's great, no issues there." He waves a hand dismissively and I relax. "I was just going to tell you we decided on a name. For our *romantic retreat*." He pumps his eyebrows and laughs.

"Oh, right," I say, turning to look for Olena in the crowd. I catch sight of her standing with Sam, laughing hard. She's beautiful. I turn back to Charles and Carol. "What did you decide?"

Carol leans in. "*Starscape Manor*," she says, dramatically sweeping a hand across the space between us. "What do you think?"

I smile. "It's perfect. Olena will love it." Visions of our unforgettable night on the dock a few months ago swim into my mind. I clear my throat. "Make sure to tell her when you see her," I say. "I won't ruin the surprise," I add, holding up my hands with a smile.

"You'd better not!" teases Carol. She and Charles both chuckle.

I gesture over at the bar, explaining I need to grab drinks, and we part ways.

I catch the eye of a pretty bartender with turquoise hair and order two glasses of white wine.

"The guests of honor seem pretty adorable," she says, setting out the glasses. "Friends of yours?"

"Yeah, the blond one is my girlfriend's ex-roommate."

"Ex-roommate?" She raises her eyebrows as she pours. "Sounds like there's a story there."

"No," I say, holding up my hands with a chuckle. "No drama, honest. I just stole her away."

She slides the first glass my way. "Good." She pauses. "But, if the party gets dull later, I've got a *killer* roommate drama story for you."

"Noted," I say with a smile, then pick up the glasses, nodding my thanks before turning to go.

Wine in hand, I wind my way back toward Olena. She's standing with Nat, Graham, Wyatt, and Sam. The guests of honor grin, looking incredibly happy, as they hug an assembled throng of guests one by one.

A shouting chorus from behind me kicks off. I stop, turning to look at the source.

"Kiss, kiss, kiss, kiss, kiss..." A group of about eight young men dressed up in stylish party attire claps along with the chanted demand for the two fiancés.

I turn back to look at Sam and Wyatt. The crowd erupts in cheers as they share a long, dramatic kiss, holding their champagne glasses aloft. I smile and my eyes meet Olena's as I finally reach her. I place her wineglass in her hand, leaning down to press a kiss to her cheek.

"Jude," Graham says, shaking my hand, "good to see you, man."

Nat smiles at me from beside him. She and Graham are both dressed to the nines for the party, looking sharp.

"Looks like you've got a fan club, Jude," Nat says, grinning and eyeing the group that was just chanting behind me.

I turn and catch them staring before about half of them turn away, pretending to be looking elsewhere. The other half don't bother hiding it. One of them waves at me and I awkwardly wave back, smiling politely.

Wyatt appears at my shoulder. "Don't mind them, they're shameless," he says in my ear, then winks at me, and takes a sip of his champagne. I exhale and rub my chin, not sure how to respond.

Olena smirks at me, clearly enjoying the attention I'm getting.

"Hey, congratulations again, Wyatt. This party is... incredible." I cast my eyes around the room, hoping to change the subject.

"Thanks, Jude, I—"

Sam jogs over to us, cutting him off. "Excuse me, I need my fiancé!" he intones with a flourish, pulling Wyatt toward the dance floor.

Olena places her glass down on a nearby table and slips her arms around my waist, kissing my cheek. Hearing someone whoop from behind me, she raises an eyebrow, and pulls me into a deep, long kiss to a resounding mixture of cheers and booing, everyone laughing by the time our lips part. I throw a glance over my shoulder.

"I think they're a little disappointed I get you all to myself," she says in my ear, still laughing. She turns around in my arms to face her friends, and I pull her close, pressing a kiss to her neck. I have to remind myself to stop there.

A moment later, she pulls away.

"Mom! Dad!" She runs over to hug them both, bringing them back to our group.

"Jude, nice to see you again." David shakes my hand.

"Likewise," I say, giving him a genuine smile.

Lynn hugs Nat, then pulls back to admire her shimmering dress.

David glances at Olena, who is huddled with her mom and Nat, then motions to me, pulling me aside.

"Listen, I wanted to say... I was so glad you and Olena worked things out between you." His tone is serious.

I raise my eyebrows and exhale. "Uh, you and me both, David." I smile at him. "She's..." I look over at her. "She's incredibly important to me." I return my attention to her father.

"I can see that," he says. "You know, Lynn and I can see how good you are for Olena. Ever since you first came over for Marchmas, we've really gotten a good feeling about you."

"Thank you." I drop my gaze for a moment and smile, then meet his eyes again. "I feel the same way, to be honest." They'd been nothing but warm and welcoming to me that night, as well as every time I've seen them since; they've treated me like part of the family.

He nods, smiling. "We got the feeling you're... let's say, in it for the long haul." He gestures at me with the glass in his hand, watching my reaction.

I pause for a moment. "Yes, sir," I reply sincerely. "I'm not going anywhere."

"Good man." He nods. "In that case, welcome to the family." He holds out his glass, smiling.

His words hit me hard for reasons he doesn't yet understand. "Thank you," is all I can say, touching my glass to his, trying hard to maintain an air of casualness.

I turn to find Olena, but she's not with Nat and her mother anymore.

Suddenly, she appears beside me, out of breath. "Starscape!" she shouts over the music, breathing like she's just run across the room. "Starscape Manor! That's what they're calling it!" Her eyes are dancing with excitement. "I just talked to Carol! Isn't it perfect? With the lights and everything?" She squeezes my hands, David still watching us.

"Yeah, it's perfect," I say, smiling, as she reaches up to my neck and pulls me into a hug.

"My girl, are you going to dance with your old man, or what?" David interrupts, putting down his drink, and holds out his hand to Olena.

She smiles up at me, raising her eyebrows, then kisses my cheek. "You're next," she says in my ear, then takes her dad's hand, following him onto the dance floor.

EPILOGUE
OLENA

One year later

The sound of the river burbles along in front of me as I sit cross-legged with a book in my lap, swaying gently in the new swing. Jude installed it a few weeks ago under the arbutus tree and I can't get enough of sitting down here. The light is fading, and I reach over to the switch nearby, flicking on the fairy lights above me. I look up and smile at the twinkling of stars above my head—our own private little slice of Starscape Manor. I stretch out my limbs; my bare legs and feet are tanned from working outside in the summer sun, my sandals discarded on the rocks below me. I twist around when I hear footsteps on the stairs.

Jude descends the zig-zag of steps that connect our house to this place, smiling as he approaches me. "I'm never gonna get tired of you wearing those," he says, grinning, as I pull my reading glasses up to rest in my hair.

A light breeze catches wisps of my hair from my messy bun, drawing them over my face. I brush them back and grin at Jude, scooting over on the bench swing to make room for him.

"Hey." I press a kiss to his cheek as he sits down beside me, slipping my arm under his.

"I have a surprise for you." He puts his hand in his pocket and pulls out a small white card, handing it to me.

I turn over the business card, pulling my glasses back down to read it in the dim light. I catch Jude's arched eyebrow as he watches me. The card reads *"MacMillan & Sharpe Landscape Services"* in a classy modern script.

My eyes snap up to his. "Jude!"

"What do you think?" He smiles at me. "The truck goes in for a new decal next week."

I look back down at the card in my hand, running my fingers over the embossed lettering. My eyes well up as I meet Jude's gaze once more, pulling off my glasses and placing them on the bench beside me.

"It's perfect," I breathe, holding the card to my chest. "Are you sure?"

"Yes, I'm sure." He chuckles and kisses me.

"You won't miss the old name?" I search his expression.

"No, not at all," he says quickly. "*Sharpe Blades* sounded kind of badass when I was twenty-five. But it's time for an upgrade."

I smile at him.

"And time to make this working together thing official," he says, running a hand along my thigh. "The card's just a sample. The name isn't final if you want to change it."

I lean in and kiss him softly. "No, I love it," I say, beaming as I look at the card once more before tucking it into my book before turning to him again. "And I love you."

"I love you too." He grins at me. "Oh, shoot, that reminds me," he says, snapping his fingers. "I wanted to ask you something else too."

I furrow my brow and look at him quizzically, as he reaches into his pocket again.

"Marry me?" He holds the ring out in front of me.

My eyes widen and my jaw drops. The book slides from my lap, fluttering to the rocks below us. My heart is beating a mile a minute as I look between the ring and the man I love.

"Olena?" He chuckles at my stunned expression. "Oh boy, she's speechless..." He grimaces, then laughs again. "Come on. You gonna give me an answer, or—"

"Yes! Oh my God, yes. Yes!" A tear runs down my cheek as I throw my arms around his neck, pulling him in and kissing him hard. I draw back, searching his eyes, then furrow my brow. "I can't believe you led with the *business card!*" I swat his arm and he flinches, laughing. I'm still in shock.

"Gotta keep you on your toes." He kisses my forehead, then slides the ring onto my finger.

The ring is beautiful and simple, the gold band hugging a bright green emerald. I move it around and watch it glitter under the twinkling lights.

"It's beautiful."

"It was my grandmother's," he explains. "Then my mother's. She loved it because it matched her green eyes."

I look up into Jude's own green eyes and kiss him again. I could do this forever. And then I realize, as he pulls me closer, that I get to do this forever. I get to have *him* forever. And it feels... perfect.

BONUS EPILOGUE

Want more Jude and Olena?

Subscribe to my newsletter to get a FREE bonus epilogue featuring Jude and Olena on their wedding night!

Get your FREE bonus epilogue:

https://BookHip.com/XPVPCCQ

Enjoy cheeky callbacks to the book, tipsy Jude, a return of the french braids, and some seriously spicy moments (including toy play), all from Jude's point of view!

ALSO BY HANNAH BRIXTON

Loved *Hey Jude?*

Read book two in the *Lennox Valley Chronicles* series:

Jesse's Girl

Get Jesse's Girl:

https://mybook.to/jessesgirl

ACKNOWLEDGMENTS

I want to thank so many incredible people for their help with shaping this story from beginning to end. What started out as my raving and scattered thoughts has been touched and molded by so many incredible friends and fellow authors into what's now an actual, finished, readable novel. The feat of accomplishing this alone is wild to me; I still can't believe I get to share this story with actual people—and that it's not just a swirling chaos that lives in my brain alone.

Andrea Bugslag: I never would have started writing without your encouragement to do it—just to see what it was like, to see if I liked it, to have fun, and to play. You talked me through endless ideas and let me be messy. I cherish every chapter I got to read to you out loud over the phone. Thank you for always loving me—wild new hyperfocus adventures and all! Thank you for reminding me to eat and drink water and take breaks to move my flesh vessel. Never stop reminding me to use my strategies. And thank you for all the gold stars! I love you!

Nicole Taylor Eby: Having your eyes on my first draft was so critical in taking this story to a whole new level and I am so grateful for your thoughtful feedback for a story that still felt so new and vulnerable to share with friends. You helped me feel like less of an imposter and you lifted me up, showing me I could really do this writing thing. Thank you also for guiding me through the chaos of the indie publishing world.

Genesis Bird: The unlikelihood of us finding each other online is matched in scope only by the beautiful connection we've made in the process of getting our first books out into the world. I treasure the thoughtful and thorough way you approached reading this story and the empathy and understanding you've been able to show both me and the fictional humans I created. Your care and attention to detail is unmatched and I am so grateful to know you and to count you as my friend. You are a beautiful soul!

Maggie Francis: Thank you for answering all my newbie indie author questions and inspiring me to take the leap and write this book. You lead by example, showing me that doing what you love and creating stories could be a worthy, fun, and creatively fulfilling endeavor, and I am so lucky to have you as a friend. You give the best, squeeziest hugs!

Laura Duncan: Thank you for getting me and my brain—and for coming along for my wild info-dumping tangents in true ADHD fashion! Your feedback on this book was wonderful and I am so grateful to know you. I hope one day we can end up on the same continent and have a cheeky chat in person! Never stop never stopping.

Cherry Keeley: Thank you for all the late night and early morning chats, ridiculous memes shared, and support you've shown me as this book took shape. I'm so grateful for your thoughtful feedback and your friendship-from-afar. I couldn't have done it without you. May all your book boyfriends be tattooed Golden Retrievers.

E. B. Slayer: Thank you for your thoughtful feedback and the many brainstorming sessions you jumped into with me over the course of revising this story. *And* for reading this book *twice*, which was really going above and beyond! You are a gem. May your dreams always be full of lumberjacks who look like Henry Cavill.

To the rest of my wonderful beta readers: Becca, Dok, Sarah, Jesslou, Emily, Bella, Emelia, Dani, Juli, Christine, and Tabatha, I thank each of you from the bottom of my heart for taking a chance on a new author and for helping me craft an even better version of this story from your most excellent feedback.

To my editor, Myranda Bolstad, who literally navigated a full-city evacuation in the middle of this project and still got the edits done *a day early*: You are incredible and I am forever grateful for your dedication and keen eye. Thank you for all our chats, for your grace, for your humor, and for your confident guidance when I forget how to use a comma because I've stared at it all for far too long.

To my husband: Thank you for loving and supporting me through all my zany creative exploits, for sharing your man-brain thoughts when I needed to get inside Jude's head, and for making dinner every night so I didn't fall apart while I wrote (and re-wrote and revised and edited) this book. I love you more than ever.

To my three incredible children: Thank you for understanding all the times my writing stole my brain away. I hope you remember this time as a period where your mother briefly lost touch with reality, but it was worth it because she showed you that doing something you really love is important and worth-while. I love you and I hope you all find what you love to do and get to do it.

And finally, to my mom: Thank you for raising me. You have always been a strong, self-sufficient woman and you've shown me first-hand that women can save *themselves*, thank-you-very-much. Thank you for inspiring me and encouraging me in my writing, and for showing me that being a writer is something you can start doing at any age. I love you!

ABOUT THE BOOK

This story came out of nowhere and swallowed me whole. Like some kind of fever dream, I wrote the first draft of *Hey Jude* in a five-week whirlwind during which I often forgot to eat because I was so wholly engrossed in imagination land. What started out as an experimental foray into writing soon became an obsession that overtook all my free moments. I quickly discovered I loved it.

I live in a beautiful part of the world and wanted to tell a story that captured some of the natural beauty of the Pacific Northwest; this desire is what helped me create the fictional town of Lennox Valley, Washington, and the Faulkners' cliff-side property in particular. The outdoor setting of the landscaping project really let me dig into the atmosphere—the weather, the plants, the trees, and the natural experiences that are so common here in our temperate rainforest.

Jude and Olena were both very important characters to me and close to my heart. With Olena, I wanted to tell a story about a woman with yet-undiagnosed ADHD who felt like a failure due to her challenges pulling off adult life. It was important to me to show this—to provide this representation for readers who may relate—because I have been that person and I know first-hand that it can feel very lonely and exhausting to be trapped in your busy mind, constantly overthinking and over-analyzing every little thing. I hope Olena made you feel less alone. You are enough. Now go get a snack and hydrate.

With Jude, I wanted to give Olena a love interest who accepted all of her as she was, messy baggage and all, and who saw her brilliance shining through. I also wanted him to be a steady, capable, empathetic, and *safe* person for her to have in her corner. While I didn't want him to swoop in and save her, I did want him to support her. This warmth and safety was what I once needed in my own life, and Jude's character represents what I needed back then. Jude is all the good things I hope every neurodivergent woman is lucky enough to find in a partner—someone who brings a perfect complement of skills to help out wherever you may struggle. And who both *is* a snack and has some in his truck for you.

To every Olena out there: may you find yourself a Jude.

Hannah Brixton

Note: If you related to Olena's story and wonder if you, too, might have ADHD, you can find a free self-test checklist to bring to your doctor at: https://add.org/adhd-test/.

ABOUT THE AUTHOR

 Hannah Brixton lives with her husband, three children, and two cats on beautiful Vancouver Island in British Columbia, Canada.

In her spare time, she loves to read, listen to podcasts, and sing along loudly to music that embarrasses her children.

Hannah Brixton's books are available on Amazon

Contact Hannah:
Email: hannah@hannahbrixton.com
Website: www.hannahbrixton.com

Subscribe to Hannah's Newsletter:
https://hannah-brixton-author.ck.page/f8158e2beb

Follow Hannah:
@hannah.brixton.author on **Facebook**
@hannah.brixton on **Instagram**
@hannah.brixton.author on **Tiktok**
@Hannah Brixton on **Goodreads**
@hannahbrixtonauthor on **Pinterest**

Printed in Great Britain
by Amazon

56603670R00219